OUTSIDE THE ROPES

ASHLEY CLAUDY

To You. You're awesome.

~Thank you

1: The First Punch

THE FIRST PUNCH THREW ME OFF BALANCE, but the second drew blood, exploding my vision as I was slammed to the canvas. My jaw throbbed with every heartbeat; a burn spreading just under the skin. I pushed against the mat, lifting my body up, and ignored the pain.

The room around me split, blurred, and then came back into focus. Bright overhead lights shadowed everything beyond the red ropes surrounding the ring.

"Two…" The referee's voice broke through the deafening buzz in my head.

Wiping my mouth with my gloved hand, the smear of blood didn't surprise me. She'd reopened the cut on my lip.

"Three…" He held three fingers in front of my face.

My vision tunneled on my opponent. She was standing with her arms in a V, playing up the crowd. That was her mistake.

My mistake had been looking towards Silas for guidance. I had been unsure of myself, and that got me hit. Twice. Now, I'd put my faith in my instincts. I rose to my feet, never taking my eyes off her.

The referee stepped in front of me, lips moving, but his voice never reached me. I sent him away with a nod.

Facing me now, her smile dropped, along with her arms. She bounced around, hands up to strike or block, her eyes intent on me.

The sound of my steady breathing filled my head, the beat of my heart keeping time.

She jabbed, and I stepped back, avoiding the blow. She had expected that and followed it with a left hook.

I ducked and took a swing, my arm vibrated down to my bones as I landed a punch to her jaw. Her head jerked up and back at an odd angle as she fell onto the ropes. Before she recovered, I lunged towards her, swinging my fists. Blow after blow connected with her body and head; the impact shook my muscles until they were numb.

The ring disappeared, and I was fighting back for all those times I couldn't. I was no longer in control of my thoughts or actions. Each punch fueled another, and I didn't want to stop. I couldn't stop.

The referee forced himself between us, shoving me back. I knocked his arm out of the way, gaining control just before swinging at him. Stepping back, I sucked in ragged breaths and watched my opponent slide down the ropes, her body folding as she hit the canvas. The ref pushed my shoulders, nudging me further away before going to her side.

My senses returned, bit by bit, with each flick of the ref's finger as he counted. The sound in the room wavered. The referee returned to my side and raised my arm. I pulled my vision from the girl crumpled on the ground with a bloody nose as her team surrounded her.

Silas stood in the corner of the ring, his feet wide and his arms crossed. His dark face remained like stone. He hadn't moved from when I last looked to him, except now the side of his mouth tugged up. Meeting his gaze, I returned the small smile. He inclined his head towards me as a pair of hands came down on my shoulders.

Dexter was behind me, shaking me, congratulating me, and everything snapped back into the present. Sweat and the metallic tinge of blood burned my nose, and the bright lights blinded me.

Only then did I recall Silas's instructions from earlier. "It's all a show, and if you win, you have to put on another one. Make the crowd love you."

I raised my hands towards the audience, but there wasn't one. I was the opening act; no one cared to watch the unknowns, especially the girls. But I had captured a few people's attention and smiled to them. Then Dex was pulling me from the ring.

We wove between groups of people making their way to their seats, to the little room we had claimed outside the gym. Dex hadn't shut up yet. He was going on about the fight, swinging his fists in the air as he recounted it.

I stepped into the small room, my eyes adjusting from the bright lights, and froze, adrenaline spiking. Gage sat in the corner, wearing only his boxing shorts, as a girl massaged his bare shoulders. Even in dim lighting, the lines of muscle stood out on his tattoo-covered torso. He leaned forward in the chair, his thick forearms resting on his knees, and raised one dark eyebrow at me in question.

Dexter nudged me from behind, setting me on the path into the room. I found the nearest chair and sat, stunned from my fight, and yet a nervous energy was now pulsing under my skin from Gage's presence.

I tried to resist peeking a glance at him, but couldn't. He rolled his head to the side, giving the girl's hands access to his neck, but his eyes locked on mine, unreadable and intense.

Dexter blocked my view, handing me ice wrapped in a rag. I pressed it to my cut lip, letting the sting focus me back on my fight. A fight I won. He stooped beside me on the balls of his feet and started to remove my gloves. He cut away the tape supporting my wrists and hands, his wide smile causing his eyes to wrinkle.

I returned the smile as realization hit. "I did it," I breathed, stretching each hand while keeping the ice to my lip.

"Hell yeah, you did." He laughed. "How do you feel, Rea? Anything besides that lip hurt?"

"Nah, the lip ain't even bad. I feel great." I stood up, pulling the ice away; bright red blood spotted the rag. I walked over to the mirror to check out the damage.

A rumble of a laugh made me stop. "I heard you got hit." Gage's voice was deep and rough with disapproval.

All the adrenaline from the fight must not have worn off because for some stupid reason I stepped towards him with my chin raised. "Did you hear I won, too?"

"That's one fight, a nobody at that, and she hit you. Twice. Don't celebrate that. You need to train, and do, better." He smirked and leaned back in the chair, pulling the girl behind him onto his lap. She landed on him with a giggle and he hooked his arms around her waist before looking back to me "Think about that. Now get out of here and let me get ready for my fight. Oh and you should stick around for it. Maybe you'll learn something."

All I could do was walk away. I knew better than to speak up in the first place. I was usually good at keeping my mouth shut. The bleachers surrounding the ring were full now, the noise adding to the energy of the room. Electric excitement filled the air, lighter than the oppressive fog that came from Gage.

Dexter followed behind me, and when the door closed, I turned towards him. "What time does Gage fight?"

His blue-gray eyes were soft as he looked down at me. "It won't start for another hour at least; he's the main fight. Let's get you changed in the locker room." As he walked through the crowd of people, towards a back hallway, he turned to me. "Don't take it personal. He's harder on himself. I think he actually likes you… thinks you've got something."

I half snorted. "Yeah, right." I shook my head. "He's right, though. It's my first fight, I shouldn't be overly confident." Because the one thing I knew was that whatever I had done in that ring, I wanted to do it again.

Alone in the locker room, I checked out the cut on my lip. It hadn't reopened all the way, so I wouldn't need new stitches. Shadows of bruises were still on my eye and chin, but there were no new ones from tonight.

I nodded to myself. Yeah, I wanted to fight again. Hitting back felt good. But I needed those guys out there to help me, more than they already had, because I didn't want to just fight—I wanted to be good. No, I wanted to be the best.

I wouldn't let anyone hit me again.

2: Darkness Circling

I REACHED FOR THE CASH IN DREW'S hand, but he raised his arm, keeping it out of my reach.

"Whadya say you give me a little kiss first? Right here?" He pointed to his cheek with his other hand.

Half smiling, I shoved him. "You wish, now give me my money." I jumped up, snatching the bills from him.

"People are trying to work here," Trichelle reprimanded, turning sideways as she slid between us, tray in hand.

Drew threw his hands up in repentance, and then repeatedly thrust his hips forward. "Come back and let me apologize, Trichelle."

She smacked the back of his head as she passed by again, weaving through patrons to get to her tables.

"Regan, do you have a ride home?" he asked, untying his apron and crumpling it up. He tossed it like a basketball into the wash bin just inside the kitchen. The apron draped over the edge, half in, half out.

Walking to the laundry pile, I threw mine in and scooped Drew's into the basket. "I'm good, thanks," I lied.

I didn't know where I was going for the night. I counted the bills in my hand, reorganizing them so the little heads all faced the same way. It was my first shift off of training, and I'd made one hundred and twenty dollars. I could get a hotel.

I paused, considering as I folded the bills into my pocket. Or maybe I'd go to Nan's again. There was always someone there to let me in; I just wasn't guaranteed a bed, but I'd save some money. A warm place to stay for the price of breakfast. Worked for me.

Shrugging into my winter coat, Drew and I walked out the door. The cold racket of the city replaced the warm clamors of the restaurant.

He slid on a ski cap and turned towards me, his breath fogging up in the icy air. "I'll see you tomorrow. You work, don't you?"

I pulled my hood up to protect my ears from the bite of the wind, the tip of my nose beginning to run and freeze. "Yeah, see ya then." Turning from him, I jogged across the street before the traffic light had a chance to change on me.

Nan only lived a few blocks away. I'd save the cab fare for tomorrow when I'd have to close late. It was a little after 10:00 pm, early for the city. The streets were lit up and alive with people walking every which way.

As I made a couple of turns, the crowds began to thin. I took my keys out of my pocket, arranging them in my fist so the thin points stuck out like I was Wolverine. I only had three keys, but that was enough. One for my P.O. Box and two for my locker that held the stuff I couldn't keep at Nan's. I didn't have much besides a change of clothes at her apartment, and I didn't plan to leave much more. Not with her friends in and out all the time.

A large shadow moving over me signaled something coming from behind, and I gripped my hand on my keys. Adrenaline tightened my muscles as the stampede of footsteps grew louder. I turned as a fist flew at my head and ducked, avoiding the blow. I came back up swinging and made contact with an arm. The keys bit into my palm with the force, causing me to drop them.

"What the fuck?" he snarled as he grabbed his shoulder.

Four more circled around me, laughing. They all had ski masks covering their faces. My brain was several painful heartbeats behind my body, frozen with fear. My muscles pulled with the need to flee, but there was no way to escape as they closed in.

"You didn't even hit her? Try again," one boy encouraged with a laugh.

"Knock her out," yelled another.

"Hit the bitch."

I breathed through my rising panic, staying focused on the one I had hit. Behind him, another had his phone out, filming. Fear surged through my veins.

Everything slowed as the boy closest to me swung again, but he was hesitant and my reactions were fast. I had been dodging punches all my life.

I stepped back, trying to stay calm and find a break in the group so I could run. He swung again, but this time I sidestepped and threw one of my own, hitting him in his temple. Pushing him to the side, I took off through the opening I'd created.

Hands snatched my jacket and yanked me back, slamming me onto the dirty concrete sidewalk. A flash of pain exploded from hip to toes.

Screaming, I yelled with all I had, hoping someone would hear. A swift, hard kick to my ribs silenced me, paralyzing my breath. Rolling to my stomach, I gasped for air, forcing my lungs to work through the blinding pain. But one, two, three more kicks shook my body.

I grabbed a foot, before it struck my head, and pulled. The boy fell to the ground, and I scrambled to stand, the chance of running overpowering the aches radiating through my bones.

But another snatched my hood off and fisted my hair, jerking me back with a lightning bolt of pain. His other hand covered my mouth and nose, suffocating me. Brick walls streaked past me and any hope I had left faded along with the city lights as they dragged me deeper into the alley.

I strained to breathe, fighting down my panic. Anger coursed through me as I focused on the guy with the phone still standing back, recording.

A pair of hands yanked on my purse. "Stupid bitch, give it up."

So I did. I dropped my bag. But they still had hold of my hair while another one tore off my jacket.

"She works at Johnny's, check her pockets," the one with the camera commanded.

Hands pulled everywhere, yanking me from one side to the other as they searched for anything of value. Even after they took my money they continued to deliver kicks and punches that threatened to push me over my limit. The blows to the head were nudging me out of consciousness, my vision darkening.

I used all the strength I had left to slam my body into the person holding me, forcing him into the brick wall at our back. His grip loosened, and I ran, desperate to get away. When another one grabbed me this time, I turned and rammed my knee into his groin. He collapsed, and I swung my fist, hitting the other masked man in front of me.

But arms still closed around me. The world bled as tears burned my vision, my heart sinking as I realized there were too many of them to escape.

Reaching up and behind, I pulled the mask off the one holding me. I wanted to at least see who they were, in case I survived. No, when I survived. He was young, perhaps 16, with skin the color of midnight and curly, dark hair. Heedless of the fists still pounding at my body, I focused my wavering vision on the telling tattoo on his neck: a horseshoe with a vine.

As the group enclosed around me, I no longer heard the threats they shouted. With one last burst of mad, wild energy, I fought, throwing punches in every direction. I had to; otherwise I would submit to the black unconsciousness that wavered just behind my anger. It seemed to work for a moment, but when they threw me to the ground and kicks shook me as quick as rain, all I could do was roll into a ball.

My head snapped back and blood gushed in my mouth and nose, drowning me. It took all my energy to stay rolled up as lightning bolts of pain thundered inside me, jerking my body, but it was my only defense.

A loud shot broke through the roar. It was pointless to fight the darkness circling me when there was a gun. I gave up and everything went black.

3: Small Kindness

THE DARKNESS HELD NO PEACE, ONLY PAIN. A liquid fire ran through me and surrounded me, consuming and destroying. I didn't know if I was still being attacked or who it was this time: strangers, foster parents, or bullies from the group home. It all bled together. Past. Present. Pain. I didn't even know if I was lying down. Everything burned, and the dark prison was terrifying.

I struggled to open my eyes, to see what was going on, but I was trapped in my body. My mind, long conditioned for survival, wouldn't shut off and fought for awareness. Muffled sounds reached me. Someone yelled something about an ambulance. I had to get up. Now.

My eyes cracked open. A shadowy form was above me, patting the air surrounding me, but I don't think his hands made contact.

"No," I croaked out.

The figure jumped back, and then leaned in towards me. "What? Just rest, you're safe now. You're going to be okay."

I moved through the strong grip of pain and sat up. The man in front of me yelled to someone else for help as I attempted to stand. My legs were shaky and ached, but I couldn't go to the hospital. I couldn't afford those bills. I needed to get to Nan's. I pushed his hands away as he grabbed for me, but the movement was slow and my arms were too weak.

"Stop, you're hurt. You need to sit down. The ambulance will be here soon," the panicked man said as another one joined him.

It was like being submerged in mud. Sounds were muffled and movements were difficult. Talking was near impossible; something was wrong with my mouth.

"You need stitches, but you'll be fine," a new man said to me. He was calm as he turned to his friend. "I think she's going into shock."

They were on either side of me, blocking my escape. My head was heavy. It swayed on my shoulders, making everything around me disjointed.

The anxious man was wearing shorts. Way too cold for that. And his composed friend's shiny head needed a hat.

Thick, dark blood pooled in the spot I had been. Was that mine? I tried to bring my hand to my face, but a shot of pain radiated from my shoulder. That arm wouldn't move. It made me light headed.

The other hand worked, and I lifted it, but didn't recognize the feel of my face. It was sticky and lumpy. Disgusted, I pulled my hand away and studied the blood that now covered it. That couldn't all be mine; it was too much.

"Catch her," someone yelled.

I was sat against a brick wall, shaking and unable to stop.

A jacket covered me and a pair of arms held me, stilling me.

A voice spoke from far away, "You are going into shock, but you'll be fine. Everything's fine. Rest now. Rest."

This time, the darkness wasn't as terrifying.

* * *

"How is your pain?" My nurse was too speedy. I couldn't keep track of her as she moved from one end of the bed to the other. She checked my monitors, IV's, and then wrote something on the chart she placed on the table.

I nodded, but don't think she saw. She probably didn't care for the answer anyways. She pulled open the blinds, and I closed my eyes against the bright daylight streaking through.

"The police are here and have some questions for you. They will be in shortly." She zoomed out of the room, and sure enough, two officers in uniform stepped through the open door.

"Ms. Regan Sommers, how are you feeling?" the female police officer asked.

Of the two, she was the one I would trust to protect me on the street. She was solid, tall, and looked every bit of an authority. Her partner was a sad case. His tiny frame drowned in the uniform; he looked like a kid playing dress-up.

I nodded. My swollen lips made it hard to speak. The officers must not have realized how pointless this interview would be.

"My name is Detective Andres, and this is Officer Grand. He will assist me with this investigation."

I half laughed at his ironic name, but the force of air hurt my bruised ribs.

Detective Andres' eyes seemed to soften and the corner of her mouth tugged up in a knowing smile. She got the joke.

Officer Grand stared at me, eyes wide. I must have looked as bad as I felt. I turned away, not wanting to see that look anymore.

"Let's see." She flipped open her notebook and scanned several pages. "Citizens on the scene detained two of your attackers. We have a good idea who the rest are based on that. So rest assured we will get the perpetrators. The three gentlemen there also gave us their account of the story, but they only saw the end. Can you tell us what happened?"

They caught two already. The news encouraged me.

My lips were sticky and crusty; the skin pulled apart as I separated them to talk. I licked the corner where the stitches were, feeling the hot pain. "I as ahki o ma eeehsou." I couldn't form the necessary consonants for intelligible speech.

Officer Grand's head whipped towards Detective Andres. "Did you understand any of that?"

She narrowed her eyes at him before turning back to me. "It's alright, no need to talk just yet. Can you write?" At my nod, she gave me a pen and paper from her notebook. "Write down what happened. Everything, even if you think it doesn't matter, write it down. Take your time. You can give it to the nurse when you're done."

In the middle of writing the events, the speedy nurse returned. "Your Aunt Mary will be coming tonight to take you home. You'll be discharged at 7:00 pm as long as all your vitals stay stable. Let's go over the doctors' orders and medication."

She pulled up a chair, took out the medicine, and explained each dosage and side effects. I was only half listening. Aunt Mary wasn't my aunt; she was the last foster parent I had—my last known address. But I hadn't lived there since I was released from the system over a year ago. The police, or hospital, must have called her. I didn't know what to expect, but she'd agreed to come, and I had to have someone pick me up to be discharged. I couldn't get in touch with Nan; you never could during the day. She was a creature of the night.

* * *

"Girl, what trouble have you gotten yourself into now? I've got babies at home, and you have me driving into the middle of the city for you. Do you know how much—Good lord, you look awful. Are you prostituting yourself? Is it drugs?"

Ms. Mary's shrill voice woke me up from my nap. The pain medication made me drowsy. I swung my feet off the bed and stood up to leave.

I wore sweats the hospital gave me, a small kindness I was thankful for since the clothes I came in were stained with blood.

"Well, hurry it up. I don't have all day. Do you have your things? Do you need to sign something? Where is someone to help us?"

As if on cue, a nurse pushed a wheelchair into the room. "We'll take you to the entrance of the hospital." She turned to Ms. Mary. "You can bring the car to the front for patient pick up."

"She's fine. I just saw her standing. She don't need no special treatment. It's her own fault she's here anyways. Always been up to no good, now it's caught up with her."

The nurse nodded, tight lipped. "It's our policy, for insurance reasons. Everyone uses the wheelchair when leaving."

That stopped Ms. Mary, and she smiled. "I understand that crazy insurance stuff. They always trying to cover their own asses." Her laughter boomed in the tiny room. "I'll go get the car and meet you all out front."

I slid into the passenger side of the station wagon, and Ms. Mary pulled away before I even got my seatbelt on.

"So where can I take you? I ain't got any free beds at my house. Those damn social workers won't give me money to expand like I wanted."

Thank God for small blessings. That lady didn't need any more foster kids. "Turn right," I managed intelligibly, pointing to the intersection.

I would go to Nan's, but I wasn't sure what my reception would be like now that I had no cash to offer.

* * *

Bass seeped from within the apartment, vibrating the walkway leading to the door. Luckily Nan lived on the first floor; my bruised ribs made walking even this short distance a struggle.

I knocked and rested against the frame, waiting for an answer. The music cut off and James, Nan's older brother, opened the door. His stringy hair hung over his red eyes.

"Damn girl, what sort of trouble you bringing here?"

"None," I mumbled, looking down the hall and into the room behind him. Several people lounged, different stages of high if the smell in the air was any indication. "Is Nan home?"

He stepped back, letting me walk in. "You must've pissed someone off to end up like that." He walked to his recliner and threw himself back, popping out the footrest. Laughing and pushing back his greasy hair, he turned to his friends. "Check out Regan, she got the crap beat out of her." He turned to the far door and yelled, "Nan, come get your friend before she falls over."

The room erupted as I walked out of the shadow of the hallway.

"Damn!" Ty exclaimed, hopping up to get a better look at me.

"What the fuck happened?" Miguel asked, sitting back with a bowl in his hand, his eyes glued on me.

"You should sit down, you don't look well." Sienna nodded her head towards an empty seat on the couch.

I sat, needing to rest. I knew I looked a mess, but I'd have to get use to this reaction for a while. Nothing to do about it. Nan came out of the back room, stretching. Her baggy shirt lifted with her arms, showing her tiny tattoo-covered waist. She stiffened when she saw me.

"What the hell?" She was at my side in a second, studying my face. "Regan, where have you been? Were you at the hospital?"

James perked up in his seat. "Get any good pills for your troubles?" His eyes narrowed on the white paper bag in my hands.

Nan cocked her head, still looking at me. "Come with me, Regan, we need to talk."

I rose to my feet, careful and slow, trying to minimize the pain that seized my lungs. James stood, too.

"We need to talk, Nan. Your friend better not be putting us in the middle of some shit without me getting a kick back. I live here, too. You remember that."

"I remember, let me find out the details bro, then I'll talk to you. Have some fuckin' sympathy; she obviously needs a place to rest."

Nan took a cigarette out of her pack on her dresser, lighting it as she watched me situate myself on her bed. She walked to the window, banging on the edges to get it to slide up. "You planning to stay here for a while?" At my nod, she released a stream of smoke out the open window, plopping on the worn down chair beside it. "Figured as much." She pointed her cigarette at me. "I want to hear what happened, but first let's work out our arrangement." She blew out the window again before whipping around. "Wait, are people after you? That's going to affect the price..." She chewed on her lip as she considered.

I wasn't sure what had happened last night or what the repercussions would be from the arrests. Maybe those boys would be after me, but they didn't know who I was. The purse they took had no forms of identification. They only knew where I worked because my shirt had said Johnny's.

Work. I was supposed to work tonight. Damn, Johnny's had been my first decent serving job. Maybe I could explain everything to them tomorrow.

I focused back on Nan and shook my head. "No one's after me. I was robbed."

Her eyes widened. "Jesus, you even sound awful."

The medicine helped with the swelling and pain, making it easier to talk. Now it was more like a mouth full of marbles than golf balls.

"Alright, so down to business then. What pills did you get?" She placed the cigarette between her lips and walked over to me, grabbing the bag. Her eyebrows rose as she pulled out my large bottle of pills. "Oxycodone. Well, alright. Ah, 30 milligrams controlled release. Damn, doctors could have done better." She walked back to the window and threw her cigarette out before continuing, "There's fifty in here. How many do you need?"

"Leave me ten, just in case."

She counted out my share and placed them in an empty cigarette pack. "Don't let James see that." Handing me the box, she sat on the edge of her queen size bed. "Alright, so you can stay here and take twenty percent of what we make."

"Forty," I countered. I knew she'd tell me she sold them for less than she did anyways. I needed some money to live off of while I was out of work.

"Thirty and I'll run to the store for you this week for whatever you need. You don't look like you could make it." She kept her lips tight when she smiled.

"I get the bed, too," I added.

She rolled her eyes to the ceiling. "Well of course. You look like crap; you need it more than me. So we have a deal?" She waited for my nod before continuing. "You know this is all just business, right? If things were different, I'd just let you stay, really, you're my girl. I have to look out for myself first, though. You know, nothing personal."

Just like Nan, she ripped me off but smoothed it over with a "nothing personal." It never was with her. She had a deceivingly sweet face that appeared younger than her twenty-one years, but she was ruthless. I knew she'd always look out for herself first. But so did I. Our mutual understanding of each other was what made our friendship work.

"I know." I nodded to her. "Now get off my bed, I need to sleep."

She stood up and walked backwards out of the room, my meds in her hand. "Fine, but when you get up, you're telling me that story."

4: Not Even Close

"I'LL WEAR A BAND AID OVER THE cuts. Johnny told me on the phone I could work today!" It had been three weeks since I worked and I was going crazy sitting around Nan's, not to mention my need for a paycheck. My face had healed surprisingly fast for the most part, but I still had visible bruising and scabbed over cuts on my lip and eyebrow.

Louisa stretched out her sigh, eyeing the almost empty restaurant, avoiding eye contact with me. "Perhaps you can do dishes tonight, but we can't have you on the floor." She clicked her tongue and her leathery hand floated to rest on my shoulder. I tensed, uncomfortable with the sudden contact. "Are you sure you're up to working?"

I stepped out of her grasp and met her soft gaze. "I'm fine. Thanks, I'll go roll silverware."

The walk here panicked me more than I had anticipated, and I was still a bit edgy. I concentrated on keeping my face neutral as I made my way to the kitchen; my ribs ached constantly, but it was nothing I couldn't handle.

The kitchen was bright and noisy, a stark change from the dim interior of the restaurant.

"Hola, Regan," one of the chefs yelled from behind the grill.

Unable to recall a name, I nodded in greeting and gave a half smile. I pulled a stool up to the stainless steel table and rolled silverware sets in napkins, letting the mindless, repetitive task relax me.

Trichelle leaned her willowy arms on the table in front of me. "Hey, I'm glad you're back. How are you feeling?"

I shrugged and gave my typical response. "I'm fine." I continued rolling the silverware, hoping to end the conversation.

"Well, you've been popular around here. The police showed up the other day wondering how to get a hold of you. Have you spoken with them?"

I nodded. James drove me to the police station last week. They had a few follow up questions for me and told me they'd already made two more arrests.

She pulled her hair back into a ponytail as she spoke, "The cops told us it was that stupid Knockout Game. Makes me sick that these teenagers are so fucking ignorant. I heard the game's killed people in other places. Stupid YouTube."

"The Knockout Game" was a dangerous game that went viral on the Internet. Only I had been too stubborn to get knocked out, so it became a beating and mugging. I couldn't decide what was worse: knowing they targeted me because I looked weak, or that I could've ended it by rolling over and playing dead.

"Damn, you're lucky it wasn't worse."

Lucky? Is that really what she said?

I took a breath, testing the pull on my ribs, and let out a short puff of a laugh. "Yeah, real lucky," I snapped, and stood up with my hand pressed against the ache on my side. The silverware was done.

Trichelle paused, staring at me for a moment. "Um, right, well... You also had some other guys stop by looking for you. Did they get in touch with you?"

I walked past her to rinse the incoming dishes. The dinner rush was just starting, and the kitchen buzzed with activity. Plates clanged and fried food sizzled, usually making my mouth water, but the tingle of dread overpowered it.

"I haven't talked to anybody. Who were they and what'd you tell them?" Nobody here knew Nan, so at least they couldn't tell anyone where I was staying.

Her lips curled in a sultry smile. "I don't know, but there were two of them. An older guy and another about our age. They're both cute, but the younger one's really hot, like, he had the prettiest eyes ever—"

I cut her off. "Trich, who were they?" I stopped rinsing the dishes and crossed my arms, pinning her with my gaze.

She smiled, unfazed by my attitude. "Oh, right. They left a card, I'll get it for you." She grabbed a tray from the pile and leaned out the kitchen door. "I just have to get this table first, I'll be back." She winked as she disappeared through the threshold.

She came back later with a card for "The City Center Boxing Club," but apparently they never explained who they were or what they wanted. I got the impression she was too distracted looking at them to ask.

"Really, you should go see that boy; I'll go with you. Mm, I'd do anything to see those eyes again." She leaned back on the table next to me, a tray crossed over her chest. "God, I'm telling you Regan, you've never seen anyone with—"

"Don't you have work to do? Because I do," I fired at her, letting the frustration show on my face.

She swallowed. "What the hell's wrong? If you don't want me to go, just say so. Is he a boyfriend or something?"

"What the hell is wrong with you? I don't know who they are. I got jumped, and you didn't think to ask strangers why they came looking for me? Go do whatever the hell you want, but stop talking to me about it!" I pushed away from the sink and went out the back of the restaurant, escaping her look of hurt and confusion.

She didn't get it. Maybe hot guys would come to her work just to see her, but not me. These people wanted something. I tried to breathe away my anxiety, but the cool evening air only reminded me of that night. The darkening sky was closing in on me, pain in every shadow. I stepped back into the bright kitchen and shut the door on my panic.

Trichelle hesitated when she returned to the kitchen later.

I gave a ghost of a smile and swallowed my pride. "Hey, I'm sorry. I'm—I don't know, I haven't been myself lately. I'm sorry for snapping at you."

"It's okay, I get it," she said with pity in her eyes as she lifted plates of food onto her tray.

She didn't get it, not even close. "Do you think you can give me a ride home tonight?"

Her smile was genuine. "Sure." She walked out of the kitchen with her tray raised high.

* * *

The heavy doors of the police station slammed behind me, cutting off the wind whipping through my shoulder length hair. Running my fingers through my knots, I approached the window for assistance.

"What's your business today?" the uniformed man behind the glass asked.

"I need to see Detective Andres." Still shivering from the cold outside, I pulled on my book bag straps, redistributing the weight to my other shoulder.

"Andres? She's on juvenile crime, I think. Hold on." He was talking to himself as he picked up the phone beside him, fingers pressing a few buttons. "Hey Fields, this is Ritter. Is Andres in?" He lifted his chin to me. "What's your name?"

"Regan Sommers."

"A Regan Sommers is here to see her." He sat back in his chair, swiveling it from side to side. "I see. Alright." He hung up, cracking his knuckles. "You have an appointment? Because she's gone for the day," he questioned with a raised brow.

I hadn't thought this through, just stopping by on a whim while running errands. I felt stronger than I had since the attack, and with a little extra pocket money from the pills I dealt with my lost keys. Now, I had my possessions from my locker and P.O. Box in my backpack. Anything of value that I owned was on me. Even as little as it was, I had to fight the urge to cradle my bag in my arms.

"No, can you just tell her I stopped by. She can reach me at work."

"Wait now." He raised his hand. "Someone's coming down from her office; you can give them the message."

"Thanks." I stepped back, standing off to the side of the small lobby.

Another lady came in, stepping up to the window, and I turned away.

The heavy security door opened, and an officer in uniform stepped through.

"Hi, I'm Anthony Fields." His warm hand shook mine with a firm grip.

He was a head taller than me, I'd guess six feet with broad shoulders, but his smile put me at ease.

"Mr. Ritter told me you were here for Detective Andres." He encased my hand in both of his and took a step closer. "I had to introduce myself. I was the responding officer that night. It's good to see you now. You have healed exceptionally well."

My eyebrow shot up; it seemed an odd compliment. "Um, Thanks." I pulled out of his grip.

"Is there something I might help you with? I know you came for Andres, but I'm well informed on the case." He crossed his arms over his chest, but his unassuming smile stayed on his face, showing off his perfect teeth.

A little flustered by his attention, I retrieved the card from my pocket and handed it to him. "Some guys came to my work looking for me. They left this card."

He nodded as he looked it over. "This guy, Silas Tillman, he was one of the men that found you. His friends called the police."

It wasn't till the brick of anxiety lifted from my chest that I realized I'd been carrying it around. I sighed with relief as more questions bubbled in my mind. "Do you know why he would be looking for me?"

His lips slid into a crooked smile that showed off a cute dimple; I averted my eyes to the floor.

"Probably the same reason I wanted to introduce myself." He ducked his head, catching my eyes with his warm brown ones. "It's hard to see something like that and not want to know how it turned out." The sympathy on his face made him look young. I had thought he was late twenties, but now I wasn't sure.

I nodded, unsure of how to respond to that.

He handed me the card back. "Was there anything else you needed?"

"No. Thanks." I slid the card into my pocket and turned to leave.

He walked ahead and held the door open for me. I glanced up at him as I passed by. "Thanks, again." Something about the way he smiled at me made me uncomfortable, but not in a bad way, just unexpected.

I heard him follow behind me, but peeked over my shoulder to be sure. His smile stretched when we made eye contact.

"I'm off work now," he explained, quickening his pace to walk beside me.

I lowered my head as I jogged down the steps.

"Where are you parked?"

"I took the metro." I pointed towards the station across the street and pulled my hood up on my jacket. The sun sank behind the buildings, turning the sky a dusky pink. I needed to hurry to make it to Nan's before dark, but Officer Field's smile had me frozen.

He tilted his head. "Let me drive you home. Save you a fare and some time."

My heart quickened with excitement, but getting involved with a cop was a bad idea. I took a few steps back, still facing him. "That's okay. I already paid for the day pass." I waved as I spun away from him.

"Wait." He jogged to my side and fell into pace next to me.

I bit my lip to hide my smirk as I walked to the crosswalk. A part of me, the part that led me into trouble, hoped he would pursue.

"If you insist on riding the Metro, I'll ride with you."

I whirled towards him. "Why?"

"Because I have some questions I need answers to."

That wiped the smile off my face. Maybe he wasn't flirting?

His smile was slow to come. "Like, are you dating anyone? Where do you like to eat? Would you go there with me one day?"

And my smile was back. I looked at the dimming sun, hating my new fear of the dark. "Would you've really ridden the metro with me?"

"Yeah, I still will if you want to. But I'd prefer to drive."

* * *

"Where to?" he asked as he pulled out of the parking lot.

There was no way I could show up at Nan's in a police cruiser; I hadn't expected him to take it home.

"Um, I have to go to work soon. Did you, maybe, want to go get something to eat before my shift?" I attempted a pretty smile, even fluffed my mousy blonde hair for good measure, hoping to appear like I was only flirting.

"How much time do you have? I need to go home and change if we go out to eat, do you mind?" He stopped at a red light and directed his good boy smile at me.

Letting go of my nerves about Nan's, I smiled back with a raised eyebrow. "You're inviting me to your house already? A little forward Mr. Fields, don't you think?"

I laughed as he turned an unexpected shade of pink.

He looked down at his hands as he responded, "I can't go out in uniform when I'm not on duty." He lifted his shoulders, like his jacket was uncomfortable, as he pulled out into traffic. I almost felt bad for teasing him. "But if you have to be at work soon, we can get fast food and eat in the car." He glanced at me. "Not much of a first date though."

I rolled my eyes to the roof. This was a bad idea, now he thought we were on a date. "I have about an hour, let's go with fast food."

We parked behind Johnny's Restaurant, our meal spread out on our laps.

I dipped my nugget in sweet and sour sauce, unsure of how to break the silence. We hadn't done much talking. It was a little awkward sitting in the front of a cop car with an officer dressed in his uniform.

He cleared his throat. "How do you feel? You look like you've healed well, but are you in any pain?"

I touched the rough scab on my eyebrow. "I'm good. My ribs are still sore."

He stretched his arm out and cupped my chin, his thumb gliding over the cut on my lip. "That doesn't hurt?" His touch was warm and desire clear in his eyes.

I shook my head and parted my lips, taking his thumb into my mouth. I grabbed it between my teeth and sucked, tasting the salty mix of French fries and skin.

He sucked air, pulling his hand away as if I'd bitten him.

The moment had been fueled by lust, but the way he turned pink made me suspect he was new to this game. I couldn't help but smile at his embarrassment.

He paused before taking a bite of his burger, his voice strained as he spoke, "I'm glad you're feeling better. I've been worried about you since that night."

I ran my hand through my hair several times; he was obviously trying to ignore what just happened. I would play along for now. "What's going on with the case and the boys that were arrested?"

He shook his head and shrugged with agitation. "All four had their arraignment hearing the day we brought them in and posted bail. Their court date hasn't been set yet; the case is still being built against them. I wish I could give you more news, but the system is slow."

My insides coiled with disgust and anger; those boys were out free to do what they wanted. "Could you fill in the blanks for me? I don't remember much of that night." I looked out the passenger side window at nothing. There was a large brown dumpster in the shadows of the stained brick wall of the restaurant, but I wasn't seeing it.

He picked up the remnants of our meal, stuffing it into the bag it came in. "By the time I arrived, Silas had you wrapped in his jacket and you were unconscious. And Gage and Dexter Lawson were with two of the boys responsible."

I paused from cleaning up my trash. "Gage and Dexter?"

He pushed his light brown hair back. "They were with Silas, the guy who gave you the card. I thought they fought the two boys to detain them, but Gage said all he did was catch them running and they gave up. Their bruises had come from you." He smiled at me and his hair fell back on his forehead. "I was impressed. That was dangerous, and officially I should say you shouldn't fight back like that, but…" He shrugged.

I looked at my lap; now it was my turn to be embarrassed.

"I saw the video the boy we arrested last week had. You yelled, and you tried to run, but you fought when you had no other options." His fingers were light as he guided my chin to face him, his voice even lighter. "I've never seen anything like that, like you."

I didn't want to talk about that night anymore. Lust was back in his eyes, and I had the same desire. My heart fluttered in my chest. We weren't compatible; we came from two different lives. But I could have this moment with him. I had nothing to lose if I acted on the impulse. It's not like we had a tomorrow anyways.

Plus, I needed some fun in my life.

In slow motion, I leaned towards him and our lips met. When he deepened the kiss and swept his tongue into my mouth, I raised myself up and crossed the seat to straddle him.

His grip on my shoulders tightened and he pulled back. "What? We can't do this." But the look in his eyes said otherwise.

Excitement danced in my stomach as I ducked my head to kiss along his jaw and neck, his stubble rough against my lips and cheek. "Sure we can," I whispered against his skin.

His head tilted back and his hands dropped to my hips, gripping them as he sucked in air. I knew he wouldn't stop me now.

He continued with the meaningless words, words to make him feel better about this, like he wasn't expecting it. "You don't have to do this. This wasn't my intention." But his fingers massaged my hips, over my jeans, under my shirt, and his head stayed rolled back, giving me free rein to his neck.

"Mhm," I responded as I ground my hips against him. His finger tips pressed into my skin as he tightened his hold. My fingers moved to his belt buckle, undoing the strap.

His hands left my waist and grabbed the back of my head, pulling me into a hungry kiss. He lifted his hips, allowing me to pull his pants down a little.

My heart pounded as he released me and slid them to his ankles. He left his boxers on, his hardness peeking through the front flap. The exhilaration of the moment made me light headed but unstoppable. I was close to bursting with anticipation as I stroked the smooth length of him.

His breathing was shallow as he watched my hand move between us. "This is illegal."

I moved off his lap, back to my seat, but kept him in my hands, continuing the up and down strokes. I smiled up at him. "So arrest me."

He shook his head, and I dipped down, sucking him into my mouth.

"Ahh," he groaned. One hand dipped into the back of my jeans, his other wound in my hair.

He only let me continue for a few moments before he pulled on my shoulders, bringing me back up to him. He kissed my lips as his fingers moved over the buttons to my pants.

I slid them off and he rolled on a condom; maybe he wasn't as new to this as I thought. I straddled him once more and he guided my hips over him, sliding inside me. He pulled his jacket around me to cover us up from behind.

I smirked at the gesture; it seemed pointless, but sweet.

He pulled on either side of the jacket, pressing me to him, kissing my neck as I rocked on him.

When his hands glided up my shirt, I pushed them down, keeping him away from my scars.

He grabbed my hips and moved me faster. I took over the rhythm, muscles straining, and let all thoughts go. Soon he was panting, his orgasm building. He let out a strangled groan as he spasmed beneath me, gripping my arms to hold me still until his body stopped jerking.

Breathless, I pushed off him and slid back to the passenger seat, pulling my underwear and pants back on. When we were both in order, I opened the door to leave. Reaching for my book bag, I gave him one last look over. Even in the shadows of the evening, he was cute, but I was glad to be leaving. It had been an impulsive and fun moment, but it was over now and I didn't want to deal with the aftermath.

"I've got to get into work. Thanks."

He grabbed my hand before I could back out of the car. "Can I call you sometime?" His brown eyes were already muddied with guilt.

I flashed a lopsided grin and shook my head. "I don't have a phone. Bye." I closed the door before he could respond. There was no need to pretend like we were anything more than a one-time thing.

I jogged with my book bag into the back door of work, leaving my exhilarating afternoon behind me.

5: I Could Imagine

"IF YOU CLOSE MY SECTION TONIGHT, I'LL let you have this tip." Drew lifted the money off the table, holding the bills between the tips of his fingers. He waved it back and forth in front of my face.

I straightened, with a full bin of dirty dishes, and glanced at his section. He hadn't cleaned all night; food pieces littered the floor around the tables and all the condiments needed refilling.

"Twenty dollars to clean this mess." I turned with my bin, walking back to the kitchen.

Drew followed me. "Okay, Deal. But you have to sign off on it now. That was my last table and I need to go." He rubbed his hands together with excitement. "I've got a hot date tonight."

"Alright, go. I'll let Johnny know." I still couldn't serve, and even though bussers are tipped out at the end of the night, it's not much.

"You're the best." He squeezed my shoulders, and then jogged out of the kitchen, whipping his apron off and tossing it into the wash bin.

I dropped the dishes off and went to the dining room to clean up Drew's section.

"Cleaning up for him again?" Johnny questioned from the bar.

"Not for free," I assured, spraying a table down with cleaner.

He went back to mixing drinks for the few patrons left. It was near closing time and business was winding down. Johnny was the owner, but also tended the large mahogany bar that was the center of the restaurant. He had built it himself and often reminded us of that fact.

Louisa, Jonny's wife, was also working tonight. She walked out of the kitchen with a slice of chocolate cake balanced on her tray, dessert for her last table.

I'd be able to go home soon. I was hoping to hitch a ride with Drew, but now that idea was out the window. Johnny and Louisa lived above the restaurant; they couldn't drive me.

I walked back to the kitchen to retrieve the broom and dustpan. The only other worker still on duty was the cook.

"Hey Marco," I started sweetly. When he looked up from scrubbing the grill, I continued, "Do you think you can give me a lift home tonight?"

He tilted his head in apology, and my stomach dropped.

"Sorry, Regan, I live across the street, so I walk."

Walk. The air in the room froze, and it stung to inhale. I was choking. My nails bit into my palm, and I steadied myself.

I'd call a cab. No need to panic.

What was wrong with me? I needed to get a grip on this anxiety. All those stupid therapists I had to see while in foster care should have taught me something; I should be able to cope with this, but my fear of the dark since the attack seemed to be escalating, not improving.

Still trying to steady the erratic beating of my heart, I went back to Drew's section to clean and nearly bumped into Louisa.

"Whoa girl, watch where you're going." She grabbed my elbow with care in her eyes. "You alright?"

"Sorry," I mumbled, pulling out of her grasp.

She nodded behind her. "Some guy is asking for you out there." She walked past me and into the kitchen before I could question her.

I closed my eyes, inhaling, and went to face whoever was here.

It took a moment to recognize him out of his uniform, but it was Officer Fields in dark denim jeans and a leather coat. He sat at the bar, watching me walk towards him with a broad smile on his face and his hair styled back in a messy wave.

I tried to cover my groan and rearrange my face into a smile, but fell short of removing the disapproval from my tone. "What are you doing here?" I questioned low once I was standing in front of him.

Johnny nodded from the other side of the bar, "Your friend's here to give you a ride home. Just clean Drew's section and you can go. Your portion of the tips will be ready tomorrow."

Officer Fields raised his eyebrows at me, and his grin widened, daring me to say something.

"Alright, thanks," I responded to Johnny.

I finished cleaning with an odd mixture of excitement and dread. I was glad to not have to call a cab, but I wasn't looking forward to the pending conversation. That's not what I signed up for when riding him earlier. That was supposed to be the end of our talking. This was one of those moments where I wanted to punch myself in the face.

We walked to his truck in silence. He opened the door for me and leaned in a little too close for comfort. I dodged him and hauled myself up into the seat, setting my book bag on the floor in front of me.

I had been trying to formulate a plan while cleaning, but had come up with nothing.

He climbed into the driver's side and shut his door. The interior lights dimmed with each second, washing us in shadows, but he kept his eyes forward, unmoving.

Just when I thought he would start the truck, he banged his hand on the steering wheel. "What the hell was that today?"

Surprised by his outburst, I tensed and sat up, grabbing my bag. "It was supposed to be fun," I bit back, reaching for the door handle.

"Wait, don't leave." The anger vanished from his voice.

I sat back with relief, not wanting to step out into the darkness.

"I, uh, I've never done anything like that before," he began, looking at his tangled hands in his lap. "It was fun." He looked at me with a shadow of a smile, "But, in there, you weren't happy to see me. I could tell."

My eyes rose to the gray lining of his roof. Ugh, I had hurt his feelings. I thought he had understood *that* was a one-time thing. I wasn't the type of girl he would want a relationship with. He probably had career women with college degrees lined up for him.

"It was spontaneous and fun." I swept my eyes down to meet his and smiled, confused. "Nothing serious. You and me," I gestured between us, "We're not a thing. Never could be."

"So why do it then?" He leaned forward on his steering wheel and shook his head, eyebrows knitting together. "I thought you liked me. I like you."

For a moment, a half second, my heart melted. It seemed so sweet. He liked me. This guy, who had to be at least five years older than me, had a job, a car, and a home, liked me. He was the type a girl could take home to her family, I could tell. But I didn't have a family, and I wasn't the girl you'd want to show off to your parents. He must be dense to not realize that I'm not that girl. I didn't fuck him because I was in love; I did it because I could. Because he wanted me.

But then he continued, "What we did today, I can't get it out of my head. I can't get you out of my head." He gripped my thigh, his hand inching up my jeans.

My heart hardened, and I pushed him away with a bitter laugh. Yeah, he liked me alright. He liked that I did things the girls he knew wouldn't do. "Are you planning on driving me home?"

He nodded, stunned by my reaction. "Yeah, okay."

I sat in silence after giving him directions to Nan's apartment complex. My emotions were all over the place, but mostly I was angry with myself. I had done it again. Slept with someone out of my league, which would have been fine if he never showed back up. But here he was, and I had let myself, for half a second, believe he wanted me. But all he wanted was sex, just like the others.

Not that there had been a lot. Since I lost my virginity at 14, I've only had a handful of guys, and only one had ever gotten to me. I wouldn't let that happen again.

The fleeting moment I had with Officer Fields was enough to make me want to scream. I hated the desperate girl in me that wanted a man. Better to use them than let them use you.

As we pulled up to a stoplight, he started again. "Look, I'm sorry. I didn't come here for that. I just wanted to talk to you. To see you again."

Still facing the window, I peeked at him from the corner of my eye. The lights of the city lit up odd parts of his face, but his eyes were pleading with me, and when I didn't respond, he grabbed my hand.

"Please. You're different from anyone I know."

I pulled away, annoyed. "Please, you don't even know me."

"But I want to get to know you. How about a real date?" His smile seemed hopeful as he accelerated the truck when the light turned green.

I turned towards him, watching the streetlights illuminate the car in waves. He kept looking back towards me with flicks of his head as he tried to split his attention between me and the road.

My head fell on the cool glass of the passenger window, and I stared straight ahead, tired of this conversation. "No."

He didn't respond as we made the turns into Nan's neighborhood. I directed him to the first complex, even though Nan's was two buildings back. He parked in the middle of the lot, but kept the engine running.

"Well, good luck with everything, Regan." He managed to make it sound a lot like a "fuck you."

"Thanks, you too," I mumbled as I gathered my belongings and hopped out of the truck, slamming the door behind me.

The rumble of his truck faded as he pulled away, and I walked towards the buildings, breathing through my fear of being alone in the night. I pulled my book bag and jacket tighter around me, like a shield, and ran around the apartment complex towards Nan's.

My heart pounded in my ears, and my skin tingled as all my senses went into overdrive. I couldn't keep up the pace and had to slow to a walk. Shadows were everywhere, and I kept turning to scope out my surroundings. The grassy field between buildings appeared empty, but the rustle of tree limbs in the wind played tricks with sound and I couldn't shake the fear that surged inside me.

By time I reached Nan's door, my heart was crashing in my chest and I was close to throwing up. My arms shook beyond my control as I knocked on the door. I tried to fight the tears just behind my eyes as I waited for someone to answer. I needed to get inside. Now.

James cracked the door, and then swung it open for me, his too large clothes hanging off his slim, tall frame. "Hey, did you bring home any tips, or food, or anything?" His eyes, their typical shade of red, scanned over my body.

I walked past him, escaping the dark. "I didn't get any tips tonight and no food. Sorry, the kitchen was closed when I left. Where's Nan?" He had one friend over tonight, zoned out on the couch, staring at the television.

"Wait." James grabbed my arm. "You have any more pills? I heard you sold some yourself. Everything's gone now. You owe us rent. It's not good business going behind our back."

I hadn't liked taking my pills; they made me disconnected, so I opted to take Ibuprofen for pain, and sold some to make extra money. But Nan knew about that.

I kept my appearance calm, but my heart was pounding, sending nervous energy through me. "Nan and I worked out our arrangement, talk to her about my rent." I pulled my arm from his grip and walked away with more bravado than I felt.

"Nan's not here, so I'm talking to you." He followed behind me.

That was my cue. I went into Nan's room and locked the door before he had a chance to stop me.

He pounded on the door twice. "You can't hide forever."

"I'm not hiding, I'm going to bed," I said to the closed door. The last three pills were in my backpack; I took them out and slipped them into the third drawer down on the dresser. I'd give them to Nan in the morning. Maybe they'd buy me a little more time.

* * *

I awoke and sat up, grabbing the clock on the nightstand table, ready to bludgeon someone.

The shouts continued in the other room, and I scooted off the bed. Tiptoeing to the bedroom door, I strained to make sense of James's tirade.

The door flew open wide and a shock of light blinded me from the other side. I froze, gripping the heavy clock in my hand.

Nan crossed into the room and whirled, slamming the door close as she shouted, "Go kill yourself!" She flipped on the lights, illuminating the room and her anger.

Growling, she flung her clothes into the corner and threw drawers open and shut as she snatched out shorts and a t-shirt.

I sat on the edge of the bed, waiting for the hurricane in Nan to calm. When she was fully dressed, she perched on the chair beside the window, smoking her cigarette.

She was vibrating with anger as she spoke between drags, "Fucking junkie doesn't care about anything but his next high. He would have kept all your pills to himself if I hadn't taken some and sold them. Still, he ate most of 'em. And now he's mad that you sold some." She shook her head and met my eyes. "Thanks for not telling him that was my idea. He'd be pissed I kept that from him. But, shit, he can't be trusted with money." She pulled her thin, brown hair over one shoulder and picked at the ends of it. "I just don't know what to do with him." She dropped her hair and stood, looking at me. "Do you have any pills left?"

I took a deep breath and nodded to her dresser. "Third drawer down. There's three of them."

She knelt in front of the drawer and searched for the pills, scooping them up in her hand. "I'll give him these, then maybe he'll calm the fuck down."

I didn't like her plan. "Nan, are you sure?"

She stopped on her way to the door and turned towards me with a shrug of her bony shoulder. "No, but it's all I can think to do for now."

I leaned back on the bed after she walked out. I needed to get out of here. When I started serving again, I'd be able to afford a cheap apartment. Until then, this was it. Even though it sucked, it was better than nothing.

Nan walked back into the room and flopped next to me with a sigh. "He should be good for now. I can't keep doing this, though."

I looked at her out of the corner of my eye. "I'm going to get my own apartment; you can move in with me."

One side of her mouth pulled up. "Thanks, but no. I can't leave him alone, he's family, ya know?"

I shook my head. I didn't know, but I could imagine.

* * *

The Boxing Club was an open warehouse with two boxing rings in the center. Mats, bags, and weights lined the perimeter. There were several dozen people around the gym at different stations working out.

I hesitated by the door, unsure of who I was looking for. Or more accurately, who was looking for me.

A man smiled at me while pounding a body bag.

"Excuse me," I called to him. "Is Silas Tillman here?"

He steadied the bag in his hands and nodded his head to one of the boxing rings. "He's over there."

There were two kids in the ring with helmets and gloves on, sparring. At one corner, a tall, muscular man gave directions to the miniature boxers.

There are strange bits and pieces that I remember from that night, and his bald head was one of them. I recognized him as the calm one.

"Can I help you?" he asked as I neared the ring. His eyes followed the boys jabbing at each other. "Keep your hands up, Derek."

"Mr. Tillman?"

At my question, his eyes swept over me with eyebrows raised.

"I wanted to thank you, and I was also told you were looking for me."

"Practice on the bags for a minute boys, I'll be right back." He climbed out of the ring and his narrowed eyes scanned over me. "Regan?" At my nod, his full lips spread into a smile. "Well I'll be damned, I wouldn't have recognized you."

"Thank you. Thank you for your help that night." My voice strained with more emotion than I'd expected.

He shook his head and continued staring with wide eyes. "Come with me."

Walking to the next ring, he patted on the canvas. "Gage. Dexter. Look who decided to show up."

The two shirtless men in the ring paused and swept their gazes across me.

One was young and lean with trim muscles and definition. His clear, pale eyes stood out against his light brown skin. His smile was friendly as he scanned me, but I only spared a second to look at him.

The other man was large and cut, a head taller than the boy in the ring with him. The dark ink of his tattoos stood out on his tan skin, several spotting his right arm and ribs. But when his cool blue eyes met mine, they squeezed the air from my lungs and sucked the warmth from my body.

The younger guy jumped over the ropes and hopped off the canvas, landing in front of me, effectively pulling my gaze from the other.

"Hey, I'm Dexter." He pulled a glove off his hand and tossed it back in the ring, and then looked me over once more. "Wait a minute, are you—You are, aren't you?"

Before I knew what was happening, he was hugging me. "How are you?" He held me at arm's length, and then squeezed me close again. "Man, I'm glad to see you."

Wide eyed with shock, I stepped out of his grasp.

"Calm down, Dex, you're scaring the girl." The deep voice stopped Dexter from hugging me again.

The man in the ring climbed out of the ropes. My nerves pulsed the closer he got, urging me to flee. His mere presence overwhelmed me, more than the other boy's over eager greeting.

"Hi, I'm Gage Lawson." He nodded his head to me.

My heart raced, making up for the beats it skipped at the sound of his voice.

I didn't recognize either of them from that night, but I assumed the younger one was the nervous guy in shorts. I don't know why I couldn't place Gage; he didn't seem like the type you would forget.

But I recalled Officer Fields words; Gage had chased the boys and caught two of them. No wonder they gave up, his every pore radiated strength.

I nodded to each of them, finding it hard to look at Gage but even harder to keep my eyes away. "Thank you. All of you. For helping me the other night."

They nodded back, not saying anything. I shifted on my feet, unsure of what else to do.

"Come back to my office, I'd like to talk with you," Silas broke the silence.

I followed him, but snuck another look at Gage as I walked by. His light brown hair was spiky with sweat, and his strong jaw clenched as his cool eyes followed me.

Silas sat on one side of his desk, and Dexter and I sat in the wooden chairs on the opposite side. Gage leaned against the wall, an ominous presence shadowing our meeting.

"How have you been, Regan?" Silas asked, leaning back in his chair.

"Good." I shrugged. "Mostly healed. But that night's still a mystery."

Dexter leaned towards me. "I bet. That was the craziest thing I've ever seen, and I've seen some shit. But man." He shook his head, and for the first time his smile melted into a grimace. "I'm just glad Silas had his gun on him to scare them away. Although I wish we could've kicked their asses. Fucking cowards."

"So there was a gun." I looked towards Silas. "I thought I heard a shot, but I wasn't sure if I was remembering right."

Silas met Gage's eyes, and something passed between them before Gage focused on me. "I had a fight that night. We were leaving out the back when we saw them," he paused, swallowing some words, "attacking you."

Silas picked up the story, "It was bad. I shot my gun into the air, hoping to get them off of you. It worked; they ran away and Gage chased 'em. Dexter went to check on you, and I called the cops."

Dexter smiled and tipped his head to me. "One of the boys Gage caught had a broken nose. You did that."

I nodded again, trying to mesh their story with what I already knew. "You were the one with me when I got up?"

He laughed and shifted his eyes to Silas. "I was freaking out. I thought you were going to die, and then you just stood up."

I cringed. "That bad, huh?"

Silas gave Dexter a look that silenced him. "No, not that bad." He stepped in front of me, leaning on the edge of his desk. "You were attacked by a group of boys and fought back, injuring several. And you still stood up after." He nodded around the room. "I saw that video—we all did. Where did you learn to fight like that?"

I shifted in my seat. I had taught myself; I was tired of getting beat up, so I googled defensive moves and practiced them. But I skipped answering, and focused on something else they said.

"How did you see the video? I still haven't seen it."

Dexter pulled out his phone. "The cops released it; it was on the news and the Internet. Here, I've got it if you want to see it."

"No," I responded before he could hand me his phone. I wasn't ready to see it, not yet, and not in front of people. I hated the idea of others, people I didn't even know, watching my attack.

Gage's eyes narrowed as I fidgeted in my chair. His quiet, but dominant, presence seemed too large for the room, making me claustrophobic.

"Thank you, really, I wish I could do more, repay you somehow. But... thank you." I stood to leave. I needed to see that video, away from these people, away from Gage.

Silas straightened. "Wait; there is something you can do. It's more for you though, but it will help us as well."

Dexter was smiling, his blue eyes alight with excitement, but Gage wouldn't look at me; his hard gaze locked on Silas. Then he turned and walked out, pulling the door shut behind him.

Silas shrugged and resumed the conversation. "You have a talent for fighting, for boxing, and I'm a trainer and manager. I propose a partnership. What do you think?"

My eyebrows rose in question. "You want to train me? I don't have money for that." Was he trying to sell me a gym membership?

"I want to train you, but it's more than that. If you're up for it, you could fight this Friday and earn some money."

"Friday?" I sat back down in the chair; that was only two day's away. "How much money?" Anticipation pulsed, tingling my skin. This sudden turn of events was exciting, even if I wasn't sure I could actually do it.

"You would get three hundred dollars. It's a professional match, but your opponent's new to boxing, too. We'd have to act fast if you want to do this. You need to be licensed and see our doctor."

I looked from Dexter's encouraging grin to Silas's neutral face. "Can I fight that soon? Don't I need to practice first? Why the rush?"

I wanted to do it and the money was tempting, but my suspicion was building.

"The girl that's supposed to fight dropped out last minute. Someone needs to fight or we lose money. You'd be doing us a favor."

Dexter scooted his chair closer to mine, leaning forward. "I could help you practice. Like Dexter's boxing boot camp." His eyes sparked with energy. "For future fights you'd need training, which is where Silas can help. But knowing what you can do, I think you could win this."

I nodded, considering. Thinking about winning relit my excitement. Pain didn't scare me, and I knew I could handle a one on one fight, win or lose. "Would I still get paid if I lost?"

Dexter's grin stretched even further, and he was almost out of his seat. "Hell yeah, but I don't think you'll lose."

His encouragement pumped me up. "And you'll train me after, so I can keep fighting? Professionally?"

Silas nodded. "Do we have a deal?"

"Tell me what I have to do."

6: Fight Night

THE NEXT COUPLE OF DAYS WERE A blur of activity. If I wasn't working, I was at the gym. Silas sent me to a nearby doctor's office for a physical and then disappeared. Gage was nowhere around.

Dexter stayed true to his words, giving me a crash course in boxing. He practiced with me, helping me prepare with tips on form and blocking, but my nerves increased to rapid fire as fight time came near. I wanted to keep practicing and expel the nervous energy I felt, but Dexter insisted I rest before. He introduced me to his girlfriend, Leona, a tiny Latina with energy to match his. She brought me a sports bra, shorts, and boxing gloves for the fight.

When the time came to go to the gym holding the match, I was all energy, but it swirled between fear and excitement in an intoxicating mix. I sat in the small room off the main gym with Dexter and Leona. I wanted to throw up.

Silas walked in, and I stopped in mid pace, bracing myself for bad news. I was sure something would go wrong.

He smiled at me. "You ready?"

I forced myself to swallow, hoping to keep down my lunch. "Now?" I looked around the room, not sure what I should take or do.

Dexter laughed. "Chill, you'll do fine. Just remember what we talked about."

I shook my head, eyes wide; I couldn't remember anything.

Silas squeezed my shoulders. "Everything's ready. You'll do great, you've already won this. But remember, when you win, keep up the show and smile for the crowd. You want to win fans tonight."

I nodded again, and then let him guide me out the door.

The music blared, drowning out the announcer's voice as I entered. None of it reached me. The mix of adrenaline and nerves had me high.

My opponent was full of confidence, jumping around as she came into the ring.

The bell rung to start the fight and I couldn't think—I couldn't get it together. I wasn't ready. I looked to Silas outside the ring, hoping for direction; instead, I got hit.

The first punch threw me off balance, and the second drew blood. But it forced me to focus, bringing me back into the present moment. I fought back, the only way I knew how. Before I knew it, I was walking out of the ring a winner, more euphoric than ever before, but still wanting to throw up.

* * *

After a quick shower, I dressed in my standard jeans, t-shirt, and hoody, throwing my wet hair back into a low ponytail. The shorter front strands fell loose, but I didn't care. I gave myself one last proud smile before exiting the locker room.

Dexter was waiting for me outside the doors.

"There's the champ!" He pushed on my shoulders with excitement.

More people filled the seats in the gym, and the buzz of conversations made it hard to hear.

Dexter leaned into me. "Leona's saved us seats up front."

I followed him through the crowd.

Leona stood as I approached. "You did great out there."

Someone behind us patted my back. "You made it rain. Way to bring it."

I nodded and smiled at the odd statement, and Dexter cracked up laughing.

Leona shook her head. "I can't believe you chose that song for her. I almost peed my pants when they announced "Regan 'Make It Rain' Sommers"

"What the fu—I didn't even pay attention. Am I stuck with that name now?" I was too stunned to be angry.

He shook his head, still laughing. "No. You can change it, but for last minute I thought it was great. Rain. Sommers. Summer rain." At my narrowed eyes, he put his hand on my shoulder. "We'll work on it."

We took our seats; Dexter sat in the middle so he could explain things to me. I had already missed the other female fight, and the next two were men. Both the fights were won by mere points, reinforcing Dexter's advice about the importance of scoring.

As they set up for the last fight of the night, the crowd grew and the room pulsed with anticipation.

Dexter stood. "I have to go help Gage for his fight, I'm his corner man." He bent down and kissed Leona, then scooted out of our row.

Leona bounced on to the chair next to me. "Have you been to Gage's fights before?"

I shook my head. "Never been to any fights before. Only watched on T.V."

"Oh man," she giggled, "And you had to be the opening match at your first time to the fights." She shook her head in disbelief. "You've got balls!"

The light's lowered, and a Latin rap song started as Gage's opponent walked out with a big smile and large entourage. He disrobed and jogged around the ring, bouncing back on the ropes at all four sides. Then the music shifted.

Gage entered to some electronic mix with a hard beat that could be felt under the roar of the crowd. His gaze was cold and hard as steel, never leaving his opponent as he climbed between the ropes. Silas and Dexter followed him, copying his menacing manner.

An announcer in a suit jacket paired with street clothes and a baseball cap began introductions, his voice drowned out by the music and crowd. "In the red corner... gold shorts... 196... six wins via knockout... Pablo 'Piranha' Sanchez." He extended his arm towards the fighter who raised a gloved hand to his ear and waved his tattooed arm, encouraging cheers.

He was large, no doubt; taller than Gage, but with a layer of softness over his muscles that made Gage's chiseled body stand out. Gage smirked, watching his opponent pump up the crowd.

The announcer stepped towards him and I strained to hear his statistics.

"... Blue corner... silver and black shorts... weighing 194, six foot three... four wins, undefeated... Gage 'Lighting' Lawson."

Leona leaned into my ear, speaking over the crowd, "He only switched to professional boxing a couple of months ago, but he already has a reputation from before."

I barely registered what she said as I watched the two fighters bump gloves and begin the match. Gage stood on the defense with his arms up as the other boxer circled around him, throwing jabs and testing his reflexes.

Gage blocked a combination shot with slight twists of his body before striking with a quick, straight jab to the face. Pablo's head snapped back with surprising force; it hadn't seemed like Gage had hit him that hard.

Pablo came back a little more wary, keeping one arm raised to protect his face as he threw punches that Gage blocked with pivots and steps back.

I was on edge, waiting for Gage to do something. But all he did was block punch after punch, never reciprocating with any of his own. I couldn't believe he was letting Pablo lead them around the ring in their slow, odd dance. The bell rang, signaling the end of the round, and both fighters returned to their corners.

Dexter hopped up into the ring with Gage, wiping his face and re-applying Vaseline, his lips moving a mile a minute. Silas stayed to the side but patted Gage's shoulder at the start of the next round.

Gage resumed his same defensive stance, but the moment Pablo attempted a right cross, he rolled his shoulder with it and hooked his left arm in an effortless punch. Pablo fell to the ground as quick and smooth as the punch he received.

The referee counted each second; at five it was clear the fight was over. Pablo raised his head at six, but dropped it back down, not even trying to raise himself up.

I sat stunned at the quickness of it all. Leona grabbed my arm, pulling me to stand with her. She'd been standing during the fight, and now she was jumping up and down with excitement. Everyone in the room was on their feet, yelling as Gage was announced the winner.

Leona tossed her long, wavy hair over her shoulder as she raised her arms in a little dance. "Woot. Woot." She bit her lip as her smile crinkled her nose. "We are going to party tonight. I love fight night parties! You're coming with, right?"

I shrugged, unsure. I was up for celebrating, hell I had enough energy to party all weekend, but I needed more details about where we would go.

She gave me a sidelong look as she hooked her arm around my neck. "Of course you are, Chica! Come on, Dexter will meet us at the car."

I stepped back, out of reach, and gestured for her to lead the way.

In the parking lot, I questioned, "So where's the party at?"

She sat on the trunk of her car and pulled out her phone. "Not sure. Sometimes we go to the clubs, but sometimes we just go to a house, usually Dexter's." She looked beyond me and slid off the car. "Hey Jase, what's good for tonight?"

A frat boy type parted from his group of friends to give Leona a hug. "Depends, what's Dex getting into? I was waiting for him to tell me. Tell him we should go to his place. I need a break from the clubs."

He waved his friends over, and they discussed the highlights of the night, mainly Gage's knockout punch. When one of the boys mentioned my fight, I had to pinch the inside of my hand to keep from exploding with pride.

"Who was that new girl? She was raw. It was badass the way she let go. Were you here in time for that?" he asked his friends.

Leona nudged my shoulder. "Meet Rea, she's that bad ass."

I'd been called Rea a few times in my life, but it never stuck, and it wasn't frequent. Dexter had been calling me that all day, and now it seemed like that's what I would go by with this group. I liked it.

I bobbed my head as I gave a small wave. "Hey." For once I didn't mind being the center of attention. I soaked up their compliments and adulations; I felt larger than life. The cold of the night couldn't even touch me.

Dexter appeared in the center of the group. "Alright Scrapper, let's go celebrate that win. My place everyone, but bring your own drinks. I'm looking at you Danny." The boys cheered as they dispersed to their own cars.

"Where do you live?" I asked before agreeing to go.

"Not far, Harborview," Dexter responded.

"You live in Harborview, or just near Harborview?" They didn't strike me as the money type, but you had to be to live in Harborview.

Even in the dark, his sly smile showed and his light blue eyes lit up. "In Harborview."

I slid into the backseat of the car. Dexter drove and Leona sat in the passenger seat.

I was stuck on this new information. "Do you live with your parents?"

He met my eyes in the rear view mirror. "Nope, just my brother and me."

It's not that Harborview was millionaire rich, but it was close to it. Never had I met someone who lived there, let alone been there myself. It was within the city, but it might as well be a different world from mine.

"Who's your brother? What does he do?" I couldn't contain my curiosity.

Leona laughed and twisted in her seat to face me. She rested her chin on the top of the seat, her large brown eyes bright with amusement. "Gage is Dexter's brother."

I guess I remember Officer Fields saying Gage and Dexter Lawson, but I hadn't connected the dots. They looked different. Dexter was a coffee and cream color, and Gage was white. Tan, but still white. Also, their build was different, Dexter was lean and Gage was thick. Now that I thought about it, their eyes were a similar grayish blue, but Dexter's held a warmth that Gage's lacked.

Dexter stopped at a red light and twisted to me, his expression serious. "Gage is probably adopted, but don't tell him that. He hasn't figured it out yet."

I narrowed my eyes; I knew he was teasing me, but on which part? Were they really brothers?

He laughed, a full, melodious sound that made me smile, even in my confusion. "I'm fuckin' with you. He's not adopted. We just have different dads. It's funny, people are always so surprised. I know I'm much better looking, but damn, he's not that bad."

I shook my head with a slight puff of laughter. Dexter was attractive, in a pretty way, and his energy only helped, whereas Gage had a darkness that made him intimidating, but a primal sex appeal that couldn't be denied.

Dexter pulled in front of a liquor store and turned to Leona and I. "What do you ladies want?"

"Get me soda and Rum," Leona requested.

"Soda please." I stretched my arm between the seats to hand Dexter several dollars.

He shook his head. "Just soda?" At my nod, he continued. "I'll get a handle of captain, and we'll all share."

I didn't drink, but was used to people assuming they could talk me into it. It wasn't that I had anything against others drinking, I found their antics amusing, but I couldn't stand the out of control feeling I had the two times I tried it. I already had my plan—I'd walk around with my soda in a glass and let them assume what it's mixed with.

As Dexter walked into the store, Leona explained, "He has a fake ID, but his friend works here so he doesn't even need it. How old are you anyways?"

"Nineteen, and you?"

"Nineteen, too. Dexter just turned twenty."

After he returned with a case of beer, Coke, and Captain Morgan, we made a few more turns, then pulled up to a gate. He pushed some buttons, and the bars slid open to his community. He let several cars pass through before following them in and parking at a corner townhome right on the water's edge.

His friends walked down the street from a nearby parking lot with their own cases and bottles of alcohol.

Dexter led the way up the steps to the front door and entered first. Beyond the foyer, Gage was descending the stairs with a stunning woman. She looked straight off the pages of Vogue. Tall, thin, and well dressed. Only her hair was less than perfect, knotted in a just got laid sort of way.

Gage paused mid-step as Dexter and his friends streamed in and then resumed his path. My position at the back blocked him from view once he was off the steps, but his deep, honeyed voice was enough to make my skin tingle.

"Make sure to keep your party in the basement and have them all out by one. I've got training in the morning and so do you."

Dexter's lighter voice responded, "Will do. You gonna hang with us tonight? Celebrate that win?" He nodded to Leona. "Take them downstairs, Baby. I'll be down soon."

As the group filed past them, Gage's Vogue-model grabbed his hand, speaking in a soft, whispery voice, "I'd love to hang out a bit longer, help you celebrate some more."

He tilted his head considering her, then his eyes flicked over me as I passed by. "Regan?"

I paused and gave a slight nod of acknowledgment before following the group down the stairs.

Gage's smooth voice spoke from behind, "We'll hang out."

7: Static

I LEFT BEHIND THE OPEN, BUT TIDY foyer, descending into a sports bar. Framed sports posters of knockouts and football plays covered the dark gray walls. Three big screen TV's were mounted above a fireplace and an oversized playpen sofa was in front of them. A bar stretched across the opposite wall with leather stools and wood trim. A pool table was in the center of the room and several boys surrounded it, racking the balls.

I took a seat next to Leona on the bench facing the pool table.

"Do you play?" I asked.

"Sometimes, but only when these idiots aren't taking it too seriously." She nodded at the boys who were throwing money down on the green felt, wagering bets on who would win.

Her eyes lit up as Dexter rounded the corner of the stairs, his liquor store bag in tow. She stretched her arms towards him, making grabby motions with her hands. "Ooh. Ooh. Ooh. Gimme."

He kissed Leona, holding the bag out of reach with one hand while patting her in a calming gesture with the other. In a mock attempt not to be heard, he dropped his voice. "Chill, babe. I know I'm hard to resist, but we've got company."

She slapped him away. "Oh yeah, so hard to resist. You know I only keep you around for one reason." With a raised brow, she stood up and grabbed the bag from him. "To make the drinks." She winked in my direction and sashayed to the bar with the bag in her arms.

I laughed as Dexter grabbed his heart and followed her. "You're killing me, Lee Lee."

When Gage walked into the room with his model trailing close behind, the group at the pool table immediately took notice.

"Gage, you want to play?"

"Hey man, good fight tonight."

"Here you can take my spot if you want. I can get next game."

He took one of the pool sticks pushed in his direction as his eyes swept around the room. "Yeah, okay, I'll play. Who's up first?"

The frat boy, Jase, started racking the balls again; they had already started one game, but abandoned it when Gage arrived. "That'd be me. You can break first."

The girl with Gage reluctantly released his hand and went to sit on a nearby stool, her eyes glued to him like he was all there was to see.

I couldn't contain my eye roll at how they fell all over him. I guess it wasn't only me who he intimidated. Although with his just washed hair sticking up in tufts, his casual jeans, t-shirt, and zip up hoody, his scary vibe was muted. Just a tad.

"Was this your first fight tonight?" A boy sitting next to me asked.

My smile stretched as I nodded. I was still amazed at myself. A few days ago, I would have never thought this possible. Now it was all I wanted. This week had taken a turn, but I was used to the unexpected.

The boy's name was Danny and he went to UMBC with Dexter and Leona. My first impression of them being frat boys was right. Dex never joined, but many in the group were frat brothers, including Jase.

As the night continued, everyone loosened up with alcohol, becoming more social, and I had to start adjusting my prejudice of college kids. They didn't seem that stuck up. In fact, they just seemed crazy.

"Show her the hug cam." Danny laughed as he nudged Dexter.

We were watching different YouTube videos on one of the big screen's. Dexter went to his channel and clicked on a compilation of Vines, with Dexter as the star. He hugged random people in different settings. Their reactions ranged from pushing him to laughing to hugging him back.

His friends were all cracking up laughing as the video played, and I couldn't help but laugh along with them; it was so random.

When it ended, Dexter turned to me expectantly. "Kinda funny, right? You should try it some time."

"It looks like an excuse to hug a bunch of pretty girls to me," I answered wryly.

Leona pushed his shoulder. "See. I'm not the only one who says that."

Dexter popped out of his seat and pointed at me, excitement lighting his face. "Challenge accepted! Tomorrow, I'm going out and hugging dudes. Then let's see what happens. In fact," He looked around the room, "I'm going to practice now." He marched over to his brother, who had his back to us, lining up a shot on the pool table. He threw his arms around him and squeezed him, hard, his eyes shutting as he snuggled up to his back.

I let out a shocked laugh and vibrated with suppressed laughter.

Gage straightened and twisted around, looking down as his brother pressed into his chest. His confused expression softened as he glanced around the room, taking in the laughter. His face transformed with a small, soft smile, and his chest shook with his own amusement. He pulled his brother off of him and held him out at arm's length.

"How the hell are we related? You are a lunatic." It was almost a whisper.

"Alright, well if I can get away with hugging you, I think I can take on anyone." Dexter walked away to stand in front of me. "So since you presented this challenge, you have to come with me tomorrow to witness it."

I straightened up and pressed my hand to my chest in confusion. "Me? I didn't tell you to do anything."

Gage walked over and sat in the open seat beside me, looking towards the TV. "Oh, now I get it. This is all part of those videos you're always taking." He shook his head, but the low rumble of his laugh vibrated through me. "Show that one you did at the gym the other day."

Everyone on the couch seemed to let out a sigh of relief at Gage's response, including Dexter.

Another video started. A guy at the gym was punching the body bags when Dexter leapt into the shot and straddled the bag, sending it flying. The bag bounced into the original guy, flinging him to the ground and knocking Dexter off the bag.

It was official. He was crazy. But he had me laughing more than I ever had before.

We watched more videos, and as others joined us on the couch, Gage scooted closer to me. He didn't say anything, but I could feel him, like static electricity. The closer he got, the stronger it was—an ever-present fuzzy warning between us. Even when his model sat on the other side of him, linking her arms with him, I couldn't shake the feeling. I tried to focus on the videos, but he wasn't the type you could ignore.

Jase turned to his friends. "We need to go soon. Gage said everyone out at one."

Gage shifted, leaning over me slightly to respond to him. "No, you all can stay longer."

His heavy warmth was suffocating, the fuzz of electricity spiked, and I pressed myself back into the couch. When he straightened, I hopped up and asked to borrow Leona's phone. I needed to call a cab. It was getting late, and even if Gage was alright with people staying now, I knew it was the alcohol that changed his mind. He had wanted us gone. Plus, I wanted to start training in the morning, too.

"Sure." Leona slurred as she wobbled to her purse. "Here, I'll write the address for you, too."

"Thanks." I took the phone and address and walked to the stairway to make the call.

After the arrangements were set, I returned to the room and found Dexter. "Hey, a cab is coming in about 10 minutes. Can you let them in your gate when they buzz in?"

His face fell with disappointment. "You're leaving already? Alright, I'll let 'em in, but we're still on for tomorrow, right? I have a hug cam mission."

"I'll be at the gym in the morning and then I have to work after that."

"You're not escaping that easily. We'll work something out."

When the house phone rang, signaling that the cab was at the community gate, I said my goodbyes and walked upstairs.

I could feel the cold night air through the windowpane by the door as I watched for the lights of the cab.

"You're leaving?" Gage's deep voice came from behind.

I spun towards him and cringed at being taken by surprise.

He leaned against the doorframe to the basement steps, a beer bottle dangling from one hand, and his lip turned up in amusement.

His eyes zoned in on me as he pushed off the wall and took an easy step closer.

"You don't have to go. You could stay here."

"Uh, thanks." I broke his gaze to check outside. No cab yet. "Cab's already on its way." My voice sounded shaky, even to my own ears.

His slight smile inched up a bit more as he watched me, and he took another step towards me. "Do I scare you?"

I straightened at his words, remembering myself. I'm not sure what to call what I was feeling; it was something very much like fear, but I wouldn't let him know that. I raised my chin, defiant, and shook my head, not trusting my voice to keep up the act.

He licked his lips, and his smile stretched just a bit more. "Then come a little closer." He took a step of his own, now only an arm's length away. That sizzle of electricity charged the air between us.

At the same time, the lights of the cab streaked through the window and relief surged through me. "My rides here," I said in dismissal, putting the door between us in an instant.

I jogged down the steps to the waiting cab, sliding into the warmth of the back seat. I rattled off Nan's address and slumped back.

I had no clue what that was in there or what he was trying to do. Whatever it was, I didn't like it. Nor did I like my reaction. I had to be careful with him.

* * *

Nan met me at the door. She linked her arm through mine, partially for balance and partially to whisper to me, "I need the bedroom tonight. You're probably going to want to take the couch."

I leaned back, evaluating her. She was all smiles, a sure sign she was wasted, but I wasn't sure it was just alcohol. It didn't seem likely.

Their typical weekend crowd, with a few extras, were in the living room. Liquor, beer, and weed paraphernalia littered the coffee table, but something about the way everyone held themselves, a bit too loose and close together, suggested more.

My attention pulled back to Nan as she stroked my hoody.

"I love this sweater, it's so soft," she mumbled. Raising her eyes to mine, she smiled. "I love you, too. Can I please wear your sweater? I'll love it and take care of it." She nodded her head with sincerity.

I leaned away from her and pulled my hoody over my head. She wore a crop top and skirt; she needed the sweater more than me. Although I bet she wasn't feeling the cold air. "Let me just use your room to change first, then it's all yours for the night."

She was too busy rubbing the sweater against her cheek to pay attention.

After changing into sweat pants and another hoody, I hid my book bag away in Nan's closet.

Returning to the living room, I spotted Nan sitting on Dean's lap, cuddled into his neck, only one arm in my sweater. I figured that's who it was; he was her occasional bed partner, but not quite boyfriend.

She stood up and pulled him with her. "Come with me." She faced me with her sweet, drug-induced smile. "I saved you this couch." She narrowed her eyes, pointing to everyone else in the room and warned with a hard voice, "You all leave Regan alone. She gets this couch, and none of you bitches better bother her or you'll answer to me." Breaking away from Dean, she leaned on me. "I've always got your back, Babe. God, I love you."

I nodded, indulging her. "I know. I love you, too."

Satisfied, she turned back to Dean. "See, I told you she was my best friend," she pouted as they made a clumsy path to her bedroom.

I wasn't worried about Nan; unlike me, she was a fan of recreational drugs and had never once mentioned regretting anything she'd done on them. And since she had been with Dean before, I was sure everything was consensual.

But now I was stuck in a room with six others, all in different stages of oblivion. Hopefully everyone stayed in the mellow states they seemed to be in now.

I grabbed a comforter from the hall closet and claimed my sofa, spreading myself out and covering up. But I didn't dare lie down and close my eyes, not that I could if I tried.

Family Guy was on, and I zoned out to it like everyone else.

A couple of episodes in, noises from the couch next to me competed with the show. James had a girl, Sienna, cuddled up with him. He stroked her long braids as she kissed a trail on his neck. Her hands groped down the length of him shamelessly, making him moan, drawing even more attention.

I tried to block them out and watch TV, but the escalating scene was stirring my anger as much as it made me uncomfortable. Just as I was about to say something, another boy I didn't know eased himself over to my couch, stealth like.

"Don't even think about it," I warned, pulling the edge of my blanket out of his grasp.

James raised his head at the sound of my voice and smirked. "Yeah, Sam, don't even try it. That one there bites."

Sam looked towards me with wide eyes, frozen in place. I snapped my teeth at him and he shuddered in revulsion before slinking away to the other chair.

The girl pulled on James, trying to return her lips to his neck, but he shook her off and stood up. "My room?" He nodded in the direction of his door and she scurried to it.

He looked around at those left and said, "Alright, I'm going to bed now. Sam and Reggie, it's time for you to go. Miguel and Ty, are you staying?"

Ty stood up. "Not tonight. I'll be around tomorrow, like we talked about."

Miguel stayed on the recliner. "I'm crashing. Regan, can you get me one of those blankets, too?"

"Seriously? You can't walk ten feet and get it yourself?" But I stood up anyways, grabbed another blanket from the closet, and tossed it to him.

Miguel caught it. "You're an angel."

James returned from locking the door behind his friends. "A damn dark angel." He ruffled the top of my head as he passed by.

The TV was still on, but James flicked off the light before he went to his room. I nestled deeper into the couch and relaxed.

I wasn't worried about Miguel sleeping opposite me; he wasn't necessarily a friend, but I knew him well enough. Even earlier, that other boy who tried to slide under the covers didn't faze me. These were my people. I knew how to handle myself with them, including James, the wild card.

I closed my eyes, recalling the thrill of connected punches and the feeling of power that came with it. Gage was the unknown entity in my day, the one part that didn't feel within my control, but I didn't want to focus on him. Today had been a great day, and for once I was looking forward to tomorrow.

* * *

I walked into the gym at 9:30 and was surprised to see Gage and Dexter already covered in sweat at the bags.

Sliding my sweatshirt over my head, I felt stiff. My muscles were sore from my fight and recent workouts, but I'm sure the couch for a bed didn't help either.

Dexter slid onto the bench beside me. "Wasn't sure if you would show today."

I narrowed my eyes at him, pulling my hair back into a smooth ponytail. "Why wouldn't I?"

He shrugged easily. "Just wasn't sure. Thought you might need a rest day."

I slid my book bag into a locker and stood. "Well, I'm here, so what now? Will I start with Silas?"

His smile was bright. "Go to his office first; he might have something for you. But if not, you can work out with me again."

Silas gave me a sheet that listed my workout and helped instruct me. I tried to push myself as hard as possible, but still fell short. I had a lot of work to do if I wanted to get in shape. Two hours flew by, and I felt drained and discouraged when it was time to shower, but my resolve was still strong. I would do better tomorrow.

I caught a glimpse of Gage and Dexter sparring as I walked out, but couldn't pause to watch, as much as I wanted to. I had to get to work.

* * *

I was still stuck bussing, but Johnny promised I could start serving on Monday, so I sucked it up and hustled.

"Whoa, what are you doing?" I questioned, pivoting on my feet to keep from spilling my bin of dishes on Trichelle.

She was peeking around the kitchen doorframe.

"He's gay!" She slapped her leg, pouting.

I set my bin down on the dishwasher and twisted to look at her. "Who?"

She dragged me to the door by my hand. "That hot guy with the gorgeous eyes. He's gay. He's been all over Drew." She pointed to where Dexter was sitting with Jase and another boy.

Drew returned to the table with drinks in his hand. When he set them down, Dexter popped out of his seat in a flash and hugged him, rocking side to side. Drew patted his back, hesitant, before pulling away.

Walking back to the kitchen, he mouthed, "What the fuck" with large eyes.

Trichelle threw her arm up in frustration. "See."

I covered my laugh with the back of my hand.

She rounded on Drew when he entered the kitchen. "I can't believe I'm saying this, but I am so jealous of you right now."

"I better get a good tip from that table is all I'm saying." He went to the computer and typed in their orders.

I shook my head and walked out to Dexter.

He leaned back in his chair as I came near. "Hey Rea Rea, I was wondering when you would notice us."

"Don't ever call me that again. And you are creeping Drew out, stop hugging him." I couldn't hide the laughter in my voice.

The boys laughed and Jase raised his head, scanning the restaurant. "Give him another target. Who else should he hug?"

I rolled my eyes. "You're hopeless, I've got to get back to work."

"Wait." Dexter's serious tone stopped me. "Isn't that the cop from that night?" He nodded over towards the host stand.

Sure enough, Officer Fields was standing there in uniform.

I sighed and nodded. "Yup."

Dexter rose out of his seat slowly. "I think I'm going to hug him."

A burst of surprised laughter escaped me. "Go for it. Bye boys."

I escaped to the kitchen, peeking out the door in time to see Dexter hugging Officer Fields. His head rested on his shoulder as he held him in a soft embrace. The officer's eyebrows furrowed, and his arms stayed stiff by his side. Jase had the phone out at the table, videoing the entire thing.

Loading the dirty bin of dishes into the washer, I attempted to ignore the agitation creeping under my skin. I knew it was useless, but I wanted to avoid Officer Fields. Maybe I'd get lucky and he'd just leave a message.

No such luck.

Trichelle came into the kitchen. "Regan, you lucky girl! There is a delicious man in a uniform requesting you."

At my groan, she rushed next to me. "No. I don't think you're in trouble. He just wants to speak with you."

I rinsed my hands in the sink, wiping them on my apron as I made my way to the front of the restaurant. He was seated at a small table by the door.

I gave him a tight smile and crossed my arms as I stood in front of him. "Hello Officer Fields. Can I help you with something?"

He flicked his eyes to the seat across from him. "Can you sit down?"

"I'm working. I don't really have time to chat."

He nodded and rubbed the back of his head. "I wanted to give you something."

I waited.

"Here." He tried to hand me a phone with a charger wrapped around it.

"I can't take that." I took a step back.

He extended the phone to me again. "I want you to have it. It's prepaid for the month. I saw you run behind the apartments when I dropped you off." He raised his hand, keeping me from interjecting. "I'm not going to ask any questions, but that's not a safe area. You need a phone. Please, take it."

"That's crossing the line. You can't give me that."

His eyes widened and he leaned forward on the table, speaking low, "You crossed all my lines. But I liked it. Let me cross this one."

I shifted my eyes around the area. Dexter was watching me from his table, and Johnny kept looking over while he mixed drinks at the bar.

I approached Johnny. "Can I have a ten minute break to talk to him?"

"Of course, of course. Use my office in the back." He gave me a questioning look, but didn't say any more.

"Thanks." I signaled for Officer Fields to follow me with a nod of my head.

The minute he entered the space, I closed the door. The office was small, but it would do. I needed this conversation to stay private.

He turned towards me, pulling at the collar of his fitted shirt. He really did look good in his uniform. It was almost a shame I was going to have to turn him away.

"I know you don't want to date me, but I thought we could come up with some other arrangement."

I shook my head. "I don't think we can. I don't know why you're here. I—"

"I want you to be safe. Take the phone." He tried to hand me the phone again.

I hesitated, curious about his intentions. "And what do you get?"

His smile was shy, but showed off his dimples. "My numbers in it. You could call me. You're wild and I like that. You bring out my wild side. So, since you don't want to date, we could just..." He shrugged, letting his words trail off.

I was amused at his bluntness. At least he was being honest, finally. The other night he had gone on about relationships and caring, but today he was laying it out straight. I could respect that.

I cocked my head, considering him. "I think I should be offended. You're saying I should call you when I want to fuck." I went for shock value to see if he could handle it.

He didn't flinch, but watched me intently with his brown eyes. "You should be, but you're not. That's why I'm here. Don't worry; I won't ask questions, I won't make demands. I just want you to keep me wild, and I'll keep you safe."

I was about to take the phone until that last line. "So you have a prince charming complex? I don't need anyone to keep me safe; I can do that on my own."

He rubbed the back of his neck again "Alright, I know. However you want it. I just meant, take the phone, and call me when you want to."

"How old are you?"

He dropped his eyes. "26." He hesitated to look back up at me. "But I know you're 19, so it's all good."

I took the phone from his hand, holding it between two fingers. "Why is this so important to you?"

He shrugged. "I had to do something. I can't stop thinking about you. So you'll call?"

I slid the charger off and slipped it into my apron pocket. Turning the phone on, the screen lit up. It was a generic smart phone, but still nice.

"No questions?" I wanted to be clear on the rules.

He smiled and shook his head. "And no demands. Not from me anyways."

"Uh," I paused, considering everything. For some stupid reason, I couldn't resist. He was offering a no strings relationship, and I think I could handle that. I knew I could handle him. "Okay, Officer Fields. Maybe I'll call you later." I slid the phone into my pocket and turned to go.

"My only demand."

I froze, back still to him, reaching for the phone to return it.

"Call me Anthony."

I smiled, sliding the phone back into my pocket. "Okay, Anthony."

* * *

"You're early. I never expect you here at the start of the night." James stood back, letting me pass into the apartment.

He kicked the bottom of the door closed and grabbed the Styrofoam container of wings from me. "And you come bearing gifts?" He opened the lid and his smile grew. "Old Bay wings."

I walked into the living room and hesitated as I spotted Damien, a notorious drug dealer, on the couch with Ty.

"Regan, been a minute since I've seen you." Damien's eyes crawled over me.

I nodded and turned to go to Nan's room to get away from him and whatever deal he had going on with James.

The doorknob to Nan's room wouldn't budge, and my heart squeezed. It was locked.

"Nan's got company; can't go in there yet." James confirmed what I suspected.

My insides protested against sitting with them, but there seemed to be little choice. I took off my winter coat and chose the seat farthest from Damien.

"You just get off work?" Ty asked.

I looked down at my outfit—dark denim skinny jeans and a green t-shirt with Johnny's written across it in bold print. "Yup."

James set a stack of paper plates and the wings on the edge of the scratched coffee table. "She brought wings if you want some"

Damien shot a disgusted look. "Let's fuckin deal with our business first. I don't want that grease on my money or supply."

James head bobbed on top of his long neck as he closed the lid to the wings.

Damien flicked his eyes from each of us in the room before resting on James. "We all good here?"

I tried to ignore them and watch the commercial for some floor cleaner on TV. I knew what he meant though; could they make the deal in front of me.

James continued to bob his head. "You know Regan, don't you?"

He smirked. "Yeah, me and Regan got some history. But it's just that. History. Wasn't sure if she changed."

I stiffened infinitesimally, still trying to play off interest in what was on TV. I knew him from around. He lived near my last foster parent, Ms. Mary, but I never really spent time with him. I went to school with his sister, but she hated me. He would occasionally talk to me, usually to hit on me like he did all females. He was one of those guys that thought he could, and should, have every girl.

Ty spoke up, "She's good. So you think you can help us with what we talked about?"

James perked up and stilled his bouncing leg

Damien leaned forward on his knees. "That's why I'm here. But I don't give loans, not to start. You prove yourself and maybe in the future. But today, right now, you have to pay the full amount. Then whatever you make is profit. Charge whatever you want, hell if I care, but don't use my name to anyone. And you don't want to charge less than J.R., although it's your ass if you do. Remember, my name doesn't leave your mouth after this."

James and Ty exchanged glances and nodded.

"Alright then, where's the cash?"

I couldn't fake it anymore; I got up to walk to the kitchen. I had already heard too much and didn't want to be part of the rest.

"Regan? That goes for you, too. You're not gonna talk about this, right?"

I looked at Damien, not hesitating with my answer, "No. I won't talk."

"Then where are you going?"

My heart was beating in my stomach. I should have stayed seated. "To get a drink. Anybody else want something?"

They shook their heads and I walked out of the room. I scanned the kitchen, not really needing or wanting anything, just trying to distract myself from what was going on in the living room. I wonder if Nan knew what her brother was getting into now. He was still on parole; this could send him back to prison.

"Regan?"

I closed the refrigerator and turned to face James.

He crossed his arms. "Let me get one twenty."

My eyebrows flew up. "What?"

"We're one hundred and twenty short. Let me get it."

I shook my head. I had the money, but not to give. I didn't owe him anything.

Ty walked into the kitchen, looking eager. "Can she help?"

"No, I can't." I backed into the refrigerator as Damien walked in.

The space was small and crowded with the four of us standing.

"So no deal?" Damien looked between James and Ty.

"Can't we work something out? Maybe we only get some now? Make it a smaller order?"

Damien shook his head and adjusted his ski cap low on his head. "Nah, it don't work like that." Then his eyes focused on me and he paused. "Although, we could work something out; another form of payment." He licked his lips and cocked his head. "Regan, what do you say? Help your friends out?"

I shook my head and struggled to find my voice. "No, I can't help."

James looked between the two of us. "You mean something other than money?"

I glared at James. I wasn't willing to give them money; I sure as hell wouldn't sleep with someone to pay for their drugs.

"She wouldn't do that. If you know Regan, you know that," James said.

At least he hadn't lost his mind.

Damien smirked. "Yeah I remember Regan. She was always one uppity bitch. Only giving time to those boys with money, never one of her own. I just thought those boys might have knocked her down a notch."

I bit my cheek to keep quiet, but a fire started burning in my stomach.

Damien's wicked smile spread as he chuckled. "I have seen you recently, on a video. But it cut off before they got to the good part. They had you on the ground, so don't tell me none of those boys knew what to do with you. Did you—"

"Shut the fuck up." I couldn't stand to hear any more from his foul mouth. My emotions crashed violently inside me, looking for a way out.

James gave a nervous laugh, eyes bouncing between Damien and me. "Let's go back to the living room. I'll check with Nan. She'll help."

"Wait." Damien took a step towards me, filling all my senses. "I want to hear what happened. I could make you forget their touch, Baby. And then we'd all be happy."

He stepped closer, reaching for me, and I shoved him away, hard.

"Stupid Bitch," he spoke low, his voice laced with hatred.

It was all the warning I needed. Just as he lunged at me, I punched him in the face and kneed him in the stomach. As he folded, I ran out of the kitchen.

James grabbed me by the shoulders and I turned on him, still swinging.

"Whoa," he yelled, but anger transformed his face as my fist connected with his lip.

He pushed me back to the wall in the hallway, his hands wrapped around my neck, rage clear in his eyes.

I pushed at him and clawed at his hands. I was struggling to breathe. My vision wavered and darkened at the edges. James' angry face blocked everything out.

Then he was gone, and I sucked in much needed air. I looked around wildly, still with my guard up.

James lay on the ground, and Nan stood to my side with a gun in hand. She moved it in a wide arc, keeping everyone back.

Damien's cold voice broke the silence. "You better be willing to shoot. You've done lost your mind pulling a gun on me."

She shook her head and lowered the glock, sliding it into the back of her pants. "I'm not going to shoot, but he was going to kill her. I had to do something."

Dean put his arm around Nan, pulling her back as James stood up.

"So you're gonna fuckin' choose her over me. I'm your brother."

She sighed, deflating. "No, but I had to stop you and you weren't listening." She turned towards me. "Regan, you need to go. Now."

I nodded, still feeling the danger in the room. "Let me get my things."

"Make it fuckin' quick," James ordered.

I grabbed my book bag, shoving in as much as I could make fit, in under a minute. Then I braced myself to return to the living room and grabbed my jacket. They were all still in the hall way and kitchen. James was apologizing to Damien, who laughed.

I avoided looking at them as I walked by, but Damien spoke before I closed the door.

"Stay safe, Regan."

My heart crashed into my stomach.

8: Cat And Mouse

I MADE IT TO THE CURB BEFORE I stopped to put on my jacket. I was shaking and fumbled with the puffy coat and backpack in my arms. Tears burned, blurring my vision. I told myself the lie that it was just the cold.

I couldn't peel my eyes from Nan's apartment door and my damn jacket wasn't going on. Frustrated, I threw my bag down and shook my jacket out, shoving each arm through. I picked the backpack up and began moving again. I needed to put distance between me and the people inside that apartment.

"Regan, wait," Nan called.

I stopped walking only when I saw that she was alone, but I didn't dare walk closer.

She jogged to where I stood. "In a couple of days, maybe you can come back."

I shook my head, unable to find words equal to the fucked-up-ness of the situation.

She threw her hands up in frustration. "What happened in there?"

I kept looking to her door, anticipating when it would open next. I couldn't stand here and have this conversation. Not now, maybe not ever.

Tension pulled at my muscles and my hands balled into fists just thinking about what went down.

"You saw what happened. Your brother and his friends..." I shook my head; I couldn't come up with the rest. I couldn't think through the panic in me. This place was dangerous, and not just for me. "Don't go back in there, Nan. We can go somewhere else."

She crossed her arms. "No. I have to go back in. My brother—"

"He's bad news. Ever since he's gotten out he's caused trouble. You can't keep living like this."

She shook her head, strings of her hair blowing in her face. "It's not just him. You don't fucking think sometimes. What the hell were you doing in there? What did you say to them? Why? When you know he has a temper." Her voice was turning shrill. "You get yourself in trouble all the time, even before James came home."

I had no response; a small part of me saw a sliver of truth in it, but only a sliver. I knew tonight was not my fault. "Okay. Go back inside then. I'm leaving."

"Wait." She wiped the side of her face and nose with the sleeve of her sweater. The slick trail of tears shone on her cheek under the streetlight. "Where are you going to go?" Her voice was small and weak.

"Are you crying?" I was annoyed. "You kick me out, tell me it's my fault, and now you're crying? Stop."

She stiffened. "I'm worried for you, just come by on Tuesday."

The door to Nan's apartment opened and my flight response went into overdrive. I took two steps back, about to run.

Dean stuck his head out and yelled, "Nan, everything good?"

She looked to me and back to Dean. "I'm coming in. One sec."

"Be careful, okay. I mean it." She gave me a sad smile.

"Yeah, you too," I said, turning to leave.

Everything settled on me—the darkness, the cold, and Damien's veiled threat. I quickened my pace; my only goal was to get out of the area, but then what?

I made it to the front of the apartment complex and saw a group of teens walking on the sidewalk along the main road. I crouched on the curb, hiding myself between two parked cars. The group was laughing and yelling as they walked by, but I couldn't bring myself to stand.

I was stuck, struggling for air. I put my head between my knees and tried to think of something to do. Remembering my phone in my back pocket, I leaned forward to slide it out, saying a prayer as I pressed the on button. It lit up with a full charge still. It took several seconds for my numb and shaky fingers to navigate the screen, but I finally saw the number I was searching for and pressed dial.

"Regan?"

I nodded my head, tears prickling my eyes. "Yeah."

"Do you—Can I come pick you up?"

Everything was tight; I could barely get the breath to reply. "Yeah."

"Those apartments?"

The darkness was suffocating, but I forced enough air to whisper, "Yeah, come now." And then I clicked off the phone.

I let it fall into my lap as I curled into myself, struggling between wanting to see my surroundings and wanting to squeeze my eyes shut. There wasn't enough air. I gulped lung-fulls of the frigid night, feeling the prickly burn in my lungs, but it wasn't enough. I was choking.

Cradling my head in the crook of my arm, I kept one eye open to look for Anthony's truck. Every car that drove by relit my panic and sent a new surge of toxic energy through my body. I couldn't fight off the tears. My stomach flipped and I dry heaved, retching nothing but spit and bile onto the pavement.

Hearing the loud rumble of an engine, I raised my head, spotting Anthony's truck pulling in. With relief, I jumped up and ran to it, climbing into the passenger seat. I pressed back into the fabric, eyes squeezed tight, trying to calm myself. My bones hurt as they shook, and it took all my effort not to throw up again.

Recalling a trick my therapist in foster care taught me, I counted to ten as I inhaled and ten as I exhaled, slowing my breath and calming one body part at a time. I started with my toes, flexed them, and then counted until I felt them come back under my control. Then I moved up, ankles, calves, knees. By time I reached my chest, I felt calmer and opened my eyes.

We hadn't moved.

Anthony was twisted in his seat, watching me. When our eyes met, he nodded slightly and silently pulled away.

With my breathing under control, I realized that I was freezing. I put my hands against the vents and absorbed the heat into my fingers. I focused on the needle-like pain as they defrosted; it was a welcome distraction.

"It's really cold out," I said lamely, knowing it wouldn't explain the way I'd acted, but hoped he would play along.

His jaw tightened, and he blew out a long breath. "They're calling for snow later this week."

I wiped the tears from my eyes, the last evidence of my panic.

"Where are we going?" We were taking an exit to the highway, out of the city.

"My house. I don't live far."

Alright. My strength was returning; I could handle this. Nothing had to change. Anthony and I had an arrangement and that's what this was. If he were smart, he would keep to his end and not ask questions.

I blocked out the doubt that tried to force into my thoughts. I wasn't using him; we were just in a mutually beneficial situation.

He took the next exit and as he made turns, I recognized where we were. I knew where the metro station was and studied the route he took to remember the way, just in case.

"This is it," he said as we pulled up to a one story, brick home. It had a cute porch but no landscaping that I could see in the dark.

"Do you want something to drink or eat?" he asked as we walked into the living room, a small space with a mish mash of furniture.

"Yeah, please. Do you have anything warm, like coffee or tea or hot chocolate?"

He smiled with questions in his eyes. "I have coffee or hot chocolate."

"I'll take the hot chocolate, thanks." I followed him into the kitchen, just off the living room.

The space was cozy, a dull yellow with dark wood cabinets. The counters were cluttered with bags of chips, mail, and half full liquor bottles.

He made our drinks, and I busied myself with looking around the kitchen and living room. He had a few pictures, him with his family most likely. I gathered he had a brother and sister, and his parents were all smiles and hugs in the pictures. Just like I thought, a nice family with nice kids that took vacations on cruises and ski resorts. There was one of him in his uniform, and his father next to him, both smiling at the camera.

"That's the day I graduated from the police academy." Anthony handed me my drink and sat on the couch, nodding for me to join him.

I sipped the hot drink, feeling my insides melt a bit, and sat. It felt good to sit, to let my tense muscles relax.

"Are you alright?" he pushed my hair back on my shoulder with one finger.

I cringed and reluctantly met his gaze. "I'm fine."

"I have a friend who has panic attacks. I've seen it before. Do you get them often? Is it because of the attack?"

I set my mug down, parting with the warmth in my hands, and then turned to face him. "No questions, remember?"

He nodded. "I just thought you might need tonight to be a safe night."

His words made me want to cry all over again. But I knew he couldn't deliver that, it wasn't possible. I didn't want to talk anymore; I didn't want to feel anymore. I wanted it all to go away. And he could help with that.

I shook my head and inched towards him till our lips met.

He didn't resist. Instead, his arms wrapped around me, pulling me into him. I straddled him, as I had in the car that day, and tried to focus only on where our bodies touched and the warmth coming from him.

He pulled away from me. "Let's take this to the bedroom."

I stood and he led me down a hallway to the last door. He lay back on the bed, pulling me on top of him. I lifted my work shirt off, keeping my tank top on underneath, and then lifted his shirt off. Our jeans ground against each other.

He sat up, trailing his lips down my neck and shoulders, pushing my tank down until my boobs spilled out. I moved his hands away, keeping him from sliding the top any lower. That was off limits.

I stood up and slid my pants off as he did the same, pulling off his boxers, too. He reached into his night stand and pulled out a condom, tearing the corner of the pack with his teeth, a wide grin spreading on his pretty face.

His eyes traveled over me. "Damn, you're sexy." He hooked one arm around my waist and pulled me back to him.

He was as eager as I was to get to it. His hands slid my panties down and then rolled the condom onto the length of him.

I rode him with mounting frustration, never finding the escape I sought. The tightness around my heart eased slightly, but not enough. Closing my eyes, I focused on the physical only, trying to give my mind a moment off, but it never worked.

He found his escape, shuddering and convulsing under me, and I relaxed my body on top of his. I had exerted energy and had some fun. But now I only felt empty, and not the emptiness I had been seeking.

I rolled off of him. "Do you mind if I shower?"

He pulled me back into his arms and kissed my neck. "Go ahead. You can use the one in there, towels are hanging up." He nodded to the door straight ahead and released me.

I showered, taking time to let the warm water massage my aching muscles. Anthony called out that he was leaving clothes for me outside the door.

I changed into the large shirt and shorts that I had to roll several times to make fit. Running a brush through my wet hair, I returned to his room. He was lounged on the bed, fresh from his own shower.

He patted the spot beside him. "Come over here. We can watch a movie if you want or just go to bed. I'm assuming I don't have to drive you back tonight, right?"

I shook my head and joined him tentatively.

He hooked his arm around me and pulled me closer to him on the bed, laying us back to watch a movie I couldn't focus on. This didn't feel right. Cuddling. It felt too personal and not what we were supposed to be about.

I pulled away. "I need to go to bed. Can I sleep on the couch?"

His face pinched with confusion, but he didn't voice it. "You're welcome to my bed with me, but if you'd prefer I have a guest bed you can use."

I nodded and stood, following him through the hallway to a smaller bedroom. He left me there with an awkward hug and I settled into bed. Sleep didn't come easy; when I did sleep, it was only in short bursts.

When the first traces of daylight broke into the room, I folded the borrowed clothes on the bed I made and left before Anthony woke up. Walking to the metro station, I organized my day; I had things I needed to do. First thing was to talk to Silas about when I could fight again; I needed the extra money more than ever.

* * *

I could hear them talking, Gage and Silas, as I walked towards the office. I didn't think anything of it until I heard my name. Curiosity won and I paused to listen, not wanting to interrupt the conversation.

"Regan told me she wanted another fight," Silas explained.

I had, yesterday, when Silas asked if I wanted to continue boxing.

"What does she know? She's not ready, not for that fight. Find someone else." Gage's voice was ruff with disapproval.

I tensed as anger began to simmer in my gut. He had no right to speak for me, to cancel a fight and keep money from my pockets.

"C'mon, if you would've seen her, you would know. She can handle it. She can take punches. She can—"

"I didn't see," his angry voice cut off Silas's and a hollow thump followed.

"Exactly. I did and I think this is a good arrangement." Silas wasn't backing down.

"For you or for her?"

I couldn't take it anymore. I walked around the corner of his office and stood in the open doorway. "Silas? Dexter told me you wanted to speak with me."

Gage and Silas were standing on either side of his desk; they both turned their heads to look at me when I interrupted. Silas's face broke into a smile; Gage's didn't.

"Speak of the devil; we were just discussing your next fight. It seems Gage and I disagree on this matter."

I looked between Silas's smiling face and Gage's hard one. He hadn't budged. "It seems like it should be my decision."

Silas's smile widened and he laughed. "I think you're right." He extended his arm to the chair opposite him. "Let's talk."

I took the seat next to Gage, but he continued to stand, his gaze sliding between Silas and me. He radiated anger, but I wasn't going to let him intimidate me today. I was still numb over all that happened yesterday. I had reached my limit, and I wasn't about to let Gage take this away from me.

Silas sat and began, "You could fight again next month, against another boxer starting her career for the same money you made before. Or, you could fight in two weeks, against an established fighter for triple the money if you win."

"Could I do both?" I asked.

Silas laughed and rubbed his chin, appraising me. "That's what I'm talking about. You're eager, I like that. Hell, I can have you fighting almost every week if you want."

Gage's eyes narrowed, drilling into me. I didn't like the way he was looking down on me from where he stood.

"Do you want a career? Are you serious about boxing? Or do you just want money? Because if it's the money, then go do something else. Female boxers don't make that much."

I sat back, trying to curb the anger building in me. Who did he think he was? "I want the career and the money. I like boxing, but I won't do it for free, and I'm sure you wouldn't either."

"Gage, she's made up her mind. You should get back to your training; you have a month till A.C."

His jaw flexed, but his glare was focused on Silas as he stalked out of the room.

Silas continued, unfazed by his departure. "You will need to commit to training these next two weeks and clean up your diet to be at your best. But don't lose weight; you want to stay in your weight class. We have a lot of ground to cover in a short amount of time, so let's get to it."

What I had been trying to achieve with Anthony, I found in the bag. I gave it all I had and completely spent my energy. After an hour of punching, blocking, and jump roping, I was drained and my muscles exhausted. I hadn't had much sleep the past two days and it was catching up with me, affecting my stamina, but releasing my anger and frustration felt good. It was the therapy I needed.

With a sheen of sweat covering every inch of me, I sat to rest and drink water. I relaxed back in the chair, closing my eyes, and enjoyed the liquid feel of my muscles, a sure sign that I was working hard and getting stronger.

Silas had been pleased with my workout today, and Dexter had popped in between his sets to give his energetic encouragement.

"You done for the day?"

I opened my eyes, but didn't move as Dexter sat next to me.

"I'm taking ten, then going to decide if I can do more. Right now, I think I have to be done."

I turned towards him to get a full view. He was shirtless and shiny with sweat, but as high energy as ever. It was evident even in the way he sat, perched on the edge, like he would pop up any moment.

"What about you? You working out more today?" I cocked my head, curious about his boxing status. "Do you have any fights?"

"My next fight isn't for six weeks. So I have time to help you, isn't that great?" His smile was big and genuine, and I was helpless to do anything but return it.

"Okay, so what do you know about this Dreya Welch I'm going to fight?"

He shrugged. "I don't know really. I've heard of her, she's good and she's aggressive, but I've never studied her. We'll have to do that tomorrow. I have to take Leona out today, for Valentine's Day. You got plans?"

I leaned forward, resting my arms on my knees. I had forgotten that today was Valentine's Day, and my mind flashed to Anthony. I quickly punched down that wayward thought. I definitely would not see him today.

I shook my head. "I don't have any Valentine's plans, but I do have stuff that needs to get done." I was going to check in to a motel somewhere and start looking for apartments. I didn't have enough money for them, I knew, but I could find out what I needed.

He nodded. "Yeah, like buying your own gear. You should take your money from the fight and invest it in yourself."

This conversation was bringing back my frustration. It slid to anger as I caught Gage watching us from the weight bench, still dark with disapproval. Maybe I would work out a little longer. I stood up, stretching.

When it was evident Gage was walking to us, I stiffened, prepared for a confrontation.

Dexter stood up, facing his brother. "I have to meet up with Leona at eleven, are you going to be ready soon?"

He nodded, but never took his eyes from me. His path stopped directly in front of me, and he crossed his arms, showing off his biceps.

"So you think you're ready to fight Dreya? Did you even pause to learn anything about her?"

I was done with his disapproving tone and judgment. "Silas thinks I'm ready, and he's my manager, not you."

"Rea," Dexter's voice was soft, "He's only trying to help."

I turned on him, amazed that he didn't see what a jerk Gage was being. "Help? He doesn't want me to fight, how does that help? He hasn't even seen me fight, but he thinks he knows what I'm ready for. He doesn't."

Gage took a step towards me, so he had to look down on me to meet my eyes. "You haven't even been here a week and you think you know everything. This isn't a joke; you don't just decide one night to be a boxer. It takes perseverance and commitment. You have to want it. You have to live it. The girl you're fighting does, and that makes her better than you."

It felt like a slap to the face, and I was tired of his assumptions. He didn't know me, and I wasn't going to let him bully me. What did that rich boy know about me and my struggles and how much I needed this? I resisted the urge to step back, out of his electric field.

"I may not have known to want this last week, but now that I've tasted it, I do. And it's more than wanting. I need this. It's all I've got, and I won't let you take it from me. So if you're not going to help me, then at least stay out of my way." I brushed off Dexter's hand as he tried to pat my back.

Gage's full lips tugged up on one side, but it didn't make him look any less fierce. If anything, it made ice run through my veins.

He lifted his chin. "Okay, I'll help. Gear up, I'll show you some things in the ring."

Dexter looked between the two of us. "Are you sure? I thought we were going to leave soon."

Gage started walking to the ring. "We will, but I have time for one lesson. She's got less than two weeks till her fight."

I had to unglue my feet, the switch in conversation made me dizzy. I wasn't sure what was about to happen, but I wasn't convinced his motive was to help.

Dexter shrugged at me and walked after his brother.

Once I had gloves and headgear on, I stood in the ring. Nerves tightened my exhausted muscles some, but not enough.

Gage stood nearby, arms loose at his side. He wore gloves, but no headgear. He didn't appear angry anymore, his face was relaxed, almost bored. The dark lines of his tattoos wrapped around his right arm, and the ones on his torso peeked through the cut off sleeve of his white t-shirt.

"You've been practicing punches on the bag, but defense is important. This girl charges, and a good block is key. You're going to want to time your own counter punches, but never leave yourself open. Let me see your stance."

I held my arms up the way Silas had showed me.

He nodded and stepped forward, placing his gloved hands on my back and stomach, twisting me. "Always keep your side to your opponent." He adjusted my shoulder. "And raise your shoulder up. Use it to help block your face."

My breathing was shallow. I tried to concentrate on his instructions, but the static was back, his gentle touches and soft voice were unexpected. I could smell his sweat, a clean musk, almost feel it evaporating in the heat between us.

He stepped back, and I cleared my thoughts. I needed to focus.

"Okay, you ready?"

At my nod, he jabbed. I twisted too late, my reactions too slow to block the punch. He didn't hit hard, but it jarred me, and I became more alert.

He jabbed a couple more times, landing each one. He was too fast, and every time I tried to block, he found a new open spot to attack. I wasn't giving up though and began moving around the ring, using the space to evade some of his jabs.

He wasn't putting much effort into this, I could tell, and he laughed as I circled him.

"You're going to tire yourself out before you even throw a punch." He jabbed again, lightly hitting my stomach.

I tried to strike him, but he deflected it.

We continued this way for a while, my frustration mounting. It was like a cat and mouse game. He was the cat and had me under his paw, batting and toying with me, never giving me a chance.

When he hit my face again and laughed, I erupted. "What? What am I supposed to do? You're better than me, we both know that. So what's the point of this?"

I pulled my gloves from my hands and undid my helmet. "I'm done with this. I'm glad you got to get a good laugh."

He watched me with that slight, cool smile on his lips, the one that sends ice through me.

"So you're giving up? I knew you didn't want this. It's like I said, you're not serious."

I rounded on him. "I am serious, but this wasn't helping me. You were just trying to embarrass me, and it worked. I know I'm not great, but I'm trying. And I want this more than you can imagine. You may have been at this longer, but I can guarantee you I want this just as much, if not more, than you."

"Then why are you taking the fast track to ending your career? A loss stays on your record and it's hard to recover from. Check out anyone who made it and you'll see the loss column is zero, sometimes one, but never two. And you're setting yourself up to lose."

His words made me pause. I hadn't known this, or even thought about it. I had thought win or lose it was an opportunity to learn and make money. But I wasn't prepared to admit he was right, not with his smug attitude.

"I don't intend on losing. I have a lot to learn, but you weren't trying to make me better, to teach me. You just wanted to put me in my place. I don't want or need help from someone who doesn't believe in me."

I climbed out of the ring, not waiting for his response. I didn't have time for this. And I was afraid of what would come out of my mouth next because I knew he was right, and I was possibly making a big mistake.

I escaped to the locker room, relieved to be away from Gage's disapproval. I don't know why it bothered me so much, but it did, and that only made me angrier.

Needing time to cool off, I sat on the bench with lockers surrounding me and took deep breaths. I reminded myself that Silas approved; he thought I did good and believed I could win. And he had seen me fight. A fight I won. In the first round. With a knockout.

But all the positive self-talk in the world couldn't wipe away his words, "she's better than you" and "you're going to lose."

"You were in the ring with Gage Lawson, right?" a voice broke through my thoughts.

I side glanced at the pretty girl standing next to me. She had her long white hair pulled up in a ponytail and wore the tiniest workout outfit possible for a public place.

I nodded, not wanting to talk about it. The fact that the gym was full of people only added salt to the wound; that anyone had seen how weak he made me look reinforced my anger.

Her eyes widened as she sat next to me, gripping the edge of the bench with her hands. "How? I haven't seen you around here before. I come every week and he's never spoken to me. How did you get him in the ring with you? Is he a trainer now? Where do I sign up?"

I rubbed my temples, trying to ease my headache. "Believe me, you're not missing out. He was being a jerk, trying to make me give up." I stood up, cutting off my self-pity; it was time to move on with the day.

She stood up too and begged with her big blue eyes. "My name's Becka. Could you introduce me? I'd love to just meet him. I've tried to introduce myself but he's always so focused when he's working out. Please."

The headache was back. "I'm going to get a shower."

She nodded her head with excitement. "I'll wait. Thank you so much." And she sat back down with a smile plastered on her face.

I shook my head, but didn't say anything as I walked to the showers. Maybe she was a boxer too. Her tall, slim body was tight, but she didn't come across as the fighting type.

Sure enough, Becka waited while I showered and dressed for the day. Since I had to walk in the cold to work, I took the time to blow dry my hair and slide Chap Stick across my dry lips. She stood up with a little squeal as I exited the room.

The only thing that kept me from turning around and telling her to go away was that she could be my buffer if Gage still felt the need to lecture me.

Gage and Dexter were standing by the front door, talking to some guy. They wore track pants and zip up hoodies, ready to leave.

A smile pulled at my lips, I hadn't expected them to be the type to wear matching outfits. As I walked closer, I saw that Dexter's shirt underneath said, "I would hug you so hard" and my smile grew.

"I like the shirt," I greeted him as Becka hovered behind me in her barely there outfit.

Dexter's eyes lit up and he pulled me into a tight squeeze.

I stiffened and my words muffled in his sweater, "Alright, that's enough."

"One day, you'll be asking for my hugs," he promised as he let me go.

"Hi!" The blonde behind me greeted.

Gage's eyes had been locked on her since I started walking over, his face unreadable.

"Becka, this is Gage. Gage meet Becka, she's been wanting to talk to you." I mimicked her peppy voice.

She gasped, and I sidestepped the nudge she tried to give. Gage's eyes narrowed with interest.

"Bye." I waved, walking past the group and out the door, all too happy to be rid of the girl and Gage.

Dexter followed me. "Wait! I wanted to ask you, can I get your number?" He had his phone out.

I stepped out of the way of people on the sidewalk. "Umm..." Recalling my phone, I brightened, and pulled off my book bag to retrieve it. "Sure, I'm just not sure what my number is. It's a new phone."

He laughed, shaking his head. "Call my phone now, then I'll have it. I have classes Monday through Thursday so I won't see you at the gym in the mornings. But we need to research your fight."

I nodded, digging through my stuff to find my phone in the bottom of the bag. "Do you think I'm making a mistake?"

He shrugged. "I don't know. Silas is smart, but so is Gage. They just... I'm not sure."

My hand found my phone and I pulled it out. Seeing a missed call and text from Anthony made my stomach dip, but I didn't pause to check out what the text said. I dialed Dex's number as he called it out.

"Alrighty then, I'll call you tomorrow." He walked backwards, still facing me, until he reached the gym door.

I zipped up my bag, slinging it on my back, and turned to walk down the street. At least today wasn't below freezing, only the occasional wind brought a chill.

My pocket vibrating made me slow my pace. Pulling out my phone, I saw Anthony's name lit up across the screen.

"Hello," I answered.

"Where are you? I've been calling. What happened this morning?" his voice sounded harsh and accusing.

I watched for traffic as I crossed the street. "I'm just leaving the gym. I didn't have my phone on me."

"Why did you leave without telling me? I could have driven you. Don't ever do that again." His voice was softening, but still sounded like a reprimand.

I bristled. "Whoa. Don't tell me what I can do."

He paused. "Look, I was worried, that's all. Give me enough respect to let me know when you're coming and going in my house."

"Alright, fine." I was tired of disappointing everyone. Over the last twenty-four hours I had destroyed several relationships, knowing I didn't have that many to begin with. What was one more? Burning bridges seemed to be a talent of mine.

"Don't worry, that won't ever happen again."

He sucked in air with a hiss. "That's not a dismissal is it? I'm not mad. I still want you."

I couldn't respond to that.

"Can I see you today?"

I shook my head, silent. Maybe this bridge was stronger than I thought, on his side anyways. "I'll call you later."

I hung up the phone.

* * *

I walked around the bed in the small motel room, unsure what was safe to touch, let alone sleep on. I pulled the comforter off the bed and threw it in the corner; there was no way I was sleeping on that.

The motel was a modern day brothel with rooms you could rent by the hour. I had little choice in where to stay though. I didn't have much money to waste, not if my goal was to afford a more permanent place. Not to mention, the nicer hotels in the city were reluctant to rent a room to someone my age, with only cash to pay. They wanted adults to sign for it or a credit card on file.

I could hear shouts from outside my window and checked the curtains, making sure no one could see into the room. It was only the girls walking up and down the street yelling to each other, but it made me uneasy.

They gave me prime real estate, first floor, front and center. The stares of those outside the building didn't go unnoticed as I walked from the front desk to the room. The smile from the clerk and his tone when he said, 'Good luck Doll,' made his assumptions clear.

I peeked out the window, the daylight was dimming and the people traffic outside the motel was increasing. I turned on the TV and tried to relax, tried to ignore the musk seeping from the carpet, tried to block out the noise radiating through the walls. But I failed at it all.

Today had been a disappointment. My search for apartments only made me realize how far away that goal was. The cheapest thing I found still required two months rent and utilities up front, plus a security deposit and a little more because of my age. I had four hundred dollars to my name, and I needed quadruple that. There was no way I could turn down the fight next week. I only hoped that Johnny would keep his word and let me start serving again, and I needed weekend shifts.

I tried to rest. Using my book bag as a pillow, I kept as little of my skin from touching the bed as possible. I hadn't slept well the past two nights and tonight was shaping up to be another sleepless one.

The hollers from the street taunted me, reminding me how far I had to go, how slim my chances were. I had hoped the cold of the night would have kept most people inside, but it didn't. And the silence in my room didn't help, even with the TV on, I felt alone. At Nan's I would often be alone in her room, but there were always people around, and the voices I heard were ones I knew. Even before Nan's, growing up I was always in homes with lots of people. Now, there was no one. And that knowledge pressed heavily on my chest.

The book bag under my head vibrated. Pulling out my phone, Anthony's name across the screen gave me relief this time, with a slight mix of wariness.

"Are you at those apartments?" He asked.

"No." I was alert now. Was he there?

"Where are you?"

"Why? What's going on?" I avoided his question.

"I'm on night patrol, but I wanted to check on you, after last night. Even though I'm working, I'm still here for you if you need me." He paused, "So are you alright?"

I paused, letting his words sink in. He was just calling to check on me. I sighed with relief. "Thank you. I'm fine." That wasn't true, but I wasn't going to tell him that.

"So, if you're not at the apartment, where are you?"

I sat up on the bed, leaning against the wall behind me. A loud peel of laughter and a thump came from the room on the other side. "No questions, remember?"

He released a heavy breath. "Maybe I need to clarify that rule. You don't have to answer my questions. I won't make you. But I will ask questions. I want to know you, whatever you'll let me know." He paused and the police radio crackled through the phone. "I have some time tonight to talk on the phone. Will you talk to me?"

I liked that idea. There was no pressure on the phone, and it kept my loneliness at bay.

"Sure, you start. Tell me about you."

We talked on and off through the night, in between his calls and work. I didn't reveal much, except that I was now boxing with Silas. But he shared stories about his childhood and what it was like being the youngest of three.

Mostly, I just liked listening to his voice, knowing that someone was there and I wasn't alone. It muffled the bumps, yelling, and city sounds that were just outside my room.

I went to bed glad that my past attempts at setting fire to our connection didn't work.

9: Sleep Deprived

I SLEPT BETTER ON THE BUS THAN I had in the motel room. I needed sleep and hoped tonight I'd be so tired I could sleep through anything, even fear.

The gym was only a block away. I pulled the wire signaling I needed off, and the bus began to slow. Lifting my bag, I stood and made my way down the aisle, trailing my hands on the bar above me for balance.

An icy wind met me at the door, shocking the sleep from my system. The sky was a blanket of gray and I could practically smell the frosty snow in the air.

Ugh, I hoped it would hold off until my shift at the restaurant was over, even if I wasn't sure how I could physically get through the day. My body was heavy with pain and exhaustion. Every bit of me was sore. I rubbed one side of my ribs, uncertain how much of the ache was because of my workouts or my still healing bruises. Either way, I had to keep going.

It must have shown on me, my fatigue, because Silas took one look at me and said today was a light day. I was to run, and stretch, then rest, because tomorrow we would get back to training. It worked for me, because I only had an hour before I needed to get ready for my shift at Johnny's.

Walking out of his office, I covered my jaw-popping yawn with my fist.

"Tired?" Gage's eyebrow lifted in question, a small smile played on his lips.

I didn't trust the kind tone and stifled the next yawn that tried to follow as I stepped past him.

He grabbed my elbow, pulling me to face him, so close our loose shirts touched and I was eye level with his chest. The tingle of adrenaline pulsing my muscles made me want to run, but I stiffened, freezing my reactions.

"Did you back out?" The warmth of his breath brushed against my face.

"What?" I jerked my arm out of his grip. I didn't like him being so close; it forced me to have to look up to meet his eyes.

"The fight next week? Did you cancel it?" He asked conversationally, but the look in his eyes as they locked with mine contradicted his indifference.

"No," I scoffed, taking a step away.

"What a waste," he grumbled through a clenched jaw.

"What the hell is your problem?" I couldn't contain my instant reaction; my filter wasn't working in my tired state.

His response was just as immediate. Taking a threatening step towards me, he towered over my 5'6 height. He grabbed my arms, blocking me from pushing him away.

"I'd ask you the same thing? Look at you. Have you even gone to bed yet?" He dropped my arms, taking a step back, shaking his head. "Glad to see you're taking this so seriously."

I gritted my teeth, and my fists curled. "You don't know anything about me, Rich Boy. So just back off."

He crossed his arms with a puff of laughter, one side of his mouth tugging up as he watched me. "Rich Boy? You say it like it's a bad thing." He shook his head as he leaned in slightly, his voice dropping. "I don't need to know you 'cause next week, after you lose that fight, you'll be done."

He walked away, and I sucked in much needed air. My head fell back as I wiped the frustration from my face. I ignored Silas's directions for today and started on the punching bag, determined to prove him wrong and release the anger he caused.

* * *

"You can start shutting down your section. We'll close up early, it's piling up fast out there," Louisa said as she walked past me.

I watched the large clumps of snowflakes swirling out the window, a lacy layer of white covering everything in sight.

Texting Dexter back, I let him know I was getting off early because of the weather and I'd see him another day. We had made plans to meet up after my shift, but the snow started sooner than forecasted. I had to cancel.

I cleaned my section and cashed out for the day. It had been slow, but I was leaving with twenty-four dollars more than I'd arrived with and the promise of serving again on Wednesday.

After sliding on my jacket and book bag, I scooped up my to-go container and walked out the front door.

Dexter was just getting out of his car in the parking lot. Noticing me, he knocked on the hood. "Come on, Rea, quick get in." He hopped up and down in place. "It's freezing out. We got to get back before the blizzard really starts."

I didn't know what the plan was, but walked to the car anyways. He looked like fun, and his smile could talk me into almost anything. Plus, I wasn't in a rush to get back to the motel.

"Hey Leona. Jase," I greeted, sliding into the backseat.

Leona bounced to the music in the front and turned towards me. "We're going to ride out the snow storm at Dexter's. I hope you don't got plans." She clapped her hands when I shook my head.

"We can swing by your place first so you can get some things. Got to make it quick though, others are meeting at my house in an hour," Dexter explained as he started the car. "So where to?"

I tried to think fast, I needed to return the key to the motel if I didn't want to pay for an extra night. Who knew when I'd be able to get back if the snow were real bad. They were calling for up to a foot.

I put money in front of my pride and gave directions to the motel.

As we approached the motel, Dexter met my eyes in the rearview mirror with a look of concern, but he silently followed my directions. I could feel Jase fidgeting beside me.

"You can turn in here," I said, leaning forward in my seat and pointing to the parking lot.

When he parked the car, they all traded uncertain looks, but I avoided meeting their eyes.

"Stay here. I'll be right back." I shot out of the car.

A door slammed behind me, and then Dexter was at my side, hood pulled over his head. "I'm coming with you."

I hadn't left anything in the room, so I went straight to the front office.

A girl leaning against a nearby door called something out to Dexter in a slurred voice, and he grabbed my arm. He stayed silently attached to my side until I returned the key and we were walking back to the car.

"Do you live here?" Dexter asked, voice low.

I lowered my head against the snow blowing around us. "It's only temporary."

"Damn straight." All humor was gone.

The silence in the car was heavy, a stark contrast from the excited banter they had before.

"One last stop... the liquor store. Gotta keep warm in the cold." Dexter broke the tension with the return of his usual excitement.

The further we drove from the motel, the more their conversation returned to normal. But something had changed; it was evident in the careful way Jase and Leona talked to me. I wasn't who they thought I was. Well, too damn bad, they were stuck with me for now.

I was use to this shift, it always happened when people at school found out I was a foster kid. They became tentative and a little more closed off. Like they couldn't trust me, like I might steal from them. I can't say I blamed them really. Not that I would ever steal, but I knew plenty who would.

Anyways, it was better than the other reaction that I sometimes got; pity. Pity was the worst. I hated pity.

* * *

"Can I use your microwave? I haven't eaten all day." I lifted my to-go container towards Dexter. "You can have some if you want."

He nodded as he stood from the couch. "It's alright, we ate earlier."

I followed him up the stairs and down the hall. The kitchen was a large open space with a window overlooking the harbor. Icy flakes floated around, only to be consumed by the choppy water beyond the snow covered deck.

Dexter pulled out a plate and handed it to me.

"Do you want something to drink? I've got beer, soda, tea?" He scrunched his nose. "But it's unsweetened."

"Tea, please," I said as I laid my chicken tenders and fries on the plate.

The alarm system beeped as the front door opened and closed. Heavy boots thumped in the hallway.

Dexter handed me a glass of tea and looked around the corner. "Hey, glad you made it home in time. Looks like it's picking up."

I closed my eyes with an internal groan. I thought I had gotten lucky when Dexter said Gage wasn't home, that perhaps he had gotten snowed in somewhere else.

"I know better than to leave your crazy ass here alone. No telling what I'd come home to…" His voice trailed off as he rounded the corner of the kitchen.

The microwave beeped and I busied myself with my food, never looking up.

"Regan." The soft way he spoke my name sent a current threw me, causing all my hairs to stand on end.

"Are there others here, or is it just you two?" He asked Dexter, leaning on the island in the center of the kitchen.

I looked up through my lashes. He was watching me, face blank.

"Jase, Danny, Lee, and Aliya are downstairs."

He nodded, eyes narrowing on the chicken tender I bit into. "What are you eating?"

I washed down the chicken with a sip of tea. "Dinner." I kept my answer short, still holding a grudge from this morning.

He pushed off the counter, standing to his full height, just so he could look down on me with that obnoxious small smile of his.

"Great dinner for someone trying to prepare for a fight. Good to see you taking care of yourself, putting in that effort," sarcasm dripped from every word.

"Leave her alone," Dexter defended.

I dropped the food, honestly confused. "What the hell? I thought you were done lecturing me, giving up." I threw up my arms. "And anyways, what's wrong with my food? Its sweet potato French fries and chicken tenders. I cut out the bread and I'm drinking unsweetened tea."

Gage's lip twitched as he watched me. "Do you really think that food is good for you? That it gives you the nourishment you need?"

I looked between Dexter and him, doubtful, and shrugged. "It's better than my typical hamburger and onion rings, right?" I had thought I was eating low carb…

Dexter laughed and put his arm around my shoulder. "Oh Rea, you have a lot to learn."

I dropped my head to the table, evading his arm and blocking out Gage's judging glare. "I haven't eaten today; I'm hungry. What the hell am I supposed to be eating?"

"I have some leftovers you can eat, it's better than that crap." Gage grabbed some containers from the fridge.

I straightened up. "Really, Thanks." I didn't want to push my luck and say anything else. I was surprised he was willing to help.

He heated up Teriyaki glazed Tilapia with stir-fried vegetables and watched me expectantly as I took the first bite.

I nodded. "That's good. I could eat stuff like this. Where did you get it?"

Dexter hopped up onto the kitchen island. "Gage made it. He's the cook of the family. Without him I would starve. Or live off fast food."

"Help yourself while you're here. If you would actually listen to me I'd help you, but you won't." He turned away from me, placing the containers back in the refrigerator.

We were back to that, my decision to fight next week. He couldn't get over me not doing what he thought was best.

I shook my head, but kept silent as I finished my meal.

"Thanks." I rinsed off the dish and placed it in the dishwasher.

"Alright, well we're all downstairs if you want to hang out," Dexter said to his brother as he hopped off the counter.

"Sure, I'll be down later."

I followed Dexter to the basement door.

"You can go down Rea, I'll be right there." He opened the door, waving me through before closing it on me.

When Gage walked into the basement the others gravitated towards him. Jase and Danny wanted him to play pool with them, while Aliya wanted to talk and flirt. Gage barely glanced her way though, and she eventually sat back down with Leona and me.

After the boys played a couple of games of pool, Leona stood up and got their attention. "It's the girls turn to play," she demanded.

Jase was already racking the balls again.

Dexter pulled Leona in to him and kissed her neck. "Alright Lee Lee, how about teams? Me and you, and who else?" He looked around.

Aliya shook her head. "Not me, I suck." She laughed, winking at Gage. "Maybe you could teach me later?"

Dexter looked towards me. "Do you know how to play?"

"Sure." I stood, looking between Jase and Danny.

"I'll play," Gage said, grabbing the pool stick from Jase.

I licked my lips, agitated, hating that he could make me nervous about playing a friendly game of pool. I didn't want lectures on what shots I lined up.

After a bit, I loosened up some. I was sinking balls, not giving Gage any reason to criticize. But when I missed an easy shot I braced myself.

He patted my hip as he passed by me and murmured, "Good try."

The brief contact jump started my heart, but he continued to the bar unfazed. He leaned back on the stool, sipping his beer, scanning the table as he waited for Dexter to shoot.

Gage ended the game on his next turn and nodded to me. "Good game," he said with his slight smile.

"Thanks to you." I nodded, wary that his judgmental side would return.

He went for another drink, and I walked to the couch.

Leona and Aliya had turned on music and were dancing with each other, loose with alcohol. The boys played PlayStation but divided their attention between the screen and the girls.

"Come dance with us," Leona attempted to coax me.

"No, I'm gonna sit for a bit. It's been a long day."

I sunk into the couch, and my exhaustion consumed me. After a while, the heavy tiredness of my limbs was replaced with weightlessness as my mind disconnected from my body on the verge of sleep.

The tip of a finger trailed behind my ear, over my tattoo, and I shuddered as a wave of sensation shot to my toes.

My eyes snapped open as Gage sucked in air between his teeth.

"Sorry. I hadn't noticed that before. A flame?" He lifted his eyebrow in question as he leaned back on the sofa, eyes intent on mine.

I rubbed my own hand over the small flame tattoo behind my ear, trying to wipe away my strange reaction, and sat up. He was too close; I could feel his body heat surrounding me. And I was a little creeped out that he had been looking at me while I slept.

Struggling to swallow, I attempted to laugh it off. "I'm the girl on fire."

"Seriously?" His eyes flicked over me as his smile grew.

My stomach twisted and I shook my head, looking to the floor. I felt dizzy, still half asleep. "No. Not seriously."

His smile faded at my words. Leaning into my ear, he whispered, "I know you're tired. Come on," he nodded to the stairs, "I'll take you upstairs; you'll sleep better. It'll be quieter than down here."

Looking over to where Dexter was wrestling Jase over the PlayStation remote, I huffed a dry laugh. Letting my tired weight pull me back on the couch, I rolled my head on the cushion to face Gage. "I'm fine down here." I closed my eyes, blocking his surprised look.

His weight shifted next to me, the heat from him increasing, and I felt his breath against my lips as he spoke. "That's good. Smart." He tugged lightly on the bottom of my shirt.

I opened my eyes. He was only inches from me, his head rested on the couch mirroring mine. Every part of me tightened, shrinking away. I didn't like not knowing what to expect, from him or from my body. My heart pounded and my breathing intensified.

His eyes lit up as he leaned into my ear again, and his finger still played with the end of my shirt as his whispered breath tickled my skin. "You don't have to be scared. I won't bother you, nobody will. Not tonight."

Then he stood up, cold air filling the space he had been. And I struggled to regain control of my breathing and body.

"Leona, take her to the room upstairs. She's falling asleep," Gage ordered.

My muscles rebelled against moving, but I slowly sat up.

"Don't worry Lee, I can take her," Dexter said.

"No. I want to play you in Madden. Let Leona do it."

I got up in time to see Dexter nod in assent, taking the control from Gage.

"You ready?" Leona asked, extending a hand to me.

I nodded and pushed myself to standing, following Leona up the stairs.

I glanced back at the room once. Aliya sat beside Gage and squeezed his arm in encouragement. He never even looked towards me, and I began to wonder if my sleep-deprived mind had dreamed any of that up.

10: Tiny Storms

I SLEPT HARD, THE KIND OF SLEEP that leaves you with no sense of time passing.

I had followed Leona to the second floor and she had wavered between two rooms. "Gage's room or the guest room?" she asked with a raised eyebrow.

I guess his whispered words to me hadn't gone unnoticed by others.

Walking past her, I pushed open the door she had gestured to as the guest room.

The moment I settled in the sheets I was out. Gone to the world. No dreams, no nothing. And in the next moment I opened my eyes. The room was lit with bright, clear light from outside. Out the window, tiny flakes swirled in the wind, moving every which way, defiant to gravity.

Lying still on the bed, I listened for noises in the house. There was a faint scraping sound from below. Perhaps others were awake. The clock on the nightstand read 9:24.

Sliding out of the sheets, I stretched and smiled. I felt good today. My muscles were sore, but the good kind, the kind that meant I was working hard.

I paused, spotting my book bag against the wall. I had locked the bedroom door last night, but had not brought my bag up. It made me uneasy that someone had been in the room. I was typically not a deep sleeper and would have woken, but I also would usually never leave my book bag out.

I checked the bedroom door... it was locked. When I checked the bathroom, I discovered it connected to the hallway as well, that's how they got in.

Kneeling by the bag, I did a quick inventory. Nothing seemed out of place or missing and the prickle of anxiety began to recede. Pulling the phone out of the front pocket, I saw several missed calls from Anthony, and text messages asking if I was okay, and telling me to call him if I needed him.

I sent a quick message letting him know I had went to bed early last night and his response was almost immediate.

Good. I kept you up too late Sunday, sorry. :)

His text brought a smile to my lips. I liked staying up and talking to him. It was easy. He was easy, and I was beginning to appreciate that more and more.

Gage set me on edge, I couldn't figure out what he wanted, and didn't know what to expect when I saw him. He flipped from angry to helpful to flirty at dizzying speeds. It was exhausting.

I hope you're safe and warm. Call me if you need me. I'll get a sled to pick you up if I have to.

Anthony's text vibrated the phone in my hands, returning my smile. I knew he didn't have genuine affection for me, that his interests were purely physical, but that just made it better. There was no pressure and he made no demands. I sent a quick thank you text and made my way downstairs.

"Rocky? Where are you?" Dexter's voice trailed up the stairs.

I turned the corner and spotted Leona crouched down, looking under the couch in the living room.

"He's here," she yelled over her shoulder and then turned back to the couch, her long hair falling over her and spreading on the floor. Her tone morphed into a high-pitched baby voice. "Come on Rocky. It's alright I won't let Dexter put you outside in this mess"

Dexter walked into the living room, snowsuit undone from the chest up.

"Don't make that promise Lee." He saw me, and his smile grew. "Rea you're awake. Just in time. We're testing Rocky's hunting skills in the snow."

I raised my eyebrows, still confused. "Who's Rocky?"

"My cat," he said as he lowered himself by the couch to look under it.

Leona's head popped up as she sat back on her feet. "He's smart; he won't come out for you."

But Rocky did come out, almost immediately, and Dexter scooped him up in his arms. He or she was pretty. All gray with a big bushy tail.

I walked over to the cat in Dexter's arms and ran my hand along its soft fur.

"Rocky, like Rocky Balboa?"

"No." He scoffed. "Like Rocky and Bullwinkle." At my confused look he continued, "You know Rocky, the flying gray squirrel? Never mind. Come see what Jase and I have done. We've been busy this morning."

Dexter whispered things to the cat as he walked towards the kitchen.

Jase stood by the sliding glass door to the deck, dressed in layers of sweaters and sweats. Snow gloves on, and a scarf wrapped haphazardly around his head.

Gage sat back in a chair at the kitchen table, watching his brother, a plate piled high with eggs, ham, and toast in front of him.

"Look Rea, we made a maze for Rocky. I want to see if he can find the treat I put at the end of it," Dexter excitedly explained. "You got the video ready?"

The snow was about eight inches high, but rounded mounds showed where they had built tunnels on the deck. The maze was mostly enclosed, but holes spotted the top of the paths.

Jase took off his gloves and pulled out his phone, holding it up towards the maze. "All set."

I walked to the side of the sliding glass door to get a good view, but still stay out of the shot.

Dexter kissed the top of the cat's head. "Good luck buddy." He released him at the start of the tunnel. Rocky patted at the snow a couple of times, and then crouched low, taking off into the maze. At the first hole he popped out, and ran on top of the course to the end. He dipped his head into the hole, coming up with a piece of ham, and jumped onto the deck rail before sailing off the other side.

I gasped as I saw him spread his arms and legs, disappearing out of sight.

"Is he okay?" I followed Dexter, Leona, and Jase outside. I peeked over the edge and saw him running down the pier. Relieved, I hopped back inside, my bare feet freezing in the snow.

"That wily bastard foiled our plans," Jase said.

"Good for him," Leona declared.

Dexter just laughed.

"Regan, eat some food and then we'll train." Gage pointed to the stove. A frying pan was filled with eggs and another with ham. He stood up and walked to a cabinet. "Here's the plates and toast is here."

"Thanks, but I can't eat in the morning. I'll take coffee though." I could smell the coffee in the air and began scanning the counters for it.

He shook his head, his face showing his displeasure. "No. You need to eat to have energy for our workout. Make yourself eat." He forced the plate in his hands towards me.

My face pinched in frustration, but I kept quiet. I could feel all eyes on me and didn't want to start a fight.

"Fine. I'll have some toast," I relented.

So much for my good mood this morning. Thirty seconds of talking to Gage wiped that away. I tried to shake off my frustration, but him watching me eat with his self-satisfied smile made it hard.

I restrained the retorts that popped in my head. He said he would train me today and as angry as he made me, I couldn't pass up the opportunity to learn something. I needed to win next week. I tried to focus on that as I forced the toast down my throat.

When I finished, I raised my eyebrows to him. "Better?"

He nodded, smug. "Now go get dressed. I've got a gym downstairs we can use."

I did as told, but was still hesitant to approach him in the hallway upstairs when he came out of his room. He was dressed in a form-fitting Under Armour shirt and loose shorts.

"Can I use your washer and dryer? I mean, I could give you some money, it's just I can't get to the Laundromat today…"

"Don't worry about it. That's fine. Go get your clothes, we can start them now," he cut off my rambling.

I hated that smile he had. He knew I needed him, and it showed. It didn't feel like a good position to be in with him.

His gym was legit, equipped with a weight bench, speed bag, punching bag, treadmill, mats, and free weights. He had me show him my form on the punching bag first.

"Stop," he ordered. "You started off good, but now you're getting sloppy. Keep your wrist straight." He grabbed my arm, running his hand along my forearm and over my gloves. "Always keep this a straight line. Don't increase your speed if you're not in control." He met my eyes, looking for understanding.

I nodded and swallowed down the lump in my throat. He wasn't being condescending or judging, just helpful, with an even voice. I wanted to prove I was good enough, better than he thought. But he made me feel inferior without even trying.

I pulled out of his grasp and went back to the bag.

"Good. Better." He nodded in approval.

I hit harder, but kept control, focusing on the line of my arm and the strength of my punch.

Dexter sauntered in. "Hell yeah Rae, work that bag." He walked over to Gage, who was lifting weights. "Figure I'll put in a little time. They're all up now watching TV. Maybe we can go on a drive when we're done."

I did a cycle of strength training and skill moves, ending on the bag again. I felt good about the workout, already able to do much more then my first day at the gym. My good mood from this morning was back.

Gage and Dexter were at the weight bench spotting each other, so I took the opportunity to let loose on the bag. After a combination punch, I lifted my leg in a roundhouse kick.

"What the hell was that?" Dexter laughed.

I smiled to him. "Just getting a full body workout."

"You do know there's no kicking in boxing right?" Gage asked dryly.

I couldn't read him to know if he was teasing. "Yeah, I know that. But you know in real life you need to be prepared. Maybe I should switch to MMA."

Dexter groaned. "Don't even get Gage started on that. He's a purest."

Gage narrowed his eyes at Dexter. "I don't mind the UFC. I like watching it. I'm not going to do it though. Boxing's all about the strength of the punch, I focus on that." He nodded towards me. "But you're right, in real life you got to know more, especially if you're a girl."

I nodded in complete agreement. "So you've thought about the UFC?" I asked, looking at both of them.

Dexter smiled and nodded to Gage. "He has, I never would put this body through that." He ran his hands over his shirt, down his torso.

"Just your face?" I semi teased.

"Boxing is straight forward. And at least I don't have the danger of broken limbs," Dexter responded.

"I've done some training with UFC fighters, but it's like Dexter said, I prefer boxing. The pure battle of strength."

I contained my eye roll. I didn't want to poke the bear. Of course Gage thought his choices were best, he couldn't just be honest like Dexter.

"So you've got some kicks. What about escaping, do you know how to break free of holds?" Gage questioned, taking a step towards me.

My mind immediately flashed to that night last month, when the one boy had his arms around me, and then James's hands around my throat. The blood drained from me, leaving me cold. I thought I knew,

I had studied videos about how to escape different scenarios, but it hadn't worked.

I shook my head, stepping away from the bag and Gage. I didn't want to think about this anymore. "We're done right? I'm going to get a shower." I left without waiting for a response.

* * *

I dressed in my warmest hoody and jeans, and made sure to put on two pairs of socks with my chucks.

A knock came from the bedroom door.

"Regan?" Gage's voice was low from the other side.

There was just something about my name coming from his lips that sent a shiver through me every time.

"Come in," I called, sitting on the edge of the bed lacing up my black shoes.

I focused on tightening the laces, to avoid looking at him, and wondered which Gage was visiting. The sexy flirt, whose touch affected me more than it should, or the jerk, who criticized my every move. Tiny storms of chaos swirled through my veins. He caused them, and I didn't want him to see.

He sat on the bed next to me, and I tensed slightly, still moving my fingers over my laces, doing nothing really.

"I'm sorry."

I looked to him, surprised at his words. I raised my eyebrows, questioning. There was plenty I could imagine him apologizing for, but I didn't expect one.

"For yesterday." His eyes locked with mine.

I shrugged, unclear if he meant last night's flirting or his harsh words at the gym.

"I was wrong to accuse you of not taking this seriously."

I swallowed, pushing my heart back down my throat.

"Dexter told me about yesterday. Have you been staying at that motel for a long time?"

Sweeping my eyes to the ground, I broke our eye contact. I didn't like the look in them. He felt sorry for me, and I didn't want his sympathy.

"Only one night," I said in a measured tone.

"Why?"

His question irritated me; I didn't want to explain anything. "To have a place to sleep," I stated the obvious.

He sighed, lowering his head to catch my eyes again. "Where would you sleep tonight, if not here?"

His icy blue eyes demanded answers. I broke away again. Standing from the bed, I shrugged.

His fingers wrapped around my wrist, keeping me from walking away. Everything in me focused on the spot where he touched me.

"You can stay here." He tugged on my arm, urging me to meet his eyes again.

I should have felt relief, but instead I felt like I was hit with a ton of bricks, and the weight was crushing. I lifted my eyes to meet his, not wanting to give anything away.

"You can stay here as long as you need to. And I'll help you train. I know you need this."

I closed my eyes, waiting for the "but" or "if". There are always conditions. No offer comes string free.

"All you have to do is tell Silas you're not taking the fight next week."

I jerked my arm free. "What?" It took a few moments for my mind to catch up with the anger he lit in me.

"I'm not doing that. You can't say you know what I need in one breath, and tell me not to take that fight in the next. I have to fight. I need that money."

He stood up suddenly and rounded on me; I took a step back, bumping into the bed. His face twisted with confusion and anger. "I'm offering you what you need; all you have to do is listen to me."

His next step forced me into sitting on the bed, anger lighting his eyes as he hovered over me.

His anger surrounded me, his breathing intense as he tried to pull it back in. And I stayed still, barely breathing.

He took a step back, eyes glared down on me. "Think about it." Then he left.

Alone, I wrapped my arms around myself, trying to subdue the panic in me, breathing and focusing on each body part until I had myself under control.

11: In For A Penny

I BRACED ONE HAND ON THE CEILING and gripped the seat with the other as the SUV glided sideways across the snow. Nervous laughter rolled from me, joining the other screams and yells.

We slid to a stop just at the edge of the parking lot.

"Holy shit, that was close," Danny exclaimed.

We were in a large, empty, church parking lot, forcing the SUV into slides, fishtails, donuts, and pretty much anything it would do in the snow.

"I don't think I should do this anymore," Leona said from the driver's seat. "I almost ran us off the lot."

Dexter patted her shoulder from the passenger seat. "It's alright; you would have only gone into the snow. Rea you're last, ready?"

"Uh." I cut off my laughter. "I don't have a license. I shouldn't."

Gage twisted in the seat in front of me, eyebrows raised. "No License? Got to fix that."

Leona hopped out of the SUV, and Dexter called back to me, "Come on Rea. There's no one out anyways. You can drive here and have a little fun."

A giddy adrenaline was fizzing in me from just being in the car while they twisted it into slides, now it bubbled over.

"Alright."

Gage got out and lowered his seat for me to climb over.

"Your ass looks great in those jeans," Aliya said from the other side of Danny.

I laughed off her compliment. I had no choice but to bend over while climbing out, and since Danny and Aliya were in the back with me, they got the view.

Gage tried to grab my arm as I stepped down, onto the snow, but I shrugged him away. I had been ignoring him since his ultimatum, but he frustratingly didn't seem to notice or care.

I walked around the vehicle to the driver's side, my shoes absorbing the wet, cold snow. The snow had stopped and the day was warming up fast, but the wind was ice. It wasn't until I was in the warmth of the dry driver's seat that I paused to admire the tracks covering the parking lot, like toddlers artwork.

After buckling up, I turned in the seat. "Everyone ready?"

"Let's do this," Jase exclaimed from behind me.

My arm twitched with excitement as I put it in drive and the vehicle crept forward.

Dexter laughed next to me. "You're going to have to go faster than that."

So I pressed on the gas and cut the wheel hard. The SUV moved out of my control as it continued its spin.

"Ahh," I squealed as I hit the brakes.

We continued to spin over the snow for a moment before the brakes took traction and stopped us.

I looked to Dexter with wide eyes. "Wow"

The bleep of a siren cut through my excitement and dropped my smile. Dexter's face melted just as fast. Looking to the rearview, I could see the cop car blocking the exit to the parking lot.

"Uh, maybe we can switch spots Rea." Dexter reached for his seatbelt.

"No!" I pressed back against the seat, stomach clenched with nerves. "He'll see us moving."

"Oh no. I can't go to jail," Aliya cried from the back.

"No one's going to jail, we'll just get a ticket," Gage explained.

"We won't, Rea will," Jase clarified.

I couldn't listen to them. I wound down the window and put my hands on the steering wheel, waiting for the cop to make his way over.

I kept checking the rearview for his progress. When he finally stepped out, I gasped. It was Anthony. Initially this caused relief, but the tension quickly returned. What would he say in front of everyone?

A static voice from his walkie-talkie grew louder as he approached. He said something back to them and then he was at my window.

"Ma'am, Do you...." He leaned on the open window, surprise and amusement flashed on his face. "Regan! What are you doing?" He looked into the SUV taking in the full load.

"Dexter, Gage, good afternoon." His voice wasn't as light now.

"Thank God it's you. We promise never to do this again if you just let us go with a warning." Dexter crossed himself and put his hands up in prayer.

Anthony looked directly at me, no longer smiling. "Regan, can you step out of the vehicle for a moment?"

I followed him back to his car, hands shoved in my jacket pockets. He opened the passenger door for me and I hesitated.

"I just want to talk for a moment," he explained, still holding the door.

I slid in and he closed it.

Once he was in the driver's seat, his smile returned. His hand reached across me, and slid behind my neck, pulling me in for a kiss. Our lips met, his pushing for more, but I pulled away.

He nodded to the SUV parked in front of us. "What are you doing here with them?" It came out like a sigh.

I shrugged. "Having fun."

"That's not funny, but alright." He looked so pitiful. His eyes cast down to his lap where his hands were knotted together.

He must have been thinking about when I told him that's what him and I were doing, having fun.

"Not that I owe you an explanation, but I'm not sleeping with any of them."

His warm brown eyes lit up as he raised his head. "Yeah? Well I wanted to talk to you anyways. I found some stuff out that could help you."

I stiffened. "Really? About the case?"

"Something like that. Can we talk when I get off tonight? Or tomorrow? I can pick you up since I know you don't have a license." His eyebrows lifted at the last part, making it clear that I could have gotten in trouble today.

It also made it clear that he had been looking up things about me; we had never talked about my license or lack of one.

I ignored the last part, for now. "Sure, we can meet up. But can't you tell me now?"

He chuckled and leaned forward in the seat. "Don't look like that." He moved his hand across my forehead, trying to smooth the lines. "It's nothing bad, but I can't tell you yet. Insurance that you'll have to see me again."

I smirked with a small breath of laughter, raising my eyes to the ceiling. "Fine."

He opened the door, stepping out of the car. "I'll call you when I get off work."

I got out and he followed me back to the SUV, stepping in front of me to open the back door.

"No more driving for you," he said, a soft smile on his lips.

"Yes, sir," I saluted.

Jase slid over and I got in, and then Anthony leaned into the car, his hand braced on the seat behind me.

"You all go home now. No more four wheeling." In that moment he sounded extremely old. He winked at me and closed the door.

"Oh. Em. Effing. Gee," Leona exclaimed, deflating the tension in the car.

Dexter hopped out, jogging to the driver's seat. "That was close, let's go home."

"Did he kiss you? It looked like he kissed you," Aliya shrieked from the back seat.

I felt all eyes on me, but Gage's gave the most heat. His typical icy glare seemed more like smoke from a fire. Even Jase between us couldn't block it.

But his anger only reminded me of my own. I wasn't going to let him cause me to panic anymore. I wasn't going to show him any fear. I needed to take back control in whatever this was between us.

"Yeah," I said matter of fact.

"Damn. I wish I was a girl so I could get out of trouble by flirting," Jase said.

Dexter pulled the SUV slowly back onto the street. "I knew there was something going on that day I saw him with you at Johnny's."

Excitement was high as everyone chatted on the way back, except Gage and me. We both stayed quiet for the rest of the ride.

* * *

"Haven't you two studied enough for one day?" Leona whined, shaking Dexter's shoulders.

"Babe, Regan needs to see how her opponent moves. Learn what to expect."

"But you've been watching the same fight for-ev-er!" She groaned.

"Yeah dude, you two can take a break for a while. The snow's going to be gone quicker than it got here with this crazy warm weather," Danny plopped on the seat next to me, pulling Aliya down with him. "We might even have class tomorrow. Got to live it up tonight."

Dexter looked at me, giving me the choice.

I shrugged. "Fine by me. I think I've seen enough for now."

Draya, the girl I was going to fight, was tough. She was fast and came out swinging; I would need to block. In the fights I saw she was only hit twice, but both times she went down easy. I just needed to find an opening and take it. I was encouraged because I knew my strength was that I could take a hit, and hers didn't seem that hard.

"Where's Gage at?" Aliya asked.

Jase hit a ball in on the pool table. "He said something about an interview."

Dexter changed the TV to his YouTube channel and started a funny video. "He has a big fight in Atlantic City next month, probably doing some promotion for that."

Jase walked over with a liquor bottle and cups. He looked at the TV and pointed. "Did you upload Rocky's suicide jump this morning?"

Dexter grabbed the cups and lined them up. "Not yet. Danny get up and get the soda. I can't drink this straight."

"Me," he cried, unwrapping himself from Aliya. "Fine, but I get to choose the next video."

They poured drinks for everyone and put a cup in my hand, even when I tried to refuse. I gave up protesting and set the cup down when their focus went back to the TV.

We laughed for a while watching stupid videos, and then a compilation video came on that made my heart stop. It was 'slap cam', and everyone around me found it hilarious. Granted no one was really getting hurt; I still couldn't stomach watching it. It was too close. This stupid game was too close to the game that sent me to the hospital.

I cringed as I saw a person walk unsuspectingly through a doorway, only to be slapped by his friend on the other side, falling to the ground with the impact.

The laughter in the room scraped an already opened wound.

I burst up, unable to take anymore. "That's disgusting."

They all froze for an instant.

"Oh man, sorry Rea. I really wasn't thinking. I'm turning it," Dexter apologized, pressing buttons on his remote.

Danny groaned, "Really?"

I took a deep breath, unsuccessfully trying to calm myself. "It's fine, watch what you want. I've got to… make a phone call." I walked up the stairs, out of the basement.

It wasn't a full-blown panic attack, but it was something close. It took a while to even my breathing and calm the bile that bubbled in my stomach. This was the second almost panic attack I've had today. It was exhausting and I desperately didn't want to be that girl.

I had no control over my body and the fear that surged in me. I felt weak. My life had always been screwed, but now, as an adult, it was supposed to be better. I just didn't know how to make it better.

My phone vibrated with a text from Anthony:

I'm off in an hour. Pick you up?

I wavered on my answer, unsure if I should put him off till tomorrow.

My fingers slid over the keys to reply when a sudden knock on the door froze me.

Gage walked into the room without waiting for a response.

I slid off the bed as he sat on it.

He shook his head slightly, his lip curling into a smile. "Regan, are you still scared of me?"

I crossed my arms, keeping myself still. "More like appropriately cautious."

His eyebrows popped up in surprise. "Really?" He reclined on the bed, leaning back on his forearms. "What do you need to be cautious of?"

Lounged back on the bed in relaxed jeans and Henley tee, he didn't look too bad. In fact, he had my body clenching in a way that had nothing to do with nerves, but I wasn't falling for it and I'd make that clear.

"You. You're like a wild animal. Unpredictable and dangerous."

He paused, eyes connecting with mine. "I'm not dangerous. I would never hurt you." He sat up and patted the spot next to him. "Come sit. We need to talk."

Part of me didn't want to listen, to stay standing, but my legs felt like Jell-O and serpents were coiling in my stomach. I had to sit to keep up the bravado, but I made sure not to sit where he patted.

"The cop's a little old for you, isn't he?"

I snapped my head to him. "That's none of your business."

He shook his head, his jaw tightening. "You've got to know I like you. I think I've made that clear."

"No. You've made it clear that you want me, there's a difference." I wasn't prepared for this conversation. I hung tight to my anger for support.

He reached his hand out to me and I jumped off the bed, avoiding his touch.

"There is a difference. And believe me, if I only wanted you, I wouldn't be talking to you right now. I don't need to chase anything." He put his hands up, palms out. "I won't touch you if that makes you feel better. Not until you want me to. I know you're not like that, and that I have to go slow with you. I will. Just…" He reached out to where I stood frozen and grabbed my hand in his. "Relax. Sit back down." His warm grip pulled on me as he tried to bring me back to the bed.

Confusion swirled in me, and I pulled out of his grasp. This man was dangerous. He wanted to control me, and I wouldn't let him.

I stepped back and spoke through shallow breaths, "Stop pretending. You don't know me to like me, and all we've done is argue."

His lips slid into a sly smile. "Maybe I like that. There's a fire there." He stood and took a step towards me, snaking his arm around my waist. His movements were quick and fluid, and before I knew it he was holding me against him. "Feel that heat?" His eyes looked down into mine as his other hand stroked the length of my hair to my back.

I didn't feel heat; I felt white cold shock.

"This isn't normal. We could be good together." He nodded his head, confident in his words. His hands tightened around me, pressing me to him. His lips touched the top of my head as he spoke into my hair. "I want to help you, take care of you."

His words made my stomach clench in revulsion. I had heard them before, many times. My childhood was filled with those promises. And it was never true. Never. If it had been, I would have had a different life.

I tried to push him away, but his arms tightened around me. "Why? You see some charity case you can help, so you can feel better about yourself? I don't want it. It's like I said, you don't know me." I was able to break free at my last words. "You don't know anything about me. I'm not who you think I am." I could feel the words mounting in me, the anger growing. I knew what I could say, but hesitated for a second.

He took the pause in my speech to reach for me again and I laughed harshly as I stepped back. I had already started this, might as well finish. It's like they say, in for a penny, in for a pound.

"You think I'm innocent? I fucked that policeman within an hour of meeting him. It's you I don't want." The look that flashed over him shut me up, and I chocked on further words. Perhaps I had taken it too far, but he had to know he had it all wrong. He didn't have me figured out.

His hands curled into fists at his sides and he glared at me. His chest heaved with his deep breaths. After a moment he said, "Maybe we're more alike than I thought."

My phone vibrated from its place on the nightstand. I only noticed because Gage's eyes flashed to it. Anthony's name lit up the screen.

I picked it up and answered, never breaking my gaze from him. I was proving a point.

"Yeah. I can meet you tonight. I'm at Harbor View. I'll meet you at the gate."

His face turned to stone, his cool mask back in place, giving nothing away.

"See you soon." I hung up the phone as Gage walked out of the room.

12: Dazed And Confused

THE SMELL OF ROASTED CHICKEN AND GARLIC filled the first floor, making my mouth water. An Eminem song blared loudly, covering the sound of me leaving.

A large hand grabbed my shoulder and spun me around, just before I reached the door.

"You're leaving? With him?" Gage spit out between clenched teeth.

I masked my fear of being this close to his anger with indifference. I knew now he liked getting a rise out of me, whatever the emotion, and I wasn't playing into it.

Looking past him, I shrugged.

His tightening grip on my shoulder could be felt through my coat. "You leave now, and my offers off the table."

I flicked my eyes back to him and pushed his arm away. "I was never going to accept it anyways."

His face dropped, resignation clear, and he stepped back from me. "Then go." His voice was ice sliding down my spine.

Reaching behind me, I opened the door. It was difficult to pull my eyes from him. This moment felt final, and I suddenly had doubts and regrets I couldn't put a voice to. All I could do was keep going, even though the look on his face shredded something in me.

It wasn't until I was out the door that I allowed myself to feel the sadness, but it was short lived. The full moon and streetlights cast a pale glow, but the night was ripping my last bit of confidence from me, leaving me with nothing but fear.

The snow made running difficult and slow, but I was thankful for it. The white blanket reflected light, keeping out the darkness. The conditions kept others indoors, leaving me alone.

When I made it to the gate, Anthony's truck was idled, waiting for me.

"They made you walk down here? I could have picked you up from their house." He was angry as he pulled away. "Or did you not want them to see me?"

I couldn't deal with his feelings right now, and my frustration must have shown on my face as I set my book bag at my feet and slid on my seat belt.

He squeezed my thigh. "Hey, sorry. I'm not mad at you. I just don't like you out running around on your own. Are you alright?"

I nodded and turned up the radio. I needed a moment to recover from everything, the night, my feelings, but mostly Gage. His words echoed in my head. He liked arguing with me, he liked me, he wanted me. But he wanted it all on his own conditions, conditions I couldn't handle.

I looked over at Anthony. His light brown hair was messy, lying across his forehead, and the way he kept sneaking glances at me was sweet. He was willing to give me the space I needed, but still checked up on me. He gave me control, while still putting in effort. He knew what I needed, more than Gage. Anthony was proving that point with his actions.

"Uh, is it alright if I spend the night tonight?" I asked, looking out the window.

His hand slid to my leg again, running over my jeans in a soft caress. "Of course, just no running in the morning. I'm off tomorrow, we can spend time together."

"I have to work and go to the gym before, if they're open." The roads in the city didn't look too bad, but as we drove into Anthony's neighborhood they became snow covered.

His smile was genuine and lit his face, showing his white teeth. "I can take you there."

* * *

"I have pizza, spaghetti, or tacos? You decide." Anthony looked over his shoulder from the refrigerator.

My stomach revolted against spaghetti, I could never eat it again. One foster home only ever fed us spaghetti. Breakfast, lunch, and dinner. Ms. Mary was probably the best home I ever lived in. I had thought I was unlucky with placements, but from talking to other kids, my experiences weren't that bad. The scary thing was, some homes were much worse.

"Tacos." I wondered what Gage would say about this dinner, then I drop kicked that wayward thought.

I sat on a stool, chopping a tomato while Anthony browned the beef.

"So, what's the news?" I asked impatient, placing the tomato pieces into a small bowl.

Anthony laughed as he slid the meat from the frying pain to strainer. "We can talk about it over dinner." He set down the pan and walked to me, sliding his arm around my waist. "Don't worry, it's all good." He kissed my forehead and slid his lips to mine.

Adjusting himself to stand in between my legs, he gripped either side of my thighs, pulling me closer till our bodies were flush. His tongue slid in and out of my mouth. His hands slipping under my shirt, and I pulled back.

"I'm kina hungry. Maybe we should eat first."

He sucked in air and kissed my lips one last time. "Okay. Later." He patted my hip with a lustful smile.

"So? Can you tell me now?" I asked in between bites of my taco. We ate in the living room, watching the news

He nodded, chewing. "I talked to a defense attorney that was at the station. He said you could sue for emotional damage. You could get more money that way."

I frowned, setting down my taco. "I thought they were already going to have to pay for my medical and stuff. Detective Andres said I should turn in any bills that come from the hospital, that it would be covered when they were found guilty."

"But you could get more money, for yourself, if you sue. Then you wouldn't have to box anymore."

The last line surprised me. "I'm not just boxing for the money. I like it." I shook my head. "And anyways, I don't want to drag any of this out. I don't want to have to go to courts and speak to lawyers any more than necessary. Let the state deal with them. I'm not going to sue."

He sat back, shaking his head. "Well I know you don't have insurance, that you're not signed up for any support." He set his plate down and walked into the kitchen. A moment later, he came out with a packet in his hands. "You should fill this out. It's a simple application and you could qualify for insurance, financial assistance, possibly housing, although there's a wait list for that."

He extended the papers towards me. I grabbed them, chest tightening at the familiar header of Maryland Department of Human Resources.

"I was surprised to see you weren't receiving services still. It should have carried over from foster care."

I tore my eyes from the paper. "What have you been doing? How do you know any of this about me?" My agitation was rising.

"I saw your file from Detective Andres. I was checking up on your case." He scooted towards me, talking softly, trying to calm me.

I stood up, evading his touch. "Then you should know that I emancipated myself at 17. The state completely dropped me. I'm not going back into that system."

He stood too. "It's different now that you're an adult. They don't do anything but give support. You won't be ordered to see therapists, told where to live, or monitored by social workers. It's not like when you were a kid. This can help you."

"You could even go back to school. Get your GED."

My eyes widened. "You shouldn't have looked at my file. That wasn't for you to know." I grabbed my head in frustration. What else did he read? What else did he know about me? I felt vulnerable, and exposed, and betrayed. I was shaking with anger.

"Whoa. I didn't mean to make you mad. This could help you, that's all."

"You couldn't just leave it alone. You had to step in and try and 'fix' me. Well I don't need anyone helping me. I've got this."

Tears prickled my eyes. I didn't know what to do. Everything in me wanted to run, but fear kept me still. I couldn't go out into the night and find a hotel.

"I'm sorry. I thought... I don't know, I didn't think." He stepped to me, movements slow as he wrapped his arms around me.

I stood in his embrace, unmoving. Dazed and confused.

"I didn't mean to overstep. I won't mention it again." He rubbed his hand in circles over my back.

I shrugged him away. "What did you find out about me? How far back did my file go?"

"I only looked at the summary sheet, all the basic information. I didn't dig deeper. The rest you can tell me on your own, when you're ready."

Unsure of the truth, my eyes narrowed. "Alright." I didn't have a choice. I had to let this go if I wanted a place to sleep.

Picking up my plate of tacos, I took it to the kitchen, cleaning up to avoid conversation.

Anthony brought in his own plate and put away leftovers. We moved around the kitchen in mutual silence.

The papers still lay on the coffee table; it was the first thing I spotted when I returned to the living room. I scooped them up and put them into my backpack. After my reaction to it all I didn't want to admit that it could be a good idea. I could keep them for later.

Anthony kept quiet, but I saw the ghost of a smile cross his face as I zippered my bag up.

As much as I fought it, I needed help, and I was beginning to think the faceless state could be the best option. I had been so determined when I got out of foster care; I had the delusionary thought I could do better on my own, and was only realizing now that I was wrong. This past week had made it clear.

Anthony sat in the middle of the couch, arms stretched out on either side, waiting for me to join him.

"I started my period." I blurted it out. He needed to know, it effected what we could do.

I was on the depo shot, making my period infrequent and light when it came, but he didn't need to know that.

His face dropped slightly. "Do you need medicine or something?"

I shook my head, sitting on the far corner of the couch, feet curled under me, just out of Anthony's reach. I wasn't ready for him to touch me, the sting of his betrayal still present.

He began drumming his fingers on the back of the couch. He was uncomfortable and it showed.

"I think—I'm going to go to bed." He stood up. "Come lay with me. We can watch TV in there if you want."

I stood, avoiding his eyes. "I'll sleep in the guest room."

"No. Not tonight. Sleep in my bed. I want to know you're here." He slid his hands into my hair, cupping my head. "Please."

I felt like I had been fighting all day, and I couldn't do it anymore. So I gave in and let him lead me to his room.

I lay next to him, his weight pressed into the mattress, and his body heating the covers. But he didn't touch me, and I didn't touch him. It made the arrangement tolerable, and I fell asleep fast.

* * *

I made it to the edge of the bed, feet on the ground, when his long arms wrapped around me, pulling me back into the warmth of the covers.

"Where are you going?" He said, voice raspy with sleep as he spooned me to him.

"I was just going to start some coffee," I lied. I had full intentions of leaving.

"Nu-uh, not yet. I let you sleep last night. But now I want you." He kissed the back of my neck. "I want to kiss you, and hold you, and feel your body."

I grabbed his hands, keeping them from roaming up my shirt. "I'm on my period, remember?"

"I'm not talking about sex, we can do other things." He shifted me so that I was under him and then brought his mouth over mine.

Gage's disappointed face when I left last night kept replaying in my mind, and I wanted to erase it from my memory. I knew what I needed: a good workout to sweat out my feelings and never ending frustration.

I could feel his erection against my stomach and pushed him away. I wasn't in the mood for his touches.

"I have cramps. You said you had medicine?"

He eased off of me, his pretty smile melting with disappointment. But he quickly covered it. "Sure." He hopped out of bed and ran into the bathroom, returning with a pill bottle. "Here's Ibuprofen."

I grabbed the bottle and escaped to the kitchen.

Anthony showed me how to start the coffee and went to get a shower. He tried to hint for me to join him, but I declined. Guilt was eating at me though, I know he didn't bring me here for company, and I wasn't living up to my end of the deal.

I made eggs for breakfast, hoping to smooth things over with food. Although, really he didn't act angry. He took my brush-offs in stride and chatted happily as we ate breakfast together. He kept to the safe topic of himself and told me he used to be a prison guard before joining The Baltimore Police Department. Now he was in school to advance from patrol to criminal investigations.

We cleaned up and then got ready to go; the gym was open.

"When can I see you again? I don't work till tomorrow. I could pick you up tonight after your shift." His warm eyes met mine, and he tugged on the collar of my jacket, pulling me to him.

I couldn't handle it. He was willing to keep seeing me, even when I refused him. I was changing the rules, and I didn't want to do that. I didn't want this to become something other than what it was. I slid my hands inside his coat and pressed my lips to his neck, walking him back to the couch. He sat down and I kneeled in front of him, sliding his pants down to his knees. His hands tangled in my hair as I took him in my mouth and sucked hard. Within moments he was done, and it was over. And I felt a little more right, like I had finally stepped on solid ground.

After cleaning up he kissed me. "That was… great!" He kissed me again and mumbled, "Thanks," into my lips.

* * *

I stared out the window, watching the stream of water run like a river through the parking lot from melting snow. The sun shone bright, high above.

I only had two tables, but that was more than earlier. Then I saw a familiar SUV pull up, Dexter was here. He walked up the path with Jase and Danny, none of them with coats on.

He wasn't at the gym this morning, neither was Gage, and I'd been there several hours.

Dexter scanned the restaurant as he walked in the front door.

Trichelle immediately perked up at seeing him and walked around the host stand. "Hey, how many?" Her hand hovered over the menus.

"I'm actually here to see Rea." He spotted me and walked past her, leaving Danny and Jase behind.

I gave him a hesitant smile. "Hi, what are you doing here?"

He wrapped me in his arms without responding, squeezing me tight.

"I'm sorry Rea. I should never have played that video. Never will again, you're right, it's wrong. Are you mad at me? Don't be mad." He held me at arm's length, eyes begging forgiveness.

"It's alright, really."

"But you left without saying anything."

I shrugged him off. "Yeah. Sorry."

He narrowed his eyes. "You're not at that motel are you? You have somewhere else to stay?"

"I'm at a friend's," I admitted.

His smile grew. "Okay, good. Now we're hungry. We want a table in your section."

I dropped off the bill and another soda for Jase.

Danny nudged Dexter. "Ask her to go." At my raised eyebrows Danny continued, "We're going out Friday to Fells Point. It's Jase's birthday. You should come."

Jase and Dexter both nodded in encouragement.

"I don't know." I rocked on my hip. I'd have to see what sleeping arrangements I could work out by then.

Danny turned to Dexter. "Well whether she goes or not, tell Gage she is. Then he'll come with us."

I straightened. If Gage went, I wasn't going.

Dexter laughed. "What are you talking about?"

"Come on." Danny leaned back in his chair. "Gage never hangs out with us, but since she's been around, bam, he's around."

Jase nodded. "He's got a point. But why do you want him to go? He's not much fun."

Danny rolled his eyes, like they were idiots. "Because girls flock to him, and I'm not above scooping up the rejects. And if he's focused on her." He jabbed his thumb in my direction. "There's bound to be lots of them to choose from."

I groaned and raised my eyes to the ceiling. "Well, I'm not going. Tell him whatever you want, but I doubt he'll go if you tell him I am."

Dexter's eyes met mine, questions glowing in them. "We'll see." He turned back to Danny. "But it doesn't matter how many rejected girls are around, you ruin all chances when you open that mouth."

Trichelle came over to me after they left, bursting with excitement. "Thank God hot boys hang out in packs. The pretty eyed one's friend, Jase, asked me out with them this Friday." She bounced in front of me. "Are you going? We can go together!"

That sealed it. I was not going.

13: Nice

ANTHONY WAS SITTING AT THE BAR TALKING to Trichelle.

She braced her hand on his shoulder as she leaned into him, laughing at whatever he said.

His face was bright with amusement and interest as he watched her.

She didn't remove her hand when her laughter stopped, but leaned in to say something in his ear.

I watched this exchange as I cleaned up my section, my shift over.

Trichelle had to stay for the later crowd. At the moment there were only a few scattered customers at the bar, allowing her plenty of time to flirt.

The agitation I felt wasn't jealousy, but something else, confusion. What was he doing with me? He obviously could get other girls, ones that would fit into his world better. I couldn't figure out why he was still around, why he still showed up.

I recorded my tips and had to give Louisa a portion to tip out the supporting staff. And unfortunately, she was at the bar.

Anthony straightened up, pulling away from Trichelle as I approached. She looked confused at his sudden shift but continued talking.

After I closed out with Louisa, I walked past the two, waving in farewell.

The sun was beginning to set; if I hurried I could make it to the motel before dark. The evening air was unseasonably warm, so I didn't mind waiting for the bus.

"Regan, what are you doing?" Anthony stopped me before I crossed the street.

I shrugged. "Letting you try your game with someone else."

He shook his head, a half smile on his face. "What? That in there? She was flirting with me. I'm here for you."

I sighed, pushing hair out of my face. "You shouldn't be. Go back in there." I lifted my chin in the direction of the restaurant. "She likes you, you might get somewhere."

Disbelief was evident in his face and posture, his smile tightened. "What's going on? Are you jealous?"

I rolled my eyes. "Oh Please. You can go do whatever you want. I don't care. That's—"

"Damn you," he interrupted me, anger morphing his pretty face as he grabbed my arm. "What the hell, Regan? I know we're not serious, but can you at least pretend to care? Even just a little."

I couldn't contain my amusement. "Wow. You really don't get it. We are not anything."

I looked around at the few people walking by. The crosswalk symbol changed back to walk. "I have to go. I'm gonna miss the bus."

"Stop. I'll drive you."

I turned back to him, stunned. He was still sticking around, even after this? My curiosity got the best of me. "Okay."

"I'll take you to those apartments, but can we get dinner first?"

His determination left me dumbfounded. "Why are you being so nice to me, especially since I'm being a bitch right now?" I didn't feel bad about laying out the truth, but I could have been nicer about it.

He turned the key in the ignition and gave me a shy smile. "I don't know; you've been pretty nice to me."

I pressed back into the seat with a dry laugh. "Is that really what this is all about for you?"

He swallowed, the muscles in his neck moving with the force, and nodded. "That's all you'll let it be, right?"

I searched his eyes, trying to understand. The engine was on, but we still hadn't pulled out of the parking spot.

I nodded in return, just as slow as he had. "That's all I can offer. But I need you to understand that's all it will ever be. You seem like a good guy, I don't want to hurt your feelings. But I need to be clear. This will never be anything more than what it is now, don't expect differently."

He looked away for a moment, when he turned back to me his smile returned. "So does that mean we can go to dinner?"

I laughed, letting go of the serious conversation. He had been warned, if he didn't listen that wasn't my fault. Then I remembered my situation and sucked in a breath for confidence.

"Before we go, I have a favor to ask."

His smile grew. "Sure, shoot."

I pressed my lips together, thinking of how to word this without taking back everything I just said. "I need—I don't have—" I sighed and he grabbed my hand, trying to encourage me, but it only made me feel worse. "I am not staying at those apartments anymore."

"Why? What happened?"

I shook my head. "I just can't stay there anymore. I don't really have a place to stay yet. But next week, next Saturday, I should have enough to get my own place, if I can save my money till then." And if I win that fight, I couldn't think of the alternative.

His eyes were sharpening as I spoke. I think he knew what was coming next, but he didn't drop my hand.

"I can stay in a hotel, but I don't want to spend money if I don't have to. And you've been wanting me to spend the night." I shrugged, uncomfortable with the request. "I'm not asking to move in; just maybe we could work out what nights I can stay, so I don't pay for a hotel room if I don't have to. I could also—"

"Alright." He cut off my rambling. "When I'm home you can stay. I have to work nights sometimes, so you'll have to arrange something else then, but I can help with that too. We can work this out till you have your own place."

He really was too nice for me, too good. I felt miserable.

"Let's discuss it over dinner. There's a really good Italian restaurant down the road. Do you like Italian?"

I wasn't in the position to say no. So I nodded and pasted on a smile. "Sure."

His schedule was confusing, rotating shifts. Two day shifts, a day off, two night shifts, a day off, and repeat. So I had to find a place for Thursday and Friday, but could stay with him until Wednesday next week. And hopefully I would be in my own place after that.

The restaurant was small, but nice, dimly lit and tables spaced far enough apart to offer privacy.

We sat in a rounded corner booth and I was able to show Anthony my gratitude, with my hand, under the table. He wanted wild, I was making sure I delivered on my end, because he was more than keeping up his side of the deal.

* * *

Pulling in front of the gym, Anthony stopped me from climbing down from the truck. His hand gripped my waist, stilling me as he leaned in for a kiss.

"I like having you in my bed." He murmured into my hair as his lips moved to my neck. "I'm going to miss you these next two nights." He pulled back, still gripping my waist. "But I'll see you on Saturday? I'll pick you up after you get off work?"

I nodded, uneasy with his affection, and slid out of the truck.

"You have your hotel key, right?" He yelled out the window.

I rolled my eyes, understanding a bit more what teenagers with doting parents must feel like.

"Yes." I pulled it out of my pocket to show him.

His smile widened. "Good." And he pulled away.

He had gone with me to a hotel near my work and signed for the room, since I wasn't old enough to. I paid for it, and it was more than I made these past few days at Johnny's, but I hoped to make it up on my shifts this weekend. The snow was nearly gone and the warmer weather was sticking around. Perhaps the sunshine would bring back customers.

* * *

I rolled silverware, my mind wandering to places it shouldn't. But Gage hadn't been at the Gym again today. It made training easier, but I didn't want to be the reason he wasn't there. Silas hadn't mentioned him to me, but he wouldn't. He preferred me to stay away from Gage, and I had to agree that was probably the best tactic.

"Have you decided about tomorrow?" Trichelle popped up next to my arm.

I turned to her exasperated. "Do you ever have a day off?"

"I picked up some extra shifts. But I'm off Saturday. Which make Friday night a great night to go out. I have to work first, but should be off early enough. You could meet me here and we could get ready together." Her eyes brightened with the idea and she gripped my forearm as she bounced with enthusiasm. "Oh, you could spend the night, it could be fun. We can split the cab, so we can both drink."

I had been ready to say no and dismiss her, but I paused considering. It would be fun to hang out with Dexter, and with the relief of my living situation worked out for now I was ready to let off some steam. Plus, if I stayed with Trichelle, I could save a few dollars on the room, but I had to cancel now. The only thing keeping me from agreeing was Gage.

"Maybe."

She froze, and then began shaking slightly. "Really! Eeeeee. Oh you have to go. I don't want to go alone. They're your friends. Please. Please. Please. I'll clean your section today. Please."

I shook my head and threw my hands up, blocking her excited attack. "Alright, let me work out the details with Dex. Just don't ever squeal like that again."

She nodded and ran her fingers across her lips, zipper like, before skipping away.

* * *

Trichelle rolled her eyes at me as her mother pulled the van up to the curb of Corner Pocket Bar and Billiard.

"You girls be safe. No alcohol," she continued, as we climbed out of the van. "Oh, look at that cute guy there. You should go talk to him Trich! It was nice to meet you Regan. Have fun, but remember no S.E.X before—"

Trichelle slid the door closed on her mother's ramblings, and linked her arm through mine. "Gah, I am sorry about that. She can be..."

I smiled, tight lipped. "She's cute; I don't mind." She seemed like a great mom. She'd even driven us here so we didn't have to pay cab fare.

It was past eleven and the sidewalks were packed with people bar hopping. We weaved through the crowd into Corner Pocket. I flashed my state ID at the man guarding the door and he let me in, but I didn't get the stamp that Trichelle got.

She put her fake ID in her purse with a smug smile.

Arms encircled me and I knew it was Dexter. I braced myself for the tight bear squeeze.

"Finally you two made it. We're over here." He hugged a thrilled Trichelle, then led the way to where everyone else was.

Gage was the first thing I noticed, he was leaning over the pool table to take a shot.

"You said he wasn't coming," I spoke low to Dexter.

"What?" he yelled above the noise of the crowd and balls breaking, then his eyes followed mine, and he nodded with understanding. "He changed his mind." He threw an arm around me. "He's spontaneous like that sometimes. But don't worry, or get your hopes up, or whatever it is you're doing, he brought them."

I followed the direction Dexter pointed and saw two girls sitting together. One was Becka, from the gym last weekend. She wore a bold, skintight dress with a pink and orange pattern. Her friend was similarly styled and they pulled off the playboy bunny look perfectly.

The bar had several pool tables horseshoed around a dance floor. High tables and chairs lined the outside of it all.

Walking to where the group was seated at, I introduced Trichelle around. There were some new faces in the crowd though, Leona and

Aliya had their roommate Zoe with them, and Jase had brought other friends.

"Who would have thought Rea had a body under all those sweaters?" Danny waggled his eyebrows. His flushed face made it obvious they had been drinking for a while.

Trichelle beamed with pride. She had leant me her top, a black, boat neck, long sleeve shirt, that I paired with my dark skinny jeans.

"If you would've seen her in the ring you would've known," Jase added.

I ignored them, uncomfortable with that type of attention, and signaled a server over.

"I'll have an ice tea." I pointed to Trichelle who ordered a margarita, and everyone else took the opening to order more drinks.

Trichelle pulled on my arm and whispered low in my ear, "Who is that guy?" She pointed to Gage.

I took a moment to drink him in. He was standing arms crossed, watching the other guy line up a shot. He wore dark jeans and some button up top I barely noticed; He stood out, not the clothes. He had a power that radiated from him and forced others to take attention. When his eyes met mine, I looked away, flustered at being caught staring.

"He's trouble. Stay away." I wasn't even sure why I gave her that warning.

After we got our drinks, most of the party went off to dance. I watched them moving on the dance floor, taking the last sip of my tea before joining them.

"Where's your cop?" Gage asked, suddenly appearing in front of me, his clear blue eyes shining with amusement.

I shook off his question, deciding it best to just walk away. His bunnies bounced over to him anyways, saving me the trouble of responding.

"You dance like a white girl. Come on Rea, use those hips," Leona instructed, shaking her own in example.

My dancing was limited to bouncing in my own contained area; these girls moved, dancing in circles with smooth, fluid, rolls of their body. They all tried to get me to mimic their moves, with varied results.

Dexter grabbed Leona from behind, eyes scanning our laughing group. "You ladies having fun?" At Leona's nod he continued, "Did you ask her?"

I paused when Dexter nodded to me, but Zoe brightened. "They were waiting on me to decide, but she seems cool and we're in a bind, so why not?"

Leona's smile widened, and she broke free of Dexter, grabbing my hand. "Come with us, we need to talk."

We left Trichelle on the dance floor with Jase, and sat around a high top table.

"Our fourth roommate just found out she's pregnant and is moving out at the end of the month. We're looking for a renter and Dexter said you were looking?" Leona explained.

I was stunned. "Oh. Yeah I am. Where and how much?"

"It's on University Boulevard, right near campus. We," Aliya spun her finger encompassing me, Leona, and her, "pay three fifty a month and split utilities. Never more than five hundred total. Zoe gets the basement to herself so she pays the rest."

"Now this is just to see if you're interested, not official yet. But you can come by and check it out. We all get along really well, we want to make sure you would fit in," Zoe added.

Leona rolled her eyes. "Zoe's the cautious one. We all have our own label in the group. I'm the fun and nice one." She stood up tall, taking pride in her title.

Aliya stood up, affronted. "Hey, I thought I was the fun one?"

Leona and Zoe laughed, and then Zoe said, "No, you're the slutty one."

Aliya's lip twitched. "Same difference. I'm just open and a forward thinker. Who needs restrictions on sex?"

"Obviously Roxy did." Leona turned to me. "She was known as..." They all looked at each other and broke into drunken giggles. "The Mom. We should have never given her that name, look how it backfired."

I took in all the silliness. Could I handle living with them? Yes. They might become slightly annoying but I could handle it. Plus, the rent was half what I would pay if I got my own place.

Dexter leaned on the table, looking around. "So it's all worked out then? Are you going to be the new fourth, Rea?"

I shrugged, downplaying my excitement. "Yeah, I'm interested. I'll come by and see what we can work out." I nodded to Zoe, the one who seemed to hold the control of the situation.

Danny nudged Dexter as he bounced on his toes. "Dex, check it out. I told you it was good to invite him."

We all looked to where Danny was gawking, and my stomach turned.

Gage was sitting back in a chair while Becka and her friend leaned over him to make out with one another. Both girls had one hand braced on his leg, the other hand running through each other's hair as they pressed their bodies together, tongues tangling with their kiss.

From my angle, I couldn't make out Gage's face, but every other guy was glued to the show. Well that's one way to get attention. I had to turn away as Becka's hand moved up his leg and to his torso.

But what I saw in the opposite direction was even worse.

Adrenaline and shock pumped through my veins, and my mouth went instantly dry, making the air hard to breathe.

Nan met my eyes, noticing me at the same time, and stood up. Damien's hand reached for hers, and she leaned over to whisper something to him. Her lips were close to his ear, practically touching, and I wanted to rip his hand off her back.

But I stood frozen for a moment, watching it all unfold, unable to comprehend.

It had only been a week. One week since I last saw her. But it must have been a rough one for her. She looked like she hadn't slept in days and her eyes were void of their typical spark.

Damien looked past her as she continued to speak in his ear. He scanned the area till he spotted me, a sick smile spreading on his face. His eyebrows rose as he pulled Nan in for a kiss, but his eyes continued to drill into mine.

When he released her, she walked to where I was. From behind her, Damien nodded and crooked his finger, calling me over.

14: Interfere

A NUDGE FROM BEHIND BROKE THE SPELL I was under.

I looked for who had bumped me, but it was only someone trying to get a better look at the scene I no longer had room to think about.

I took the few remaining steps to get to Nan.

"So weird seeing you here," She said in a daze.

"What are you doing? Why are you with him?" My hand sunk into her slouchy shirt sleeve as I pulled her out of the way of a passerby.

Her eyes widened and her face hardened. "Too much has happened since you left. We need to talk." She nodded her head in Damien's direction. "He wants to talk to you too."

"No, I won't."

She shook her head, a small tight movement. "He won't do anything. He promised."

I looked at her with disbelief. You can't trust a promise from him. "I don't care. He makes me sick, and I'm not going anywhere near him." The way her eyes shifted set off all kinds of alarms. "Nan, what the hell is going on?"

She sucked in a deep breath. "Let me get my cigarettes and we can go outside and talk."

I nodded, my stomach twisted in knots.

She walked away, swimming in her clothes. Her pants hung loose on her hips and her cropped top was sloppy, and not in the intentional way. It had only been a week.

I wouldn't look past her to Damien, but I didn't want to turn my back on them either, so I scanned the group, looking for James. He wasn't anywhere that I could see.

When I glanced to check on Nan's progress, my heart stopped. Damien was walking towards me, only feet away. Covering my fear, I raised my chin and stood up tall, waiting for him.

His smile was smooth but treacherous. "Nan must not have given you the message; I have something to say to you."

My blood turned to ice; I didn't want Nan getting in trouble for me. "She told me."

He cocked his head, giving me a side look. "Then maybe you need a lesson in listening." He grabbed my elbow in a vice like grip. "You must not realize how lucky you are, how much you owe me."

I struggled in his grip, then Nan pulled at his other arm. "Damien, remember?"

He dropped my arm and flicked his eyes to Nan with disgust before focusing back on me. "You better thank your friend. I don't let people get away with hitting me, but she can be persuasive." He looked past me. "Those your new friends? They better back the fuck down."

I turned; Dexter was focused on our group. I mouthed, "It's okay." And he stayed put, but continued watching us.

Nan flicked her eyes to the back of the place. "Regan and I are going to have a cigarette. Give us a minute, okay?"

"Five minutes. I'm done here."

We walked away from him, weaving around people and tables as we made our way to the back door. I didn't spare a glance to Gage and his girls, but could tell something was still pulling everyone's attention.

Outside, the patio was full, but nowhere near as crowded or loud as inside. A large heater warmed up the space and wide wooden stairs went to the second floor. The top deck sounded packed. Even with us sitting side by side on the stairs there was plenty of room for people to get by.

I waited in silence as Nan took out a cigarette and lit it. Only after a couple of drags did she speak.

"You look good Regan. You always were one to land on your feet. I'm glad I saw you tonight, you never showed up on Tuesday."

I didn't know what to respond to first. This didn't feel like landing on my feet, but looking at her made me realize it was all subjective.

"It snowed. I didn't have a way of getting there," I explained.

She frowned, focusing on the lit end of her cigarette. "Snow? Oh, yeah," she mumbled, not sounding sure.

"What's been going on Nan?" I couldn't take it. Damien said five minutes, and I was sure Nan would be jumping soon.

She shook her head, taking a long drag, exhaling smoke into the frigid night air. "James went crazy. Tore up the place the next day and found everything. Took everything." She spread her hands out, cigarette between two fingers. "I have nothing left. No money. Nothing."

"God, Nan. You need to get away from him."

She nodded. "I do. Are you still looking for a place?"

My heart tightened, remembering my earlier offer. But if Nan needed to break free of her brother I'd be there for her first. "Yeah. You want to be roommates? But that means a clean break from James, and no Damien either."

She nodded slow, pain evident in her face. "I know. I have to."

I never thought this would happen, that Nan would finally realize she couldn't help her brother.

Damien's shadow caught my attention first. "Nan. Are you done?"

Her eyes flicked up, and I saw a glimpse of the hatred she held for him. "Give me one minute. Almost ready."

"Make it quick." He surprised me by walking back inside.

Nan's knee began shaking and my chill was bone deep. I didn't want her leaving with him. But I felt helpless; I could barely make arrangements for myself right now.

"When can we move?" She asked.

"I'm thinking next weekend. But I can come by this Tuesday and we can check out spots together." James only worked on Tuesdays, the bare minimum to keep in compliance with his probation.

She licked her lips, putting her cigarette out. "That's good. Look, I hate to do this. But, do you have anything you can lend me. I don't want to owe Damien anymore."

My heart broke looking at her. Asking for help wasn't Nan's style. She was a shell of the girl I knew.

Standing with her, I reached into my pocket and pulled out two twenty's. I shoved it into her hand. "Here." My mind raced, thinking of any other option to get her to stay. "But you don't have to go. Stay. We'll figure something out together."

Her face hardened. "I can't. Not now."

"Then I'll see you Tuesday?"

She gave me a hollow smile and nodded before walking away.

I took several breaths, trying to make the tears prickling my eyes retreat. I couldn't stand to see my friend so broken.

After a moment, I attempted to walk back into the bar, only to be blocked by Gage's large body. I stopped myself short of bumping into him.

"Some friend you got there," his tone was cutting.

"You don't know what you're talking about." I couldn't deal with him and attempted to walk past.

He grabbed my elbow, pulling me out of the doorway, back outside.

"I saw and heard. Why would you choose to live like that? With her?"

I ripped my arm away, too full of overwhelming sadness to filter any of my words. "Live like that? Who the hell is living? Me and her, we're just trying to survive, one day to the next, and it's a little bit easier when we do it together." Or at least it had been before James was released.

I wiped my hand over my face, trying to reign in my emotions. I was breaking and struggling to hold my jagged pieces together. "I wouldn't expect you, of all people, to understand any of this. So don't you dare talk about her."

The few patrons on the patio were staring. I hadn't meant to cause a scene, but for the life of me I couldn't muster any more cares. Fuck them and this stupid life that throws away girls like Nan.

Gage didn't move any closer, but his voice was soft and careful. "I understand that more than you think."

Why wouldn't he just leave me alone? "Sure. You with your cars, and home, and food, and clothes, and career, and stupid girls. And stupid tattoos. And—" I cut myself short, knowing that I was grasping now, and not making sense. "I don't want to argue with you. I can't do this. Please."

He nodded, with a look so serious, but somehow absent of his typical intensity. "I didn't come here to argue with you."

I took my chance to take the focus off of Nan, and laughed bitterly, trying to walk past him again. "No, you certainly didn't come here for that. I saw what you came here for."

He shook his head, face pinched slightly. "Not that either." Grabbing my hand, stopping me from walking past, he added, "Don't go in yet; you're upset. Stay out here and calm down. I'll stay with you. No arguing or anything."

I took in a ragged breath. He sounded sincere, and my head was swimming. My stomach ached, twisted with worry for Nan. I needed a moment. Nodding, I walked back to the steps and sat.

Gage's overwhelming presence made me feel small, but radiated much needed warmth.

After a while of sitting in silence, he rocked into me. "So you think my ink is stupid?"

I let my head fall into my hands and laughed, embarrassed. "No. I hadn't even really looked at them. It's just, people like you find it so easy to judge people like Nan and me," I said matter-of-fact.

Narrowing his eyes, he looked directly at me. "I don't think you two are the same type of person." At my flash of anger he spoke up, "but I do get it. I fought for what I have, literally. Dexter and I never had much growing up, except a mom who was high more than home and let her boyfriend of the week run the house. I got us out as soon as I could. So yeah, I get what it's like to not know when or where you're going to sleep or eat."

I turned my head, resting it on my palm, seeing him in a new light. "How old are you?" I asked, staggered.

A small smile tugged at the corner of his lips. "Twenty three. But I moved out when I was sixteen; Dexter was thirteen."

I sat up, floored. Questions swirled in my mind. Long, sleek legs interrupted before I could voice one.

Becka leaned forward, bracing her hands on Gage's shoulders. "Baby, they're closing soon. Are we going somewhere—"

He pulled her hands off him, dropping them in front of her. "I'm talking." She stepped back at his shortness. "Go back in. I'll be there soon," he added with a bit more control.

Spotlights flicked on, flooding the patio with light, and the music shut off. People were flowing to the doors, and Becka reluctantly followed.

I stood up with one last calming breath, checking my emotions before facing everyone.

"Things will get better." Gage stood up, too close to me. His eyes searched my face, too intense. I watched his full lips as he added, "You're a fighter. You'll get through this and get to living, not just surviving."

His words cracked the dam holding in my emotions, and I had to step back to protect myself. I nodded, running my hands through my hair to avoid reaching for him.

Too much had happened tonight, and I wasn't thinking clearly. My worry for Nan made me too emotional. I walked around Gage, back inside, needing the buffer of a crowd.

The lights were bright, the place clearing out, but many people still milled about.

Trichelle wrapped my arm in hers as we followed the group out. "I was looking for you. Everyone's leaving. Tonight was so fun." Her liquor breath whispered into my ear, "I think I might go home with Jase."

I pulled back. "But I was going to stay at your house."

Her face crumpled. "Shit. That's right. I forgot."

She dropped my arm and sulked to where Jase was waiting.

Dexter walked beside me as we inched our way to the exit, his face serious. "Everything okay?"

I nodded, tight lipped, not wanting to talk about Nan anymore.

"I think your girl hit it off with my boy." Dexter's typical smile returned as he nodded to Jase and Trichelle.

I smiled in return. "Yeah, I'm sure I'll here all about it tonight."

Taxi's lined the street, waiting for customers.

Danny opened the door to one. "Jase, you coming back to the house?"

Jase grabbed Trichelle's hand. "Can Rea stay with one of you tonight so that Trich can come with me?"

"My bag and things are at your house," I interjected.

"Calm down Dora. You can go without your backpack for one night."

I dropped my head, to hide my amusement while giving Dexter the middle finger.

Humor was clear in his voice as he continued, "I've got maps. We can get it in the morning. It's all good, Boots has this under control."

I lifted my head, meeting his eyes. "Did you just call yourself my sidekick?"

He rolled his eyes and slid his arm around me. "You must not watch Dora. Boots runs that show." He nodded to Jase. "Take your girl and go. We'll call in the morning to get Trich and Rea back."

They slid into the Taxi with Danny, and another pulled up in its space.

Gage opened the door, letting his two guests slide in. He paused, turning to Dexter. "Are you coming home tonight?"

Dex dropped his arm from me and wrapped it around Leona. "My car's at Lee's. We might stay there."

Gage looked towards me. "You can stay in the guest room again, if you want to ride back with me."

The way he offered, with a soft, shy voice, churned emotions in my stomach. But the girls in the Taxi made my stomach turn in a much different way. "I'll go with them." I nodded to Leona and her friends.

Gage slid into the cab and shut the door, cutting off the trills of laughter from within.

Leona shot a dark glance at me, pulling on Dexter's arm as she swayed on her heels. "You two stay at my house. I think its best I keep my eye on you."

"Babe, don't be like that." Dexter pulled her in tighter, giving me an apologetic smile.

She pulled Dexter into the cab first, sitting herself between us.

* * *

It wasn't the worst couch I've slept on. It wasn't anywhere near the top of the list either, but it was free so I had no complaints. My mind raced with thoughts of Nan, and Gage, and my fight, and Anthony, and anything I ever had to worry about.

I wanted to know more about Gage and Dexter, how they had managed, how they overcame, especially how Dexter came out so carefree. He wasn't hardened and jaded, and I envied that.

At some point, my thoughts slowed and I fell asleep holding onto the only thing I knew with certainty; I had to win next week. I couldn't afford to lose and neither could Nan.

* * *

Jase picked me up the next morning, taking Trichelle and me back to her house. From there I went straight to the gym, hoping to squeeze in some training before my shift at Johnny's.

"You've lost two more pounds." Silas shook his head with disapproval.

I stepped off the scale, unsure of what this all meant. "I can still fight this Friday right?"

He sighed. "You'll be fighting out of your weight class. You can do it, but you can't lose any more weight. I told you, you need to eat and eat well." His eyes flicked over me. "We've got to cut back on the workouts this week. I don't want you sore on Friday anyways. We'll focus on technique until then."

We went into his office and made a plan that fit with my work schedule. He also gave me a diet plan. I needed to make sure I ate every three to four hours; it seemed like an impossible task. But I would do it.

* * *

The lunch shift was busy and stayed that way, merging with the early dinner crowd. I ran nonstop from table to table. I dropped off the bill for one table, set down extra napkins for the next, and gave a refill on soda to the third. Making my way back to the kitchen to pick up meals for a table with screaming children. Drew stopped me.

"Some dudes up front for you," he said as he passed by, just as busy as I was.

I looked to the front and saw Dexter waiting. He was alone, which was odd for him, and set off small warning bells. I finished my path to the kitchen and dropped off food for my table, giving them extra crayons and pictures for the kids, then met Dexter up front.

He smiled and greeted me with his typical hug. I was reluctant to return it since Leona's comment last night.

Dexter extended a grocery bag to me; it was weighed down with Tupperware containers inside. "Here's some food for you. Silas told me you dropped to a lower weight class."

I took the bag and narrowed my eyes. "You do realize I work at a restaurant? I'm surrounded by food?"

He laughed and pointed to the bag. "Yeah, but that's the good stuff. Gage made it. He cooks a crap load at once, so his fridge is always full. Enjoy." He crossed his arms with a smug smile. "I bet you haven't even eaten yet, since you've been here."

I looked around. "We're slammed right now. I'll eat as soon as I can. It's only been…" I did the math in my head and paused, it had been six hours since I last ate. Damn. "I'll eat as soon as I can. Thanks. I've really got to go now." I lifted the bag with a smile before turning back to work.

* * *

"What's in the bag?" Anthony asked as I closed the door on his truck.

"Food. It's supposed to make me strong for my fight."

His eyes narrowed. "When is that again?"

"This Friday at 6:30."

He laughed. "I can't get over it. You're a sexy bad ass." He started the engine. "I've got a thing planned already though. I won't be able to see you fight."

"That's okay. I can still stay the night after, right?" He had told me it was his night off. If the fight went well, it would be the last night I had to stay.

He smiled at me. "Yeah, of course. It should be done by then."

He pulled up to a light and slid his hand into my hair, leaning in for a kiss. When the light turned green he released my lips, but kept my head in his hand, guiding me to his neck. I caught on quick and continued the trail of kisses, moving my hand to his pants. He was already hard, bulging against the zipper. I stroked over the fabric until he undid the zipper himself, allowing his penis to spring free. I took him into my mouth, while he drove us to his house.

* * *

I trained with Silas Tuesday after work, a switch from my typical morning sessions. I told Anthony not to pick me up till much later though; I was planning on meeting with Nan and knew James worked Tuesday evenings. I didn't want to go there when he was home.

"You were angry today. That's good. Use that, harness it, but don't let it cloud your focus. Your punches were strong, and you need that on Friday." Silas encouraged as I took off my training gloves.

I was angry and pictured Damien's face while punching. It released some emotions, but my dread was building as I thought about going to Nan's now.

Silas looked past me, confusion wrinkling his brow. "Gage, the meeting's not till tonight, right?"

I froze, all of a sudden uncomfortable. I hadn't seen him since Friday.

"I'm here to see Regan." His soft rasp sent chills through me, followed quickly with electric heat.

I turned to him, wary, catching Silas's disapproval from the corner of my eye.

Silas crossed his arms. "We talked about this. You said you wouldn't interfere."

My eyebrows flew up. "What?"

"I'm not here about the fight," Gage said.

At the same time, Silas explained, "We had agreed he would let me and you manage your career. He's going to stay out of it." His eyes never left Gage's and the tension between the two was clear, a wall I couldn't cross.

I wondered briefly when they had made that deal, before or after he tried to get me to stay at his house. But I dismissed the thought for now. "Why are you here then?"

Shifting his eyes to me, he asked, "Are you done your training?" At my nod he continued, "Go get dressed. We can talk when you're done."

I didn't like the dismissal or that he ignored my question. But there was obviously something between him and Silas, and I took the opportunity to escape. A part of me wanted to stick around and see what was up, but the tension between them was a ticking bomb, and I was certain it was more than me that caused it.

When I came out of the locker room Silas was gone.

Gage waited by the door, talking to another guy who was sweaty from working out, gloves still on.

He noticed me walking towards him and nodded the guy away in dismissal. He stood tall, hands in his black coat pockets. He wore a hat that read OBEY on it, and I laughed internally at the irony. He would have a hat that says that, but I had to admit it looked good on him, the dark fabric made his eyes stand out even more.

My stomach clenched as he smiled at me, it was a shaky smile, like he was maybe a tad scared of me too, and the vulnerability in it was surprising.

"Have you gone to your friends yet?" he asked, his head ducked down to meet my eyes.

I swallowed, wondering exactly how much he had heard of the conversation between Nan and me. "Not yet. I was going there next."

He nodded. "Good. That's what I thought. I'm coming with you." He cut off the start of my protest. "I won't say anything. But you shouldn't go there alone."

"She's my friend. I'll be fine."

"She may be. But will she be the only person there?" He raised his eyebrows, his hands in his coat pockets lifted slightly.

I shook my head, thinking. I had tried to call her already, with no answer. But that was typical for Nan. "I'm not sure." My biggest fear was Damien being there. But I didn't think that was likely since he was never around before. But, just in case, having someone there on my side would help.

"You won't say anything? We're going to look at apartments."

He nodded, a slight smile touching his lips. "I don't mind."

15: Safety

RUSH HOUR TRAFFIC IN THE CITY SUCKS. Nan's apartment complex wasn't far from the gym, but it took a good twenty minutes in the SUV.

Gage turned down the volume on the radio. "I have to meet Silas at eight. If things are all good with your friend then, I might have to leave."

"We should be done by then. I'm supposed to meet my ride at the gym later, so I've got to be back too." I pulled my hair into a low ponytail, just for something to do with my hands.

The closer we got, the more anxious I became. I think Gage made it worse. I couldn't separate my nervousness about going to Nan's from the tingle of adrenaline being near him caused.

His eyes dragged over me as I took down my ponytail and shook out my hair, again.

"Is there anyone in particular making you this nervous? Someone I should look out for?"

I took a deep breath, stilling my hands in my lap. "Nan's brother, James, but he should be at work. Or the boy that was with her at the bar, Damien. I think it should be alright though. I'm not really sure why I feel so jumpy, maybe too much caffeine." I tried to smile and failed. My leg bounced, unable to keep still.

Gage didn't say anymore, just turned up the radio and kept glancing at me when he could.

* * *

Nobody was answering the front door, but the TV was on inside.

Gage stood just behind me, waiting; hat fitted low on his head, shading his face.

I turned to him after knocking with no answer.

He cocked his head and shrugged his shoulders. "What do you want to do?"

"I have stuff in there I need to get." I had left clothes in my rush to leave last time. "I'm going to walk around back and knock on the slider."

"I'll come with you," he said simply.

We walked over the muddy ground to the back of the brick building. Dark red curtains blocked any view inside the apartment. The rattle of the door was loud when I banged on it, an echoing boom that shook the glass.

"Nan," Miguel yelled from the other side of the door. "Someone's at the back door." His voice was farther away this time.

A few moments later, a small section of curtain was pushed aside and Nan peeked out. The latch clicked, and the door slid open, just enough for her to squeeze out.

She was in boxer shorts and a tank top, her hair thrown up in a messy bun that looked slept in. Dark circles shadowed her eyes blending with smudged eyeliner.

"Regan?" She smiled sleepily at me, seemingly oblivious to the cold. She shook her head slowly. "What are you doing here?"

I narrowed my eyes. "We made plans to look at apartments, remember?"

She nodded, smoothing stray pieces of hair back. "I thought we said Tuesday?"

My patience was growing short. There was more going on than her being tired. "It is Tuesday."

Her mouth popped open, and she rubbed the heel of her hand over her eyes. "Really? Well why did you come so early?"

I sucked in air, trying to calm myself. "Nan, it's five o'clock. If you've changed your mind, fine. But let me at least get the rest of my stuff while I'm here."

She straightened and frowned. "No. I'll go. Let me get dressed." She stepped back through the slider, but turned before I could enter. "Wait here."

I stopped her from shutting the door on me. "Can I get my things now? Before James comes home from work?"

She paused, eyes widening for a second, and then nodded, stepping back to let me pass. She blocked Gage from entering. "No, you wait here. I don't know who the hell you are."

He raised his chin, looking down on Nan, and his jaw worked under the skin. "I'm Regan's friend."

"He's a friend." We spoke at the same time.

Her nerves were showing as she looked between us, but she shook her head. "He can wait out here." She gave me a meaningful look. "Regan come on, we'll only be a minute."

"Who else is in there?" Gage asked, holding the door open with one hand.

"Only Miguel." Nan narrowed her eyes at me. "Did you bring a body guard? Come on, you can trust me."

"It's fine, we'll be out in a minute." I begged him with my eyes to listen.

The lines of his jaw deepened, but he stood back as the door closed on him.

I went straight to Nan's room, wanting to get out as soon as I could. This place no longer felt like the safe haven I had once seen it as. Nan's room was a mess; I was the one who kept it clean before. Soda cans and food debris littered the floor and dressers.

I opened the drawers I used when I stayed here, looking for any of my clothes. Nan disappeared into the attached bathroom to get ready.

"Have you seen my boots? The short ones?" I opened the bathroom door to check for any of my things, and rage surged through me.

Nan had several pills spread on a tray, crushing them with a card. Residue of lines already taken streaked the surface.

I flipped. Without thought I knocked the tray away from her, sending it flying into the bedroom. Pills and powder exploding in every direction.

You would have thought I hit Nan too, the way she dove after it all.

"What the fuck are you doing?" She said from the ground, searching for the pills that scattered.

"Leaving. I'm getting my things and—"

The slam of the front door silenced me.

"Where's my dirty girl?" Damien's voice made every molecule in me scream. "Daddy brought you some candy."

I heard laughter from whoever was with him, and jumped into action, picking up the little bit of clothes I had gathered and heading for the door.

Damien stepped through it first. "What will you do—"

He cut off his own words as he scanned the room, taking in Nan on the ground picking up pills, the spray of white powder streaking the carpet, and overturned tray. "What happened?" His voice was frighteningly low.

Nan sat up, pointing at me, tears running down her face. "She did it. She—"

The back of his hand slammed into my cheek in an instant, whipping me around, the clothes from my arms spreading on the floor.

His hand was in my hair before I could react, dragging me to him.

I screamed, grabbing his arm to keep him from yanking my hair any further. He tossed me away, sending me bouncing on the bed.

"Shut up you fucking bitch." He pounced on me, using one large hand to cover my mouth and pin me down.

I kicked at him and tried to hit him, but he released my mouth so he could pin my arms. I managed to get my knees up between us, keeping him from pressing his full weight on me. Bringing up one foot, I kicked him in the stomach. But he went flying off of me with a force that I couldn't have caused.

I scurried off the bed, the moment his weight was removed.

Gage picked Damien up by his shirt and slammed him into the wall, fist pounding his face over and over, blood spraying from his nose.

Nan was standing, screaming at me, "Do something."

"Gage. Stop. Let's go," I yelled.

But he didn't listen. He kept hitting Damien, holding him up with one hand and punching him with the other. Damien was slumped against the wall, convulsing with each blow.

Two guys I hadn't seen before jumped on Gage, knocking him off balance. He staggered back, letting go of Damien. He charged one of the guys, knocking him to the ground. Standing over him, he kicked him several times. The other guy tried to jump in again but Gage swung and hit him, sending him to the floor.

With all three down, it was the perfect time to leave. I grabbed his shoulder, trying to gain his attention. "Let's go," I pleaded.

I heard the click first, before I saw it, and the room silenced, everything slowed. I dropped my hand from Gage's shoulder as he straightened himself up.

Behind him, Damien was rising to his feet, gun aimed steadily on Gage. "Don't move motherfucker." He used one hand to wipe the blood from his nose, smearing it across his swollen and cut cheek. "Who the fuck are you?" He stepped suddenly towards him and kicked him in the back of the legs, sending Gage down onto his knees.

Gage's eyes met mine, an eerie calm, as he stayed still.

I closed my eyes as Damien brought the back of the gun down on Gage's head.

But when I opened them, Gage had Damien's arm twisted behind his back, and a different gun pressed to the back of Damien's skull.

"Regan, pick up that gun," Gage commanded.

I picked it up quick, before anyone else could react.

Gage kept the gun pressed to Damien's head and dropped his arm. Then he reached his free hand out to me, and I gave him the weapon I picked up.

Damien's friends watched wide-eyed from their spots on the ground, and Nan stood with her jaw dropped, an expression that matched how I felt.

"Are any of these three Miguel?" Gage asked.

"No," I managed even though I felt like I was choking.

"Miguel. Come in here now." Gage's voice was calm, but demanding.

Miguel walked in, palms up and shaking. "Man, I'm not any part of this. I just crash here sometimes."

"Sit down. On the bed," Gage ordered. "You too." He pushed the gun into Damien's head, in the direction of the bed, and Damien walked to it. "Everyone on the bed."

They all obeyed, sitting on the long edge of the mattress, facing Gage.

I attempted to disappear into the wall.

"This is how it's going to work. We're going to leave, and none of you are going to try anything. Ever," Gage explained in a measured tone.

He took a step towards Damien, gun pointed in between his eyes. "And in case you don't fully understand, let me explain. You work for Rock."

Damien's scowl flinched at that and Gage nodded, pointing his gun at the tattoo on Damien's neck. "What type of pussy lets another man brand him? I know that mark. Ask him about Rusnak."

Damien's eyes flashed wide and he moved back just slightly.

But Gage smiled. "Ah, so you've heard the name? Well then you'll know I'm not one to fuck with."

Gage stepped back and pulled the magazine from Damien's gun, tossing both pieces in opposite corners of the room.

He looked to Nan. "You going to come with us?" She shook her head, and Gage flicked his eyes to me. "You ready then?"

I nodded, unable to speak. I felt ill and couldn't breath.

"Wait. Did you get your stuff?" His voice was too calm.

I picked up my scattered clothes as quick as my shaky arms allowed and walked out the bedroom.

He caught up to me at the front door, when I faltered with the knob. He opened it for me and kept his hand on my back as he ushered me into the passenger side of the SUV. He even slid my seatbelt on before shutting the door and jogging to the driver's side.

I was frozen to the seat, forcing myself not to think. I couldn't think about what just happened. I didn't know what just happened. I didn't know who this was in the car with me. I couldn't think. And I couldn't breathe. Everything hurt. Energy crashed through me, breaking me. I gasped for air and closed my eyes, trying to block out everything.

I didn't even realize the car had stopped, but the zip of Gage undoing his seatbelt pulled me from my panic. I opened my eyes, just as his lips crashed into mine.

He sucked the little air I had left out of me.

His arms wrapped around me, and his lips moved, aggressive and demanding.

I choked, literally gagged, and pushed with everything I had to get him off of me. But it wasn't enough, he was too strong.

He pulled himself away though. Pressing back on the driver's side window, he watched me like the wild animal I once accused him of being.

"Don't touch me," I strained, opening the passenger side door to wretch up whatever I could.

It burned to breathe and tears blurred my vision. I was going insane and prayed to wake up from whatever nightmare I was in.

Gage put his hand on my back and I whirled around.

"I said, don't touch me," I growled low at him.

He pulled his hand back and watched me for a moment, his chest heaving with his strained breaths. "Everything's alright now."

I shook my head. Nothing felt alright.

"They won't bother you."

"Why? What was that name you said?" Then I thought better of it and covered my ears. "Don't tell me. I don't want to know anymore.

I don't want any part of any of this." I didn't want to add any other names to my list of people I had to watch out for.

"Take me back to the gym."

When he started the car, I changed my mind. "I'll walk."

I opened the door and he reached over me, pulling it shut.

"Stop, I'll drive you." He slammed his hand on the steering wheel. "Fuck. I have to be at that meeting, but Dexter's home. You're staying with me tonight."

I sat back in the seat as he pulled away from the curb, too scared to protest.

"I can't stay. Someone's expecting me. I need to go. I don't want to stay." My voice cracked at the end. I needed to get away from all of this.

Gage inhaled and exhaled, hand gripping the wheel. "Okay. I know you're scared, but you don't have to be. I meant what I said, everything's going to be alright." He looked towards me, but I stayed looking forward, wanting to avoid him. "I can explain. I will."

I shook my head and squeezed my eyes, my body shaking beyond my control again.

He sighed. "It's okay. Not tonight, we'll talk when you've calmed down."

We pulled up to the gym, and he put the SUV in park. He twisted in the seat to face me. "Regan, this is important, look at me." When I met his eyes he said, "Don't tell anyone what just happened, for your own safety."

I nodded, a tingly numbness taking control as I got out of the car, pulling my overfilled backpack with me.

16: Habits

I PULLED THE HOOD OF MY JACKET up and walked, head down, to the bathroom.

Lowering my face directly under the cool stream of water, I tried to drown the chaos in me. When my need for air forced me to come up, I rinsed the acid from my mouth and spit into the sink.

I reluctantly raised my eyes to the mirror, not liking the girl I saw. Bracing my hands on the edge of the sink, I breathed deep, fighting down the remaining spasms of panic twitching my muscles. I angled my face to get a better look at my cheek. Damien's back handed slap left a shallow gash, but otherwise I was unmarked. Unharmed.

I tried to convince myself everything was alright now, just like Gage had said. But I didn't buy my lie or his. Nothing was alright with what had happened. Not a thing. And I had to accept the fact that it had been my own stupid mistake. It could have been avoided.

Pulling out my phone, I texted Anthony to come get me, and I waited in the bathroom till he texted that he was out front.

The red layer of the gash stayed wet, not allowing makeup to cover it, so I pulled my hood back up, trying to cover my face as much as possible.

Gage walked beside me the moment I stepped out of the restroom, but he didn't touch me. I increased my pace, wanting to run away.

"Regan stop," he demanded as I reached for the main door.

I turned to him, controlling my voice and movement. "Thank you."

He flinched, surprised, and nodded with narrowed eyes. "Of course, but we need to talk."

"No. No we don't. I'm leaving now, and I don't want—" I looked around the gym, hesitating, struggling to find the right words. I couldn't say I didn't want this, the boxing. "I won't talk," I promised low and turned away, walking into the cold night.

Anthony's truck was running at the curb. I climbed in and buckled up, saying nothing.

Gage watched us from the gym door, arm's crossed and face stern, not even trying to hide it. And I just wanted Anthony to go, to pull away.

But he brought his hand to my chin, turning my face to his. "What happened?" His voice was as soft as his touch.

I pulled away and shook my head. "Just go, alright."

His face hardened and he looked past me, nodding towards Gage. "Did he do something?"

"No." My response was immediate. "Please, just go. Now."

He nodded and pulled away.

He didn't question me further. We went through our evening routine, cooking dinner with him recounting his day, and I listened, silent, trying to block out my own thoughts.

When I crawled under the sheets that night, in one of his too large shirts, I curled up next to him, trying to absorb his warmth. To feel connected. I had lost the only person who had been a constant in my life today. And I still worried for her, even if she didn't share the concern for me.

He stiffened at first, surprised by my touch. I never cuddled. Then his arms wrapped around me and he pulled me in tighter, tucking me under his chin. One hand drawing circles on my back.

Closing my eyes, I shuddered at his touch. He wasn't demanding anything, but I felt more vulnerable like this than in any other position he had me in before.

"What happened?" He whispered into the top of my hair.

My heart squeezed, nearly stopping, tears prickling my eyes, but not falling. Instead of answering, I trailed soft kisses over his collarbone and neck.

He rolled to the side, holding me back slightly, searching my eyes.

I froze, feeling my pulse pound through my veins. He couldn't turn me away. I needed this. I needed him. I needed him to want me, and my desperation must have shown.

He pulled me in against his chest, stroking the hair away from my face. "Tell me something. Is someone hurting you?"

I let out a shuddering breath, running my hands along his shirtless body, wanting to be the girl that could talk to him. I didn't want to be Regan, the girl who made too many mistakes and never got anything right, always choosing the wrong people, doing the wrong things, making the wrong choices. I wanted off that ride.

He moved over me, bracing his arms on either side of my body as he looked down at my face. He pleaded, "I can't help you if you won't talk to me."

I shook my head. He was wrong, he could help me. By touching me, making me feel worthy of something. Anything.

I slid my hands behind his head and pulled him down to me. Our lips met, whisper soft, and he pressed into me, deepening the kiss, stroking my tongue with his. His hands roamed over my shirt, sliding down my panties and kicking off his shorts in one quick motion.

He slid back over me, bringing our lips together again, groaning into my mouth. He reached one hand into the nightstand table and took out protection, sliding it on himself without breaking our kiss.

He rubbed the tip of himself over me, spreading the slickness and I wrapped my legs around him. He pulled back looking into my eyes, questioning me silently.

I knew what it was; I never let him on top. I pushed my hips to meet his, wanting him to take control. I didn't want to lead; I didn't trust myself, my decisions.

He groaned while kissing down my neck and sliding into me. He rocked his body and moved his hands over my hips and stomach, sending chills through me. His hands slid higher under my shirt, testing how far I would let him go.

I tried to stop myself, but I couldn't. I pushed his hands away before he reached the start of my pain, scar's that proved I was born disposable.

Anthony kissed away the tears that I didn't even realize were falling, shuddering inside me as he found release.

He pulled me back into him, not letting me go till he fell asleep.

I got up and showered, only allowing myself to release my sadness when I was safely wrapped in the steam of the hot water.

* * *

Anthony wrapped his arms around me while I sat at the kitchen table drinking coffee. "You can stay here tonight. I'm calling off work."

I sat up. "Don't do that for me. I'm fine with the hotel."

He trailed his nose over my cheek and down my neck, his warm breath tickling the skin. "I'm not fine with it. Not after last night."

The familiar spiral of sadness was consuming me. I had been here before, the aftermath of a tornado, left to pick up the pieces. Except, I was beginning to realize I walked into the storm willingly.

Anthony was the only person I had left. The only person not touched yesterday. Silas and Dexter may not have been there, but I didn't know what role they played with Gage, what they were involved in. I needed a break from it all.

"So, what do you want to do today?" Anthony asked pulling a chair closer to mine.

I shrugged. "I don't want to do anything."

He smiled. "That sounds nice."

We spent the day watching movies and lounging on the couch. He wouldn't let me go long without touching me, caressing me, or just holding me. And it broke my heart. Each and every time.

"I don't want to push, but I have to know something. I let it go the first time you came here panicking, but last night was different. And you've been hit. What happened?"

"I box. I get hit." I tried to end the conversation.

He narrowed his eyes skeptically. "What about the other thing. Why were you so upset?"

I shook my head, but saw the determination in his eyes. I wanted to change, to be different. So I went against my instinct, and I let him in, just a little. "It's Nan. She was my friend. And now," I shrugged helplessly, "she's not. Maybe never was, not really."

"Nan?"

I bit my tongue, mad that I had said her name to a cop. I had forgotten for a moment; seems I couldn't stop making wrong choices.

"I'm only talking as a friend right now," he reassured, speaking to the thoughts that I hadn't voiced.

I slid my arms around him, fighting the part of me that wanted to leave, fighting the old me. But old habits are hard to break.

"I don't want to talk," I whispered into his neck, my hands sliding into his sweat pants.

* * *

Sometimes, sleep is what you need most and it didn't fail me now. It defeated my sadness and replaced it with a new determination. After spending a day in hiding, I was ready to get out and get back to the gym. I was done letting bad circumstances rip away what mattered most.

When I looked at my life, boxing was the only thing I had that made me feel good, that gave me any hope.

I slid out of bed, careful not to wake Anthony up. A pang of regret tugged at my heart. It was wrong of me to have used him like I did yesterday, to let emotions mingle with what we had. The lines were blurring, and it was my fault.

I was tempted to walk to the metro, but Anthony was going to help me get a hotel for the night while he worked.

I took my phone to the kitchen table and checked my missed texts. There was a series of them from Dexter, the earliest ones silly, just for fun, and progressively becoming more serious. My favorite being a middle one that said:

Are you lost Dora? Call backpack.

I couldn't imagine this boy being involved in whatever Gage was into, but it didn't matter. I was going to fight tomorrow and then try and find a new gym. But first, I had to win.

I texted Dexter, letting him know I would see him today. We had a fight to prepare for.

* * *

"You should take off tomorrow." Dexter frowned at the shorts he picked up. "Do you like pink?"

"The singer or the color?" I asked, flicking through a rack of sports tops in florescent colors. I stepped away from the hangers, frustrated. All the clothes were so bright, a psychedelic rainbow of color everywhere I turned. Then I saw black and went to the table that had items laid out, neatly arranged.

"Either. What about this?" Dexter lifted his arm, displaying a stringy black top with pink trim.

"I don't' mind pink, but I can't fight if I have to worry about a wardrobe malfunction. I need more coverage than that."

He set it down with a goofy grin. "Wait, you actually don't mind pink? You are a girl."

I gave him a sidelong glance. "Shut up, I meant the singer. Just choose a top. Silas gave me the gym's black and silver shorts, and I've got the shoes, this is the last item right?"

I didn't mind the color either. But when you have a limited wardrobe, color is not your friend. It's best to stick with neutrals that don't stand out so you can wear it often.

"Here, this will work." I picked up a full-length black spandex top with thick straps. The price tag wasn't bad either. "Are you thinking Pink for my introduction? We have to discuss all that. No more making it rain."

He put his hand on my shoulder. "Whatever you say. Do you want to go to Leona's now? Talk to them about moving in?"

I felt stuck. This was a good opportunity, cheap rent that I could afford, even if I didn't win the fight. And my roommates would be college kids who didn't seem to walk with trouble. But what did I know? I wanted to ask Dexter about Gage, but didn't, remembering

Gage's warning. Not that I needed it. I knew never to talk about crap like that.

"Sure, but I can't stay long. I want to go to bed early and rest up for tomorrow." I paid the cashier for my top and followed Dexter to his car

* * *

I signed the contract.

It was a month-to-month lease. It gave them the flexibility to replace me with another college student come the fall or sooner. But it also allowed me an opening to leave if I needed to, If this was too close to Gage, if they weren't as innocent as I assumed.

I could move in on Monday.

* * *

I sat back with headphones on, trying to keep calm, letting myself get lost in the beat, to be empowered by it. The anticipation was sweet and I embraced it, enjoying the vibration through my muscles. Whatever happened, I was giving this my all, and I couldn't wait to meet the girl in the ring.

Dexter tugged on one cord, knocking my ear bud out. "Let me hear. I want to see what's got you smiling."

We sat side by side listening, bobbing our head to the music. Outside the room a fight was going on. I wasn't the first fight tonight.

When the chorus played Dexter smiled to me. "This is it. This is going to be your song."

The door opened and Gage walked in, scattering my composure.

He looked between Dexter and me, eyes stopping on me. "You ready?"

I was. Before he ruined me. I pulled myself together and nodded.

Gage jerked his head to the door, signaling Dexter to go.

And the bastard got up and left, without a pause or a glance back. So much for loyalty.

Gage ran his hand over his hair. The short sleeve shirt showed off his muscles stretching under his tattoos.

"Do you need anything?" he asked.

I narrowed my eyes. "To be left alone. I need to focus."

He dropped his arms by his sides. "Okay. That's why I came in. I don't want you distracted. I'm sorry, for everything. You can do this. You can win."

His words hit me, affecting me more than I cared to admit.

He bowed his head low and left me alone.

I put my headphones back on and turned up the music.

* * *

I walked out with Silas and Dexter, surprised by how calm and confident I felt. I had done all I could to prepare and now was the moment of truth.

This place was bigger than the last, more people filling the bleachers surrounding the ring. But I put them out of my mind. They weren't important.

Draya came in next. She was bigger than me, had more definition of muscle and radiated anger.

She stalked in a circle around the ring, scowling as she took her corner. She was in red and black, with cornrows tight in her hair.

Then the referee stepped in the center, signaling the start of the fight with a flick of his hand before he stepped out of the way.

I bit tight on my mouth guard as Draya charged at me. She covered the distance before I even took two steps. But I had my hands up and blocked her first assault, absorbing the punches into my arms and side. I almost laughed; they were nothing. I had been hit harder and taken much worse.

I took a step into her punches, taking her off guard, and hit her in the stomach.

She stepped back with a grunt. Shock registered on her face; she had felt it.

That put her on guard. She had been loose, not bothering to protect herself, but now she postured to block.

We circled each other for a second, and then she attacked again. One hit stinging my ear. But she left herself open with her wide swing. I took the opening to hit her again, once more in the stomach, followed by a left hook.

She dropped to her hands and knees, and the referee started counting. I never took my eyes off her. She moved to one knee, using the time to catch her breath. She stood at nine, and then knocked hands with the ref.

She was easy to figure out. She lunged at me again with another bout of punches, a little more wild and fast, but not nearly hard enough.

I shook with each landed punch, small jerks forcing my body to move. I stiffened, using my strength to still my reactions and stepped into her again. But she moved back, distancing herself from me.

I kept coming though, not even throwing punches, just walking towards her. She was retreating, jabbing the air to keep me away.

When she was backed into the corner, I bent my knees and stepped in to her punch. Her fist connected with my right shoulder, but I struck her chin with an uppercut from down low. She bounced against the ropes, and I stepped back as she slid to the canvas.

My excitement built with each number the referee counted. She raised herself up on her arms and knees, but left her head hanging. She shook her head at eight and I knew it was over. She stopped trying to stand.

I let my head fall back with relief, a smile stretching my cheeks. The referee lifted my arm and announced me as the winner.

This time I was prepared for Dexter's excitement as he jumped in the ring. I spun around towards him as he picked me up in a hug.

"One round, Rea! Damn girl, you are good."

I looked past him to Silas, who smiled at me with a nod.

* * *

Dexter spun me around as I exited the locker room. "What are we going to do tonight to celebrate?"

I looked between him and Leona. She was smiling, but not her typical smile that reached her eyes.

"Rain check? I've got plans already," I explained, checking my phone. Anthony would be here in ten minutes to pick me up.

Leona's smile brightened as she wrapped an arm around Dexter's waist. "Sure, we'll see you later, probably Monday when you move in." She looked up at him. "Let's go, Danny's waiting on us. Good job tonight Rea."

* * *

Anthony sat on the couch with a small smile, as I relayed the fight. He interrupted my story by wrapping his arms around my waist and pulling me to sit with him.

"I like how excited you are." He kissed my neck and whispered in my ear, "Let me help you celebrate."

"I haven't finished the story though. She got back up after that and—" I pushed him away as he kept nibbling at my ear. "Are you even listening?" I was so proud of what I accomplished. I had to talk about it or burst. But he didn't seem to care.

"Sorry, sorry." He sat back, amusement in his eyes and gestured for me to continue.

The doorbell interrupted me and he jumped, a frown marking his pretty face.

He cracked the door, standing in front of the small opening, blocking the visitors from my view.

"You left your hat tonight," a girl's voice said. "Plus, you left so early and haven't really been around lately. We wanted to check on you."

I hadn't even asked him what his plans had been tonight. But now I was curious and couldn't help but listen.

"Thanks for dropping it off. I'll call you guys later." Anthony reached for his hat, and the girl pushed open the door he was leaning on.

"You can't get rid of me that easily, Anthony. What has been—"

A pretty brunette stepped through the door and I recognized her from the pictures on Anthony's wall. Her eyes lit up with surprise as she spotted me.

"Hello, I'm Anthony's sister, Janet." She began unwinding her scarf from her neck and unbuttoning her jacket. "And this is my husband, Jason." She gestured to a slightly balding man that walked through the door.

She looked back to Anthony with amusement. "So you haven't been in hiding this entire time, or at least not alone. Who is this?"

Anthony wasn't smiling. "Sure come on in Janet. Take off your coat, stay a while."

Jason laughed. "Sorry man, you know how your sister is, might as well give in."

Anthony rolled his eyes and sighed. "This is Regan." His eyes met mine briefly. "She's just a friend."

Janet raised an eyebrow. "Well good, because I'm no lawyer, but I think it would be called adultery if she was anything else."

17: Trust Me

ANTHONY OPENED THE FRONT DOOR WIDE, HIS face transformed in anger. "Get the hell out of here with that crap. And you wonder why I haven't been coming around?"

"You shouldn't give up so easily. This is a marriage were talking about." Janet turned towards me. "I'm sorry. You might be nice, but you shouldn't be here."

I was stunned by the new revelations and stared wide eyed as Anthony grabbed her shoulder, turning her away from me.

"You have some nerve accusing me. She's the reason the marriage is over." He let go of her arm and stood by the open door, his face flamed red. "Take her home, Jason."

Jason put his arm around his wife, trying to usher her out. "That's enough, Janet."

She stopped in the doorway and turned to her brother. "She's not with him anymore. She knows it was a mistake. Forgive her and—"

"He ended it, not her." Anthony shook with anger. "She made her choice eight months ago. She may be your friend, but you're my sister. Act like it."

She shrunk, melting into him. She wrapped her arms around his stiff waist. "Of course I'm your sister first. I love you. But you're making a mistake. She made one too, but you made promises to each other."

He pulled her arms off of him. "Leave now."

Jason pulled his wife out the door, and Anthony shut it behind them. He rested his head against the door for a moment, back heaving with his breaths. Then he turned to me, emotion wrinkling his face.

He crossed the room to the couch, grabbing my hands as he sat on the coffee table in front of me.

"I am sorry. I was married, but she cheated on me and left me, and we've been separated—"

I pulled my hands away from his, lifting them up as I sat back, shaking my head. "You don't need to tell me this."

He flinched back, affronted. "That's right. Cause you don't talk, and I'm not supposed to talk about anything real. I could never talk about this with you. Screw you."

I popped up, hands balled in anger, and spoke through clenched teeth, "I'm leaving."

Anthony glared at me, silent, as I left to the bedroom to get my things.

Sliding out my phone, I sat on the bed and tried to think of where I could go. Dexter was my first thought; maybe I could still go out with them tonight.

The bedroom door squeaked on its hinges, and Anthony walked through, his head lowered. "I'm sorry. Don't go, you don't have to. You can stay in the guest room if you prefer, but you don't have to go. I should have told you. I'm sorry, can you forgive me?"

He sat on the bed by me, eyes full of remorse and sadness.

"I'm not mad about what your sister said. I'm mad about what you said to me, you were being an asshole." I gathered enough from their argument to know he wasn't in a relationship with his wife, and I'd been here enough to know she wasn't a presence in his life. We weren't hurting anyone else by being together. But what he said after bothered me. I knew he wouldn't be content with what we had, and now he'd just admitted it.

He cocked his head, disbelief evident. "That's all—I thought—" He looked to the ceiling a smile growing. He smoothed his features before looking directly at me. "I'm sorry for taking my anger out on you. I was mad at my sister, not you. I care about you, and I thought she just destroyed whatever we have going."

A chilly fear began creeping in my muscles. Did he just say he cared about me? Looking at his sincere face made me feel awful about myself. He was a good person and had done so much for me. All I ever did was take.

"I'm sorry." I meant it. I was deeply sorry for all of it. "I never meant to make you feel like you couldn't talk. I may not say much, but you can say whatever you want. I'll listen." It's the least I could offer him.

His eyes scanned over me, excitement building in them. "Maybe I don't want to talk just yet either." He licked his lips and moved over me, causing us to fall back on the bed. He covered my giggles with his lips as his hands began unbuttoning his pants.

He lay on his side, facing me, telling me about his soon to be ex-wife. And I lay on my back, listening.

"We started dating in high school and my family was thrilled. They loved her and her family. I think they loved her name the most. Her dad is a prominent surgeon at Johns Hopkins; her mother heads a lot of charity events. I was lucky to land her; everyone kept reminding me of that." His eyebrow raised and voice was bitter at the last line. He sighed. "So six years later, I had ticked off everything on my families to do list. Got a good job and married Sophie. And maybe we were happy, or maybe we just made everyone around us happy by doing what was expected." He shook his head, eyes squinting as he thought about it. "But eight months ago I came home to her sucking off our accountant on our couch." He rolled onto his back and pushed his hair out of his eyes. "And she told me she was in love with him, had been for several months." He shrugged. "It was all pretend. I had fooled myself into thinking this was the life I was supposed to have. I'm done with that now. You came at the perfect time."

He rolled back to his side and picked up a lock of my hair, a confident smile brightened his face. "I don't have to plan with you. We just do. And it's fun. To hell with what everyone else wants."

I could agree with that last line, but the tingle of joy I felt scared me more than anything else.

* * *

"One, two, three, four," I mumbled to myself as I hit the speed bag with rhythmic punches. Music blared from my headphones.

A tap on my shoulder pulled me out of the zone. And I turned, frustrated at the interruption, only to be suffocated by the atmosphere surrounding Gage.

I stepped back, my rapid fire nerves making me jumpy.

Amusement shown in his clear blue eyes as he tapped his own ear, signaling me to pull out my headphones.

When I did, he crossed his arms and tilted his head to me. "I'll give you this one time. Go ahead and say it."

My mind swirled. What was I supposed to say? I looked around the crowded gym. Surely he couldn't mean anything about the other day. "What?"

He smirked. "I told you so. Go ahead and say it, I know you want to. I was wrong, and you were right." He lifted his hand, waving it at himself. "Go on, let's get it over with."

I shook my head, flustered by this teasing side of him, not sure how to respond. "I don't need to say it. You already know."

He chuckled low, a real smile spreading his full lips. "You're right." The way his eyes dropped over me set me on fire. "So what's next?"

Heat filled me, and I had to look away, get away. I couldn't process his question, unsure if he meant my fighting or us.

Thankfully, Silas caught my attention. He waved me over to his office.

Gage stopped me from walking away. Grabbing my elbow, he stepped into me and spoke low, "We'll talk later."

I pulled away and nodded, knowing I couldn't avoid the conversation forever. I didn't want to make any more enemies and had to let him know I would keep his secret.

Silas waited for me in the doorway, stepping back as I entered, eyes narrowed at Gage. His frown deepened as he closed the door and addressed me.

"So now tell me Regan, what did you mean this morning when you said you wanted a new gym? Are you not happy here? I'm sorry if you don't feel like your needs are being met, you are important to us. I had to finish a previous meeting or I would have talked about this right when you said it. But know that I have been concerned since you said it. So please explain."

I had tried to come up with a believable excuse, but I knew it was weak. "I'm moving and thought I might be able to find a closer gym."

He sat back and pressed his fingers together under his chin, considering me. "Just a new gym, not a new manager?"

I shrugged, not sure what was best. I respected Silas and appreciated his trust in my decision-making, but I didn't necessarily trust him. He had something going on with Gage; I could feel it when they were together, some sort of undercurrent of tension. It was possible that Silas could be just as shady as him.

"I need to know what you want. Your performance last night caused a stir. I've had another offer for a fight. Next month, two thousand dollars. If you win this one, big things will start happening, and I think you have a great career in front of you. I want to be there for that. So tell me, what do you want?"

His words thrilled me. I pushed down my reservations, blinded by the lure of success. So what if he had a shady side, as long as he kept me out of it.

"I want what you just said. I want to fight. I want big things, and I want you to get me there."

His smile was dazzling, showing off his white teeth. "We can get there together. Let's get started."

* * *

Silas's praise and encouragement reinforced my dedication. This is what I needed, what I could build a life with. Boxing. That's all I should be focused on.

The only obstacle I could see was standing by the exit of the gym, blocking my way out. The lightness I felt leaving Silas's office was weighed down at the sight of Gage. An anchor tethering me to a world I didn't want to be part of. Time to cut him loose.

He was leaning against the front wall, watching me walk towards him. His smirk evaporated as I got close, maybe he could see the determination in me. Whatever he saw, I don't think he liked it.

He pushed off the wall, standing up straight as I stopped in front of him.

"You leaving?" he asked.

"I've got some time before I have to be at work. We can have that talk now?"

His eyes flicked behind me and back down. He shifted on his feet and grabbed my elbow, pulling me closer to him. "I want to. Trust me, I want to, but..." he tugged on my elbow again, moving me slightly to the side so we were both parallel to the wall. His head ducked down to meet my eyes. "I can't right now. How about later? After work?" He scanned my face, pleading with me.

I stepped back, trying to escape my own reactions to his touch, to being near him. The rush to my head made it hard to think.

I licked my dry lips and swallowed hard, trying to take back control of my traitorous body. "I can't tonight." I had plans with Anthony. We only had two more nights together, I couldn't abandon him now, especially not for Gage.

The intensity in his gaze scared me. I felt like his prey, but I wasn't going to let him devour me.

His eyebrow glided up. "Tomorrow?"

I nodded, feeling a little more confident as I took another step away. "In the morning, here. Before my work out. Seven." Anthony had to work tomorrow, too, so he could drop me off early.

He nodded as his closed lip smile grew, and I got the sinking feeling I might be walking into his trap.

* * *

"What are you doing?" Anthony pulled his hand back, avoiding the phone I extended to him.

"I'm returning this to you. I got my own phone today. I can pay you back for the minutes, too." I shook the phone, encouraging him to take it from me.

He hesitated before grabbing it, his forehead creased in wrinkles under the soft sweep of his hair. "Do I get your new phone number?"

We were in the police cruiser, both having just got off work.

I patted the firm material of his uniform, smoothing the black collar. "Do you want it? This might be a good time to jump ship."

He shook his head, with a slight, sad, smile. "Is that what you want? What's going to happen on Monday when you don't need me anymore?"

I shrugged, leaning back in the seat, looking out the window at my own dark reflection. "I'm not thinking that far ahead. Whatever we want to happen can happen."

His hand slipped into my hair, turning my head to look towards him. "I know what I want—"

"I know what you want, too." I interrupted, leaning across the console to meet his lips, my hands moving to his belt buckle.

* * *

My nerves were exploding. Little bombs going off one after another, increasing rate and intensity the closer we drove to the gym.

Anthony pulled the car to the curb and I scanned the area for Gage. A slight relief relaxed my muscles when I didn't see him.

"Give me a call when you get off work. I'll be there."

I pulled my attention back to Anthony, throwing him a smile and nod as I opened the door to leave.

"Hold up." He leaned over the passenger seat.

Standing outside the car, I leaned back in and gave him the kiss I knew he was requesting. I pulled back before he could grab me and extend it, and then I shut the door on any further delays.

I took a deep breath, letting the crisp morning air fill my lungs. Preparing myself, I wasn't sure if I was more scared of Gage himself, or my reactions to him. The worst thing was he knew he had an affect on me. I was going to end that today.

The gym was nearly empty; a few people spotted the open room, getting their early morning workout in. Gage was at the body bag, pounding low on it, back to me. He was shirtless and glistening with sweat. The muscles on his arms and shoulder flexed with each blow. He was amazing to look at.

Stilling the bag, he turned slightly, spotting me. He reached to the ground and picked up his towel, wiping the sweat from his body.

I was frozen, staring at the tattoos extending down the side of his ribs and stomach, dark thick lettering with a flame at the top. His gray shirt dropped into place, covering the words before I could read them.

He smiled, like he knew he had me. He nodded his head towards Silas's office and walked in that direction before I even moved.

Giving myself a mental chastising, I followed him. I needed to do better if I was to pull this off.

"Silas won't be in for a while. We can talk in here." He stood at the door, inviting me into the room.

I hesitated. "Are you sure Silas is alright with people in his office?"

He cocked his head, and his eyes assessed me. "It's half mine. I just don't use it much." At my confused look he continued, "The entire gym is half mine." He nodded his head inside the room. "Come on."

I pressed my nails into the soft skin of my hand, trying to focus on something other than my racing heart, beginning to regret my decision to show up today. But I couldn't back down now. Against instinct I stepped into the small room with him, and my heart skipped when he closed the door.

Reminding myself that this was a public place didn't help to quell my rising panic. This closed room didn't feel public.

He narrowed his eyes and crossed his arms. "You don't need to be scared of me."

I stood up straight at his words, trying to burry my fear. "You keep saying that."

"Because it's true." He stepped towards me, and I was thankful for the chair between us.

"Who should be scared?" I thought about the look of fear that crossed Damien's face.

He shook his head, eyes not leaving mine. "My opponents. Anyone threatening the people I care about." He took a step to the side of the chair, and I gripped the back of it, to keep from moving. "Anyone threatening you."

I swallowed down the lump in my throat and stomped the butterflies in my stomach.

His next step forced me to turn my back to the chair so I could face him. His body was almost flush with mine, but not touching, although I felt him as if we were.

"But not you." His hand rose towards me.

The shock of his fingers on my cheek made me jump back, nearly stumbling over the chair behind me. I pushed it out of the way, allowing myself room to move.

"Quit that shit," I reacted with anger.

He paused, shock freezing him, his arm still dangling in the air. Then his eyebrows knitted together, and he curled his open hand into a fist. "What?"

"Breathing on me." I wasn't thinking. I just knew I had to make it clear that he didn't affect me. That he didn't have the upper hand. Even if it was a lie.

He straightened up to his full height, confusion lining his eyes. "Breathing on you?"

I stepped further away, putting the chair between us again. "Yeah, you get too close, too often. And you breathe on me. It's fucking annoying. Stop it or I'm leaving."

He let out a stunned puff of breath and a ghost of a smile played on his face. "Well, damn. That's—" he shook his head and sat in the other chair behind him, the lines of his jaw working. "You're cold." His eyes locked with mine. "Ice."

I pressed my lips together to hide my own smile. His reaction encouraged me. He wasn't getting scary angry, and the fact that he sat down made me sure I had shocked him. Maybe now he'd listen.

I scoffed, continuing the show. "Because I don't fall all over you? Well get over it." I sat in the chair in front of me, trying to pull off relaxed, even though I felt anything but.

He narrowed his eyes. "Fine. I'm over it. That's not the point of this talk anyways. The other day," he leaned forward in the chair, forearms resting on his knees, "What went down at that apartment, I've got to explain."

I shook my head. "You don't have to. I won't say anything to anybody. I'm sorry I brought you there."

He leaned back like I slapped him. "You're damn lucky you brought me. What are you doing with people like that?"

My spine stiffened at his accusatory tone. "You seem to have known them too, and people much worse."

He ran his hand over his face, frustration clear in the way he moved. "I can handle myself around people like them."

My heart squeezed at that. What he implied was loud and clear, I couldn't handle them. And he was right, somewhat. "They're not all bad," I said with a soft edge.

He watched me for a moment before responding. "I know, people usually aren't. She was your friend, but you've got to see she's no good for you."

I was done talking about me and what I should be doing. "And what about you?" I snapped. "What about your friends? Are they good for you?"

He leaned back, running a hand over his hair, making it stand up in a mess of spikes. "I'm not involved with them anymore. I was before Silas and I partnered up, but not now."

Fear spread like wildfire in my stomach. "So your threat to Damien was empty?" I didn't want to be around when he found out, and thinking of Nan still with him scared me. What if he took it out on her?

He scooted closer and almost reached for me, but thought better of it. "No. They would still have my back if I called them. It's complicated, but it's my family."

"So Dexter too?" I held my breath for the answer. If he was involved than my judgment of people was crap.

Gage sat up, indignant. "I would never let my brother get involved. He's not part of it. I did it for him, so we could get away."

Relief drained some of the tension in my shoulders, but confusion throbbed in my head.

"It was my dad. His family, his life. He was in prison for most of my life, but when he got out, he helped out."

I didn't want to know the details. I didn't want to hear names. But I had to ask, "You're not involved anymore?"

He swallowed. "My dad died. I still talk to my uncle sometimes, but they understand that's not the life I want. They're not bad people."

I nodded and stood up. Still unsure, but feeling slightly better. "Alright. Thank you."

"Wait." He stood up. "Silas said you were moving gyms. Don't do that because of me." The corner of his mouth tugged up, just barely. "I promise not to breathe on you."

I eyed him skeptically, my own smile mirroring his. "You better not. Now that I know you and Silas are partners, I know you have to behave. Silas said I could do big things and that would benefit both of you. You can't afford to push me away."

He crossed his arms, full of smug confidence. "I can afford," he stretched out the word afford, "to do whatever I want. But I won't, because you don't want me too."

* * *

Aliya held tight to the bottle while Zoe tugged at the wine opener until the cork slid out.

"Now I remember why we always get the boxed kind." Zoe untwisted the cork from the screw.

Aliya giggled, already loose from wine with dinner. "But this is a special occasion. We have a new roommate." Her smile turned to a pout as she faced me. "But you're not even drinking. We're supposed to be celebrating together."

I held up my water glass. "I'm celebrating. Tonight's been fun and dinner was great."

Leona stood up. "Thank you. You can thank my mom though; I had her cook the empanadas."

"So Rea, will we be seeing that police friend of yours around?" Aliya questioned as she refilled her wine glass.

I sat on the couch with Leona. Zoe sat with her legs curled under her, on the opposite couch. She held up her glass and Aliya topped it off and sat down next to her. All three of them watched me, waiting for my answer.

I had forgotten that they saw us kiss that day in the snow. I shook my head. "No, don't worry, he probably won't be around."

Leona's eyebrow went up. "Really? That's a shame because he was really cute."

"Especially in that uniform," Aliya added.

Zoe set her glass down. "A police officer? You were dating one? Is that why you didn't go with Gage the other night at the bar?"

The questions stumped me. It took a minute to regain composure, and I wanted to laugh. These girls were excited about me possibly dating an enforcer of the law. Nan would have kicked me out on the spot. Maybe things really could change.

Aliya spoke up first. "Ooh that's right, why wouldn't you go with Gage? He is, like, the hottest guy and super sexy."

"He also had two other girls with him that night," I responded and then regretted it; that made it sound like I would have went with him. "Plus, he's too bossy."

Aliya smirked. "He could boss me around any day. You wouldn't mind would you? If I hooked up with him?"

Leona rolled her eyes. "It's never going to happen. He barely talks to you."

Aliya crossed her arms with a huff. "There's always a chance, especially with our Atlantic City trip next week." She stared off in exaggerated dreaminess. "How I would love to be one of the girls he chooses after he wins. God, I can't even imagine how hot that would be. I'm getting wet just thinking about it."

"Eww." Zoe knocked her over with a pillow.

Aliya giggled and sat back up, eyebrows raised to me. "You wouldn't mind then, right?"

"No. Do whatever you want." I tried to excuse the way my stomach turned sour thinking of her with him. It was probably the way she was excited to be chosen out of many that got to me. She could do better than that.

"Is there anyone you're interested in?" Zoe asked me, sweeping her eyes to Leona.

I shrugged. "The police officer, Anthony is his name. He's a friend, but maybe." I don't know why I said that. Except I wanted to talk to these girls, and they had been excited by him. And I wanted to deny any attraction to Gage. There was also the look between Zoe and Leona; I needed to make it clear there was nothing with Dexter either.

"You should tell her what you told me, Leona. Get rid of any tension tonight so we can all get along," Zoe advised.

I sat back, waiting. I thought I knew where this was going.

Leona stood up with a nod. "Come with me for a minute, so we can talk."

I followed her to her bedroom down the hall. She sat on her bed and I sat on the rolling chair at her desk.

"You get along really well with Dexter. I've been trying to brush it off as nothing; I'm not usually the jealous type. I mean, Dexter gets along with everyone. I've talked to him about it and he explained your connection, about the attack, that I shouldn't worry, you two are just friends. But I wanted to make sure you weren't mistaking it for more."

I frowned as her words sunk in. "He's nice, but only a friend. What did he tell you about our connection?"

She waved her hand. "Just that because he was there that night when you were attacked he feels a bit like your protector. He wants to make sure you're okay."

I hated that I hadn't picked up on that. He was another person who wanted to keep me safe. I didn't want that. I wanted someone that was my friend, simply to be my friend.

Running my hand through my hair, I responded, "You don't have to worry about me and him. It's like he said. Also, I would never do that to you, to anyone."

She stood up with a smile. "I'm glad we had this talk then. Can I ask a favor though?" at my nod she continued, "Can you try not to be alone with him. That way there can never be any doubt."

I nodded. "Sure, I'll try."

* * *

I pulled the phone away from my ear; Anthony's voice was loud.

"...The date has been set for next month, March 25th. I'll be there to testify. You should be getting information soon. I know Detective Andres wanted to get a hold of you. Have you given her this number?"

"Not yet. I'll give her a call tomorrow." I sat in my empty bedroom with only a bed for furniture.

I gripped the soft blankets, unsure how to feel. The date for court had finally been set, but it didn't cause excitement or relief. It was a dark hole, with fear hiding in the shadows. That's what those boys had done, released the fear that I had always locked away. And now it plagued me during the night.

"So, I know I'll at least see you next month then," Anthony spoke soft. I had to press the phone back to my ear.

I was too lost in my thoughts to respond.

"Unless you want to see me sooner?" he said after a moment of silence.

"Maybe. That wouldn't be bad." I didn't know what I wanted anymore. But I knew I felt comfortable with him. He took me just the way I was, and I liked that.

I could hear the smile in his voice. "I'm off on Thursday."

After hanging up with Anthony I tried to call Nan again. I had tried twice already. It went to voicemail and dread swirled in me. It was normal for her not to answer, but I wanted to hear from her. I wanted to make sure she was alright. The last time I saw her she seemed so weak, and I was no longer sure she could stand up for herself, especially with Damien. And I couldn't really blame her for not leaving with Gage and me; we had both been shocked and scared that day.

* * *

I had my head back, drinking deeply from my water bottle after my workout. My muscles were drained, and I wanted to fall over flat. But Gage walking towards me made me stay standing, stiffening my spine.

I busied myself by picking up my towel and wiping my face. I didn't want to watch him as he made his way over, but I couldn't pull my eyes off him. He was in a tank top and his arms were distracting, especially the half sleeve of dark tattoo's on one.

"Silas told me about the offer. How are you feeling about that?"

I nodded, avoiding eye contact. Silas told me this morning that a local sports store wanted to photograph me in their clothes. It would help advertise for the gym as well, plus I needed professional pictures to advertise fights. The photo shoot was in two weeks.

I took another sip of water before answering. "Another part of boxing I hadn't expected. But I guess it's a good thing."

"You'd be surprised how many photo shoots you're going to be a part of. I've done a few myself."

My lips pressed together to hide my smile. I might have to Google that later.

"Silas also told me he wants to keep you at this lower weight class. You'll have a better chance at earning a title."

I nodded. Silas had already told me this. "I've got to get ready for work now."

"I can help. I can show you some simple recipes, take you shopping..." He shrugged and the corner of his lip tugged up. "After all, you are a good investment for the gym."

I eyed him, skeptical of his intentions.

His eyes shifted to the door, narrowing. "Hold on," he murmured as he walked past me.

A young teen boy had just walked in. He was dressed in street clothes, a puffy coat and skinny jeans positioned low to show off his boxers. He wore a Ravens hat over his braids and his face was twisted with anger.

Gage grabbed his arm and the boy shook his head, saying something as they both walked back to Silas's office.

I sat on the bench behind me, needing to rest. I couldn't stop my creeping suspicion, but I tried to push it away. Whatever was going on, I would stay out of it. Everything would be fine as long as I stayed out of whatever Silas and Gage were doing.

The more I thought about what Gage told me the other day, the more questions I had. The biggest one was about the guns. Silas had one the night I was jumped, and Gage had brought one to Nan's.

Gage came back out of the office with the boy. The teen turned around to face him and said something while simultaneously pulling up his pants. Gage pushed the back of his head in a teasing way and looked in my direction. He held up his finger, signaling the boy to wait and came over to me.

"I have to go. But we'll talk later."

Doubt must have shown on my face because Gage sat next to me and nodded in the direction of the kid. "I have to take him back to school. He got mad and walked out."

My eyebrows popped up in surprise. "Oh," I said lamely.

Gage smiled. "I help at a sports camp for boys during the summer. That's how I met Javon. He's a good kid, but sometimes he needs a little guidance." He shrugged, and his blue eyes lit up. "I'll see you later then?"

I leaned back, stunned. This man was full of surprises. "Alright."

18: Not Breathing

GAGE MOVED AROUND THE KITCHEN, OPENING AND closing each cabinet.

I sat back at the table as he made his inventory of the place. I hadn't checked out most of the pantry myself yet.

"Dude, you can't just go through people's cabinets like that. It's rude," Dexter complained, running his hands over his buzzed cut hair.

Gage turned to look at his brother. "I've got to see what they've got, to know what they need." His tone was condescending, which I hated, but he was right, which I also hated.

"I don't have anything. You're looking through everyone else's stuff."

He leaned back on the counter, arms crossed, and nodded. "Fine. Then let's go shopping."

Dexter groaned. "It's already ten, why do you have to go now?"

Gage nodded his head towards me. "She works crazy hours. We were supposed to do this yesterday, but didn't. What are you going to eat tomorrow? What did you eat for dinner tonight?" He eyed me, waiting on my answer.

I shrugged. "Let's go to the store then." I had been eating leftovers from work, not the best of choices I knew.

After shopping and unloading groceries, Gage left with a promise to show me how to meal plan tomorrow. Dexter was staying the night with Leona, so he was charged with making sure I ate breakfast, not that I needed him to enforce it. I wanted to make sure I was in good shape before my photo shoot and future fights, and I was more than willing to take Gage's advice on this topic. His body was proof that the man knew what he was talking about.

* * *

"It does taste better with the lime," Gage agreed as he took a bite of his lunch.

I sat back in the chair with a small victory smile. I had suggested adding lime to the avocado salad.

We had been cooking and packaging up meals I could grab on the go, and surprisingly Gage had been very professional the entire time. He never got too close, and he never ordered me around too harshly. He had been a good teacher.

"Thank you for your help. I feel prepared now. It's good." Who would have thought cooking could make me feel so accomplished. But as I took a bite of the salad, I felt a burst of pride. I had cooked before, but not like this.

Leona came into the kitchen, scarf and jacket on. "Mm, it smells good in here. Can I grab some food? I have to get to class, but I'm starving."

"Sure," I said as she filled a Tupperware container.

"Dex should be back from class soon if you're waiting for him," Leona directed to Gage on her way out the door.

The room was silent after the door slammed shut, and I was all too aware that we were alone in the house. I had been fine around him while we were cooking, but now the familiar swirl of tension in my muscles returned. A feeling that only Gage caused.

I stood up with my plate and went to the sink.

"That's all you're eating?" he asked, remaining seated.

"I'd been snacking while we cooked," I mumbled, as I busied myself with cleaning up the leftovers.

"Are all your roommates at class?" His voice was low.

I thought I could feel his eyes on me, but I didn't turn to find out. I started loading the dishwasher. "Yes. But Dexter, Zoe, and Aliya should be getting back soon."

"Why aren't you in school?"

I straightened up and shook my head, my back still to him. "I work instead." I tried to deflect the shame I felt; I hadn't even finished high school. "Why aren't you?"

"Life didn't work that way for me."

I turned at his words, meeting his eyes, and nodded in complete understanding. "Yeah, me neither."

After a moment, I forced myself to ask the question I couldn't stop thinking about. "You work at a summer camp for youth?"

He cocked his head, that cocky glint in his eye that he always gets when he corrects me. "I volunteer my time there. I don't need extra money, and they help a lot of kids, kids that would otherwise get into trouble. I mentor a few during the school year, like Jovan."

A wall within me cracked. I physically felt it and it hurt. He didn't have to say it, but I knew he helped kids like the ones we used to be. Maybe like I still was.

The rumble of an engine pulled up in the driveway. The others had returned.

Gage broke eye contact first and cleared his throat as he brought his plate over to the sink.

Dexter came barreling in the door as Aliya chased him.

* * *

Anthony stood from the bar as I walked towards him. "You ready to go now?"

"As long as you don't mind that I smell like grease." I looked down at my shirt that had a few stains on it from various spills tonight.

The restaurant had been slammed, but I couldn't complain since my pocket was full.

"I could take you to your place to change." He held the door open for me as we walked out into the chilly night.

I eyed him with suspicion.

"What? I could find out where you live easily enough, remember my job? And you're going to want me to drop you off there tonight, right?"

I paused; he was right. I hadn't thought much about what our new arrangement would be, but I didn't need to sleep at his place anymore. A slight pang of sadness flashed; I had gotten use to his warm body next to mine.

"What did you have planned for tonight?" I asked

He smiled, opening his truck door for me. "I was hoping we could do something, like bowling, or pool, or go to the movies."

I had a moment to think as he rounded the truck to slide into the driver's seat. This new territory was making me feel nauseous, or maybe that was the smell of onion drifting off my shirt.

"I should change before we do anything," I relented.

"Stay here. I'll be right back," I ordered when we pulled up in front of the house. There were some lights on, but Zoe's car was gone.

Aliya was sitting on the couch and I waved to her as I passed by to my room. A few moments later, a couple of car doors slammed, followed by the front door, and several giggles.

I shoved my legs into jeans and slid a long sleeve t-shirt on.

"Rea?" Leona yelled.

"Out in a minute." I ran a brush through my hair and exited my room.

"Is your cop out in that truck?" Zoe asked.

My stomach clenched, but I nodded. "We're just leaving."

Aliya hopped off the couch and ran outside, more gazelle than girl.

I followed behind her. The idea of these two worlds meeting felt like a head on collision.

Aliya leaned into his window, and her voice travelled in the thin night air. "Come on in for a little bit. We'd love the company."

Anthony opened the car door as I cut in front of Aliya. "That's alright, maybe another time. We're going bowling, right?"

He stood up to his full height, inches away from me and stared me down with narrowed eyes, before relaxing and sweeping them to Aliya.

"We're going bowling. You can come if you want."

Aliya's grin stretched from ear to ear. "Can Zoe and Leona come, too?" At his nod she said, "I'll be right back." She ran inside to get the others.

Anthony's chest vibrated with laughter as he looked down at me and his arm circled around my waist. "Don't be mad. I want to meet your roommates. This will be fun."

And it was fun, for the most part. I sucked at bowling, but everyone got along really well and Anthony charmed the girls. They kept giving me thumbs up or mouthing "OMG" when he wasn't looking.

When we pulled back up to the house, the girls said a quick goodbye and left me alone with him.

"You're not mad, are you?" he asked reaching for my hand.

"No. I had fun tonight." This felt like a date thing to say, making my stomach sink.

Anthony leaned across the console to me, almost kissing me. "I did, too," he breathed. Then our lips met, and his hands pulled me closer to him.

He deepened the kiss, leaning into me, pushing me back against the seat. His hands traveled over my shirt and curves. He broke away from my mouth and whispered to me, "Can I..." as his fingers ran along the edge of my jeans.

I pushed away, shaking my head, trying to clear the fog. Tonight had felt different at first, and I wasn't sure if I wanted different. But now that we were going back to our same routine I felt dirty, and didn't want to bring that to this house. I had hoped to be different here, and this was the first step.

"Not tonight." I kept my hand up between us. I shook my head, trying to think of words to explain.

With a small smile, he caressed my cheek. "It's alright. Tonight was good. Wait here."

He hopped out and ran around to my door, opening it for me. "Let me walk you to the door," he said with his good boy smile.

I still wasn't sure what I was doing or how this was going to work, but I pushed those worries aside and enjoyed the moment, because it was a good one. I felt normal as he walked me to the door and kissed me good night with a promise to call me soon.

* * *

I had my headphones on while I folded clothes, putting some away and packing some for our trip to Atlantic City tomorrow. We were leaving on Thursday, Gage's fight was Friday, and we would come home on Sunday.

My fingers trailed over my new clothes that the girls helped me pick out. Things really were different here, but I was still holding my breath.

This past week had been one of the best of my life. No drama, all focus. Gage stopped by frequently to help with cooking, and I had gone on a couple more dates with Anthony. And work had been really busy, which meant good tips.

I stood up and tried on a new top, looking at myself in the mirror. Training this past month had tightened my muscles, but this new diet was already changing my body, making the muscles seen. Lines of abs were beginning to show, and my triceps had a nice lean cut to them.

My phone vibrated on the bed, and I jumped to pick it up. Nan's name flashed on the screen, and my heart was in my throat as I answered.

"You have to stop calling me," she hissed into the phone.

"I wanted to make sure you were alright. Last time I saw you—"

"You made a bad situation worse, like usual," Nan interrupted. "That's what you do. And now you keep calling, and that's not helping anything. If he saw that I was talking to you…"

"Nan, I can help you. You don't have to be scared of him." I wasn't focused on her words, but the fear I heard under them. It terrified me.

"You don't know anything Regan. That man you brought here can't do anything. He can't save you or me. You're the one that needs help, not me. Worry about yourself." Her words were little razor cuts in my gut.

"What do you mean?" I asked cautiously.

"I don't want you calling me or helping me. You destroy everything! You make everything worse. So stay the hell away from me. Lose my number."

Silence. She hung up.

* * *

I kept my headphones on, music blaring for only me to hear, drowning out my own twisted thoughts. I wanted to push away Nan's phone call, lock it into the back of my mind. I didn't know what else to do and I didn't know what it all meant.

Searching the kitchen for food, I pulled out a bag of M&M's, and poured a handful into my mouth. Anthony was on his way to take me to dinner, but I craved the sugary sweetness like a drug. I needed something to make me feel better, and chocolate seemed like the safest bet, but it wasn't enough.

I reached into the top cabinet for my peanut butter, the all-natural one Gage made me buy. It took all the fun out of the creamy treat, but adding M&M's to it might solve that problem. I sat on the counter as I stirred the colorful candies into the top layer of the peanut butter and took a big bite. I hadn't cheated on my diet once since I started, but this was an emotional emergency. Creamy, chocolaty, sweetness melted into my mouth and I let all other thoughts go.

Except when I looked up, Gage was standing in the kitchen, watching me. I pulled my head phones off and swallowed my dessert. "What are you doing here?" I asked, scooting on the counter to sit in front of the bag of M&M's.

He cocked his head at me, eyes suspiciously narrowed. "I was helping…" He crossed the kitchen, walking in slow motion, stopping just in front of where I was perched on the kitchen counter. "What are you doing?" One eyebrow glided up.

I screwed the lid back on the peanut butter, my candies still stuck inside. "Having a snack." He smelled sweet, like fruit, but his natural fresh scent was just under it, making me dizzy.

He reached one hand behind me, almost touching me. The heat and static that swirled between us was intoxicating, putting me in a trance. All I could do was watch him as he lifted the bag of chocolates and set it back down on the counter, the corner of his mouth gliding up into a smile.

He braced one hand on the counter top next to me. The other inched to my face, his thumb dragging over the corner of my mouth

The feel of his hard, but smooth skin against my lip sent a surge of heat through me, but when he pressed the thumb to his mouth and licked off the peanut butter, I melted.

He put that hand on the other side of the counter top and nudged closer to me, my legs spreading to let him stand in-between without resistance or thought.

"What are you doing?" I whispered, not really wanting to break the spell between us but my heart was in danger of flying out of my mouth.

He inched closer as one hand moved to grip my waist. "Not breathing," he said low, his head moving ever so slightly towards mine.

I wasn't breathing either, and it took me a moment to get the joke, but I couldn't laugh. The adrenaline rushing to my head made any thought difficult. I moved my hands to his shirt, wanting to pull him closer, feel his heat against me.

The slam of a car door snapped me out of it. I jumped and scrambled off the counter.

Gage stopped me with a hand on my hip. "Wait—"

I pulled away from him, feeling weak beneath his touch. "I have to go. Anthony's here."

I wanted to run outside and keep them apart and that thought made my head pound. What was I doing? I had been trying to deny whatever Gage and I had, but I couldn't. I couldn't resist anymore, and

I had almost given in moments before Anthony was supposed to pick me up.

Gage frowned, looking out the window as Anthony walked up the driveway. "The cop?" he sneered. "You're still with him?"

Anthony was almost at the door, but I didn't want to leave Gage like this.

I shook my head, meeting his eyes, pleading with him. "It's complicated. I…"

Anthony knocked, and I shrugged helplessly to Gage. "I've got to go."

Picking up my jacket, I opened the door.

Gage stepped behind me. "Any news on the case?" he questioned with a hard voice, and my stomach clenched.

Anthony's smile melted as he glanced between Gage and me. He nodded. "Regan can tell you any information she wants you to know. It's not my place to share."

Gage crossed his arms. "Four were arrested? Two of them I caught. So what have you done?" The challenge in his voice made me nervous.

"We'll talk about this later. We've got to go." I turned to close the door, but Gage grabbed my arm, pulling me back to him.

"Don't go. Stay and talk to me now."

"Get off of her." Anthony stepped through the doorway.

Gage's eyes were locked on mine, but I couldn't stand the emotion in them, and I pulled his fingers away. "I have—"

Anthony slid in between us, pushing me behind him. "Stay away from her."

I pulled Anthony back, putting myself between them again and tried to lead him outside. "Let's go."

I spun around as Gage took another step forward. "Stop," I demanded. "Don't do this."

His jaw clenched and the line of his body was rigid in anger. Aliya stepped into the kitchen looking like she just walked off the pages of an Abercrombie catalogue. She approached Gage, her eyes scanning between the three of us.

She touched his arm with her fingertips and he flicked his eyes to her but then met mine again as Anthony pulled me away.

The last thing I saw before the door closed was her slip her arms around his waist, and my heart nose-dived into my stomach. Now I knew why he had been here to start with.

"What the hell was that in there?" Anthony barked as he slammed his truck door shut.

I climbed up into the passenger side and shook my head. "I don't know."

"Are you fucking him? Is that why you haven't been sleeping with me?" He glared at me.

I stopped putting on my seatbelt and let it slide off of me. "No. I'm not sleeping with anyone."

Anthony grabbed my hands before I could open the door to leave. "Wait. I'm sorry. This is driving me crazy. Please, don't leave yet." His eyes begged me to stay.

I nodded. "We need to talk."

He ran his hand through his wavy hair, messing up the swoop back style he had it in. He turned to me with a deep breath. "We do. But not here. I know a place."

Minutes later, we pulled up to a wooded park with a lake you could barely see through the leafless trees. He parked in the empty lot and leaned back against his door, looking at me.

"I'm not going to like this am I?" he asked, voice flat, and lines crossing his pretty face.

My heart pulled. "I'm sorry. I really do appreciate everything you've done for me."

He scoffed. "And I've been paid in full for it, I guess."

I deserved that, but it still stung. Staring at my folded hands, I buried my retorts. I knew I was the one doing the hurting here, and he needed to get out whatever he wanted to say, it was the least I could do.

"Seriously, Regan? You're ending this when it only really just started? I thought things were changing this week, that we were moving this relationship forward. Is it because of Gage?"

When I didn't answer quick enough, he banged on the steering wheel. "Answer me!"

I took a calming breath and raised my eyes to the ceiling. "No," I spoke loud and clear. "It's not anyone but me. I warned you from the start to not expect anything. It's not my fault if you did." But I knew it was my fault. I had leaned on him too much, needed him too much.

"You're going to regret this." He shook his head, teeth grinding. "This is a mistake. You we're lucky to have me. I'm miles above you, and you don't even realize it. I'm the best you could ever have and you're throwing it away."

He was right; it had been my thoughts of him all along. "You can do better than me. And one day you will," I said with control. His words may have been true, but they were still starting to piss me off. "Can you take me home now?"

"Get the hell out." He waved his hand in dismissal.

I climbed out of the car and he drove away the minute the door shut.

At least we hadn't driven too far away and the sun was only just beginning to set because I had left my phone back at the house.

The walk was needed anyways. I had to make sense out of my jumbled thoughts, especially those surrounding Gage and Nan.

19: You Need It

THE DETAILS OF THEIR KISS WAS A ball of barbed wire in my stomach, and every time she talked, it banged around, inflicting little cuts. And I couldn't escape the details since we were stuck together in a car for two hours.

The boys left in the morning to AC. But since I had work and Leona had class we didn't leave till that night.

According to Aliya, Gage had come over to help move her new dresser, her way of getting him into her bedroom. When they finished, he went to the kitchen for a drink, that's when I saw him, and when I left, they kissed.

I had to hear about how soft his lips were, how he pushed her against a wall, dominating the kiss. How she thought he was going to take her there on the kitchen counter.

"What happened with Anthony?" Aliya looked in the visor mirror to see me in the backseat. "Gage was hot about that, I know. I could feel it, even his kiss was angry." She sunk back in the seat. "Whatever it was, thank you."

I stared out the window as we passed cars on the turnpike. "They got in each other's face." I shrugged, not wanting to share details.

Zoe flipped her magazine close and sat up next to me. "Aliya, you do realize that they were probably fighting over Rea, right?"

Aliya turned around and counted on her fingers. "One, Rea is with Anthony. And two, she said she didn't mind if I tried with Gage. So three, I don't care what his motivation is, I'll take the kiss and more if I'm lucky." She bounced back on her seat, smiling bright. "This weekend should be fun."

I hadn't told them about Anthony, yet. I didn't want to change the dynamics, especially with Leona.

Leona met my eyes in the rearview mirror and smirked. "Smile Rea, we're supposed to be having fun."

* * *

The soft hum of silence enveloped me like a warm blanket. I was alone in our suite. Our large group had three suites side by side, and everyone from mine was still downstairs at the bars.

I walked onto the balcony, drawn by the ocean view. I had never been to the beach before. Leaning on the iron railing, I watched as the moonlight shimmered over the swells and curls of the waves, the faint sound of rolling water barely audible under the cacophony of sounds of the city at night.

The air had a touch of cold in it, but wasn't bad for February. I grabbed a blanket and curled up in a chair to watch the water from the safety of a lit up hotel.

After a while, the slider from the suite to the right opened, music and laughter spilling out before Gage stepped through.

He slid the door closed and stood scanning the ocean. Then his head turned, and he saw me.

The corner of his mouth tugged up, and he walked to the rail that separated our balconies. "Everyone back already?"

I pulled my blanket tight around me and sunk into my chair. "No. I came back on my own."

He looked towards his room. "I'm about to tell my crew they have to shut the hell up and go to bed. I can't think with them around." He looked back to me. "But, maybe it can wait. Can I sit with you?"

I took a sip of my tea and nodded before I could talk myself out of it.

He took a step back, still facing me, and put his finger up. "Give me a minute. I'll be right over."

He went back into the room, voices escaping as the sliding door opened and closed. I hadn't seen Gage since we arrived. I knew his room was next to ours, but I also knew he had his own friends with him.

When he came over, he set up a fire in the marble fire table our chairs circled. He moved easily in his casual jeans, t-shirt and unzipped gray hoody, the hood slung on the back of his head. And like a moth to the flame, I couldn't take my eyes off him.

I stayed quiet, pretending to watch the fire flames as he sat on the lounge chair next to mine.

He braced his forearms on his knees, hands pressed together. Then he looked sideways at me. "Your cop mad about yesterday? About you being here?"

His casual attitude made my gut twist with anger.

"Don't pretend to care. He's none of your business." I shifted further back in my chair, distancing myself from him.

His knee bounced under his arm as he watched me for a moment. Then he stilled and looked back to the fire. "Fine. But where does that leave us?"

I couldn't stop my response. Appalled, I leaned forward to grab his attention, my eyes wide. "You kissed Aliya, where do you think that leaves us?"

He sat back with disdain. "You're with someone else. What the hell do you want me to do? Wait for you?"

The way he sneered with the last question sealed it, confirming what I knew. He wanted me, but that was all it was. Attraction. Nothing more. And I could deal with that.

I raised an eyebrow. "I'm not with him anymore." When he looked at me and stilled, amazement clear on his face, I continued, "We ended it after I left yesterday, for good."

His eyes travelled up and down me, not much to see though with the blanket still wrapped around me.

"I only kissed Aliya because I wanted to kiss you," he confessed in a sigh.

If he didn't look so damn hot, I would have been gone with that. I should've walked away, but I had already made my decision. I needed him out of my system.

For some reason I was holding back. My body wouldn't let me move. His eyes locked me where I was.

"You ended it or he ended it?"

I shrugged, annoyed. I didn't want to talk about Anthony. "What does it matter? It's over."

"He wasn't good enough for you."

"You don't know what you're talking about. He was a good guy, too good for me. He had his shit together and I only brought him down." I pressed my lips shut, regretting speaking my thoughts out loud, but I didn't want Gage talking bad about him.

He shook his head, watching me with disbelief. "He may have had a good job, but that doesn't make him a good man."

"Just shut up."

"I'm only trying to figure out where your heads at, how you're feeling." He picked up the lounger and moved it a couple of feet closer to me, our knees almost touching when he sat. He took my hands in his. "If it was my fault he broke up with you—"

I pulled away. "It isn't your fault. I just finally accepted the truth."

Even in the fires glow his eyes still sent shivers through me.

His icy blues were locked on me. "What's the truth?"

I hesitated, wanting to make my move, but still frozen under his gaze. Instead, I talked, maybe to cover my nerves or maybe to make him understand. What I had planned was not about feelings, but something else. Something I was only beginning to realize about myself, although it had been there all along.

"I always ruin good things. I choose the path to destruction. Every. Time." I looked away, past the fire to the ocean and still barely saw that. Now that I started, I wanted to get it all out, put a voice to the thoughts I never admitted before. And maybe this man with a broken past could understand a bit.

My laugh was bitter. "I had a therapist who told me that. That I purposefully push people away and set fires to anything good. My way of taking control and avoiding the risk of becoming attached." I swallowed hard. Unsure if I could continue. My muscles were already vibrating with nerves.

"What happened to the therapist? You still see him?"

"I quit after that. Thought what she said was bullshit and never went back." The irony hit me like a truck; I had proved her right by quitting.

Gage got it, I could tell by the look that crossed his face. "Why do you believe it now?"

My heart was jack hammering in my stomach. But I had already gone this far, and the words kept spilling out of my mouth. I needed to get my body to move.

"I had two choices yesterday. One that could have led to a life I should want, but I didn't choose it. Instead, I'm here, with you. And even now…" I sat up in the chair letting go of the blanket surrounding me. "I could make a different choice, but I'm not."

Gage stiffened, face unreadable but eyes full of desire as they trailed over me like a caress. "What choice are you making?" he whispered, slow and thick.

I stood up, moving my hands to his shoulders. He placed his hands on top of mine and slid them up my arms, a trail of heat lingered where he touched. His eyes captured mine, pulling me in.

I moved like a dream, placing one knee at a time on either side of him, gradually straddling him. He sucked in a sharp breath as our body's touched, and the sizzle of electricity enveloped every part of me.

When our lips met, I imploded; everything inside me went up in flames.

His full lips moved against mine, soft but hard in all the right ways. Then he moved suddenly, flipping our position so I was below him, his hands gripping my upper arms.

I gripped his shirt, attempting to pull him back on the lounger with me. Only then did I realize he wasn't kissing me back anymore.

He jerked me away from him, letting go of my shoulders as he stood. A look of betrayal twisted his face.

I was in complete shock. Everything in me clenched.

He leaned over me, yelling in my face, "I'm not a fucking path to destruction. You're wrong. Go back to your therapist, you need it."

He kicked the chair next to us with the bottom of his boot, sending it flipping across the balcony till it banged into the rail. Then he jumped over the railing connecting our balconies and threw open his slider.

"Party's over," he commanded before the door closed, blocking out any other sounds.

I sat back, stunned. That had not gone as expected. But the end result was still the same.

* * *

Our seats were third row in a packed venue. The lit up arena buzzed with conversations as people waited for the next fight.

My nerves were snapping with anticipation. Gage would be coming out soon. I hadn't seen him since he stomped off last night, but I hadn't stopped thinking of him since.

I had spent the morning working out with Silas and the day on a chilly beach, mostly alone while the others recuperated from their night out.

But Dexter told me Gage came by the room looking for me.

My lips tingled recalling our kiss, and my heart dropped remembering his reaction.

Aliya grabbed my hand, looking to the aisle. "Oh no," she groaned. "His stupid friends had to bring stupid girls."

I followed her gaze to see a line of people coming up the aisle. Three men, who were probably early-twenties, and six girls, like an assortment of candy. They wore bright, tight dresses that showed off shiny skin and cleavage. Perfectly groomed Barbie's.

Aliya huffed next to me, crossing her arms. "If one of them end up in his bed, I'm ripping out her extensions and strangling him with them."

I sat back, feeling sick.

From the other side of Aliya, Leona said, "You look better than them Ally Cat. Don't stress. There are plenty of other guys."

Zoe leaned over from the end to add, "You knew this was the way it worked. It's always some random."

The new group filed in next to us; a blonde guy starting the line sat next to me, and the rest of the party took up the seats till the end of the row.

Looking down the line of girls, I was taken aback with how different the bodycon style could look. They wore it like a skin, whereas Leona and Zoe's dresses were more fashion. Aliya went with a circle lace skirt and crop top with a jacket. I was fine with being the odd one in my dark denim jeans, but I appeased the girls by dressing it up with heeled booties and a sleeveless chiffon top.

The blonde smiled at me and nodded to our group; he pointed to Leona. "You're Dexter's girl right?"

"Leona," She smiled tight with a nod.

"We just saw him and Gage in the backroom. Who are your friends?"

Zoe rolled her eyes. "We've met before at other fights."

The blonde laughed, taking his seat. "Oh right, I forgot." Then he looked over at me, starting from the legs up. "I haven't seen you before. I'm Ian."

"Regan." I turned my attention away from him, back to my roommates.

Aliya grabbed my hand with a giggle and whispered, "Gage's friends are hot right?"

I laughed slightly, unsurprised, she thought most guys were.

An announcer started introductions, pulling our attention to the center of the ring.

Gage was introduced first. We all stood as the music started and turned towards the doors above us to see him enter with Silas, Dexter, and one other guy. He made his way down the aisle, scanning our section.

Ian leaned over to me. "Dude's crazy. Never seen anyone as calm as him before a fight. Have you seen him fight?"

I couldn't respond because Gage's gaze landed on me, and didn't move as he continued his path. Even with a stone blank face, the intensity left little room for anything else. Everything around me blurred and dropped away, leaving only him. When he passed our seats, I was no longer in his sight, but my eyes were still glued to him as he climbed into the ring.

He stood in the corner stretching his neck and turned around, eyes landing on me again. And once again the air vacuumed from my lungs and my lips throbbed with memory.

Leona grabbed my hand, bouncing next to me. "He keeps looking over here."

Something darkened his face, making the lines stand out, and his eyebrows dropped along with my stomach.

Ian leaned in to say something, but I didn't pay attention, too absorbed watching Gage. He was my gravity, pulling me like the tide, and I was unable to fight it.

Thankfully, he released me by turning around, facing the opposite way to watch his opponent come in. A tall, rock star looking guy with a full shirt of tattoo's, and long dark hair pulled back into a ponytail.

The bell rung and Gage moved, landing a lightning fast uppercut that jerked the guy's chin up. He followed it with a left hook, and then a right that slammed the rock star to the ground.

The room exploded in cheers and everyone that wasn't already standing rose to their feet as the Referee counted.

When the Ref declared Gage the winner Dexter jumped into the ring, but Gage sidestepped him. He moved with such fierce purpose that everyone cleared out of his way. He climbed between the ropes and started up the aisle, then down our row.

I was trembling the closer he got, my feet stuck to the ground.

He stopped in front of me, and then all at once he hooked his arm around my waist and his lips smashed into mine. My body dissolved, relying on his to keep me up. His tongue slipped in to my mouth, sending shocks of lust down me. Hormones went berserk in my veins.

When my body could finally move, I wrapped my arms around him, feeling his smooth skin over hard muscle. He pulled me in tighter with his arm, and the searing heat of him pressed against the length of me. He kept his still gloved hands off me, but I craved his touch, my skin screamed for it.

He slid his perfect lips to my ear, his ragged breathing only fanning the flames, and I quivered in his arms.

"Wait here," he said between breaths; his face pressed to my hair.

He must have kissed the sense out of me, because in that moment I would have done whatever he wanted. I nodded, my head pressed to his chest, trying to regain control over my own breathing and muscles.

His arm slowly released me while he lowered me to the seat. Then he walked backwards out of the row, everyone moving out of his way.

If I wasn't already sitting the smile he sent me would have dropped me. It was a wide genuine smile that lit up his face. I had never seen him smile like that, but it was possibly the sexiest thing I ever saw. I placed it as the euphoria I felt after winning a fight; he had to be full of it after such an impressive win. He hadn't even broke a sweat.

He jogged back to the ring, Silas and Dexter crowding him before they walked off for an interview.

It took a moment for me to float back into my body.

Aliya was waiting, staring wide-eyed, mouth agape. When I looked her way, she grinned.

"Oh Chick, that was..." She sat back fanning herself. "Lucky Bitch." She nudged my shoulder, teasing.

I didn't need her permission, but seeing that she wasn't angry was a relief. To be sure I asked, "You're not mad?"

She shook her head, excitement lighting her face. "Oh hell no. I knew he was digging on you, I just didn't know it was that bad. Or that good. And I'm glad it's not one of those randoms. You can give me details later." She winked.

Leona leaned over. "What about Anthony?"

"Who cares about him?" Aliya shrieked.

"We're over," I answered. The more I talked the colder I felt. The rush was receding fast, and I wasn't sure I should wait. The intensity of my reaction scared me.

The boy on the other side of me was gone, as well as a few others from that line. People were up, walking around before the next fight.

Dexter popped into the seat next to me. "Damn Rea, what did you do to my brother?" Even his half smile was contagious, but when it dropped so did the rest of the heat in me. He looked past me to where Gage was approaching, quickly adding, "You don't have to do anything you don't want to. We're staying here to see the last fight if you want to stay too."

It sounded like a warning, and probably one I should listen to, but when Gage was there and extended his now gloveless hand to me, I took it. He pulled me into the warmth of his shirtless body and walked us out.

"Wait. Silas wanted to talk to you," Dexter called after us.

"Later," Gage responded without slowing our path to the exit.

And I must've still been drunk off his kiss because my earlier hesitation faded in his presence. This is what I had started, what I had been thinking about all day, and now it seemed he had let go of whatever stopped him last night.

20: Stop Me

MY BODY DID CRAZY THINGS SIMPLY STANDING next to him in the elevator. We both faced forward in the full car, not looking at each other; our hands our only connection. When the elevator dinged our arrival, Gage slipped his arm around me and guided me past the strangers.

Anticipation pooled sweetly in my stomach, pressure already building at just the thought of being alone with him.

He opened the door to his suite and was on me before it swung close. He trapped me against the wall by the door with his body, his lips melting into mine.

The lock clicked as he finished closing the door, and then I had his full attention. He lifted me easily, and guided my legs around his waist, walking to the couch in the sitting area.

My legs clenched around him, my center already pulsing, needing. He had just enough hair for me to grip and I did, better angling our kiss so I could dip my tongue into his mouth.

A low rumble vibrated from his chest and the fire in me flared.

He dropped me onto the sofa, and I had to hold back a whimper at the sudden break in contact.

Climbing over me with a hungry glint in his eye, he dipped his head down, licking up my neck. A hot and slow stroke that stole my air.

He growled in my ear. "You want this? You want me?" And sucked my earlobe in-between his lips.

It was impossible for me to answer. But I gripped him to me, my nails pressing into his strong back, and I brought my hips up to meet his.

He pulled back looking into my eyes. "Say it."

"I want you," I gasped.

One hand ran through the hair by my face, his other holding himself up. "Do you trust me?" His deep whisper sent a chill through me.

I searched his face, taken off guard. Why was he doing this? I could barely catch my breath as I tightened my arms around him and brought my lips to his.

He pushed me back to the couch, holding my wrists down so I couldn't touch him.

"I'm doing this. Not you." He locked me with his eyes. "Do you understand? This isn't you. This is me."

The change was dizzying. Every inch of me craved his touch. My hands ached to explore him, but he still held me still. And I couldn't think; my mind wasn't working.

He lowered himself on me, easing the ache I felt. But he still trapped my hands, and wasn't loosening his grip.

"We're good together." His lips brushed my ear as he spoke, a heated whisper, and I nodded. This was good.

Picking his head back up, he met my eyes again. "I won't let you push me away or put an end to us. Give it a chance."

"Shut up and kiss me," I pleaded, fear starting to rise.

His eyes dropped to my lips and he licked his own, making me squirm beneath him with need. The hot, heavy length of him pressed against me, his arousal hard against my stomach.

I sucked in a groan when I realized he wasn't going to listen to me.

"I want to, and I'm going to. But I need you to agree first."

My heart skipped, but I nodded, not at all sure what I was agreeing to. But needing him to touch me.

His breath quickened, and his sexy smile returned as he let go of my wrists. One hand tangled in my hair, the other gripped my waist.

"I got you. I got us. Just let go and trust me." He collapsed into me, our lips twisting together and body's melding.

His hands ran over the smooth, silky, fabric of my shirt, sending shivers through me, and his lips moved to my neck. He lifted himself up, pulling me with him and raised my shirt. I let him slide it off me and pressed myself to him, enjoying his skin on mine.

His lips trailed down my neck to my collarbone, and I moved my hands to the edge of his shorts, letting my fingers dip inside the elastic.

The moment my breast sprung free of the bra, a cold shock hit me, like ice water. I jerked my hands up to keep it in place, knowing what the wide bottom band had been hiding, but I was too late.

Gage stilled on me, the heat gone between us. The look on his face said it all.

I kept one arm across my bra and used the other to push him off me, but he wouldn't budge.

"What happened?" He asked in a detached whisper. His hand moved over top of mine, the scar underneath.

I thought I shook my head, but I don't know if I actually moved. "It was a long time ago."

He pulled himself off of me and my heart sunk. This was it. He no longer wanted me.

I couldn't decide what was worse, the initial look of disgust or this look of pity.

Scooting myself into sitting, I buckled my bra up before he could see the other scars that trailed to my back.

He wasn't looking at me anyways. His head was cradled in his hands, his leg bouncing beneath his arm.

I watched him and moved to get my shirt, steady and slow so as not to pull his attention.

His hand sprung out and grabbed my wrist, keeping me seated. "What happened?" he asked again, more demanding.

I shook my head. "I didn't come here to talk."

"You were shot. That's what that is."

I ripped my arm out of his hold, a wild panic taking control. I stood up to face him. "Yeah. Now make up your mind, you either want me or you don't. But I'm done talking." I slid my arms around his neck, desperately trying to get us back to where we were before.

He pulled my arms from him, dropping them in front of me. "What happened?" Anger was clear in his question.

I picked up my shirt and pulled it back on, leaving. I think the worst part of the entire evening was that he didn't stop me.

* * *

The next night, Dexter and his friends were drinking in the room, trying to convince me to go out with them.

The familiar comfort of anger took over my sadness, giving me the strength to face the rest of the trip. But I wasn't up for a high-energy club.

I had spent the day alone again, avoiding any questions from the girls. They got in so late they couldn't have known what a disaster my night had been.

Aliya was itching to talk to me, I could tell in the way she smiled at me with her eyes wide.

Danny stood up, already swaying on his feet. "Go get your brother and his friends. Then we can get in anywhere without having to worry about our ID's. They wouldn't turn away the champ."

Dexter was relaxed back on a chair, his fingers mindlessly playing with a lock of Leona's hair. "Already got that covered. They'll be over in a minute."

Aliya sat up tall, biting her lip. "You have to come out now. Everyone's going."

My jaw clenched and muscles tensed as the door opened and Gage walked in with three of his friends, the same guys from last night.

"Is Silas coming?" Dexter asked.

Gage shook his head. Then his eyes met mine, and I crumpled a little when he looked away less than a second later, continuing his scan of the room.

The toxic swirl of emotions made me feel sick, and I had to look away, staring at the wall opposite of me.

Dexter leaned forward to the coffee table, mixing himself a drink from the bottles arranged there. "Help yourself." He waved to the guys that entered. "Rea, c'mon girl. One little drink. It's our last night in AC. And we have important business to take care of."

I raised an eyebrow. "What's that?"

He threw his hands up in mock disbelief. "We need to come up with your new name. 'Make it Rain' Sommers isn't working for you. So help me out." He lifted up a Grey Goose bottle. "We need a brainstorm session."

Gage's friends had started helping themselves to the liquor, but Gage sat in a single chair in the corner, and I hated that I knew that. That I couldn't stop paying attention to him.

Jase took a sip of his drink, raising his eyes to the ceiling. "What about, Rea 'Raging' Sommers."

"That's good." Dexter rubbed his chin and lifted up a cup he poured for me. "C'mon Rea, what do you say?"

"She's not drinking. Leave it alone," Gage's deep voice cut into their playful teasing, and my stomach spasmed.

It rubbed me the wrong way. He wasn't calling shots on anything about me. He managed to take control last night when I was in his arms. He stole my agreement to trust him and immediately betrayed it.

Walking to Dexter, I took the drink and tilted it back until it was empty. Not a fast or impressive feat, since the alcohol seared and I'm sure my face twisted with disgust. But I did it.

The room was quiet for a moment, all eyes on me.

I breathed through the burn. "Let's get this night started." I turned to Aliya. "Can I still borrow your dress?"

She hopped up and pulled me into the other room. "This is going to be so much fun!"

It was going to be something, that's for sure.

21: More Than A Little

"SO YOU WON'T KISS AND TELL? FINE, I'll just use my imagination." Aliya grinned at me while straightening a lock of her hair.

Leona sat on the closed toilet, with a drink in hand. She pursed her lips. "But what now? I've never seen him with the same girl twice. Are you hoping for more?"

Before I could answer Zoe spoke up from her perch on the side of the tub, "It doesn't matter what she wants. They slept together. Sorry Rea, but that's probably it for him."

I pulled the mascara wand away from my eye and turned to her. "We didn't have sex," I corrected, but softened as I turned back to the mirror. "But that's probably it anyways."

Aliya clamped the straightener a couple of times, making it click in my face. "No way. He's still into you, and I can understand why. Girl, you're hot and crazy chill. I would be into you if I were a dude."

I paused with doubt but took the straightener from her.

Her smile twisted as she nodded. "You're tough, I know, I saw you fight. But you're so chill about it all. You don't give away anything, I bet Gage likes that."

I had just enough liquid confidence in me to accept her complement. "You're pretty chill too," I said with a slight smile.

Aliya shook her head, amusement brightening her face. "I'm crazy, not chill. And I like that about myself. I'm an open book to anyone, I just don't care."

Leona smiled. "Yeah Rea, you're the badass of the group." She finished off her drink. "You're like our bodyguard." She giggled. "Now hurry up. I'm ready to go."

Zoe stood up. "I'll go get us all shots. This is really our first night out as roommates. We've got to start it off with a toast."

The drink from earlier seemed to have little effect, except to smooth some of my edges. Maybe I had hated on alcohol misguidedly. I felt chill, like Aliya said. Plus, I could let go of some of my hyper vigilance with this group.

After I straightened my hair, I checked myself out one last time. I wore one of Aliya's tight skirts with a slouchy top that hung off a shoulder. It showed off more leg than I was used to, but the looser top balanced it out. Then I joined the girls in taking a shot to being young and having fun.

* * *

The Barbie's were back. I don't know if they were the same ones from last night; I didn't care enough to find out. Except the one that was dancing too close to where Gage was sitting to be anything but intentional, I kept my eye on her.

The only guy that would even get near me all night was Dexter. It's like everyone else had a ten-foot rule about me; they couldn't get closer than that. I assumed it was because of Gage's kiss at the fight last night, but that didn't seem to keep girls away from him.

That damn girl was blocking his view of me dancing. And I was twisting my hips good, another perk of alcohol. Except now there was nobody to appreciate it. I had caught Gage glancing before, but not now with her in front of him. Ugh, my smooth edges were beginning to splinter with frustration.

Time for another drink.

I went back to the table, having to cut through the plastic girls to get to our bottles. I kept my eyes focused on the glass as I poured, avoiding Gage and his friends sitting in the booth across from me.

"You know you can mix that, sip on it, you don't need to drink it straight."

I cut my eyes to Gage. He was leaned back in his seat, his dark gray top fit just right on him.

"I'm not drinking it for the taste." I held up my glass. "This works fine for me." I tried my damnedest not to cringe as the liquor went down.

He leaned forward, dark eyebrow lifted. "Why then?"

I shrugged, the burn in the back of my throat made it hard to speak. "For fun."

"I thought you didn't drink."

I pursed my lips. "You do that a lot; think things about me that just aren't true."

He nodded, leaning back in his seat. He turned his head to watch that girl still dancing too close to him. In fact, I think she had gotten closer. I went back to my roommates on the dance floor.

"She's not a Barbie, she's a troll." I squinted my eyes, appraising the girl now sitting beside Gage. "A stupid, yellow haired, troll doll."

Aliya's head fell back with laughter. "You're funny when you're drunk." She passed me a blue shot. "Here, have another."

I tilted back the shot. "I'm not drunk." I stood up from the stool and the room tilted beneath me. "Maybe I am a little drunk." I gripped the back of the chair waiting for the ride to stop. "Or a lot drunk. But I'm not funny. I'm angry." Damn, my filter wasn't working, must have been washed away with the alcohol. "I want to melt her stupid plastic face with a lighter." Maybe it was time to quit drinking.

I finally managed to separate enough from the group to get the interest of other guys, and just in time. I was tired of dancing alone and wanted to hear I was hot, and that was exactly what this guy was saying.

He wasn't dancing too close yet, but kept one hand on my hip as we moved to the beat. I stepped in closer to him, and he pulled away, eyes widening behind me.

A plaid arm draped over my shoulder, it was Dexter and his silly jacket. "Are you trying to start trouble?" He said into my ear, with a touch of amusement.

I groaned as the guy danced away, finding a new partner.

"How am I starting trouble?" I twisted in his arm and shoved him a little, or not, it sent him back a couple of paces. My muscles felt loose, must have put more force into the shove then I intended.

"Sorry," I said with a laugh and patted his shoulder. "But I'm not doing anything except dancing. Why are you starting trouble?"

His eyes widened and he shook his head. "I gave you that first drink. If something goes wrong, it's going to be my fault."

I scoffed, waving him away. My body swayed with my words, "I am responsible for my own actions. I make my own choices. It's all my fault."

With a smirk, he put his arm around me again, turning me to face the corner where our table was. "I know that. Believe me, I've figured out you can take care of yourself. But see, he," Dexter pointed to where Gage could barely be seen through the crowd, "would blame me. And I'd like to keep this face pretty, so help a brother out. Please. Stick by us." He started our path back through the crowd. "C'mon I'll get you a drink. I'll dance with you. You'll have fun. Promise."

I reluctantly moved my feet to the table. "Fine."

Leona held up a shot for me. "What about Regan 'Drunk Ass' Sommers?" She almost fell over from giggling.

"Nah Babe, that's you," Dexter teased, wrapping his arm around her to hold her up.

Aliya chimed in, "Oh, Regan 'Bad Ass' Sommers."

Dexter raised his eyes to the ceiling. "People, there's an art to this. No cuss words and alliteration is your friend. Or some sort of word play."

I laughed and took the shot Leona had handed me. Crap, I wasn't supposed to do that anymore. But I glanced towards Gage, and the look that crossed him made me want to take the shots out of everyone's hands and down them. He was angry, his face an intense mask, and I wanted to be the cause of that.

The yellow haired freak next to him ran her finger along his jaw, attempting to pull his attention back to her.

I poured myself another shot and was happy to see him respond; his face darkened even more, causing me to smile.

I slammed the shot, no longer worried about cringing; everything was numb.

* * *

I couldn't move. For a horrifying second I thought I had been jumped again and was only now regaining consciousness. But I was in a soft bed, with soft sheets.

Then it hit me. I was hung over. This is why I didn't drink.

"Hey, you've got to get up now. We have to check out soon," Dexter's whisper was loud.

My heart had an attack as the memory of him throwing me onto the bed resurfaced. He had carried me over his shoulder and tossed me on the bed.

I groaned and pulled a pillow over my face. "I am never drinking again."

He chuckled and slapped my foot from where he was standing at the end of the bed. "We've all said that before. You'll get better at this, the more you drink."

"Uh-uh, I mean it." I pulled the pillow off my face and tried to sit up. Big mistake.

I stumbled to the bathroom and upchucked any remaining alcohol into the toilet. As I hovered over the bowl, I tried to piece together last night. I remembered the club, the dancing, and the girl that spent most of her night with Gage. But I couldn't remember me. What happened?

"She's in there," Dexter said to someone from the other room.

"Rea? You need help? Dex is getting you some medicine," Aliya called out.

Another heaving wretch was my only response.

Aliya came in with a glass of water, Pepto-Bismol and Ibuprofen. "Take this when you can. Don't worry, I was doing the same thing earlier."

I sat back on the cool tile floor, resting against the tub, hoping the spasms were over. After a moment I took the medicine.

"So… Scrapper, you feeling better?"

Something about the way she laughed triggered another avalanche of memories from last night. Crap. I had tried to fight that girl sitting next to Gage. She'd made some stupid comment about all the nicknames they were giving me, and I lunged at her. Jumped over Gage and tackled her down. He had to pull me off of her. He had lifted me by my waist and set me down in a chair like I was in need of a time out.

"Oh no." I thought I might get sick again. "I… don't know what to say about last night. I was ridiculous."

She laughed and sat next to me on the floor. "You were a sloppy drunk. But so were we all. It was good times." She put her hand on my knee. "That will go down as one of my all-time favorite stories. You'll see, if you're not laughing about it yet, you will be."

I blew out air and shook my head, doubtful.

"Dexter get in here," Aliya yelled. When he entered, she said, "Tell Rea how damn funny last night was. She's feeling a little embarrassed."

I covered my face with my hands. "More than a little."

Seeing him brought back the rest. After Gage put me in my time out chair, he called Dexter over to handle me and went back to his friends. Dexter had brought me back up to our suite, but I had only made it to the couch, and he had to carry me to bed.

"I'm sorry." I pulled my hands away to look at him. He was grinning.

"Don't be. We've all had those moments." He chuckled at the skeptical look I shot him. "Well, something like it." His laugh rolled out of him, and he joined us on the ground. "When you jumped across the table, were you calling her a troll?"

My head fell back, and I closed my eyes. I was never ever drinking again.

After a quick shower I was ready to go. Not one hundred percent, but good enough to sit in a car.

I put my backpack on and came out to the living room. "Where's Leona?" Aliya and Zoe were in the room waiting.

"She's riding back with Dexter. They're going to stay a little longer. She's been trying her luck at the slots."

"It's stupid 'cause she can't collect big winnings with a fake ID, but whatever," Zoe said from beneath her large sunglasses.

As we left our room, the door to Gage's suite opened. I kept walking to the elevator, hoping it wasn't him.

But it was. He and two guys came out of the room with two girls; they stood and waited for the elevator with us. Aliya greeted them all, but I just nodded my hellos.

When we stepped off the elevator to the main lobby Gage called out, voice sharp, "Regan."

I paused my stride, but didn't turn around.

He walked away from his friends to where I was. He put his hands in his leather coat pockets as he addressed me, all business, "Your shoot is on Tuesday. After last night you have to be really strict with your diet. Drink lots of water and workout hard. Don't drink again until after this photo shoot."

He waited with his brows raised.

I shrugged. "That's it?" Breathing was tight. I don't know what I had expected or wanted him to say.

"Is there anything else?" he challenged.

I wanted to slap him, but instead I shook my head and walked away. Last week he would have been offering to cook my food for me; now he was back to ordering me around. Maybe the girls were right; I was his fight night girl and nothing more. I told myself it was best this way anyways. This is what I had wanted.

22: Man Up

THE OWNER FROM THE STORE FITNESS FIRST was running the show. She acted as the stylist and was directing the photographer on shots. Her first order of business was to demand I get my haircut and dyed.

Her curt directions turned me off at first, but the highlights, layers, and side bangs looked good. Not a big change, but it brightened my look. And as she kept the shoot moving, I came to appreciate her no nonsense attitude. After I adjusted to all the attention, it was actually fun.

"Let's change gears now. Change into this." She handed me a sleeveless zip up hoody and a bottom that wasn't quite shorts. "And we can let your hair down now. Sylvie can you fluff her hair, you know that wild, sexy look."

I didn't mind this new outfit, the mini red shorts covered more than my bathing suits and after my hair and makeup was done, I had to admit the look was hot.

My stomach dipped as I stood in front of the camera and caught Silas staring, a self-satisfied grin on his face.

"Sharon, you've outdone yourself with this one." He shook his head. "Regan, we might be able to branch out in a whole new career."

I raised my now manicured eyebrow. "As long as I can box too."

Silas's laugh was loud and echoed through the open room.

"She's a pretty girl that's for sure, as long as she's not bruised from being hit." Sharon pulled me over near the front window. "Now, I think this natural light will work better here." She pulled on my top, adjusting it, and unzipped the zipper some. "Take off the bra, you're young and perky, it's better to go without for this shot." At my hesitation she continued, "We're not taking off the top, but I don't want the bra showing."

I reached under the top and undid the bra, sliding the straps down my arm and pulling it from under the sweater. She pulled the zipper down to just below breast level and pulled on the edges so my natural cleavage would show.

"Perfect." She smiled, stepping back out of the shot.

The camera flashed a couple times and Sharon directed, "Put your hands in the pockets, and turn slightly away from the camera. Show off the design on the back of the jacket." After I did what she said, she added, "Arch your back a bit more, stick out your rump; don't be shy now."

Pinpricks of excitement and nerves crossed my skin, but I followed her directions. I found myself wishing Gage would step out of the back office now. He was there, I knew because I saw him arrive earlier, but he hadn't come out this entire time.

I cleared my head of the distracting thoughts and focused on following Sharon's directions.

"That's good." Sharon stood behind the photographer, looking at the pictures he had snapped. "Last change." She went to her hangers and pulled out a bikini. "Here put this on."

My blood drained from me as I looked at the strings. "Do you have a different one? Maybe a sports bra type top. I don't wear string bikinis," I tried to explain.

Silas's forehead wrinkled. "You wear what she gives you, this isn't about personal style."

My heart flip-flopped in my stomach, but I raised my chin in defiance. "It's not that… I won't wear it. That has nothing to do with boxing, I'm not doing it."

Sharon turned to Silas. "We agreed on the number of outfits and the bathing suit was part of it. It's part of the contract."

Hating that she was discussing this with him and not me, I interrupted. "I'll wear a different one, but not that one."

Silas shot me a silencing look. "Come with me," he commanded.

I followed him to his office.

"Get out. I need to talk to Regan." Silas's normally level voice was strained.

Gage stood up from behind the desk, eyes widening as they grazed over me.

"What's going on?" he questioned, not moving to the door.

"Sit down, Rea." Silas gestured to the chair before turning to answer the question. "She's refusing to wear the last outfit."

His back rose and fell with his deep breath, and then he turned back to me, his face back to his typical smile. "Regan, I understand you being wary about modeling in a bikini. But I can guarantee you it won't hurt your image. It's for an athletic store, not some magazine. If anything this will help. People might see you as a pretty face and underestimate you, which could be used to your advantage in the ring." He nodded like he had already convinced me.

I met his eyes, trying to make it clear that I wasn't budging. "No. I won't wear that."

"Why?" he demanded.

I couldn't answer that, protecting my scars was my top priority, no matter how angry Silas got.

"I'm a boxer, not a bikini model." I didn't break eye contact with him.

Gage put his hand on Silas's shoulder. "I'll go see if we can work something else out, maybe another outfit or something."

I let out the breath I was holding, feeling a slight relief. But Silas wasn't appeased by Gage's suggestion.

"They already paid us up front. I'll come with you." He turned back to me. "Stay here while we clean up this mess." He shook his head in disapproval before walking out.

What felt like an eternity later, Silas came back in. "Will you wear this?" He held up a sporty white and blue tankini, and I nodded with relief.

After changing, I hesitated on my way to the set up. Gage was standing there in blue and white surf trunks that matched my bathing suite. His tan body was shiny with oil, the same oil I was covered in.

My mouth went dry and I had to force myself to breathe. He watched me as I made my way over, his face blank, but an unreadable look in his eyes.

He took the few remaining steps to where I was. "They agreed to the switch of outfits as long as I stood in for this one." His voice was low and his eyes kept dropping over my body, leaving electric currents in their wake.

I couldn't stop myself from drinking him in. This close range, I could easily read his tattoo along his ribs. Big bold lettering stacked on each other: Rage, Rage. The top word was in flames. When I raised my eyes, he was smirking, eyebrow lifted as he watched me, watch him.

"Come on. Let's get this over with." His blunt words squashed the anticipation that was dancing in me.

I gave myself an internal reprimand; I needed to take control of my body's reactions to him, get this over with, and move on. Like he did.

The photo shoot was the ultimate test in my strength. We had to pose in each other's arms. Standing face to face, he hung his arms low around my waist and my arms were on his chest. The heat was there, but tempered by the multiple eyes and directions being given. After a couple of shots it was over and Gage dropped his arms too easily and disappeared to change.

I showered, washing away the makeup and oil from the photo shoot, but not able to rid my skin of the feel of Gage's hands. I put my wet hair in a no nonsense French braid, preparing for work at the restaurant. My new bangs helped to soften the look.

Slinging my book bag over my shoulder, I walked out of the locker room, almost running into Gage as I turned the corner.

He took a step back, taking in my outfit, his forehead creased. "You gotta work right away or do you have some time to talk?"

"I've got to work now," I said with mixed feelings. I wanted to hear what he had to say, but didn't want to answer any questions.

He shifted his eyes, and then leveled me with them. "Can I drive you?" He shoved his hands in his pockets, giving away his nervousness.

I nodded slow, not really sure, but knowing we needed to have this talk. Hopefully we could cut some of the awkwardness and at least have a working relationship.

He slid his seatbelt across him and paused, shooting me with a hard stare. "You can't fight outside of the ring. You can get suspended for that."

I looked away, out the window. "I didn't mean to. I won't do that again."

He tilted forward, trying to get my attention. "Drinking or fighting?"

"Fighting." I meant both, but I didn't want to give him the satisfaction of being right about me.

He pulled out of the parking lot and onto the one-way street. Checking his rearview mirror he said, "You don't handle alcohol very well, you should stop that too."

"You should stop telling me what to do," I bit back. Then pressed my lips together, reigning in my anger. This had been a bad idea.

We stayed quiet, the car filled with tension, until we pulled up to my work.

I reached for the handle, anxious to escape. No longer interested in hearing what else he had to say.

"Wait," he sighed. "I don't mean to lecture you."

I dropped the handle and turned back to him, eyebrow raised, silently questioning what it was he meant to do.

His eyes softened as they ran over me, causing goose bumps.

"You scare me," he whispered.

I froze.

"The things you say and do sometimes, it scares me. And you won't listen to me; that scares me. But I thought that was part of the adventure."

I didn't absorb the words. The way he spoke them and left them hanging between us, made it clear that a big "but" was coming next. Something that would wipe them all away, and I was waiting for that, rigid.

He swept his eyes up me again, until they locked with mine. "I thought we could be fun, something new, an adventure. I embraced the fear as part of that. But when I saw that," his eyes dropped to where my scar was, "It hit me; this is real. I'm scared to death that I might hurt you, more than you've already been hurt."

He spoke softly but his words were like razors, scraping at me. I had to look away, no longer able to take the emotion in his eyes or the emotion he stirred in me. Or the way it seemed he could see through me.

"You deserve better than that, than me. I'm no good for you."

And there it was. The dismissal. I met his gaze again, forcing him to look at me while he rejected me.

"You should be with someone who makes you laugh..."

I tuned out the rest of his words, agitation building. But his last words were a slap in the face.

"... Like Dexter."

"Fuck you. You don't want me? Fine. But man up and admit it, be honest. Don't feed me some bullshit lines, and then try and pass me off on your brother." I climbed out of the car, turning back to throw out my last words. "You're disgusting."

He popped out of the car, quickly coming around the vehicle to my side. I was trapped between two cars and he stood at the end of them, not letting me pass.

"That came out wrong. That's not what I meant." He stepped close to me and grabbed my elbow. "I'm not passing you off to anyone. Especially not Dexter. God, that would kill me. I don't want you with anyone." He took another step towards me, forcing me against the car, the heat of him penetrating through my jacket. "I should let you go, but I'm selfish. I still want you." He trapped me between his arms, bracing his hands on the car behind me. "You should tell me to leave you alone. And I'll try to." His eyes dropped to my lips. "Tell me." His breath warmed the skin on my forehead and the feeling spread through me like wildfire.

I shook my head slightly, and then his lips were on mine. They moved against me, like he'd been starving, a low growl vibrating from him. He sunk to my level as his hands left the car and cupped my face. Our tongues caressed each other's and his fingers trailed down my neck, sending shivers through me. His body pressed me into the car, but our jackets were barriers, padding between us.

A chilly wind cut through our kiss, but he only pulled me tighter to him, our heat a shield to the cold. The kiss slowed to an end, but he kept his forehead pressed to mine. "I don't want to let you go." His breathing was strained, and his breath fanned over me. "Can I pick you up after work?"

I took a few breaths, trying to still my erratic heartbeat. "Yes."

I didn't know how I was going to get through the next couple of hours after what just went down, but I was happy to have the time to sort through the jumbled thoughts and emotions warring in me.

23: Edge

"BEFORE WE GO," GAGE'S CAREFUL TONE SET me on edge.

He shifted his eyes to me, giving me a sidelong look as he started the car. He pressed some of the buttons on the console, turning the heat up and music down before continuing. "You didn't say anything, and I've got to know, where's your head at with this?"

The vulnerability he let show on his face and the way his leg bounced melted me some, but at the same time it increased my own nerves.

"I don't know," I responded with the truth. I felt lost out at sea, just waiting for the tide to push me so I knew which way to paddle.

He waited for more, but I couldn't look at him as I said the rest. Instead, I stared straight ahead, at the lights of the restaurant and city life beyond.

"We're going to hurt each other. It's only really a matter of when or how hard. And the way we are, the way we fight..." I stole a glance at him, the muscles in his jaw flexed as he clenched his teeth. "But everyone hurts each other. It's what people do."

That was the end of my certainty. I turned towards him and said what I was still trying to convince myself of. "I'm willing to take that risk though."

His hand moved to my cheek, a smile touching his lips. "I don't want to hurt you. Ever."

I grasped his hand, pulling it off me. "I think we're taking it too seriously. What was it you had said? An adventure. I liked that. Let's be that.

He nodded, eyes lit with excitement. "Where should we start? Your place or mine?"

My heart skipped, and whirlwinds of uncertainty started in my stomach. "Yours."

I figured it easier to call a cab and leave than try and kick him out if we go downhill fast. Plus, Dexter stays with Leona on school nights, so we'd be alone at Gage's.

"Have you had dinner?" Gage hung up my jacket in the hall closet.

"No." I stared at him, unsure of how to act or what to do.

He seemed nervous, too, and a part of me thought I should put us out of our misery and kiss him, but it hadn't gone over well the last time I did that.

He licked his lips, only increasing my urge to jump on him.

"I made dinner. I haven't eaten yet either." He gestured for me to walk to the kitchen.

My feet froze at the entrance. He had the table set for two with a salad, and the typically tidy kitchen was immaculate.

Gage slipped his hand to the small of my back, pressing me forward into the room. "I was hoping you'd say my house. Otherwise this would have gone to waste."

I walked to the table, out of his touch, the whirlwinds picking up speed in my gut.

"I made steak and shrimp, with sweet potatoes and parmesan green beans. I still have to cook the steak, it should only take a couple of minutes." He pulled containers out of the refrigerator and turned on the center grill of his stove.

I envied that he had something to do to keep occupied. "Can I help?"

We prepared the meal together, but the awkwardness returned as we ate. I didn't know what to say. I wanted to avoid any mention of this past weekend, but it wouldn't leave my thoughts.

"I got dessert too," Gage said, lifting his eyebrow enticingly.

"You made dessert?" I was surprised. This guy was so rigid about his eating, and here we were having steak already; I had thought that was enough of a cheat for him. Especially since he ate a lot, like usual. That man ate healthy, but in large quantities.

He shook his head, sitting back from his plate. "I didn't make it. I bought it. Figured, you're done with your shoot, so you could take a break tonight."

I smiled with excitement, no longer interested in the food in front of me. "What is it?"

He went into the pantry, and came out with two bags of M&M's. Extending them to me he said, "Ones plain, but the other one's peanut butter. I thought you might like that?" He lifted his shoulders with the question.

"I do. Thank you." I bit my bottom lip, trying to subdue the nervous laughter, but my stomach still vibrated with it as I took the bags from him.

He sat, pulling his chair close, eyes dancing over me with amusement. "It's not much, but I'm glad it made you smile."

I didn't know what to do with this version of Gage. He was too hesitant and nervous. This dating thing didn't seem to suit us.

I opened the bag and offered him some before pouring several into my hand. I ate them one by one, drawing out the time before we had to talk or act.

By the way he watched me, like I was his dessert, I knew our 'date' would be over soon and he'd get to the real reason for having me here.

His face darkened as his jaw worked. "How many people have you been with?"

I almost choked on the candy in my mouth, but forced it down, going rigid at his question. "How many have you slept with?" I returned.

He took a deep breath and nodded, visibly letting go of some of the tension in his body. "Point taken. What I really meant was, there's no one else now, right? The cop is still out of the picture?"

I nodded, still trying to subdue my residual anger. "There's no one else. And what about you?" My mind jumped to his randoms. "Even casually?"

He stretched his jaw while shaking his head. "Nope. And there won't be." His hands traveled over the top of my jean covered thighs, building heat. They moved up my legs until he gripped my hips and shifted me to face him with a quick jerk that sparked a fire. "I want the same promise from you. I can let go of our past, as long as it's only me now."

"As long as we last, it's only you." I bit back my smile, afraid to let it go. "And we'll forget our past?"

His hand gripped my hip tighter at that, like a warning, and my stomach dipped.

"Except, I have to know one thing." He paused, but I didn't respond, a slow cold fear spreading. He hesitated as he watched me for a reaction. "That," his eyes flicked to my scar, "was it someone that can still hurt you?"

I scooted back, out of his touch. Not able to handle it with the thoughts crashing in my head. I could answer this one question; I had to if I wanted him to drop it. I just had to work up the nerve and figure it out.

I carefully planned my three words and said them with even more care. But I couldn't look at him. "No, she died."

It was and wasn't the truth. She was dead, but she still hurt me. All the time.

He grabbed my hands, leaning into my space again. "Who?" his voice was desperate.

I closed my eyes, pulling everything back in so when I looked at him I was in control. "You said one question." I rose to my feet and dropped my eyes over him, slow and heated, making my intentions clear.

He pulled me into him, a good thing since my feet wouldn't budge. Letting go of my hands, he slid his to my waist, firm and strong as they circled around me. My body melted under his grip.

"You won't pull away this time?" I had to ask.

The air around us burst as he stood, chair skidding back behind him. His gaze was electric as he looked down at me. "No."

Then his lips were on me, inhaling me, hands gripping my hair as he tilted my head back. All too soon his lips left mine, but his eyes were still on fire. "Bedroom, now," he ordered, pulling me in that direction.

But he couldn't make it that far before he was on me again. He pinned me to the wall in the hallway, nibbling my lips and flicking his tongue in my ear, dissolving any of my hesitation.

He broke away to pull me up the steps, only to pounce again at the top. This time he lifted me, his hands traveling over my body in waves of heat as he walked us the rest of the way to the bedroom. Our kiss was desperate, trying to hold onto lightning.

I pulled at his shirt, trying to lift it from his body, close to tearing it in my need. He lowered me on the bed, breaking his kiss just enough to slip it off.

His hot lips ran down my neck and his hands slid under my tee, soft on my stomach, making it tighten in a delicious sensation that moved between my legs.

He tugged at the edge of my shirt, but pulled back, looking at me for approval. I sat up, sliding it off, and then ran my hand over my camisole and shook my head, setting the rules.

After a breathless moment he climbed over me, pushing me back down to the mattress.

I pulled him on me, wanting to feel his weight, be surrounded in his heat. I pressed my hand into the muscles of his back as we both tasted the skin on each other's neck and shoulders. I was lost in touch and sensation, and I needed more. I moved my hands to his pants, undoing the button. He pulled his hands off me to undo the rest, kicking them off as his fingers moved over my jeans.

We couldn't seem to move fast enough, both pulling and fumbling with the strain of wanting. There was no time for us; we needed to do this before it all fell apart. That's how it felt, an ecstatic rush of need. A race on time. Desperate to touch and know the other, every inch.

I didn't get to run my hands over him for but a second, his silky smooth skin stretched over the solid length of him, ready to go. He pressed me into the mattress as he raised up, using his hand to rub himself over me, spreading my wetness between my legs.

He groaned. "I want you so bad. I can't take my time, not this time," he panted into my ear.

"Good," was my only response and barely audible. I needed him in me, and the strain made it hard to breathe.

"Damn. Wait." He rolled away and grabbed a condom from his nightstand.

I squeezed my legs together as he rolled it on, the ache in me building with anticipation. I kissed along his neck, unable to keep off of him.

Then he positioned himself over me and slid in, stretching me to the point of almost pain, a satisfying searing heat filling me. His groan encouraged me to move, rocking my hips beneath him. He pulled me tight to him, his lips finding mine as he panted into them, in between brief, wet kisses. We breathed the same hot air through our mouths and absorbed each other's moans, collecting them like prizes. I wanted his moans, and I circled my hips, clenching the muscles between my legs until I had my reward.

His thrusts grew deeper, harder, faster, breaking the dam of tension in my core with a surge of physical pleasure. I cried out, unable to hold back anything. My mind no longer in control. I was all feeling and my body spasmed with it. And still he kept going, taking me on the ride all over again, my body in his control, responding to his every touch, every thrust. He took me to the edge of pleasure and pushed me over.

When I floated back into myself, he was laying on me, forehead pressed to my neck as he sucked in ragged breaths, his own muscles twitching with his release.

I wasn't sure if the beating I felt was my own heart, or his, but I throbbed with each pulse.

After a while our breathing steadied, but he still laid on me, his arms wound around my waist.

"I'll be right back," he broke the silence, getting up and removing his condom.

My muscles still felt weak, but I slid off the bed and escaped to the bathroom to clean up and put pants back on.

When I came out he had the covers pulled back and was lying in bed. "Come here." His voice was husky as he ran his hand over the mattress beside him.

I scurried over before I could change my mind and curled into the warmth of him, trying to ease the fear creeping back in.

His finger tips trailed down my arm, then over my hip. "You put your jeans back on," he said with a frown. "You're going to stay tonight, right?" He looked down at me, eyebrows slanted in.

"Well, I thought—"

He pulled back from me, lines marking his face. "What? You're staying tonight. You have to." He rolled to his side, hands pulling at my hip to face him. "That was only the start. I need this night with you. I've been wanting this for so long. Stay."

Knowing that his plans weren't cuddling and sleeping made it easier to agree to. "Alright."

* * *

Even after three nights of running my hands all over that body, I still wanted more. And so did he.

"I don't care how late it is. Let me pick you up after work," he murmured into my neck in-between soft kisses.

I slid my hands inside his jacket, feeling hard muscle under his soft cotton shirt, and his arms encircled me, keeping me warm against the damp wind.

"Trichelle's driving me since we both have to close. Plus, I need to go to my house." Even though I was trying to pull away with my words, my hands couldn't stop their path along his torso, trying to soak him up.

The lines of his jaw deepened as he looked down at me. "Then what about tomorrow? Cancel your thing, come with me."

I let my arms drop with a groan. "You cancel. Leona and Aliya are both performing and bought me a ticket already. I can't flake."

He pulled back some, his eyes more gray in the drab weather as they swept over me. "I can't, it's an important business night with Silas. And you have to work tomorrow, during the day?" His frown deepened as I nodded. "Sunday then?"

My lips slid to a smile. "Sunday." This small space would be good; I had been so wrapped up with him since Tuesday that I couldn't think straight.

He leaned in, trapping me against his car. His warm breath caressed my neck, and his clean sent surrounded me. I felt the now familiar tickle of need that only he could satisfy.

"Or you could call off work now and come home with me."

It was tempting. But I put my hands in-between us, a weak barrier, and shook my head. "I've got to go. I'm going to be late for work. I'll see you Sunday."

* * *

I jumped awake, alert, but unsure why. I slid from the bed, grabbing a hand weight from the corner of the room, heart pounding.

The window rattled as someone tapped on it again. That was the noise that had woken me. I tiptoed to the window and peeked out the corner, releasing the breath I held when I saw Gage. He had a ski cap on against the cold and his blue eyes pierced through the night.

He was preparing to tap again, shifting on his feet as I stepped into view of the window and pointed to the front door.

His smile was quick to appear, that same triumphant smile from after his fight, and it made my stomach spin.

"What are you doing here?" I whispered harshly, opening the front door.

He stood with one hand braced against the doorframe, his wool jacket unbuttoned, showing off his tieless suit underneath. It was kinda rumpled and the collared shirt was unbuttoned at the top. But the look in his eyes liquefied me.

When he kissed me, I could smell and taste the alcohol. He walked me back into the house, lips madly moving against mine and closed the door behind us.

I pushed away from him. "You've been drinking?" I asked needlessly.

His smile this time was more predator after prey. "Hmm." He nodded, stalking towards me.

I took a step back, hands up to stop him. "And you drove here? You shouldn't do that," I admonished.

He paused, but his smile glided up on one side in victory. "You're right. I shouldn't. Looks like I need to stay here."

"I'm serious," I whisper-shouted, mindful of roommates sleeping.

He nodded, reaching an arm around me. "I am too. I won't do it again." He pulled me in close, nuzzling my hair. "Now, about where I'm sleeping…"

I pushed away again, idea bright in my mind. "Oh, let me get you some blankets, you can stay here on the couch." I bit my lip to hide my smile.

His eyes met mine with a playfulness that I'd never seen before, and it reminded me that we were young and made to have fun.

He lunged towards me and I jumped back, elated that I had successfully dodged him. I was on my toes, ready to run at his next move, but it came so quick I didn't have a chance.

He hooked his arm around me, smile turning sultry as he pressed against me. "You'd make the future Cruiserweight Champion sleep on the couch?"

Something about his tone caught my attention, and his smile only confirmed it. I leaned back to look at him. "What?"

Excitement filled his face. "I've got a fight against Desmond Dennaki." His hands gripped my waist, emphasizing what he said. "Silas has to work out the details with his manager, but all parties agreed to it tonight. He's ranked in the top ten, so when I win, I will be too."

My heart nearly exploded for him. "That's amazing. I didn't realize that's what this business meeting was about." I slapped his arm. "You didn't tell me that. This was a big night for you."

His eyes dropped to my lips. "And I want to celebrate with you."

Silent, I walked him back to my room, closing the door behind us. Flicking off the lights, I turned to him, hands on his chest. He let me push him back onto the bed and I straddled his waist.

His hands traveled over my thighs, under the thin fabric of my sleep shorts. He gripped my legs, keeping me on top of him as he scooted himself back to lie out on the mattress. He cupped my butt and pulled me to him, kissing the top of my breasts.

Flipping me over, onto my back, he continued his hot kisses as hands roamed over the swell of my breasts, outside of my tank top. He moved his lips, biting my nipple through my shirt, and sucking through the fabric. His hands hovered at the edge, fingers running along the seam at the top.

I helped him out by pulling the top down, letting my breasts spill out. He ran his tongue from one nipple to the next, taking his time to run along the valley in between. My fingers raked through his hair and as far down his back as I could reach, before tugging at his jacket to take it off.

He sat up on his knees, removing his jacket painfully slow, eyes glued to me the entire time. I squirmed with impatience as he started undoing each button of his shirt underneath.

When I sat up to help him, he grabbed my hands, moving them off of him. "No. I'll do this." He stood up, off the bed, out of my reach. "I want to watch you get undressed too."

The rush of heat surging through me at his words took over, drowning any hesitation.

I kept my eyes locked on him as I lowered my shorts, keeping the same slow pace he had started, sliding them off one leg at a time. He pulled his shirt off, his tattoos still visible in the shadows of the room. His hands moved to undo his pants as I slid my cotton panties off.

I could hear his breathing strain as he watched me. He dropped his boxers and took himself in his hands, stroking in a way that made my legs ache, and core drip.

"What about the shirt?"

I hit a wall; every muscle felt the impact. "No." I wasn't wearing a bra underneath so my tank top had to stay on.

"Alright," he sighed, stepping back to the bed and I released my own sigh of relief.

"Alright," he said again, running one hand flat down the length of my torso, ending between my legs. Releasing my anxiety with the pressure he put there, all my thoughts centered on what his fingers were doing and the pleasure building.

My hands ran all over him, one tracing the curves of muscle while the other gripped the length of him, gliding up and down, pleased when Goosebumps broke out on his skin. Sensation was taking over and I bit the tight skin on his shoulder as I fell apart under his fingers.

In one quick motion he was in me, condom already on. His slow, controlled rock made his muscles pull and flex under my hands. His hands were running all over me.

I stifled my cries in his skin, biting and sucking his shoulder, but they still escaped. Trying to keep the noise down was dizzying.

One of his hands was gliding up and down my side and he ventured to slide his fingers under my shirt. I pushed at his hand on impulse, but he stilled, not moving his body or hand.

He had been running kisses along my jaw, he didn't move his lips away as he said, "I want to touch you, all of you. Please."

My heart hurt with the sudden constriction. I could understand his need, I wanted to touch him everywhere, but…

His kiss was gentle on my lips as he shifted to look me in the eye. "We don't have to take off the shirt. I won't look. It's just my hands."

I nodded, a small barely there consent that twisted my stomach painfully.

He moved back over me, continuing his slow rocks as his hand carefully ran along the bottom of my shirt. "Shh," he soothed. "It's okay, Baby. I got you."

It was only then that I realized I had made any noise. Every step his hand took made me tighten and squeak with fear. It was unreasonable, I knew, but it was there.

I tried to concentrate on his soft lips on my shoulder, and I wanted to run my hands along him, but I was frozen.

He cupped my breast from under my shirt, hand firm over the top of the one scar he had seen, the one just under the side of my left boob. Then his hands glided around, and my stomach clenched as he traveled over the other scars along my side and back. But he didn't flinch, even though I knew the one along my side was felt, the only one that was raised up, where a bullet had burned its path.

When his hands met along my back, he crossed them, pulling me into him in a tight hug. His lips buried into my neck and he held me still for a moment, waiting for my breathing to calm before beginning his rocking again.

He didn't touch me there anymore and I began to relax, until the pressure of him in me built and I exploded with satisfaction and a strange new relief.

* * *

I lay on top of him on the couch, letting the aftershocks of orgasm fade away. Music still playing softly in the background from our failed dinner.

It seemed sleeping with Gage had the opposite effect than I had imagined. The more we did it, the more we wanted it. And now we couldn't even make it through a meal without attacking each other.

He played with a lock of my hair, twirling it around his fingers.

"Are you nervous? About your fight?" I asked. Silas had worked out the details and it was in two weeks. Sooner than expected, but Desmond was going overseas right after so there was no time to wait.

His chest vibrated beneath me. "No. I don't take fights unless I'm certain. I know I can win this one."

I lifted my head, to look at him. "How can you know?"

His eyes danced over me, and his liquefying smile returned. "Because I know what my strengths are, and I've seen his weaknesses. I know. I don't take chances on my career." He pulled me back down to him, settling me on his chest. His hand stilled just above my shoulder. "What about you?" He was deathly quiet. "Are you nervous about tomorrow? About court?"

I had been avoiding thinking about it. "Yes," I admitted only to him. "But I just want it over with."

His strong arms tightened around me. "I'll be there with you. And hopefully those bastards get the maximum sentence."

I let out a deep breath. "You don't have to stay after you testify. It could go on all day and I know you have business things to take care of." He seemed to always be working out or doing "business" stuff with Silas, if he wasn't with me. But I didn't question it because then I might have to answer some as well.

He scooted back, looking down on me with agitation. "Are you kidding? Of course I'm staying. There's nothing else I need to do, except be there with you. I'm not leaving you alone there. End of discussion."

His tone made me bristle, but I breathed through it, focusing on his words. And if I was honest, it was a relief to know he was going to be there with me.

His hands ran up and down my arm, pulling me to look at him. "Don't you know yet? You are important to me."

There was no denying the look in his eye. He meant what he said. But I couldn't respond, couldn't allow myself to read any further into those words. So I dropped my head and rested on his chest, gripping him a bit closer. I didn't want to think about how important he had become to me, it was too quick, too soon, too much. It wasn't supposed to happen like that.

My heart crumbled as he huskily sang the words to the song playing in the background, a slow rock song about feelings that wouldn't go away.

His voice was gravelly with emotion, not the prettiest singing voice, but it fit with the moment and slid through my cracks.

I buried my head on his bare chest and closed my eyes, hoping I'd be able to keep him for a while.

24: Numb

THE CONSTANT ACHE OF ANGER, TENSING ALL my muscles and making my teeth hurt from grinding, was my version of numb for the day.

I sat outside the small courtroom, Gage at my side, while the judge called in different people one at a time. Silas and Dexter were there too, to testify as witness's. We were made to wait, knowing nothing of what was happening beyond those doors. Numb.

My attackers were held in another room while the proceedings took place, until it was their time to be called in. It wasn't even a real court hearing; they were being tried as a juvenile so what was happening was more of a conference with a judge.

Numb.

But that all broke when I was called in. Not at first. At first I stayed numb while the prosecutor questioned me. I relayed the events evenly, just as I had practiced with Detective Andres. But the defense lawyer changed that.

"So, Ms. Sommers." The short man in a suite flipped open a leather file and read some notes. "You state that these young men attacked you, but all reports, including your statement, say that you hit one of the young men with your keys and then punched him in the face." He looked up from his file, eyebrows raised. "Is that correct?"

His question sparked the first flames of anger. "They were coming at me, I—"

He raised his hand, "Please stick to yes or no while I establish the facts."

I looked around the room. The Judge sat beside me in her high chair, staring down at me through her glasses. The two prosecutors were at a rectangle table just in front of me, whispering to each other, not giving me guidance. Behind them sat Anthony and Detective Andres, and both only stared at me.

I thought my teeth might crack with the pressure put on them as I grounded out, "Yes."

"May I present to your Honor medical records from my clients that show one young man suffered a broken nose as a result, and the other had a mild concussion."

A match thrown into my anger.

"Do you have my medical records?" I demanded, turning to the judge as the beady-eyed lawyer approached her.

The judge flicked her eyes from me, to the papers presented to her, and then back to the lawyer. "Mr. Richter, do you have any further questions for Ms. Sommers?"

He pressed his jacket to him as he sat down behind his table. "No, your Honor."

Does the prosecution have any further questions?"

One man rose up slightly. "Not at this time, but we would like to request the right to call her back in later, if necessary."

"Of course." Judge Goddard turned back to me with a curt smile. "Ms. Sommers, thank you for your time. You may step down now, but please stay nearby in case of further questioning."

Flames of anger burned as I marched out of the room.

Gage was up and by my side the minute the door closed, concern clear in his eyes. "What happened?"

"Those fucking assholes." My hand shook as I pointed to the door. "They tried to say I started it. That I injured them." I balled my fist and practically grunted with anger. I knew I had to calm down, but it was all too much.

"Who said that?" Dexter asked. "Nobody really believes that. I was just in there, they know you're the victim."

"It was those boy's lawyer. Why the hell do they even get a lawyer? Why the hell are they in juvenile court? This is all fucking pointless." I grabbed my head, the reality of it crashing around me. Fiery tears burned my eyes, evaporating before they could fall. "Even if they get the maximum sentence, it's crap. Six month in a juvenile detention center, crap."

Gage tried to pull me into his arms, but I pushed away, not wanting to be touched.

I should have known when Detective Andres told me they found the other two, but because they were not visibly involved on the video they were ordered to perform community service and write letters of apology. Which I hadn't received yet and didn't want.

The door to the courtroom opened and closed, a clerk coming out. "Mr. Gage Lawson?"

"That's me," he said, still hovering by my side.

"The judge will see you now." The clerk gestured into the room.

His hand brushed my elbow as he walked by. My anger had already begun to recede back to my original numb state. It didn't matter what any of us said or did. None of this mattered. It was all a waste of time.

I slumped onto the bench beside Dexter. The wide hallway had several benches lining the wall outside of the courtrooms. People scattered the hallway, all absorbed in their own business.

"You're right, Rea. This is crap and I'm sorry." He slid his arm around me and I let him. "Just think when this is over we can go to the gym and take it all out on the bags there. Hell, I'll even let you spar with me, just don't touch the face alright?" His large smile showed his white teeth, but it wasn't contagious this time.

Thinking about the gym did keep me from grinding my teeth to nothing though, and I nodded. "The gym is what I need."

The door opened and I looked up surprised, Gage hadn't been gone long. But it was Anthony that walked out of the room, hesitant as he looked towards me.

He walked over, hands in the pockets of his black police uniform. "Regan, are you doing okay?" his voice was soft, his brow furrowed with concern

Dexter's arm tightened on my shoulder as he looked up at the man. "She's fine."

I stood up, stepping in front of Dexter in an attempt to diffuse the situation. Dex had always been nice to Anthony, but since he found out Gage and I are whatever we are, he had stepped up the big brother act.

"I'm good. Just frustrated by all of this." I gestured to the courtroom.

He nodded and ran his hand along the back of his head. "The system doesn't always work the way we want it to."

I knew this, had a lifetime of experiences that should have been enough evidence, but still felt let down.

"I hope they'll at least let me know what the end result is. This not knowing, not being in there, is crazy."

His lip pulled up and he took my hand in his, squeezing. "I'll let you know, don't worry."

He dropped my hand as the door opened and Gage came out. Gage paused, staring for a moment and strolled over, taking his place next to me. It didn't escape me the way he raised himself up and lifted his head, making Anthony have to look up at him.

But Anthony didn't look towards him. He nodded at me. "Find me after? I'll be sure to tell you." Then he turned and walked back into the courtroom.

Gage looked to me with a raised brow, and I flopped back onto the bench.

"He's going to let me know what happens, since I'm not allowed in the room." I looked up at him. "How did it go in there?"

He shook his head as he sat next to me. "Like you said, this is crap, but hopefully it will be over soon." He moved his hand to my lower back and rubbed small circles.

* * *

"The primary offender, the one that you identified, he was given house arrest for six months, has to pay a portion of your medical bills, and attend counseling. The other three have to pay the remainder of your medical expenses, attend counseling, and continue to check in with their probation officer for six months," Anthony explained with disappointment clear on his face. "I'm sorry Regan."

He looked past me to where Gage, Dexter, and Silas waited by the exit to the courthouse, and his eyes landed on mine, a small smile on his face. "I'm sorry for the things I said before too. If you need me, anytime, call okay?"

I returned his wisp of a smile and took a step back. "I'm sorry too, and thank you." And as always, I meant it.

* * *

"I'm going to stay with you. Silas can deal with it on his own." Gage slipped his arm around me and I jumped back, shrugging him away.

"Go." I was frustrated, too many emotions in me to deal with his too. I wanted to get lost in my workout, pound it all away, and he would only be a distraction. "Really. I'm going to stay here and work out. You might as well go and get work done. I need some time alone."

Lines in his face deepened, proving my point. I couldn't handle this right now.

"Go. Please. I'll see you later, once I'm feeling better."

He nodded, jaw tight, and looked beyond me to where Dexter and Leona were playfully boxing in the ring. "Dex, can you close up if I go with Silas? And give Rea a ride back to our place tonight."

I rolled my eyes at his last direction. He hadn't even asked me. "I might go back to my place. Really I'm not good company right now."

Gage dropped his eyes back to me with a heavy sigh. "Fine. I'll give you some space. But call if you need me. I'll call when we're done to check on you."

I bit back my reply. He would be gone sooner if I stayed silent, and I knew I was being mean, I just couldn't help it.

"Have a good workout." He leaned forward, giving me a peck on the lips. His intent had been more, but I hadn't responded.

"Have a good meeting." I walked away and put on my headphones, ready to drown out reality.

By closing time I was drained. I could barely lift my arms to blow dry my hair after my shower, so I skipped it. It had started to rain anyways, and I just wanted to be in my own bed. Exhaustion was better than anger though, and sleep was my next best form of therapy.

"Leona did you get your phone from the office? Don't want to leave it again." Dex asked, spinning her around as we made our way to the door.

"Oh shoot. Let me go get it." She jogged back to Silas's office.

"Were the lights off in the girl's locker room?" he asked me.

"Yup and I switched the towels into the dryer too, so they won't get moldy."

His smile brightened and he raised his hand for a high five. "Good looking out."

Leona ran back out to us waving her phone, "All ready."

"Come here girl." Dexter extended his hand to her, tucking her under his arm as he walked out the front door. "I swear, I don't know—"

My heart crashed as four men with hoods pulled low closed in on us. Their guns were drawn as they hearded us back into the gym.

Leona's shrill scream pierced through the sound of blood rushing in me.

One of the men grabbed me, pinning my arms to my side as he wrapped his around me. The cold steel of a gun was pressed to my head, just behind my ear.

"Shut that bitch up," the tallest of the men shouted, the one with his arm extended, gun pointing at Dexter's forehead.

The guy holding Leona backed up, releasing her as the fourth man stepped forward and backhanded her, silencing her screams and sprawling her on the ground.

That man flicked his hand, shaking away the sting of the hit. "Damn hoe has a hard fucking head."

I had thought I was at the height of fear, until I heard his voice.

Damien turned towards me, still gripping his hand. His face cracked into an evil smile and his light brown eyes lit up as he pulled a gun from his pants, extending it towards me.

He took the few steps between us and jammed his gun to my cheek.

I tried to keep stiff, even with the gun burning my skin as it pressed and pulled into me, and I met his gaze.

"Time to make good on some debts." Damien smirked, pure evil rage in his eyes.

25: Debt

DAMIEN'S EYES SLITHERED OVER ME AND HE used two fingers to slowly unzip my jacket.

A trail of dread ran down me at the same time.

"I can think of a couple of different ways for you to pay." The pressure of the gun never let up as he stepped closer.

The guy behind me laughed with sickly sweet breath. He no longer had his gun on me and used both hands to pull my jacket off my arms causing Damien's smile to grow.

Leona was back to crying, I could hear her panic rising and the volume increasing with hysterics. It cracked the shield I was trying to put up. This wasn't just me. I wanted her to be quiet though, she was only making things worse; I could tell by the way Damien's smile dropped.

He suddenly left me, building momentum in his strides, and he kicked Leona in the stomach.

She grunted as the air escaped her and then she was quiet. To my relief she curled herself into a silent ball and Damien stalked back to me.

Dexter had called out when Leona was kicked and the tall one in front of him pushed him down and was now kicking him in the stomach.

My stomach spasmed with each kick I witnessed, as if I were being kicked myself. The man behind me tightened his hold on my arms, keeping me up, and then Damien was in front of me and yanked me to him.

He gripped me so my back was flush with his front. His hand wrapped around me grabbing my chin, forcing me to witness Dexter being beat, and his other hand held the gun to my temple.

"Where were we?" His wet breath dripped into my ear and he ran his empty hand down my neck and over my shirt. "Ways to pay…" he pushed my head to the side with his gun and ran his tongue along my neck before sucking on a spot just above my shoulder.

I didn't even care what he did. My heart was breaking as another man joined the tall one and kicked Dexter in the face. The tall one crouched down, grabbed Dexter by the shirt and lifted him up some, saying something I couldn't hear. Dexter's head rolled slightly. When he lifted it, blood poured from his nose.

Damien's hand slid into my pants and all I could do was stand there as hell took up residence around me.

The tall one, holding Dexter up, looked over at us, and his eyes flared. "What the fuck Dee, we don't have time for that shit. Drop the girl and go check the fucking office."

Damien removed his hand, but still kept his gun on me. "She's part of it too. She runs with Rusnak's crew."

"Rock didn't mention no girl. Finish this job, we ain't got all night."

Damien dragged me to where Leona was and tossed me down, stomping to the back of the gym.

"Now, where's Rocks money?" Tall man turned back to Dexter, gun under his chin.

"I told him. After my fight Saturday," Dexter's voice was strained with pain.

My shock shook me so hard it felt like the building was collapsing. I attempted to scoot to Leona, but the man with the gun aimed at us told me to stay still.

"There ain't time for that. He's cutting all ties tonight, but first he's getting what's owed him. So try again. Where's his fucking money?"

Leona started sobbing again and the man with the gun on us, standing a couple feet away, eyed her. His face dropped into a deeper frown.

"Shhh" I tried to get her to stop, but it was no use.

The man crouched low beside her, grabbed her hair and yanked her head up, only to slam it into the ground.

And she didn't move or make a sound after that. But blood began pooling around her head.

Damien and another guy came out from the office. The other man, in the Raven's hoody said, "There's a safe back there, but we can't open it."

"Fuck's sake. Get your ass over here. Hold him. I'll get it," Tall one said as he dropped Dexter back to the ground and rose into standing. "Dee you're with him. Leave the girls alone."

Ravens jacket stood next to the littlest man, the one with his gun trained on me and only me now that Leona was unconscious.

Tall man gestured for Ravens sweater guy to come with him and they went back into the office.

Damien stood over Dexter, gun pointed down at him. "You think your running with some big boys, Regan?"

He swiftly kicked Dexter in the back. "They ain't shit no more. You choose the wrong crew. After tonight, this is Rocks world."

I just stared at him. I didn't know how to process any of this, still reeling from the fact that Dexter was the target here, not me. Dexter, my funny friend with seemingly no cares in the world, brought this chaos.

He licked his lips, tongue balanced on the top one for a moment as he cocked his head, considering me. "But it might not be too late for you. I'd take you on, give you a job." His smile glided up. "After I tried you out of course."

I didn't say anything, just sat on the padded gym floor and said nothing. Damien didn't like that.

He stormed over to where I sat, gun pressed to my forehead so hard I had to lean back, supporting myself with my arms behind me.

"That's right Bitch, you should be scared. Scared of me, scared of my boys. Scared of what I might do with this gun." He dragged the gun roughly down my face, over my eyes and cheek, and jammed it into my mouth. Forcing me to open wide or lose my teeth. "Show me how you can suck?" his voice was back to an eerie whisper.

A voice yelled from behind me, from the office. "We got it. Let's go."

Damien looked up as the two men jogged out with full backpacks. He removed the gun from my mouth, but still kept it pointed at my head as he stood up.

Tall one went over to Dexter and kicked him again, making him groan, and then put his gun to his face. "Silas will be getting his own warning. Cause that's all this is. A warning." He shook his book bag. "We're all clear now, debt's paid. But don't come around no more. Rock ain't fuckin' with your boss. Business is canceled."

As the three made their way to the door, backwards, gun's still drawn, Damien said, "Ask your boy, who can't fuck with who now?"

He tossed me one last smirk before putting his gun away and following the others out the door.

The click of the door closing was a gunshot starting my actions. I popped up off the ground and sprinted to the door, locking it, bolting it. I leaned against it for a moment and listened, there was no sound and I released an inch of tension in a single breath.

I flipped on the lights and surveyed the gym with a clinical detachment. Dexter was by Leona now. He must have crawled to where she was; a trail of blood spotted his path. She groaned as he lifted her head carefully to his lap. Her face was streaked with blood, her hair matted with it.

I dashed to the front desk and grabbed a stack of towels and the first aid kit hanging on the wall, carefully balancing it all in my hurried walk to where they were.

Dexter's nose was slowly oozing deep red blood, and I tossed him a towel dismissively and focused on Leona.

Kneeling in front of them, I scooped Leona's head in my hands and moved her to my lap.

Looking down at the blood in his lap Dexter began to rock and cry low, "I'm so sorry, I'm so sorry..." was on repeat.

I looked up, anger burning strong. "Call your brother," I demanded then pressed a towel to Leona's face, trying to find where she was bleeding. It was everywhere, thin, bright red blood everywhere, and more flowing by the second.

Dexter stilled. "I can't. He—I'll call Silas."

My heart raced, recalling what the guy said to Dexter, "Silas will get his own warning."

I pulled away the blood soaked towel and found the source. Her eyebrow was split. Opening the first aid kit I looked for anything that could be of use, not really sure what I should use.

Dexter was still sitting there, doing nothing but staring and bleeding.

"Call him then. Now. Do something," I shrieked, panic starting to rise.

I took a calming breath and dumped the overstuffed first aid kit, to better search through the contents. I found small butterfly bandages and took a handful, as well as a large bandage, Neosporin, and gauze.

Leona groaned again as I patted at her wound with the gauze and pinched the skin together to see if the bleeding would slow. It did. I tried to use comforting words as I taped her wound shut with the small bandages and put the large bandage over it all. I had forgotten to use the ointment, but wasn't about to undo everything I just did. Especially since new blood was no longer flowing over her face.

Dexter finally had his phone out. He had his head tilted back and towel held to the center of his face as he made the call to Silas.

"Gage," Dexter's voice was flat. After a moment of silence he said, "We're still at the gym." Then he hung up the phone and pulled the towel away, looking at me. "Gage answered Silas's phone." His voice was a whisper of shock. "Something must have happened with them too. He's on his way."

I couldn't worry about them yet; I would have to wait till they got here.

Focused on Leona again, who had started crying in my lap, I wiped her face with another towel, trying to clean up the remaining blood. I used a wet wipe that had spilled from the kit, attempting to clean up the already drying blood on her face.

Her small whimpers were like nails on a chalkboard. I tried to shush her and mumbled words I didn't believe. "Everything's alright now, they're gone, we're safe." But there was an edge to my voice as a hard anger crept in and I met Dexter's eyes.

"I think my nose is broken," he whispered.

I nodded my head. It was; even in its grotesquely swollen state I could see the bend in it. "Why? What have you done?" my voice was icy.

He dropped his eyes and shook his head, his shoulders slumped over.

The sound of the locks at the front door caused a white cold terror to surge through me and I pushed Leona off of me as I stood up, looking for the nearest weight to use as a weapon. But if they were back with guns, there was nothing I could do.

It receded as quickly as it came when the door opened revealing Gage and Silas. Silas was holding a blood soaked shirt up to his head, but Gage looked fine at first glance.

Gage scanned the room and in the next moment he was in front of me, eyes searching my body. "You're bleeding?" he tried to grab my blood spotted shirt.

I stepped away, pushing his hand at the same time. "It's not my blood, its Leona's."

He let out a breath of air, eyes still moving over me. "You're alright?"

"I'm fine," I lied. I didn't feel fine, but physically I guess I was.

One hand circled around my neck and the other around my back as he pulled me in, and my heart leaped to my throat. He kissed my forehead and trailed the kisses to my cheek before I pulled away.

"I'm fine," I repeated with more strength. "But Dexter and Leona were hurt."

I gestured to them. Silas was sitting with Dexter, hands on his face. Silas made a quick motion, adjusting Dexter's nose. I thought I heard a sick crunch under Dexter's yell, but couldn't be sure.

Leona's cries grew louder, and I sat beside her, trying to give comfort. She buried her head into my lap and curled up on the floor.

At least this kept Gage away. I didn't trust any of these men in the room, but couldn't think of my next move.

"What happened?" Gage asked.

I took a breath and spoke with a surprisingly calm voice, focusing on a spot of blood on the floor. "Four men came in with guns and they emptied your safe."

"Fuck." Silas jumped and ran back to the office, slapping the bandage in his hands hastily to his cut forehead.

"They didn't hurt you?" Gage asked softly, kneeling beside me.

I shook my head. "They were here for Dexter."

Dexter dropped his head, hiding in the folds of the towel he still held to his face.

"We have a lot to talk about Dexter. But first let's get the girls out of here." Gage stood up, his tone final.

Silas walked out of the office like a ghost, his face lifeless and movements slow.

"How bad?" Gage asked him.

Silas's blank eyes looked to Dexter. "We're fucking dead."

"All of it?" Dexter stood up, voice shaky and Silas nodded.

Gage looked between the two, brows furrowed. "How much money are we talking about?"

"It's not money. I was holding for Rusnak and they took it. All of it."

Gage took a deep breath. "What the fuck have you two been doing?"

Dexter was shaking. "I'm sorry. Gage, I'm so sorry. You've got to help me."

Gage charged him, pinning him to the front wall, his forearm across his neck. "What have you done? I give you everything." Gage's voice cracked with more than rage. "Why did you do this?" Dexter's face was darkening with trapped blood and Gage released him, letting him drop.

He turned to Silas, finger pointed at him. "This is your fault. Why the hell would you bring him into this?"

Silas put his arms up in surrender. "Let's talk about this later." He glanced at us, making it clear Leona and I weren't meant to be part of this conversation.

"We deserve to know, too. We were brought into this and I want to know why?" I said from the floor. Leona only gripped me tighter, trying to hide from everything.

I had been an idiot to not want answers from Gage that day we went to Nan's house. I thought not knowing would keep me safe. I was wrong.

Gage glanced at me and after a few deep breaths he said, "Let's go. We need to leave."

I helped Leona to her feet. Dexter came over to help support her, but Leona whimpered and turned into me further, avoiding his touch. I couldn't blame her. Dexter's face crumpled further than it already was and his body drooped as he walked away.

Once we were all in the SUV, Gage and Silas up front, and Dexter, Leona, and I in the back, Leona finally spoke.

"I want to go home." Her voice cracked through her tears.

Gage met my eyes in the rear view mirror. "Not tonight."

She tightened her arm around me. "Please." Her sobs escalated again. "I just want to go home."

"Maybe we should drop them off," Silas said.

"Not until I've figured out what's going on. They can—"

"They'll be safer away from us, at their own place," Silas insisted.

"And then what? Her roommates start questioning her? They go to the cops? They stay with us tonight."

My heart dropped to my stomach at what this all meant. "Where are we going then?"

"My house," Gage said, turning right onto a busy road.

A wave of panic hit me. "Shouldn't we go somewhere else? A hotel? Maybe drive far away, to another state?"

"I can't leave. I have to figure out what all went down tonight. And we can't go to a hotel like this, everyone's injured it would cause suspicion." He softened his stern voice as he looked at me in the rear view again, "My house is safe. It's protected."

I was grinding my teeth. This didn't sound like a safe plan. "Who protects your house?"

"Me. But I don't think anyone will come anyways. They already delivered their message and took what they wanted."

I held little confidence in his words. I didn't believe him. But I saw little choice except to go along. The night felt too dangerous to be alone.

Leona kept her arms around me, face hidden, even as we walked into the house.

Gage turned to me and ordered, "Take her upstairs to the guest room. Help her calm down."

I didn't want to go. I wanted to stay and hear what was going on. I needed to know.

At my hesitation Dexter stepped up. "I'll take her."

But Leona's nails cut into my stomach, through my shirt. "No. You leave her alone." My eyes locked on Dexter, steel in my tone.

Getting her to bed would make it easier to ask questions. Her constant crying was grating on my nerves.

I found Benadryl in Gage's bathroom medicine cabinet and gave it to Leona, hoping to get her to sleep. Her blow to the head concerned me, and I remembered hearing in school that you're supposed to keep those people awake, but I thought she'd feel better if she slept through this.

And she did. After ten minutes of lying with her, her breathing evened, and she was out.

I escaped from the room and went down the steps, listening to the raised voices in the living room.

"Poker? You borrowed money from Rock for a fucking poker game?" Gage's voice was incredulous.

I rounded the corner into the room. Dexter was sitting on the couch, head in his hands. Silas leaned against the front window, eyes looking out, and a rifle by his side. A metallic taste filled my mouth at the sight of the gun, acid rising in my stomach. Gage stood in front of Dexter, hands spread, questioning him.

Without his coat on I noticed that the back of his shirt was torn and blood circled around it. But it looked like dry blood at least. My mind raced, trying to understand.

"I'm good at poker. I usually win. Just this night I didn't. I had bet using the money I knew I'd get from my fight this Saturday. I've done it before and its fine. But I don't know what happened tonight. Why that all changed." He looked up at Gage. "This wasn't my fault. Something else is going on."

Gage's hands clenched and anger lined his face. Dexter moved back on reflex as Gage gripped his shirt, lifting him into standing. "You got involved with people like Rock. You did that. You took the risks." He tossed him down onto the couch and turned around trying to bring down his rage.

He spotted me at the door and turned back to Dexter. "And now you put Regan and Leona in danger. For Christ's sake, your girlfriend's up stairs with who knows what injuries. This is your fault."

Silas pulled away from the window. "Rock isn't the big problem. It's Rusnak. What are we going to tell him? I've got to get his money or shit back, or it's me and Dexter that will pay."

"Why is Dexter involved in that? Why are you?" Ice ran through his words.

"It was supposed to be easy money. Dexter is good at sales," Silas said simply.

He crashed to the floor, Gage on top of him in the blink of an eye. Gage's fists pounded on Silas and the blood on the back of his shirt began to spread, he had opened up whatever injury was there.

I just stood and watched, detached, not caring what happened to these men. They could destroy each other and I don't think I would lend a hand to any of them.

Dexter got up and put his arms around Gage, trying to stop him, without success. Gage slowed on his own. His body shook as he stood. Silas groaned and rolled to his side, spitting out blood and a tooth.

Gage stood up, an animal rage still in his eyes. Turning to me he demanded, "Go back upstairs and stay there."

The look he had scared me, especially with the spray of blood on his shirt and neck from Silas. But I needed to see what was happening. I was part of this now. "I—I want to know."

He took a few steps towards me, his fire barely contained. "I. Said. Go. Upstairs. Now."

With him towering over me, I knew I had to listen. My shaky legs carried me up the stairs. I went into the guest room with Leona. She was still asleep.

Sitting on the edge of the bed, millions of thoughts ran through me, but none of them made sense. I kept waiting for the shock to come, for my breathing to escape me, for panic to set in, but instead, all I felt was cold—a prickly, needley cold all over.

Every now and then I would hear shouting and then I heard footsteps stomp up the steps, but nobody came to the room.

A while later the door opened, but I didn't move, not even to look at him. I knew it was Gage.

"I've got to leave. But you'll be safe here. Dexter is downstairs."

I looked up. He must have showered and changed his clothes. All signs of blood gone.

"Just in case. Take this." He extended a small black gun to me but I just stared. "Have you ever held one, used one? Here's the safety—"

I stopped his demonstration by taking it, feeling the heavy cold weight in my hand. "I've used one." At his questioning look I explained, "At a gun range with Nan."

I stared at the gun in my hand, on my lap. The icy feeling shattered me.

He reached a hand towards me and I leaned away. He dropped it, shuffling his feet.

"I'm sorry about all of this. I'm going to make it better." He walked away and my heart pounded and strained painfully.

"Wait," I choked out without thinking.

He paused at the doorway, looking at me.

I looked up at him and opened my mouth a few times before I finally pleaded, my voice strained, "Don't go."

He was sitting next to me a second later, arms wrapping me up into him. "I'll be back soon. I promise," his voice was soft.

I gripped the front of his shirt, not wanting to let him go into danger. I was confused about everything, except that I wanted him safe and leaving wasn't.

Doing the only thing I could think of I pressed my lips to his neck, his lips were too far a reach.

He grabbed my wrists and held me away, leaning himself back.

I stared at his hands between us, heart sinking.

"I've got to go. This will be over in the morning." He stood up and walked away, the door not making a sound as he closed it.

Tears escaped my eyes for the first time tonight. It would be over in the morning, that's what I was afraid of.

26: Sorry

DEXTER OPENED THE DOOR AND PEEKED IN.

"How is she?" He nodded to Leona.

I stood from my cross-legged position on the floor by the window. I had been watching for anything, hoping to see Gage's SUV pull up. I set the gun on the nightstand, reluctantly parting with the security.

"She's hurt." I was pissed at Dexter and didn't want to make this any easier on him. He was the reason Gage left. He was the reason Leona was passed out on the bed with a bloody bandage.

I swallowed my anger to focus on her; it felt better to have something to do. "She must still be bleeding. She needs stitches. Do you have bandages or something so I can change those?"

We both stood on either side of the bed. Dexter brushed her hair back from her head and lowered his head to hers.

I shoved his shoulders from across the bed. "Focus," I demanded.

He stood up tall, throat moving as he swallowed. He looked to me with heavy eyes that were already bruising from his broken nose and nodded before walking out of the room.

I looked out the window and my muscles vibrated with nerves and mixed emotions. If Dexter hadn't looked so beat up, I would have punched him. I needed to punch something.

I held my breath every time headlights came up the road, but they always passed by or parked, going somewhere else. For someone else.

Dexter came back into the room with a handful of supplies and dropped them on the bed beside Leona.

"We've got super glue. Use that to keep the cut closed."

"Keep an eye out. I'll take care of her." I nodded towards the window.

Her eyes fluttered but didn't open as I removed the bandages. Squeezing her cut to keep it closed, I cleaned up the surrounding skin. I held my breath as I applied the super glue. It worked. The clear liquid dried on contact, bonding the skin together. I placed a new bandage over it and Leona's hands moved to mine as she groaned, opening her eyes.

"Rea? I hurt," she mumbled.

"I know. Try and go back to sleep," I said, too stressed to find my gentle voice.

She looked down at herself and her hand floated to her head, patting at her hair and cut. "Ugh. I need to get out of these clothes and get all this blood off of me." Her voice began rising in panic and she squeezed her eyes with the pain of it.

Dexter moved to the side of the bed, bouncing with nerves. "I'll get her some clothes." He ran out of the room.

"You can wash your hair, but don't get the bandage wet. Maybe a bath?" It sounded nice. I would love to wash the night off of me, but couldn't. I needed to stay by a window, to keep watch for what might happen next. To keep watch for Gage to return so I could breathe again.

At her nod I helped her up. She seemed steady enough on her feet so I let her walk to the bathroom on her own, the one connected to this room. The sound of water rushing filled the room as she started the bath.

Dexter returned and stared at the bathroom door. "Did she say anything? About me?"

I flicked my eyes away from him, back to the window. "No."

He sighed. "I'm sorry. I really messed things up." He sat on the edge of the bed.

"I don't want to hear sorry. I want to know what the hell happened. Why?" I snapped.

He continued to stare at the door where Leona was. "I don't know. Something went down tonight, bigger than what I did."

I waited for more, but he didn't say.

"Tell me what you do know," I demanded.

"I like to play poker. I go to games at different places, with different groups and Silas invited me to Rock's. Gage's uncle, Nick, goes too. Some other people I know as well, all people that I grew up around. A lot of the times I would win, so they'd always invite me back. Sometimes I'd lose or not have cash on hand, but they knew I was good for it. Then the other week it was a high stakes game, and I was all in. It was a different group playing, though, so Rock spotted me some money. He's done it before. He said I'd pay him back when I won the hand or when I won my fight, this Saturday." He raised his hands slightly, confused amazement clear. "But they showed up tonight."

"And what about this stuff they stole?"

"They took more than I owed Rock. Silas owed him too, but still. They took more than what was owed. And that... that's the worst part. They took more than we can pay back. And it's not Rock we owe, but Rusnak."

"Who is that?"

Dexter shrugged. "I never met him. I always went through Nick or Silas. But he's the one in charge, the one we have to worry about owing."

I tapped my finger on the gun sitting on the nightstand, unable to keep the nervous energy in. "And that's where Gage is? I still don't get why tonight happened."

"I don't know either. Gage left with Silas. That's all I know."

I went back to looking out the window and waited for Leona. When she came out Dexter jumped off the bed, going to her.

"Let me help you. I'm so sorry Lee. Please let me help," he pleaded as she stood warily. She nodded and he put his arm around her, walking her to the bed.

Tucking her in he lay beside her and I was shocked that she even curled into him a little.

"We need to talk, Dex," she whispered.

His eyes shone with tears. "I know baby. Rea can you give us a moment?"

I turned to them, looking directly at Leona and she nodded. I picked up the gun and walked out with disbelief. She had been clinging to me earlier, a crying mess, and now she was ready to forgive so easily?

Since they kicked me out I went to Gage's room. The large master bedroom stretched across the house, views of both the street and the harbor. It was probably the best room to be in anyways, for lookout purposes. And it had a chair at least. The guest room was bare minimum but his room had style. A simple dark style, but some extras like a TV and large lounger type chairs. I scooted one to the window overlooking the street and sat with the gun in my lap, so wired I was in no danger of falling asleep.

Hours later the sun began to rise, and the sky turned a muted dark gray. Seeing the familiar headlights of Gage's SUV, I hopped up, heart in my throat as the car pulled into the garage. There had only been one person driving; it was too dark to tell who, but there was no one in the passenger seat.

I was frozen in spot for a moment, not allowing myself to think anything. The stomping up the stairs got me moving. I gripped the gun and stepped out of the room, into the hallway.

All the tension in my muscles released, and my stomach spasmed, almost crumpling me, as Gage appeared at the top of the steps, in one piece. His ear was bloody, as well as the collar of his jacket, but he was standing.

I dropped the gun as we both moved to each other, wrapping each other up. I couldn't stop the tears from coming and my body shook with relief. His solid warmth reassured me as his arms tightened around me.

"You're alright?" I asked, pulling my head back to look at him. My hand went up to his ear, hovering over the dried blood.

He nodded and pressed his lips to mine, sucking me in, as necessary as air.

My hands roamed his body, more for reassurance that he was here than passion. He pressed me back to the wall, hands moving to either side of my face as he deepened the kiss.

He pressed his forehead to mine with little pecks on my lips and cheek. He gripped my hair and his breath hitched with his restrained effort.

"We've got to go. Get what you need, but we have to leave. Now."

I would have stepped away if the wall wasn't blocking me. I stiffened in his grip. "What?"

"We're going to leave. Out of state, like you said." His grip in my hair loosened and he petted me, moving one hand down my hair. A failed attempt to soothe me. "It's only temporary."

He stepped back and realeased me as he looked me over. "Change your clothes, take a shower. We have time. But we need to leave. I'll get Dexter."

My mind swam, trying to catch up. My thoughts were still stuck on the relief of him being here.

"I've got to work. I don't have anything here. I can't leave."

He gripped my arms suddenly, an edge to his voice. "Don't fight me on this. It's only until next week. I'll explain later, but listen to me. It has to be this way."

His tone scared me and I still wasn't clear on the situation, so I listened. I changed out of my blood-dried clothes and into Dexter's shirt and sweatpants; Gage's clothes were too large.

* * *

"Can we go to our place, to get some things?" Leona asked as she slid into the backseat of the SUV, Rocky, the cat, in her hands.

"No. I don't want your roommates questioning anything. You can buy what you need when we get where we're going."

I buckled myself into the passenger seat and questioned, "Where are we going?"

"New York. My fight is there next Friday. I'll get a hotel until then."

I narrowed my eyes. "Why? What happened tonight? What does it have to do with your fight?" I was surprised he was even thinking about it. For some reason I thought this night blew up both of our careers in boxing. But maybe it only ended mine, at least until I could find a manager I could trust, which may never happen.

"Where's Silas?" I whispered my last question. I may not like him, but I didn't want him dead.

"He's fine, but he's not coming with us." Gage drove out of the neighborhood, and at a red light, he finally responded to my other questions. "I'll explain, but not now." His hand gripped the steering wheel, turning his knuckles white. "I need some time with my thoughts before I explain."

My panic was choking me. "So you can make up a story? I want the truth. I want to know now, before I go off with you."

Dexter spoke up from the back, "Rea, he's doing what he thinks is best. Leave him alone for now. We've got time to talk later, everyone's exhausted."

I turned on him. "Shut up. I'm not talking to you." We were turning onto the ramp, crossing the bridge out of Baltimore. Reality was settling in, I had been holding it in all night and I was cracking. "Tell me why we have to leave now."

A low rumble, almost a growl, vibrated Gage. "Things aren't over yet. It didn't get resolved last night. So I'm getting you the fuck out of this city until it's clear." He breathed deeply, pulling back in his anger. "I've had a rough fucking night. Can you give me some time to calm down before you ask all your damn questions?"

I crossed my arms and looked out the window, anger and dread pressing on me, making it hard to breathe.

Leona leaned her head on Dexter and they both fell asleep before we were out of Maryland.

Gage's eyes flicked to me for about the millionth time when we crossed into New Jersey. "Have you slept yet?" He asked softly.

I gritted my teeth. "Oh, are we asking questions now?"

He sighed. "I'm sorry for that. I—you don't know Regan. Last night was bad."

I widened my eyes, but my voice was soft as I looked at him. "I know last night was bad. I don't know the details, but I know that. I didn't sleep; it was bad for me too. Not knowing is killing me."

"It was cocaine. That's what Silas and Dexter were holding. And lots of it. I went to Rusnak first, laid it all out, and we tried to get it back. But Rock, he had tonight planned and was hidden away somewhere. He made a new contact and cut Rusnak out of the deal. Rusnak found out last night, that's why Rock sent his men out to collect anything owed that was connected to him. But his boys took more than they should when they cleared Silas's safe."

"So Silas and Dexter still owe Rusnak?" I tried to make sense of his story.

He glanced at me, before watching the road again. "Silas still owes, but not Dexter. I took his spot. I thought I had been keeping him out, by not telling him things. But he still saw these people; he knew them. I gave him the connection but never told him about the danger. It's my fault."

I shook my head. Dexter's wasn't a kid anymore, he should have realized. "What's next?"

"I get you to New York and you stay until my fight. Then I can pay everything back." He glanced at me. "You should try to rest now."

"So should you," I countered.

He smiled slightly and nodded. "When we get to the hotel, I will."

I nodded. I would stay up until then too.

* * *

Dexter put his arm around Leona and walked her into one of the bedrooms of the hotel suite. I sat on the couch alone, unsure of what to do now.

Dexter and Leona seemed to be treating this as a vacation, they had pointed out buildings and signs as we had driven on the busy city streets. But they were crazy, and I knew better.

Gage came out of the washroom and approached me, hesitant, hand extended. "Lay down with me? We both need some sleep."

I swallowed. My heart was stuck in my throat, and I stood without grabbing his hand.

We walked to the remaining bedroom, and I lay on the bed, head resting on the pillow without comfort. I turned to the side and stared at the wall.

The bed moved as Gage climbed in behind me. His arm circled around me, severing the hold on my emotions with a painful slice.

I turned around, facing him, burring my face in his shirt. He surrounded me with his warmth, smell, and body. Tears pricked at my eyes and I struggled to make sense of my churning emotions, they pulled every which way.

"I'm glad you're okay," I said breathless, the one thing I knew. "What happened? Here?" I put my hand to his ear, he had cleaned off the blood, but it was a marbled red and blue and there was a gash behind it. "And your back?" I asked, recalling the blood through his shirt before he left.

He pulled me in tighter, resting his head on top of mine. "I was hit with the butt of a gun in the ear. But I was cut in the back. When Silas and I went to our meeting, before everything, some guys attacked us as we left. Four of them, they tried to get us into the car. I disarmed one, but another tried to cut me from behind, only a graze. They underestimated us though. Silas and I got away without much damage besides my cut and Silas was hit in the head." His body tightened in my arms. "I knew Silas was still involved with crap like this. I just ignored all the signs. I'm sorry."

I nodded, wordless. I had seen the signs too with Gage, and had chosen to ignore them. I had walked into all this and now I was stuck, wanting to push him away, but unable to.

"What happened when you left?"

He pulled away to look into my eyes, hands moving down my hair and back. "No more questions. Not now. I want to rest and hold you, and feel like everything's okay. Even just for a moment."

The pleading and sadness in his eyes pulled at all my strings, undoing me. I didn't know what tomorrow would bring, but for now I wanted the same thing. I needed it too, even though I knew it was a lie. I knew nothing was okay and I could feel the unspoken words between us. He was holding back something important, but I'd let it go for now.

I curled into him and once he became heavy with sleep, his even breathing lulled me into unconsciousness.

I woke up to an empty bed. Evening light shone through the window. A note, with not enough words, on the nightstand table, written in Gage's small, tidy print.

Stay here. I'll call soon. Sorry.

27: Abandoned

I REREAD THE LETTER AND FLIPPED IT over, but it was blank. I looked around the bed and floor; there had to be more, but there wasn't.

I grabbed my phone, heart in my throat when I saw the red icon's notifying me of a missed call and message. But the screen turned black at my touch as it drained of power, and I didn't have a charger.

Running into the room Dexter and Leona were staying in, I knocked briefly then opened the door.

"Do you have your phone charger?" I asked quickly, looking at the couple lying on the bed watching TV.

Dexter raised one arm, pointing to a black duffle bag. "In the front zipper there."

I knelt by the bag, unzipping it. "Your brother left."

"I know. He left us some money though. We can get dinner if you're hungry," Dexter spoke matter-of-fact.

My head whipped to him, charger abandoned. "You know? Where did he go?"

He sat up in bed, dropping his arm from Leona as he watched me. "He had to go back to B-more, he didn't tell you?" He asked carefully.

I sucked in a breath, fighting the choking constriction of my muscles. "When did he tell you?"

He shifted his eyes then got out of bed to come over to the bag. He pulled the charger out and handed it to me with an uneasy smile.

"He told me before we left. He was only dropping us off. He's coming back Thursday."

I was sinking. Gage was keeping too much from me and I didn't understand why. Moreover, I didn't like it. He could tell Dexter, the boy he was risking his life for, why not me?

Dexter put a hand on my shoulder and I stood up, knocking it off.

"It's alright. He's going to be back in less than a week. In the meantime we can hang out here. Look." Dexter popped up and went to the nightstand and picked up his wallet. He pulled out a card and extended it towards me. "He left us a credit card to get whatever we want."

I stared at him. Was he serious right now?

Leona had been watching our exchange. She sat up on the bed with a large smile. "We can go shopping tomorrow Rea and get some clothes. It will be fun."

"Don't make me fuckin' slap you," I said, incredulous.

"What?" She snapped, straightening up in bed.

"Whoa," Dexter exclaimed at the same time, dragging me out of the room by my arm.

I jerked free when he closed the door and brought my hand to my head, trying to grasp at any sane thought.

"Rea, calm down." Dexter stood watching me.

"Calm down? What the hell is he doing? I thought he only had to fight this Friday and then everything would be done. But he wasn't being honest. I feel like I was just kidnapped." I paused to take a few breaths, but only succeeded in feeding the flames of my anger. "And you two expect me to be happy that we have money to spend? I thought that was the problem to begin with, not enough money to pay back. Where is this money coming from? And what is your brother doing now? What type of—"

"Rea stop." Dexter grabbed my shoulders and shook me slightly.

I couldn't stand to look at his bruised face, but I did. "Tell. Me. Everything. Now," I said between clenched teeth.

He dropped my shoulders and nodded. "I don't know that much. Gage had to go back to deal with Silas and Rusnak." He shrugged his shoulders. "But I don't know what that means. As for the money... Rea, they owe over a hundred grand. What we spend isn't touching that. And he didn't kidnap any of us. Don't you get it? He wants to keep us away from it all. It's to protect us."

I pulled my hair back with frustration, wishing for a hair band to secure it. Even my hair on my shoulders pissed me off.

"They owe? No Dexter, you owe but you're letting your brother go clean up your mess and you don't even care—"

"I do care." He cut me off, anger clear in his bruised face. "That's my brother Rea. I care. But I know him and I know he knows what he's doing. He's going to be alright."

The way Dexter said the last part, a bit shaky, belied the confidence he was trying to show. And it sucked the anger out of me. I sat on the couch, hollow.

Dexter moved to sit next to me. "You'll see. It's all going to be alright. He'll be back soon, only a few days."

I could tell he was still trying to convince himself, he had no chance of convincing me that it would be okay. The phone charger in my hand reminded me of my missed call and dead phone. Leaving Dexter on the couch, I went back to my room and plugged it in.

I kept tapping on the screen, impatient as I tried to get it to light up. When it finally did, I froze. My missed call was from Nan. An all-new kind of fear started sliding down my spine. Before my mind went crazy with questions I pressed the voicemail button and listened. Her voice was a whisper.

"Regan, please be okay. I—Damien's fucking losing it, talking all kinds of crazy. I don't know what happened between you two, but I hope you're okay. Don't call me back, I'll call when I can."

My fingers shook over my screen. I couldn't call her back, she had said before Damien would be pissed to know we were talking. Even though she was calling because she was worried about me, that message made me worry about her.

I called Gage, hoping for more information, but it went straight to voice mail. I was a breath away from freaking out. My muscles were urging me to throw my phone, but I knew I needed it. Especially since all my money was left back at my house. I was stuck.

Punching the pillows and bed didn't help; neither did the push-ups I hammered out. The night had already settled on the city, but it was still bright, lit up. I wanted out of the room, but that could wait till morning. Out of options, I put my headphones on and let music drown out my emotions enough for me to sleep.

* * *

They spent the weekend in the hotel room. Dexter and Leona were self-conscious of their bruises, so mostly ordered food up. And I was out as often as I could, doing nothing but walking around. I broke and used Gage's card to buy essentials like underwear, toothbrush, and a change of clothes, but little else. I barely even ate. And Gage didn't call me until Monday.

I was in my room, doing sit-ups in bed just for something to do, when Dexter knocked.

"Rea, you decent?" He called through the door.

I sat up. "Yeah, come in."

His bright grin looked better today; the purple shadows of bruising were blending into a yellow and brown. But his smile still made me want to punch him.

"She's been good. Out touring the city." He was talking into his phone and I hopped off the bed. "Alright, Alright, here she is." He extended it to me.

I took it and paused, swallowing my anxiety. "Hello?"

"You like the city?" Gage's voice sounded casual and smooth.

My heart dropped, and I had to turn away from Dexter to hide the emotion hearing his voice had caused. He sounded fine and alive. And I let the relief wash over me for a second. The anger quickly followed.

"What the hell do you think you're doing? You left without saying anything!" I paused as I heard his rumble of a laugh. "What the hell is wrong with you? This isn't funny."

"Sorry," he swallowed his laughter, but his voice still held amusement. "I missed that fire of yours. I like hearing it. I'll be there soon and when it's all done I can explain everything. I promise."

I shook my head, speechless. I didn't believe him.

"Say something," he requested softly.

"Why should I? You're not going to tell me anything. You're going to keep making decisions for me. I want this to be over." I was desolate; nothing was in my control.

"I know and I'm doing what I can. I have to go, but I want you to know one thing," His voice dropped as he said, "I love you." Before I could respond he hung up.

With the phone still pressed to my ear, I took a few breaths, smoothing my face before turning back around to Dexter.

"What did he say? Is everything alright?" he asked as he took his phone back.

"He didn't say anything. He never does. Did he tell you anything?"

"Not really." Dexter frowned as he looked at me. "Come here Rea. I really am sorry about everything. Sorry you are involved in all this now." He attempted to pull me into one of his hugs.

Really, I kind of wanted one right now. I felt all alone and out of control, but I didn't want one from him. "Leave me alone." I threw myself back in the bed as Dexter left the room.

* * *

My phone ringing woke me up from my nap. I seemed to be taking more and more of those as the week went by.

Nan's name lit up the screen and I quickly answered.

"Regan? Oh God, I'm glad you answered. Are you okay?" Her voice was nasally, but she wasn't whispering.

"Yeah, are you?" I replied.

"Me? Yeah, I'm good." She dismissed the question. "What happened last week? He came back all kinds of crazy. Talking 'bout you and what he would do next time he saw you, how you wouldn't be so lucky. Girl, tell me you didn't do something crazy?"

My mouth went dry, and it was hard to form the words. "I didn't do anything. He's insane." I didn't want to give Nan the story; if she didn't know it, she didn't need to be involved.

"I know." Her voice came out quiet, serious. "He is insane and only getting worst. That's why I called, to warn you. He thinks he has some sort of power now, more than before. He thinks he's above the law and can't get in trouble for shit." She sighed heavily. "I'm leaving. I talked to my grams, she said I can move in with her."

"In Florida?" I asked, a small bubble of hope forming for her.

"Yeah." I could hear her voice lighten with the same hope. "Remember when we use to talk about living at the beach? You should come too. Get out of this city and start over."

I nodded, I remembered our talks. I also remember having this discussion several times with no follow through. I wasn't putting much trust in her words this time. "Maybe I will. When you get there, give me a call. When will you go?"

"As soon as I can. Things are getting bad, fast."

The fear in her voice made me speak. "I'm in New York. You could come here if you need to get out now. It's only temporary, but you'll be safe." I wouldn't give her the details, just in case, but I could meet her at the train station.

"Nah, Chick. I've got enough money for one bus ticket to Florida. That's what I'll use it for. I'm glad you're out of this city though." She laughed briefly, "I hope you will come, we could get those boob jobs we talked about, become playboy models."

I was surprised I laughed; it felt like forever since I smiled. "That was our California dream, and you wanted the boob job, not me. I've got enough."

"That's right, lucky Bi—" Her voice broke off. "Crap, gotta go." And she hung up.

I said a silent prayer for her, hoping she would be okay and make it to her grandmothers. If she actually does it then maybe I would go too, after I saw this craziness out. I was planning to stay until the fight on Friday, two days away, and then make my move.

* * *

Nan's name flashed on my screen. The sun just began to lighten the night sky. I reached for the phone on the bedside table and blinked away my sleep, a slow fear creeping through me.

"Hello," my voice cracked as I answered.

"Regan?" James' voice surprised me. "Nan—she, Oh God, please. She—He almost killed her." He was sobbing, taking gulps of breaths in-between words.

"What—Calm down James. What's happened?" My heart stopped as I waited for him to suck down his hysteria.

When he spoke his voice was small and squeaky. "I came back to the apartment and—there was so much blood. Nan was in the middle of it all. I think he thought she was dead, but she's not. Not yet. Fuck, she better live."

I was shaking. "Where is she now?"

"At Johns Hopkins, in surgery. Regan, I don't know if she's going to make it."

I hung up the phone and looked up the train schedule. I had to get to my friend.

28: Trapped

SITTING ON THE TRAIN TRAPPED ME WITH my thoughts. Thoughts I wanted to rip out and drown; thoughts that I wanted to bury and hide. Too many thoughts to keep straight or to ignore. Even my music couldn't touch them.

Dexter had tried to stop me. He even went as far as picking me up and attempting to lock me in my room, but he owed me and I cashed in. It worked to my advantage that he cared more about my forgiveness than his brother's disapproval. We all knew that Gage would forgive him for letting me go, just like he forgave him for everything else.

He tried to call Gage first, but of course there was no answer, just like every other time I had called. If everything was still on track he should be leaving for New York anytime now.

I had already called the hospital. Nan was in surgery to repair her lungs; they had been shredded with multiple stab wounds in the back. And I was having a hard time breathing.

The morning sky was a blaze of red and oranges, too pretty for the way I felt, but somewhere in the burning clouds I saw hope. Just a strand, but I clung to it. I had to.

My muscles shook with anticipation and nerves. Damien couldn't get away with this. I wouldn't let him. I pulled out my phone to call Anthony.

* * *

The train station was only about two miles from the hospital. I could have walked, but Anthony picked me up.

His honey eyes were filled with concern as he waited by his truck. I hesitated slightly when I saw he intended to hug me, but I still stepped into the warmth.

"This brings back memories. You freaking out, me picking you up…" he mumbled into my hair.

I pulled away; that's not what this was. I wasn't running to him like "old times."

"Sorry. It was supposed to be a joke. It's okay, I'm glad you called." He tried to put his arm around me again but I climbed into the passenger side of his truck to escape.

When he was buckled in, I blurted out, "This isn't like before. I really did call you for help. It's my friend, Nan; she's in the hospital. This guy, Damien, he put her there."

His eyebrows narrowed at me. "You called me to file a police report? The hospital has probably already done that."

I bit my lip, trying to find the best way to say it. "I might know more to the story. I wanted to see if you could find out any information. She may not make it." I swallowed the sadness that tried to escape with that admission. "He needs to be in jail for this so he can't' hurt her again. But he has some dangerous friends and I don't want them hurting her more." I turned in my seat, to face him. "I need your advice."

"Give me their names and I'll look into this today."

I nodded, wishing I could do more. "Nancy Baker and Damien Jallow." I wrote the names on a piece of paper.

He sighed, grabbing the paper from me. "Alright. I'll take you to the hospital now and call you later." He started the truck and turned back to me. "Are you in any danger from this man? Should you stay with me today?"

I squeezed the bridge of my nose, a pain starting just behind my eyes. "The hospital will be safe enough. I'm not going anywhere else."

He nodded running his hands over his pants legs. "So, he's a threat to you too?"

I nodded, and he sighed heavily then made the short drive to Johns Hopkins.

When he pulled up to the curb to drop me off he grabbed my hand. "I'll call soon, keep your phone on and stay here."

"Thank you." I squeezed his hand before pulling away and exiting the truck.

The hospital campus was huge, and it took too long to get to Nan's room. I took the stairs, too impatient to wait for the elevator, and practically ran down the halls till I came to the doors for the Surgical Intensive Care Unit. Once I stepped through I had to admit it all. I had played a part in her being here; I certainly could have done things differently, perhaps prevented it.

But wallowing in guilt wasn't helping Nan. I pushed through the heavy doors and scanned the door plaques to find room 322b, heart tight in my chest.

She looked so tiny in her bed. The room was filled with natural sunlight from the large picture window. I tried to focus on the view of the city because the sound of the machines attached to her was unbearable. They beeped and breathed a steady, eerie, rhythm, and her small body laid in the middle of it all, eyes closed, and still.

The sheets were pulled up to her shoulders, arms on the outside of them. I grabbed her hand as I scanned over her. She had some bruising on her face, but it didn't look too bad. She still looked like her, only pale and young. But her arms were spotted with bandages, some from the IV's and different machines, but some were covering wounds. Her hands were discolored with cuts and bruises, her nails ragged and broken. Whatever happened, she had fought.

I pulled a chair close to the bed and wrapped both of my hands around one of hers, hoping she could tell I was here. I wondered how long she had been alone for. Where was James?

A nurse came in after a moment, with a small smile and gentle presence.

"You don't have to move. You can stay there. I'm only replacing her medicine and IV."

She removed some bags from the metal hanger and put up full ones.

"Are you her family?"

I nodded. "I only just got here. Can you tell me anything? How surgery went?"

After untwisting the lines and adjusting the bags she turned to me and her eyes told me what I didn't want to know. It didn't look good.

"The next twenty four hours will be critical for her. The doctor will be in later, he can explain more. But for now they've paralyzed her lungs to give them a rest; so this machine is breathing for her." She gestured slightly to one of the machines on wheels. "They will probably take her off that tonight. Until then they will keep her in an induced coma. It's good you're here though. Talk to her, hold her hand. It helps." She squeezed my arm softly and her smile tightened. Then she left.

I tried to say encouraging words. I think I even got some out, but all I kept thinking was that Damien had to pay for what he did. The anger was the only thing keeping me from falling apart.

I jerked up straight when the door opened again. James floated into the room in his typical too big clothing and a backwards cap on. His eyes were blood shot and rimmed red. He shifted them around the room nervously, before landing on Nan.

"It's good you're here. I can't do this and Grams can't make it till tonight. I just came from Mom's house; Bitch wasn't even there so I just left a note." His voice cracked as he walked to the other side of Nan, opposite me. He picked up her hand as he continued, "Nan's in the hospital, she's going to die, you should be here. What type of note is that? We don't need her here though." Tears were rolling down his cheek as he squeezed her hand. "She wasn't around when you were living, why should she be here when you die?" He asked Nan's still body.

I broke. Stood up from my chair and pushed him away from her. "Stop saying that." I rounded the bed as he staggered back and I pushed him again. "She's not going to die. Stop telling her that." I pushed him one last time, his back hit the wall. He didn't fight it, just let his body fall back each time.

"This is your fault." I pounded on his chest, the anger in me draining fast. James stood, arms by his side, tears falling steadily. I wanted him to fight me, but he wouldn't. I hit him one last time, but let my hand stay on his chest as I sucked in breaths. I was crying too, and I hadn't even realized it.

"I know it is. I'm a horrible brother and this is all my fault." He leaned into my hand on his chest, tears dripping onto my arm. "Hit me again. I deserve it and so much more. I should be in that bed, not Nan."

My throat burned with suppressed tears. I dropped my arms, bracing them on my knees as I leaned over and squeezed my eyes, trying to pull myself back together. I stood up and walked to the bathroom to wash my tears away.

When I came out James was sitting by the bed and I went back to my seat on the other side.

James met my eyes over Nan. "I'm going to kill Damien if I ever see him again."

I nodded. "What happened?"

He leaned forward gripping Nan's arm. "She said she was leaving, moving to Florida. I was pissed that she was going." A tear slid down his cheek and he quickly wiped it away. "I left and when I came back I found her in the living room. Shit was knocked everywhere, and she was on the ground, in a pool of blood." He looked up at me. "I called an ambulance right away. I didn't even care about what they would find. I deserve to go to jail, look what I did to my sister. The monster I introduced her too. The police are all over our apartment now."

"But you didn't see Damien do this?"

His face turned hard. "I know it was him. He was there when I left. I should have never left her with him."

I nodded in agreement, but couldn't speak. We sat in mostly silence after that.

Then Anthony called, pulling me away from Nan's side.

I touched James's shoulder. "I'll be back soon." I wouldn't say I had forgiven him, but in this situation I could put our differences aside. He loved Nan too.

I met Anthony out front and climbed into his truck. "Could you take me to my house so I can get some things? I'm going to stay at the hospital for a while."

He pulled off with a nod. "Regan, I don't know too many details, but I do know this; your friend was mixed up with the wrong people. You should stay away."

My muscles tingled. "I know. But I want to get her away too. What did you find out?"

"I'll tell you at your place."

Aliya was home. She jumped from behind the refrigerator door when I came in. "OMG chick, what are you doing here? I thought you all were having some sort of couples week with Gage's fight in NYC." She closed the refrigerator door with her hip, pickle jar in her hand. "Thanks for the invite," she threw in sarcastically.

Then she really looked at me and paused. "Are you okay?" She put down the jar in her hand and hugged me.

I took in a deep breath and her fruity perfume filled my nose. "My friend's in the hospital. I had to come back. I'm only here to pick up some clothes and change."

She squeezed tighter. "I am sorry you're going through that. I have class now, but I can go to the hospital with you later."

I stepped away and shook my head. "Don't worry about it. There's nothing to do there anyways."

I changed into a fresh pair of jeans and t-shirt and packed a small overnight bag then went back out to the truck to sit with Anthony. Eagerness and dread mixing in anticipation of what he would say.

He drove to that lake we had split up at and parked the truck, undoing his seatbelt so he could face me. "I'm only a patrol officer, so my knowledge is limited, but I tried to talk to some detectives today and it doesn't look good. I think you need to drop this."

I stiffened. "Drop it, why?"

His throat moved as he swallowed. "They've already closed your friends case and Damien's name wasn't anywhere in it. They said she was a prostitute and drug abuser who was killed by one of her Johns."

"That's not true. She's not—"

"They picked her up last week for prostitution." He cut me off, his words silencing my argument.

"But even if it is true. It's strange that they would close this case before finding out who exactly it is. So I asked around some and all I got was doors in my face. The ones who talked to me, they let me know I shouldn't be asking about these people. Not Nan, nobody seemed to care about her, but Damien. He's affiliated with some people of power and won't be pursued in this case."

I took a deep breath. "What if I report he attacked me? Held me at gun point."

Anthony's eyes flashed, unreadable. "Did he? Is there more? Because that may get him brought in, but not long enough and he would know it was you. It wouldn't be safe."

I sighed, defeated. "No. That was it." I couldn't tell the rest of the story without getting Gage and them in trouble.

"Regan, I am a police officer and shouldn't be saying this but it's not safe for you to pursue this. If others found out you were even asking about him it could be bad for you." His hand moved to my hair. "I can't protect you from this if you take it further than me. Please, drop it and get away."

I closed my eyes, letting go of the small hope I had held onto. It was surprisingly easy to let go of. "Okay. I won't pursue this. Take me back to the hospital please."

He pulled up to the curb of the hospital but stopped me with a hand on my arm before I got out. "Regan, I can't help you anymore. Not if you're involved with these people. I'm sorry."

I met his eyes. "I know. It's okay. Thank you for trying."

I went to give him one last hug, but he turned his head pressing his lips to mine. He pulled away just as suddenly, eyes clouded with emotion. "Take care of yourself, alright?"

I nodded with a tight smile. "You too." And got out of the truck.

I looked up to Nan's room, the light was on I could tell and a shadow crossed the window. I swallowed my nerves and said a little prayer for her as I made my way back to where she lay.

Outside of the SICU door I was yanked into a little alcove. My reaction was immediate; I kicked at the large form. He slammed me into a wall, hands gripping my shoulders, body trapping mine.

"What the hell have you done? Why were you with the cop? What did you tell him?" Gage growled at me, voice low with anger, freezing my reactions.

But it was nothing compared to the pure rage in his eyes, a look that I had never seen him direct at me before.

.

29: Breathe

MY THOUGHTS TRIPPED OVER EACH OTHER, TRYING to catch up with the present moment. Gage had me pinned to the wall, fingers digging into my arm with anger.

He jerked me once and his grip tightened. "Tell me, now." His whispered fury turned me cold.

"Nothing that you need to worry about." I could do angry too. I tried to jerk out of his hold, but he didn't budge.

I met his icy glare. "Let me go or I'll yell. I'll scream. And then see what happens." We may be alone now, in a side alcove outside the SICU, but a scream would surely gain attention in a hospital.

He slid one hand over my shoulder, firmly. His fingers curled around the back of my neck and his thumb pressed to my lips, but not with care. He tilted my head back to look at him. "Don't threaten me. Not after all I've done for you." His other hand moved up, cupping the other side of my head in the same way. "And don't fucking lie to me. What did you tell him?"

His hold wasn't painful, but the warning was there. He was larger than me and had me in a vulnerable position. I had to choose my next move wisely. And I hated him for the fear he caused.

"I only talked to him about Nan. Nothing Else." I steadied my voice, "Now let me go."

He shook his head, never taking his eyes from me, assessing my honesty. "Why? Why did you go to him?"

"Because you weren't around." I threw at him as I tried to push him away from me again, my anger rising. "And I needed his advice. I trust him." And that was the truth. Anthony had always been honest with me.

My words caused Gage to flinch, more than any of my ineffective attempts to push away had.

He sneered. "You think I wanted to leave you alone? I'm trying my best to keep you safe. And you turn to him." He dropped his arms and took a step back, freeing me. "Un-fucking-believable. You're supposed to still be in New York, you shouldn't be here. Why won't you listen to me?"

"I didn't ask you to do anything, especially if it means keeping me in the dark. I don't just blindly follow people who think they know best. I make my own decisions. And I'm here for Nan." I walked past him, going for the doors.

He grabbed my hand and pulled me back. "We need to leave. We can't stay here. I have my fight tomorrow and need to be in New York."

I ripped my hand away. "Then go. I'm staying."

He grabbed the fabric of my coat, pulling me to him again. "Listen to me. This isn't—"

"No! You listen to me. I'm not leaving her. And I'm not following you anywhere. You go do what you need to do. And I'll do my own thing. Now get your hands off of me." I was all anger, my body rigid and venom in my words.

He let go of me, his hands curled by his side. "You don't know what you're doing."

I walked backwards, towards the double doors leading to Nan. "Maybe I don't, but that's only because you won't tell me anything. And I'm not going with you just to get left again. Fuck you and your version of caring." I spun on my toes and pushed through the doors, letting them close between us.

James' was still in the chair by Nan, his head resting on the edge of the bed as he held her hand. He sat back in his seat as I came in.

"Some guy was just here asking for you," he said emotionless.

I nodded, guessing Gage must've come to this room.

"I can't believe no one else showed up for Nan. All the people that stay at our place, and yet it's only me and you."

I sat in the same chair as earlier, taking up my spot on the other side of the bed. I put her hand in mine and willed her to fight.

James laid his head back down on his sister and fell asleep, or at least appeared to be asleep. I just sat, desolate, only moving for the nurses that came in shifting Nan, changing her dressings, and whatever other things they had to do.

A while later, Nan's grandmother and mother showed up together.

Nan's mother walked in silently, standing next to James who didn't even acknowledge her, besides sitting up in his chair. She was thin, like James and Nan, except her face was sunken, more skeleton like. She had the same thin brown hair as her kids, pulled back in a ponytail.

"Oh no. Oh no." The grandmother came in moaning. She was tall like James, but round. "Please lord, save our baby." She walked to the head of the bed and pressed her forehead to Nan's and murmured too low for me to hear.

A doctor materialized in the room, as if summoned by the family presence, or Gram's prayers.

I looked out the window at the early night sky, just a touch of dark sunlight left, as the doctor answered their questions and caught them up with the information I already knew. But I kept my ears open, tuned in for any new bits.

"I will give you a few more minutes with her and then we are going to try to take her off the respirator, see how her lungs respond."

I stood to leave, wanting to give them a moment alone with Nan. I had said everything I needed to her today. I only hoped they would use this time with her to say what they never said when she was growing up.

Squeezing her hand, I kissed her cheek and whispered, "I love you." I held back the tears just behind my eyes. "I'll be back soon."

"Where are you going?" James asked, sitting up.

"I'll be in the waiting room. I wanted to give you all time together."

Grams nodded with a small smile, hands smoothing Nan's hair.

"No. You should stay. You're more family than these people." He gestured to the two around Nan, causing everyone to freeze.

I continued walking to the door. "James, it's okay. I'll see her in a bit, once the doctors are done." I exited before he could say more.

I walked into the waiting room and took the first seat, pressing my fingers to my eyes, forcing the emotions to stay in.

I felt the air shift as a presence filled the seat next to me, at the same time an arm slipped around my shoulders, pulling me closer.

I didn't have to look up to know it was Gage.

He circled his other arm around me as he pulled me in closer, his comforting warmth and scent filling my senses and weakening my hold on my emotions.

I sucked in air, but couldn't find the strength to push away. "What are you still doing here?"

He rubbed soft circles on my back. "I'm here for you. Everything else can wait. I'm sorry."

I looked up at him, confused, with anger pricking at me. "No it can't wait. You have a fight tomorrow. An important one."

He nodded and sighed, meeting my gaze with a soft look. "It can wait for tonight. I'll have to leave tomorrow. But don't worry about it for now. What's going on with your friend?" He pulled me back into him and tucked my head under his.

I was drained from everything. I couldn't find it in me to fight with him or to pull myself away, as much as I knew I should. "They are going to try to get her to breathe on her own in a little while. Her mom just showed up though so I came out here to wait. Have you been here the whole time?" It had been hours since our fight earlier.

His hand stroked my hair. "Yeah. Have you eaten? Can I get you food?"

I held on to him tighter. "Not right now." I had been so worried about him this week, and our meeting earlier hadn't left any room for relief. I wanted a break from the misery, and his arms offered that, eased it slightly, just enough to breathe.

James, his mom, and Grams came into the waiting room moments later. I sat up and pulled away from Gage, but kept my hand clasped with his. We all waited in silence for the doctors. But at least I wasn't alone.

* * *

Someone came out in scrubs. Doctor? Nurse? I don't know. But they had little stars and moons with smiley faces on them. Not appropriate for the news they were delivering.

She had her hair back in two French braids. I don't know why I was noticing that, except they were crooked and messy. So when she said Nan had to go into surgery again, all I could think was this messy haired whatever she was better not be in there too. Simply for the reason that if you couldn't do your own hair, how could you repair someone's lungs.

"The stress of breathing caused internal bleeding. We have to go back in and find the source. We will keep you updated." She gave a nod and quickly turned to leave.

I gripped Gage's hand tighter. I had stayed seated when she walked in, but James and Grams were standing. Nan's mom stayed seated too. She reached out now for James but he walked around her and sat in a corner, looking out the window, hands flexing, face still. But the look in his eyes told me he was plotting, anger simmering just behind them.

He popped up, hands going to his pockets and walked over to me. "You got a smoke I can get?" At my head shake, he continued, "Shit, that's right you don't smoke. What about you?" He nodded to Gage.

His mom stood up reaching into her purse. "I got one, Hun. Just about to go out myself." She extended a cigarette to James.

He paused, raising his eyes to the ceiling, and then whipped around and snatched it from her. He walked out without waiting for her but she trailed behind, unfazed.

"It's probably going to be awhile. Let's go get something to eat." Gage shook my hand slightly.

I stared at him. I wasn't hungry, couldn't eat if I tried. I wasn't even sure I could walk right now.

"Or at least a tea or something for you to drink. I saw a cart on the first floor. Come on."

Before I responded he was standing, pulling me into standing too. I was disconnected, weightless, bodiless, and soulless. I only wished I could be thoughtless. I let him lead me out the doors to the elevator. The car was semi full, but he pulled me to stand in front of him, large, warm hands resting on my shoulders.

He led me to a couch facing the window and went to the nearby coffee cart to order. Moments later he returned with two red cups and a bag.

"They didn't have much for food, but we can go to the cafeteria if you want." He handed me my cup and sat next to me.

I pulled out of my trance slightly, taking the cup, feeling the almost burning heat beneath the sleeve on it. I took a sip to scald away the dry, cotton feeling in my mouth and then went back to looking out the window.

It was full on night, but no stars could be seen and the buildings blocked the moon from view. And I suddenly wanted to cry, a panic rising in me. How was I supposed to make a wish with no stars?

Gage set down his drink. Bringing his hand to my face, he used his thumb to gently wipe away a stray tear.

I pulled away before he could cause more to spill over. His touch only made me that much weaker. Taking a breath, I calmed myself. It was stupid to cry over the stars, I hadn't wished on one in years. And those wishes never came true.

"Nan and I use to wish on stars." The words were out before I even thought about them.

He was leaning forward, forearms braced on his knees, watching me with a turned head. But he didn't say anything. He didn't laugh though, and that prompted me to go on.

"Silly things, you know? We were young." I wanted to talk about her. Not what she had done recently, not the trouble we were all in. But the girl that she was, is, the real Nan. The one that took me in and befriended me. "We'd wish to have money. Go live at the beach. To be there for each other. Forever. It was never about boys or family. Never put much weight in those."

His lip pulled at the corner with a slight smile. "How old were you two?"

"I met her my freshmen year of high school. She was a junior. Neither of us went to classes much, but the difference was she still passed. She's smart. God she's smart." I closed my eyes as the reality of the present came back to me. How did my smart friend end up here? I shook it away. "But she was tough too. And for some reason she would stick up for me even when she didn't know me. My first week I somehow made enemies with the wrong crowd, a popular crowd, a large one."

I had to look away from him as his smile dropped. But I didn't want to stop talking. I wanted to invoke the strong, smart girl back. "I couldn't seem to breathe without pissing one of them off. Everywhere I turned someone was saying something, taking something, or challenging me in some other way. So I finally had enough and fought back, just happened to be lousy timing. It was in the hallway and the girl I fought had lots of her friends around. But Nan jumped in to help me." I looked back to him and my smile felt foreign. "It wasn't till we were waiting for the principal that we even exchanged names."

"How'd the fight end?"

"It got broken up before any real damage, but Nan and I, we were still standing. And those girls didn't bother me, not to my face anyway, until after Nan graduated." Once Nan graduated, shit went down fast, but that wasn't the story I was telling right now. "Everyone left Nan alone; I think because of her brothers friends. I guess they were her friends too. He was already locked up when I met her or maybe I would have stayed away too." That wasn't true. I was attracted to the street in her. She was a survivor, and I wanted to be one, so I stuck around.

"My first job was at the grocery store with her. She used to steal the candy and go to school and sell it. Said they didn't pay her enough, so she supplemented." My laugh bubbled up with tears and I turned away again.

"It's alright to cry." Gage slid an arm around me, pressing me to his chest.

I couldn't hold in the tears that had already begun to fall, but I wanted to. Before I knew it my body was shaking with sobs that I couldn't stop, so I tried to cover them in Gage's shirt. I felt too tiny and too weak in his arms. Nan needed me to be stronger than this. With that thought I pulled myself up, wiping away my tears with my hand. I reached for a napkin that sat with our untouched food and blotted my face. Gage loosened his hold enough that I could move around, but didn't remove his arm from me.

I looked up at the clock on the wall. It was 11:30. "You should go home. Get some sleep. You have a big day tomorrow."

"Are you coming with me?" His fingers were soft in my hair, tickling and soothing.

I didn't know if he was referring to New York or home. "I want to see how surgery goes first. Then maybe."

He nodded and kissed my forehead sweetly. "I'm staying too."

It was about two hours later that a different doctor came out to the waiting room to update us. This one looked like he had much more authority than the girl before and I suddenly wanted her back.

I stayed seated, letting Nan's real family do the talking. Not that I could have said anything anyways. The moment he walked in and his eyes dropped to the floor, my heart did too.

Then he shook his head and said, "I'm sorry, but she didn't make it through surgery…" and I stopped listening.

30: Drowning

I CLOSED MY EYES AND STOPPED TIME. I stopped thinking, moving, and if I could of I would have stopped myself from breathing. I wanted to delay the next moment. I wanted to delay being in a world where there was no Nan.

But I couldn't. I had to breathe and with that breath came reality. I was still alive, and I held blame for Nan not being here. I hadn't fought for her, only myself. I had left her with Damien.

I silently listened to the conversations around me; a deep, painful chill engulfing me. They weren't going to have a funeral. Why were they already talking about that? The grandmother told the doctor that the hospital could cremate her since they couldn't afford anything else. Even the doctor was telling them they could take a moment to think it over; they could go back and see her.

I stood up, chest tightening. I had to leave. I couldn't handle this or them or seeing Nan. I pushed away from Gage and whatever he was saying as James walked over to me.

"You leaving?" he asked, pulling his hood up over his head, shading his eyes.

My jaw felt tight, it wouldn't move, so I nodded.

James took a step back, meeting me with his hollow eyes. "I'll call you." He nodded, and I knew he meant what he said earlier, he wanted to kill Damien.

Gage was pulling me away. "No you won't. You don't need to call her."

I ripped my hand from his and stepped back to James, speaking quickly. "You call me. Anything about Nan, you call me. Understand?" I stood there, determined, until James slowly nodded.

"Bet. You'll get a call," he promised and I knew he meant it. I just hoped he could deliver.

Then Gage was pulling me out of the room. The elevators were empty this time, and he turned to me the minute the doors closed.

"What are you thinking?" His voice was low with concern.

I took a step back and closed my eyes, leaning against the wall of the car, running my hand through my hair. "I'm not. I'm not thinking."

I opened my eyes as the elevator doors opened to the first floor and Gage was in front of me, blocking everything from sight. And when his arms circled around me I stepped into them, wanting to hide from reality.

"I'm sorry about your friend. I'm sorry." His voice reached my ear, low and gravely as it echoed in his chest.

I pushed away. I didn't want to hear that. I should be the one apologizing to her. I didn't deserve any.

* * *

"Where are we going?" I lifted my head from the cool glass of the passenger side window as Gage passed the turn that would take us to his community.

"To New York. I've got that fight tonight." He kept his eyes on the road.

I looked at the clock on the dash; it was nearly three am. I guess the fight was tonight, and I didn't realize my stomach could sink any further then it had, but my body continued to surprise me.

"Shouldn't you sleep first or something?" I asked, trying to focus on him and not Nan.

He reached over to me, his fingers gliding through my hair. "I'll sleep when we get there. You go ahead and rest now."

This felt like déjà vu, like the last time we made this trip and he disappeared. And I was back to sinking. Head underwater.

I dug for the courage to face this new reality. "What's going to happen?"

His eyes glided to me briefly before returning to the highway. "I'll fight tonight. I'll win. And then we'll try to move on from this. Together."

"And if you don't win?" I tried to watch his face, but the shadows of the night made it hard to see his reaction or if there even was one.

"I'm going to win. That's the only option."

I didn't want to be pacified, and that's what it felt like he was doing. I wanted honesty. I needed to prepare for all scenarios and I couldn't do that without more information.

"But if you don't, you still get money? You could still pay back these people right?" I knew this was a big fight, prize money would be large, but even the loser would be paid and that should cover Dexter's half of the debt.

"Maybe," he said carefully.

We were flying down an empty highway, streetlights shining through the car randomly in waves. I let silence take over as anger grew. He still wasn't telling me anything.

When my frustration boiled over I turned back to him. "How the hell can you say we're going to do anything together when you don't include me? You don't tell me anything."

He grabbed my hand. "I don't want to lie to you."

I went still. "Then don't."

He threaded his fingers through mine and rested our hands on my lap. "I can't tell you."

I pulled my hand away and knocked his off my lap, turning my body away from his as I looked out the window.

"You have to understand. The less you know the better. I'm trying to keep you safe."

I spun around. "From what? I should know that!"

I still didn't get it. I knew Damien had it out for me, but I never told Gage of his involvement that night. So what did he think he was protecting me from?

He bobbed his head. "You should. But it's me. I'm trying to protect you from me and what I'm doing, and any fallout of that. And your friend tonight, she died 'cause of the people she ran with. I'm trying to hide you away until I'm not one of those people that could get you hurt."

The mention of Nan cut me, but I used my anger to cover it. "I'm not a damn pet. You can't just cage me up and give me water sometimes. I need you to explain things to me or I'm going to make my own decisions and they won't involve you." I was surprised by how much that declaration hurt. I didn't want to cut him out, but he was forcing my hand.

"Okay," he breathed, grabbing my knee in an attempt to calm me.

"Okay?" I repeated, questioning him.

"I'll explain some things. What you need to know."

I sat back, floored that he agreed. I had changed his mind. Well, good, I was right and he should tell me.

"It's not about the money anymore," he began and I held my breath, not wanting to miss a word, not daring to interrupt.

"It never really was, not really. These people care about loyalty and control. They actually prefer if you owe them, so they have something on you. Even if I lost this fight, it would be enough to pay them back for Dexter, but they don't really care about that. I owe them a favor so they want me to win 'cause they're betting on it. This past week I've had to slip back into who I was. I was wrong when I told you they still got my back, they don't care about me, just what I can do for them."

When it was clear he wasn't going to say more I questioned him. "So you have to win. But will they back off after or stick around?"

"When I win, I'm clear to go. Rusnak promised."

Something about the way his eyes shifted and breath hitched caused a jolt to shoot through me, a warning.

"Why wouldn't they bet on you losing? Isn't it easier to throw a fight, a safer bet?"

He sucked in air. I was getting close to what he was hiding. "More money to be made if I win. And my career will still be solid. They think long term, if I ever owe them a favor again then I'll have even bigger names to fight, with more money."

"So they aren't letting you walk away." I still managed to sink deeper, where was the bottom?

He shook his head and gripped my leg. "Once I'm clear, I'm done. I'm not going to owe them shit in the future. And Dexter's done too; I won't bail his ass out anymore if he fucks up again. But Regan," He paused, and I held my breath again, bracing myself. "I'm only out if I win in the third round."

"What does that mean? Why?"

"The biggest payoffs are for calling the round. They want me to win in the third round. That's what they bet on. They are not trying to make this easy but I can do it. I will win in the third round."

"How can you be so sure?"

"Because I've done it before. I've set up fights for them before. But this is the last time."

We sat in silence for a while, my mind shutting down from overload and exhaustion. But as I struggled to sort through my thoughts I realized the most important question hadn't been answered.

As the early morning light filled the SUV I turned to him. "What happens if you don't win in the third round?"

"That's not going to happen," he claimed firmly.

I shook my head. "What if it does?"

He turned to me, an unreadable look crossing over him before he focused on the road. "Then you run. Far away from me."

This time when I sunk it felt like I had finally hit bottom, and it nearly shattered me. A part of me wanted to take off now, not even wait for tonight and the results. And it felt like a part of me did, just tore away and bailed.

But the part of me that was left didn't care about his warning. I wasn't asking what was going to happen to me.

"But what about you? What will happen to you?" My voice came out in a whisper, unable to get enough air.

He glanced at me a few times, but I was beginning to think he wasn't going to answer. Then he ran his hand through my hair, brushing it back from my face.

"I don't want you to worry about that. I'll handle whatever happens."

I grabbed his hand and trapped it between both of mine as I brought it to my lap. "You worry about me, so I can worry about you." But I knew worrying was pointless. I had worried about Nan, but she needed action.

He squeezed my hand as we drove through the tunnel into New York City. "Neither of us has to worry because I am going to win. Let's leave it at that."

I dropped the questions. He didn't need them right now. He needed sleep, focus, and confidence. Instead I said, "You will," and then brought his hand up to my lips, sealing the wish.

* * *

Gage turned to me in the elevator and said, "When we get to the suite, go straight to our room. I don't want you to get pulled into the drama that might be waiting. You're exhausted and need sleep. I'll be right behind you."

"What drama?"

He stretched his neck to either side. "Silas will be pissed that I'm cutting it so close. Dexter, I don't know what to expect from him, but it doesn't matter. Just go straight to the room, alright?" He grabbed my hand as the doors opened and we walked two doors down to the suite.

I scanned the room as I entered. Dexter wasn't around, but Silas was waiting. He jumped up from the couch and stomped over to Gage.

"God Dammit boy, you have to be ready for press at noon. Get your head in this and focus on what's important." I'd never seen Silas so flustered; he was angry but nervousness was clearly running under his words, evident in the way he shifted from foot to foot.

Gage dropped my hand and nudged me in the direction of our room. I walked away, but slow enough so I could hear the conversation.

"Don't fuckin' think you can lecture me anymore. I know what's important and I'll be ready. Where's Dexter?" Gage's voice was low and controlled.

"He's in the room, hasn't come out since his girl left yesterday."

I paused in front of the door to the bedroom and turned to look back at them. Leona left? Dexter and her seemed to be doing fine when I last saw them.

Gage met my eyes and nodded to the door in a clear command, then strode towards Dexter's room, disappearing inside.

"Where did Leona go?" I asked Silas.

He turned towards me, his eyes narrowing as he thought. "She went home. Gage scared her off when he blew up at Dexter yesterday. I'm surprised you came back; does that mean you're still willing to fight? That I'm still your manager?"

I stiffened my spine, standing up tall. "No, you're not my manager." I finally listened to Gage and went into the bedroom, shutting the door on Silas.

I didn't even bother changing, just took off my pants and slid into bed. The cool sheets and soft mattress felt like respite to my drained body.

But my thoughts weren't given the same break. They continued to run over the last twenty-four hours, and Nan was screaming in my head. I tried to stop myself, but I couldn't. I played out different scenarios, but kept coming back to one. Nan on the floor, on her stomach, clawing to get away from Damien as he cut into her, stabbing her repeatedly in the back. Seven times.

I curled into myself, under the blankets, fighting the tears that were already streaming down my face, wanting sleep to block out these thoughts. I had always been able to sleep, even in the worst of conditions, even under stress.

Nan had questioned that before. Ever since I knew her, she relied on medicine to sleep, said she had too many nightmares and wondered how I didn't. I had always thought of sleep as an escape; my nightmares occurred when I was awake.

The bed dipped beside me and the covers shifted. I struggled to breathe without letting Gage hear my tears. He needed to sleep, and I didn't want him wasting any more time worrying about me.

A gentle touch brushed the hair from my face, his warmth radiated into my back as he shifted closer, and his soft lips kissed the corner of my closed eye.

I'm sure he meant to make me feel better, but it only made me feel worse and a sob shook me as I squeezed tighter into myself. I had to get control so he could sleep.

His arms scooped me up, turning me to face him, and he wrapped me in tightly. My tears flowed onto his bare chest as his lips brushed the top of my head.

Unfolding myself, I brought a hand up to his chest and pushed away slightly. "It's okay. I'm okay. Really. You need to sleep."

His only response was to trail feathery kisses over my forehead and cheeks.

"Please. You don't have to do this. It'll make me feel worse. You need your sleep for the fight tonight." But my hands glided over his chest and around to his back, pulling myself in tighter, letting him surround me.

He kept one arm wrapped around my lower back and the other cupped my face, moving me to look at him. His eyes searched my face, and I searched his. So many emotions seemed to fill his gaze, but mostly I saw concern and uncertainty. It was the nervous uncertainty that had me pulling him closer, practically melting into him. I wanted to fill him with confidence.

I pressed my cheek to his chest, hearing his strong steady heartbeat.

His hand left my face, trailing down my arm and over my hip. His fingertips glided back up to my stomach, running under the hem of my shirt.

"I told myself I wouldn't do this, till after the fight. But…" His voice was breathless, and he gulped in air, "I want you so bad. I don't think I can sleep with you next to me." His hand gripped my hips as I attempted to pull away. "But I don't want you anywhere else. You belong here with me. I want to kiss you. Can I do that?"

I leaned away, confused. Of course he could, but then I realized he hadn't kissed me since that night everything went down. I nodded and wiped my cheeks, trying to clean up my face for him.

He brought his lips to mine tentatively; they barely grazed. The kiss was shallow but still lit a fire that I desperately needed, pushing away the cold that ached in my bones. His tongue lightly licked at my lips until I captured it in-between them and sucked him in. The next moment, he rolled me on my back, deepening the kiss, and the fire erupted, burning all other thoughts.

His hands moved all over me, memorizing all my curves as I did the same to him. I ran my fingers under the elastic of his boxers and felt him shudder under my touch.

He broke the kiss, raising himself up with his arms braced on either side of me. His head dropped and blocked his face from view as he spoke. "I can't do this. It's not fair to you." He brought his forehead to mine and whispered, "I love you, but I can't make you mine till after my fight. It's not right."

Another piece of me was just ripped away. I had lost too many pieces and was scattered, unable to even pretend to pull myself back together.

I cupped his face in my hands and kissed his lips softly. "I'm already yours. That's why I'm here. But whatever you need, I'm here." And at the moment, it was true; all that was left of me were the parts that belonged to him, the parts that he had saved from drowning.

He moved towards me and hesitated slightly. His lips brushed my ear and his warm breath sent chills through me as he breathed, "I need you."

As his hands roamed over me and he trailed hot kisses down my neck, I gave up fighting and let him take over. He pulled my shirt over my head, but left on my bra, not pressing the issue.

Our movements were smooth and in sync, with an easy flow. He made me forget anything but this moment. Even time became a non-issue. This is what we both needed.

His naked body rose over mine as he removed his fingers from between my legs and inserted the tip of himself. He slid in, filling me, completing me. And we both held tight as our bodies joined as deep as possible. But we couldn't stay still for long.

He rocked in and out and soon pressure began mounting for us, and his attempts at control were gone and replaced with raw emotion.

He slammed into me, over and over, covering my cries with his lips. I drank in his grunts. Our bodies were slick with exertion as my core tightened and snapped, a shattering release that racked my body in uncontrollable spasms.

He slumped over me, his own body quivering as his hot release filled me. He held himself still inside me, breathing raggedly into my neck. His breathing calmed, falling back under his control, but he didn't move and neither did I. I felt him soften in me, but he only wrapped his arms around me, keeping me still. And within moments, I submitted to my exhaustion and fell asleep surrounded by his warmth.

31: Decision Made

HE WAS SHIFTING AWAY FROM ME, SLOWLY removing his arms from around my body.

"You're leaving?" My stomach twisted as I gripped his waist and kept my head on his chest.

He had stiffened when I first spoke but quickly relaxed and stroked my hair. "Go back to sleep. I have to get ready to go, but I'll see you tonight after the fight."

I unwrapped my arms from him. "Where are the tickets?"

He shook his head. "You're not going. Stay here."

Sitting up in bed, I met his eyes. "Of course I'm going. I'm not missing this fight."

"It may not be safe for you to be in my guest seats."

But he didn't sound firm, so I pressed the issue. "Then I'll get different tickets and sit somewhere else."

He nodded. "Alright. You can pick up tickets at will call."

His quick resignation made me feel sick. I was happy to get my way because there was no way I was missing the fight, but he seemed drained, and that wasn't good.

I slid my arms around him again and pressed my cheek to his chest. "I'll see you tonight after the fight. I'll be here." I didn't want to bring up the possibility of losing, but I hoped he knew I meant I'd be here no matter what happened.

His hands ran up and down my back. "I know. I've got to get ready." He pushed me back slightly to look at my face. His eyes bounced over me and then his lips pressed to mine, a brief spark before he pulled away.

* * *

Restless, I paced the common area of the suite, counting the seconds with my feet. I paused at the window, staring out at the busy city, the people going in all directions on the sidewalks, and the cars jammed on the street.

The door to the suite opened. I spun around as Dexter stepped into the room, panting and covered in sweat.

Adrenaline pumped through me, ready to react, until I saw him remove his headphones and look up at me with a slight smile.

"Hey. It's good you're back, but I'm sorry about your friend."

His words tightened the knots in my stomach. Sorry was a stupid thing to say, and I didn't want to think about her right now.

He walked over to where I stood by the window. "I went for a run. Had to clear my mind. Did you hear Leona left?" His eyebrow rose as he looked down at me.

I nodded. "Why? Where did she go?"

He sighed and sunk down on the ground. He stretched himself out on the floor, looking up at the ceiling.

"She went home 'cause I told her to." He lifted his head to look at me, the corner of his mouth lifting wryly. "But I can't figure out why I thought that was a good idea."

I sat cross-legged on the floor next to him and picked at the fibers of the carpet. "Oh yeah? So did she leave mad or what?"

"Angry. She was angry." He closed his eyes. "It's probably for the best. That's probably what I was thinking when I said it. But…" He shrugged and grabbed my hand. "What about you, Rea? You still angry with me?"

I pulled my hand from his. I had told him I would forgive him if he let me leave to see Nan. But that didn't mean we were friends. Right now, though, I welcomed the distraction of talking to him.

I shook my head. "I've got too much going on to be angry with you."

"I hear that and I'll take it." He propped himself up with his elbows behind him. "Maybe after tonight I can fix things with Leona, too."

I looked at him. "I thought you said it was better this way?"

"What the hell do I know? I miss that girl. I love her and I know she loves me. This week has been stressful, that's all."

I frowned and my face pinched in. "That's not all. It's been more than stressful."

He swallowed and cleared his face of all traces of humor. "I know, but it'll be over soon."

"I hope so." I couldn't focus on the uncertain night. "What exactly happened with Leona? Silas said Gage scared her off."

He dropped back on the ground, hands cupped behind his head. "Nah, it wasn't like that. He was mad that I let you go back, but we knew to expect that. When I was trying to calm him down and explain that you weren't in danger, that it was Gage and I who were the targets, it clicked to Leona. I think she had been shook up by the other night and clung to me to feel safe. Then I said that to Gage, and she realized I was the one putting her in danger. She freaked out, so I told her to go." His eyes cut to where I sat. "It's true, though. It's not you two that are in danger. Gage and I both were being selfish by keeping you with us."

"Except your brother didn't stay with me." Somehow jealousy found room to sit with my crowded emotions.

Dexter pushed himself up. As he stood he said, "I don't pretend to understand Gage, but I trust him. He's usually got his reasons. I've got to go shower and dress to meet up with him before the fight. You good here by yourself?"

I nodded; it wasn't like I had a choice in it anyways.

* * *

It was between fights, but the arena pulsed with music and the big screen above the ring showed clips from past fights. I walked up the steps to my seat, on the end of the row on the second tier. The guy to my left glanced at me, disappointed that he now had to squeeze in closer to his friends.

I sat down, heart in my throat, as I watched clips of Gage on the screen. His knockout punch from his last fight flashed and twisted a knot in my stomach. I prayed that this would go as smoothly.

The screen played clips of his opponent, Desmond Dennaki, a bald beast of a man. His face was hard and ugly, but intimidating. Gage's muscles were cleaner and more defined, whereas Dennaki's puffed out, making him seem larger even though their height and weight were about even. Dennaki's scorecard read twenty-two wins, twelve by knockout, one loss, and two draws. I hoped tonight would be his second loss.

A voice broke over the speakers, announcing the start of the fight and the music shifted to Gage's signature beat.

I stood, straining to see over the people in front of me, but the easiest way to see his entrance was on the large screen. Silas and Dexter walked out with him as well as two others. He strode in with his typical stone cold expression, gaze focused on the ring. The icy fury in his eyes gave me hope.

After climbing into the ring, Dexter removed Gage's blue and silver robe, revealing his solid muscles. He stretched his neck and exuded cool and determined confidence.

Dennaki put on a show, or at least the people in his group did. Dennaki walked out with the same seriousness of Gage. His eyes honed in on him and never let up as he stalked to the ring. His large group was mostly female and slinked around in their skimpy cheerleader-esque outfits. They dropped away before he entered the ring.

In the ring, he raised his arms to the crowd and smirked as they cheered. The men next to me were on their feet yelling for him, and I wanted to hit each of them.

I sat as nerves took over. They were rapid fire under my skin and made me shaky on my feet.

The ding at the start of the first round jump started my heart. I was on the edge of my seat as the boxers circled each other. Gage had his hands raised high, blocking his face, but Dennaki kept his posture relaxed, his arms barely blocking his chest. His smug cockiness was soon wiped away as he attempted to throw a hook. Gage evaded it easily and moved out of the way of two more attempts. Then he threw his own punch.

Dennaki's head snapped back as Gage's fist connected. He shook his head, clearing it of the sting. The boxers gave each other more space after that exchange. Gage walked in slow circles around him, and Dennaki backed away from him anytime he got too close.

Dennaki stepped in suddenly and threw a low punch that connected with Gage's chest. Two quick body shots followed and connected.

Instead of blocking, Gage threw his own punches, matching him on body shots. He pounded on his sides, and on the large screen it was easy to see the effect. Dennaki's body shifted under each blow, whereas Gage's body absorbed each punch without reaction.

Dennaki retreated, and they circled each other again. The bell ending the round surprised me and the boxers separated to their corners. Gage sat easily on the stool offered as Dexter wiped away sweat and applied more Vaseline to his face. Dennaki was given the same treatment as well as an en swell, a cold metal thing, pressed to his eye where Gage had hit him.

The next round started with Dennaki swinging, trying to take back control. Gage evaded most of them but one was landed on his jaw. Gage returned the punch and several others. Dennaki was stunned by the blows, unable to get away or block as punch after punch jerked his head around. Then he was down and I was standing, my heart in my throat.

The referee stepped in, pushing Gage back, as he counted. At four, Dennaki rose up to one knee and let the ref continue his count while he took the time to regain some energy. At nine, he stood up and the men next to me cheered.

Gage got in some more body shots, wearing down Dennaki, but stayed away from his head. Dennaki threw a flurry of punches, with a burst of energy, but only connected with Gage's side two more times. Then the round ended.

I was struggling for air, about to burst, as the third round started. The only round that mattered. I couldn't stand or move; I was cemented to my seat. With my eyes glued to the ring, everything else disappeared.

Gage came out swinging this time, but Dennaki blocked it, taking the hit in his shoulder. But the next one connected with his stomach, making him fold slightly. Gage followed it with an uppercut that sent him flying back on the ropes.

A quick one-two punch dropped Dennaki to the canvas. The ref stepped between the boxers, counting. Dennaki rose up at seven and I was in danger of throwing up, my vision shaking from the lack of oxygen. He was fully on his feet by ten and stayed back from Gage.

But Gage charged him, trapping him in the corner while throwing punches. Dennaki tried to block, arms up in front of his face. After a moment, Dennaki wrapped his arms around Gage and stepped in; he was too close for Gage to get a good punch in. Instead, Gage could only throw weak side punches.

The referee stepped in-between them, separating the two, allowing Dennaki a way to escape Gage's attack.

But Gage quickly cornered him again, not letting him close enough to grab him as he landed his hooks. He stepped back as Dennaki fell over, letting him drop to the canvas again.

My vision flicked between the ring and screen. Dennaki was struggling to raise himself up, and I prayed he wouldn't.

Gage watched him and wiped away sweat from his forehead with the back of his arm. His whole body shined with perspiration and his chest rose and fell harshly as he tried to catch his breath.

As Dennaki stood, blood streaming from his nose, my vision blurred and I quickly wiped away the tears that filled my eyes. I needed to see everything.

Gage's face was twisted with rage as he charged back to Dennaki. Dennaki raised his arms, trying to block the next wave of punches.

Then the bell rung, saving him but shredding me.

A strangled cry escaped me and I nearly fell out of my chair, my stomach spasming with anguish, but I pulled myself together as I watched Dennaki in the corner; he was surrounded by three men, pushing at his face, trying to stop the bleeding. I grabbed the hope that they might call it. The ref stepped over, checking out Dennaki's status, but all too quickly the bell rung again, starting the fourth round, and all hope was ripped away.

I had no reaction. I sat stunned and numb, unbelieving. Gage won in the next round, but it didn't matter. The fourth round wasn't the third. The only round that mattered was the third, and he hadn't won it.

I watched, a shell of myself, as Gage was announced the winner and the ring was stormed with reporters and others congratulating him. Everything seemed normal; he talked to the reporters as the screen replayed his knockout punch and others began streaming out of the arena.

* * *

I don't know how I made it back to the suite. But I was here; I must have been on autopilot. I sat on the couch, waiting for the doors to open. I needed them to open and for someone, preferably Gage, to walk through and tell me what would happen now.

But nobody walked through the door, not for hours. When the door finally opened, it was only Dexter.

"Is Gage coming back here?" I knew the answer already, but asked all the same.

Dexter couldn't meet my eyes as he walked to sit by me. "Rea, you're not supposed to be here. Gage told me you were supposed to leave."

I had thought he understood that I was going to be here for him no matter what. I shut the doors to my emotion and trapped them inside a locked box, as I looked back to Dexter.

"Where is he now?"

He shrugged. "He left with Silas. They were heading back to B-more. I was told to get everything and check us out in the morning. You can ride back with me then."

I dropped my eyes, focusing on the swirls in the carpet, trying to plan my next step. I had thought I would be doing that with Gage, but I should have known I would have to do this myself. Alone.

Standing, I said levelly, "Okay. I'm going to bed. I'll see you in the morning."

As I lay down, I tried to untangle my thoughts, unsure if I should listen to Gage or not. Should I run away or after him? I had lost Nan because I didn't act, and that guilt was crippling. I don't think I would survive losing Gage, too.

And I also held blame for tonight. Gage hadn't slept because of me. Instead, he stayed with me at the hospital, and to make it worse, we had sex instead of sleeping. He had been so close to winning in the third—just a bit more energy could have changed the results. I had been the one to take that away.

* * *

Dexter drove me to my house and stayed to talk to Leona, who warily accepted him into her room. He made it clear he knew nothing about where Gage was or what he was doing. We both tried to call him, but as expected, there was no answer. There never was with him.

I couldn't handle waiting for information, so the next day I slipped the gun Gage had given me into my hoody pocket, just in case, and walked to the metro stop outside the house.

My first stop was Gage's house, but nobody answered. The house was dark and empty, no cars in the drive way.

Next, I went to the gym, the only other place I could think to find him… my last resort.

It was full, which was typical for a Sunday morning. Scanning the room, I didn't see any sign of Gage, but there was a large banner up advertising his win and my heart raced. I hoped I would see him again and that he was okay.

After leaving me again, I don't think I could ever go back to what we were, but I had to know what happened. I had to make sure he was alright. More importantly, I had to say goodbye.

"Rea!" one of the employees greeted me. "I haven't seen you around in a while. Working out today?" His eyes looked over my jeans and pullover.

I shook my head. "Have you seen Gage?"

The boy smiled. "Nah, but with his win the other night I bet he's out celebrating. He usually takes a couple days off after a fight. Probably won't be in today, but Silas is in the office."

Determination made me rigid. I steeled myself and walked to the office with a muttered thanks.

Silas looked up with red-rimmed eyes as I walked in without knocking.

His smiling mask dropped into place within an instant. It took me this long to finally recognize it for what it was, a lie. All this time I had thought he was genuine and open.

"Regan, have a seat." He gestured to the chair on the opposite side of the desk.

I stayed standing. "Have you seen Gage?"

He nodded, his smile still in place. "I have, just last night actually. Have a seat, let's talk."

I felt the reassuring weight of the gun resting in my front pocket. I didn't really think I needed it for Silas, but it gave me the confidence to take the seat and sit tall.

He nodded at something, perhaps his own thoughts, and stood, coming around to sit next to me.

"Regan, I know you're angry with me, but I was hoping you wouldn't let that interfere with your career. I meant what I said. You can do big things and I want to be there to help you do just that."

I looked directly at him, unflinching. "No. I'm done working with you. I'm only here looking for Gage. I need to talk to him."

His eyebrow rose as he leaned back in his seat. "You care about him?"

His tone sent ice down my spine.

"Then help him. Help yourself. Come back to boxing."

I didn't answer; instead, I stared at him, trying to read his meaning.

"He wants to help you, too, but he can't do it on his own. If you come back to boxing for us, you'll have others protecting you, too. It'll make it easier for him."

I narrowed my eyes. "What are you talking about? Protecting me from what?" I had thought Gage was just being overprotective, but Silas's statement relit my fear, setting me on edge.

He cocked his head, considering. "From Rock's thug. I think they called him Dee?"

Damien. The fuse of anger was lit, burning quickly. But what did Silas know? "What are you talking about?"

His lip turned up. "Gage didn't tell you? That night after we left you at Gage's, we went looking for Rock. We didn't find him, but we found some of his crew and one of them knew about Gage and you. It worked to our advantage. He was so hell bent on destroying Gage he didn't even realize we brought others with us."

He paused, pointing at me. "He said a lot of shit about you, too, and it didn't sound like empty threats. You're a marked woman, Regan. You need protection. We can give you that if you fight for me again."

"By 'we,' you mean Rusnak? You're in thick with them?" I needed to know where he stood. What he said about Damien ignited all the anger I felt for him and reminded me of how I failed Nan.

He spread out his hands and shrugged. "It is what it is. They're good people to have on your side. So what do you say? I've always been honest with you about your career and let you get the final say. This would be a smart move. You get to fight and you get protection."

I nodded, my decision made. "I don't want protection. I want something more."

He lifted his chin, gesturing for me to go on.

"I want him dead."

A slow smile filled his face. "I think we can work that out."

Continued in book two: INSIDE DANGER

Acknowledgements

This book wouldn't exist without the support I had along the way and I am forever grateful.

I thank God for giving me the ability and means. I thank my family for giving me time, support, and endless love (and letting me get away with fast food and a messy house). Thank you to my Memaw for starting this all. I also thank my friends and coworkers who gave me the confidence to move forward with the story.

Also, the technical: Thank you R.B.A. Designs for the amazing covers that are better than I could imagine. And thank you T.K. Editing for your patience and dedication.

A special thank you to those who read while I wrote my first draft, this story wouldn't be the same without those comments and feedback. And I may still never have realized how perfect #rage is for a ship name!

About The Author

Ashley Claudy is a mother, wife, teacher, proud UMD Terp, and perpetual Learner with a wild imagination fueled by coffee. She's also an occasional runner, a late night book junkie, and a daytime dreamer.

She loves to interact with her readers and can be found on most social media. Go to her website for more information about her and her books, including some fun extras for this story and sneak peeks at future novels.

Please visit: AshleyClaudy.blogspot.com

Made in the USA
San Bernardino, CA
20 February 2015